The Train

Connor Harding

Published by Rogue Phoenix Press. LLP
Copyright © 2019

ISBN: 978-1-62420-499-9

Credits
Cover Artist: Design by Ms G
Editor: Amanda Armstrong

Chapter One: Eight Years Later

The shipyard was more hectic than usual. A sweeping mass of fresh faces assimilated amongst the faces of those who frequented the storefronts for years. Somehow, they all looked the same. Little Ezekiel shoved an old, rusty gate open and walked down the gravel path in the alley to the main section of the shopping district. Lugging a large bag of collectables, he trudged his way down the boardwalk to Old Sal's curio stand at the south end. The sack was nearly as heavy as Ezekiel, but he was more than experienced at lifting heavy things. The torn pages of a Traveler's Duty magazine were hanging loosely from the boy's pockets. A picture of the Grand Canyon, Ezekiel's favorite, was sticking so far out that the gentle spring breeze was nearly mighty enough to sweep the page square out of his shorts. Ezekiel looked passively at the unclean, aging shop owners as they conducted their daily business. As was the usual, people stood around the stands and kiosks, chatting about the year's crops, raids, elections, or any new parts of the city that recently got the seal of approval to explore. Expansion was an exciting prospect for many in Boston, but Ezekiel wasn't fazed by it at all. He had already been doing it for years.

Old Sal's shop was what can only be described as a pile of junk and wood which could be torn apart by the lightest breeze. The old man never really made any money from the junk he pawned off, so most citizens hypothesized he had a second, less obvious source of income. There were underground rumors he hosted dog fights by the Warf every Sunday, but that was just speculation. Honestly, little Ezekiel didn't care about what he did to make his living. He only cared that Sal would buy his goods and give him enough money to buy food and medicine for his mother. A stable source of income wasn't common in Ezekiel's part of town, or any part of town. It was up to the day if his scavenged goods would do the trick for him.

Ezekiel slung the large burlap sack onto the plywood shelf in front of the stand. The aging Italian man looked up from his book and stared down at the child with a smug grin on his face.

"Morning Ez! What glorified pieces of trash have you brought for ol' Sal today?"

Ez, with a rather bitter look on his face, replied "Just a bag of records I found at some old shop in the far western district."

"The far west district you say? Well, that's a dangerous spot. Did you waft in any of that disgusting chemical? I heard last week it was still lingering up by Charter Street."

"Yeah, there was still that awful smell around there, but nothing that could make me sick or anything."

Sal's Grin faded. "Well keep on your toes kid, you are my number one customer, and I don't want to see you become one of those wandering pale freaks like the ones in Lexington, you hear?"

Ezekiel chuckled. "Come on Sal, I know you really don't believe in the roamers. Quit teasing me."

"Don't tell me that like you know. I've seen em' before with my own two eyes."

"Forget I said anything. Just look at what I've brought you."

With a thud, a stack of once-precious records spilled out onto the planks like a line of dominos. Sal began to sift through them until he noticed a plastic, alabaster-colored disc, which was absolutely caked in dust.

"Huh. this is the White Album. My sweet god, I haven't seen one of these since before everything fell apart." The grey-haired man seemed very pleased by the find. Ezekiel became curious.

"What is so special about that one, Sal? They all look the same."

"Ah, you wouldn't get it kid. Your generation could never see the value in this. All you need to know is that you've struck gold."

"Well, if they were so great, how much is it worth to you?" Ezekiel said, pointing to the lockbox with a broken clasp.

"Well, I'll say something to the tune of twenty-five Foundercoins," Old Sal said, lifting the dust covered vinyl into the air endearingly.

Ezekiel's eyes lit up. "Twenty-five? That's enough money to buy medicine for a month."

Sal put the merchandise back down onto the table and reached under his kiosk.

"Do we have a deal? Here, I'll give you the money now."

He slid open the box under the display shelf and pulled out five large brass squares. Each was smudged by oil and skin grease, but the city label was still clearly legible in their top right corners.

"Well, I'm glad I could help out," Ez said, swiping the currency from the countertop.

"Hey kid. Keep bringing me good stuff like this, and you might even be able to afford to put a little bit of fat on those twig-legs of yours."

~ * ~

The grocery stand was only a quarter mile down the road, and Ezekiel gleefully skipped the entire way with a beaming grin on his face. He already knew what he wanted to buy with his newfound riches. The thought of something sweet made the boy salivate. Fresh grown strawberries. Only twice before in his life had he been able to afford the delicacy. Once on his birthday, when his mother gave him five dollars to spend, and once when he found a stash of jewelry in a broken lockbox. Ever since the toxin eliminated most farmers and crop fields, fruit of any kind had become a product in demand by the highest in the social hierarchy. It was naturally tangy, not like the processed pastries and stale candy which were constantly found in every corner of the ruins. People grew tired of packaged goods: the cereals, the trail mix, the boxed raisins, and it was hard to afford anything else since the few remaining growers held a total monopoly on the price of their crop. Ezekiel made quick work of finding the largest crate of berries on sale and made his way out, but only after throwing the ripest of the bunch into a beggar's baseball cap.

~ * ~

Ezekiel marched his way through the back roads and grassy patches of the district, homeward bound with a box of strawberries as long as a suitcase. He hummed a little tune from his childhood, but couldn't seem to remember what it was called. His mother used to hum it to him on cold nights to remind him it takes more than a little chill to kill a man. The Great Plague swept through not long after. The singing never made a comeback after the vaccinations took their course. As he reached the chorus, Ezekiel passed by a small, pillbox-shaped storage garage. His happy song was cut short when the child noticed the shape of a man slumped over a stack of brown bags. Curious as to who had taken shelter in such a weary, beaten down place, Ezekiel turned the corner to have a little peak at the squatter. It was a charcoal warehouse. The walls were covered in black stains and the entire place smelled of a long over-tended bonfire. Next to the man was a backpack, torn in three places, as well as two empty canteens of water.

The man was very tan, darker than most of the people Ezekiel sees around Boston. He had a long butch style of black hair and a thick, untrimmed beard. He was in very good physical condition, but also seemed exhausted and underfed, like a deprived jungle cat that learned to walk on two feet. The squatter looked to be in his late thirties, but the strange marks and scars on his face gave him the appearance of someone much older. His blue jeans and simple t-shirt were stained by an undeterminable substance. At best, it was mud. A homeless man on the south side covered in disgusting stains was certainly unusual, but it was also potentially dangerous. Ezekiel's mother always warned him folks he didn't know were usually bad, but Ez never really believed that. Ez always read that good people help people in his stories, and they only hurt bad people. Ez couldn't know which the traveler was until he asked.

Ezekiel almost pitied the man. He looked like he needed help. It was easy to get sick in a crowded place like Boston if you didn't have a roof over your head. Slowly, Ezekiel approached the husk of a man. As he drew close, the stranger's eyes snapped wide open and he flung to his feet, which did a good job of startling the boy. The traveler had a black handgun of some kind in his left hand. It was smaller, compact, and had series of scratches streaking down the barrel. The man soon realized he was only looking at a child, so he lowered the pistol and sat back down on the bags.

A few moments of incredibly awkward silence passed before Ezekiel gathered the courage to speak. "You aren't from around here, are you mister?"

The traveler wiped the sleet from his eyes and stared back down at the child. "What I *am* is trying to sleep, but I guess that's down the drain now. No, I'm not really from anywhere around here, kid. Don't you find strange folks wandering around all the time?"

"Yeah we do, but we really don't get that many new people these days, and whenever we do, it must be some kind of special occasion."

"Well, I guess you could say that me arriving here is a special occasion of some sort."

"Look mister. I'm real sorry for waking you. I just wanted to see if you were hurt. There are a lot of hurt people around here nowadays. I'm Ezekiel, but people who know me just call me Ez. What's your name?"

"Well..." The man looked thoroughly surprised by the simple greeting. "It's nice to meet you Ez. I apologize if I look stern, it has just been a while since anyone has really given me a formal greeting. The name is Jack. I just arrived here a few days ago."

"What do you mean you're not used to getting formal greetings? The folks around here always take time to introduce themselves."

"It's just not all that common where I come from to make an introduction like that."

"Why not?"

Jack stretched his narrow but tight shoulders. "Well, where I come from, it doesn't matter what you are or who you are, it is what you do that counts. People know you for what you can accomplish, nothing else."

"And where exactly do you come from, Jack?"

"I guess I come from here, and there, and a little bit of everywhere. But I started in Phoenix. We heard there was some kind of metropolis out here. Full of food, water, safety and shit. I decided to make the journey from there. I think it took us a full year to make it here, and I'm sure it could have been a lot faster than that, but we had to take some... necessary stops."

Ezekiel adjusted the magazine pages in his pocket. Things just got a little more interesting.

"Did I just hear you say you traveled to here from Arizona? How could you make a trip of thousands of miles with the gas still lingering everywhere?"

"You've never left the city before, have you kid?"

"I was born here. I've only explored this city to its outer limits, and no further. People say it's dangerous outside the city. Only the desperate and convicted ever step foot out there."

Jack leaned forward and patted Ezekiel on the shoulder. "It is, but that doesn't stop anyone from traveling through it. Have you ever heard any gossip around here about The Train, Ez?"

He nodded his head with uncertainty. Ezekiel had heard of trains as a baby, but his mother said they all rusted and died off years ago. She was intoxicated at the time, so Ezekiel wasn't sure if she was telling the truth or not. When he asked what they looked like, the best response she could manage for the toddler was "A big old metal tube that rolled around on tracks."

It was hard to learn as a youth in Boston, but Ezekiel always went the extra mile to make sure he didn't end up stupid like most of the other boys and girls in town. However, all the hard work and time he put into studying only served to make him a target. They would laugh and spit at him and call him silly names like 'book worm' or 'paper kisser', but none of it ever managed to bother Ez. He knew he was one of the strongest, fastest, and smartest kids in the colony, so things like that never managed to get under his skin.

"Alright then, make sure to picture what a train looks like in your head and keep it there. While we didn't have the luxury of riding in actual locomotives all the way here, the survivors traveling on The Train did travel in a pattern that kind of looked like one. You see little Ez, I traveled here as a part of a formation made of four distinct parts that all held their own purpose while we traveled. First, there were a few men situated far out front of everybody else in a V shaped formation. Their job was to scout out towns and roads to make sure everyone else wasn't walking into a deathtrap without a warning. Next, there was a long, rectangular section of the formation which contained most of the normal people with few special skills or strengths. Behind that, there was another set of columns which held all of the supply carts and medical equipment that was lugged around by the strongest, toughest people on board. Finally, in the back of all of that, there were a set of vehicles that were heavily armed that helped to defend the supplies in a place we called *the caboose.*"

Jack reached into his pack and pulled out a pale blue switchblade and flicked it open. He took it to the ground and began to carve a few basic shapes into the slightly mounded soil. One rectangle after another, he completed the drawing that represented his formation. Ez peered down at the set of odd, poorly-carved shapes. "Yeah, I can see why you would call it a train. How did you travel like that?"

"We walked. How else?"

"The WHOLE way?"

"Ah, a bit of cynicism I see. Well, I can assure you my old feet have stepped on unfamiliar soil almost every second of the last year."

Ez raised an eyebrow.

"Look kid, it's not like we did it all overnight. This journey took hundreds of days and thousands of hours of walking. We were on a strictly set schedule as well. We always woke up at dawn, heel-toed a dozen miles a day, and set up camp when dusk arrived."

Ez thought about the numbers for a moment in his head. Twelve miles a day multiplied by three hundred and sixty-five days would give them more than enough wiggle room to make it coast to coast.

"Alright then, how did you manage to travel in such a fanned-out pattern and still keep in touch with the rest of the people traveling with you?"

Jack scratched his chin. "Oh, that was simple. Someone would use a megaphone to signal the start and stop of each day's travels. It was loud as a tornado siren. I'm sure anyone standing within two miles could have heard that thing. When it finally broke halfway through the trip, we started using flares instead. Not as noticeable, but much more pleasant to the eardrum."

The whole idea of 'The Train' sounded very primitive, but Ez had to admit it seemed interesting.

"Yeah, a day on The Train was a hard day of work, guaranteed, but it always kept you preoccupied. You starting to get a better picture of exactly what I'm talking about, little Ez?"

Ezekiel, while hating the whole notion of being called little, nodded. "Yeah, I think I'm starting to get the idea a little better. You just walked along in a handful of long, thin lines that stretched out horizontally in three or four tiers."

"Yeah, that's a very accurate description to be made by a boy your age, kid. I'm impressed."

All this talk about moving across the barren wastes fed into Ezekiel's obsession with exploring it. This stranger drew a reaction from him, and no matter how much he told him about this strange train, he felt the urge to learn more. "Hey Jack," Ez started. "Would you mind answering a few questions for me?"

Jack almost looked flattered. "Well of course, ask away. I'm always willing to help teach someone who wants to learn. What do you need to know?"

"Well, first...I would like to ask a little bit about the old world."

"Yeah, sure kid. What do you want to know?"

"I just wanted to know what it was like before all of this, so if you could run down what a usual day used to be for you, I feel like I could maybe understand it."

"Alright kid, sure. You see, the old world was a wonderful place, with just a few flaws. Unlike today, nobody used to worry about what to eat. It was more about what you could buy and what you had to do to keep your job."

"What was your job?"

"Well, let's see...I was in my late twenties back then, I used to be employed as a night guard at an old storage facility. It didn't pay anything astronomical, but it gave me enough to help my family get by and taught me how to defend myself with a handgun, so I guess it was good enough."

"Who was in your family?"

This question seemed to strike Jack deeper, and a look of melancholy and determination grew on his face.

"Well kid, I have a daughter, something around your age by now, named Delilah, and a gorgeous wife, named Sarah. My whole world wrapped up in two beating hearts."

"What was it like sleeping on the ground out there? Was it always cold? Did the smell of the gas follow you? Did you have to look out for the feral dogs?"

"Oh boy, you sure do have a lot of questions in you, don't you Ez?

"I don't know, I have always just been really curious about life outside this place, ever since I was a baby."

Jack raised his eyebrows. "Oh, so you're an adventurer, are you?"

Ez's cheeks darkened into a rosy shade of red. "I guess you can say that. I've never been able to explore much of anything though. My mother would never allow it. She always says it's too dangerous out there for someone like me."

"I feel your pain Ez. There was a time during my life when I felt pretty trapped myself."

"I just really want to know everything about what is out there. It's all calling to me. I have a lot of dreams about being outside the walls. Some good, some bad. I love all of them though. At least they're different. At least they aren't set in this pigpen."

"Hey, don't feel so glum about the whole situation, kid. You are way too young to have a midlife crisis. I know someday, you will get your chance to take on the world. Mono e mono. You just have to wait for your turn to arrive. Until then, how about I help to answer absolutely any questions you might have about the wasteland? Would you like that?"

"Yeah, absolutely." Ez's grip on the crumpled magazine page in his pocket tightened.

"Well then, pull up a bag Ez, and I guess we can get started."

Ezekiel eagerly slid a bulky bag of charcoal dust up to the strange traveler and sat onto the top of it. Never in his life had Ez been so thrilled. He could tell Jack knew a lot about the wasteland, and maybe as he tells his stories, Ez could finally be able to paint a picture of it all in his head.

Jack started, "Now son, I'm assuming you don't know what it's all like outside of your little camp. Does that sound about right?"

"Right."

"Well, this place may be a bit dull, but it's much better here than anywhere else I've been. Out there, in the abandoned cities and forests, there isn't much pleasant to find. There is nothing more dangerous than traveling across that baron hellscape beyond those scrap-iron walls. There shouldn't be any believable reason to cross it whatsoever, but people tend to go and do it anyway. It's crazy, but the trip in some people's eyes is completely necessary. They won't let anything, even imminent death, stop them."

"If this trip is so dangerous and fatal as you say, what could possibly motivate someone to take it?" Ez asked bluntly.

Jack tapped his fingers on the paper bag and thought for a moment. "Well kid, some people go to find better shelter than they have, some come for a taste of long forgotten civilization, some just want a little safety, and a brave few go searching for love. It doesn't matter what it is Ez, but everybody on the outside has something…or someone, they keep pushing on for."

"Then Jack, what is it that you keep pushing for?"

"I came here for my beautiful little girl, but I think you already knew that. My family is alive, I know they are. I wouldn't stop searching the world until I find them or died trying. You can understand why, can't you little Ez? Do you have someone you would give everything up for?"

"Yeah, I have a mother. She lost my dad to sickness when I was very young, so she has raised me all by herself until she got sick too. Now it's up to me to get the medicine she needs every week."

"Ah, a family man. You see Ez, the idea of determination pushing survivors across three thousand miles of dirty, unsafe, and disgusting conditions is one thing. Traveling that way and enduring unexpected hardship *without a good motivation* is another. It's a survival of the fittest world out there, and some foolish people try to make the odyssey without being fit enough, either mentally or physically. They never make it. It's not a stretch to say one in every three things out there have the capability to end you in an instant."

Ezekiel cut him off. "You keep talking about dangers out there and how perilous this journey is. What actually makes it so ruthless?"

"Well, I'm glad you asked kiddo. To explain some of the many dangers out there, I will put them into two categories for you, living and non-living. I'll start you off with non-living. I'm sure you have heard of the toxin that started all this in the first place, right?"

Ez nodded. "Well, pockets of the stuff still linger around the ruins, and breathing any substantial amount in can still be lethal to anybody, regardless of age, race, or gender. The sneaky little toxin also seeps into opened containers too, contaminating the contents. Drinking any amount of infected water is just as big of a mistake as breathing it in. I learned that one the hard way. Also, some structures have weakened over years of mistreatment and have become very treacherous to walk across. Nothing out there is anything close to code anymore, so whenever you are traveling in an unfamiliar structure, you have to watch your step."

"What are some of the living threats that still exist around here?"

"Well, there are quite a few of those. The most common of those are pesky bands of raiders and bandits. There always seems to be some crew of freaks who can't survive by themselves, so instead they make a living by gathering large guns and plowing vehicles into groups of survivors to loot them for all they're worth. Besides those threats, there are also animals which suffered from the effects of the toxin, like the dogs you were talking about. Exposure is a nasty thing. Finally, in very rare cases, there are humans who suffered the same effects as animals, only to a stranger degree. People around here seem to like to call them…"

"ROAMERS?" Ezekiel shouted out with anticipation.

"Well, Yes. How did you know about that Ez?"

"The local junk shop owner said he saw one, but I always thought that they were a myth," he said with newfound enthusiasm. "You're telling me they're real?"

"They are as real as the ground you stand on, and more terrifying than anything you can possibly imagine. You see Ez, not everybody in the blast radius of the dirty air died because of its destructive effects, some weren't quite that lucky. The eggheads have a theory about how those things came around, but I'll keep it nice and simple. On the outskirts of the clouds, people were breathing in small traces of that neurotoxin, and they didn't even know it. Over the next few weeks, more and more particles of the poison gathered in their system, and soon enough, people began to lose their heads. Their skin cells died and began to flake off. First the mind, then the body. It continued until they weren't human anymore. They became something completely different."

Ezekiel, amazed and disturbed, continued on to ask. "What makes them so dangerous Jack, are they killers, cannibals, monsters? You have to tell me."

Jack looked distant and stared at the ground for a few moments. He sighed eventually and looked back at Ezekiel.

"No kid, they aren't any of those things, they are just lost souls with no competent mind or body to guide them anymore. They only attack you if they are scared, so it's not like they're killers. It's a disease really, but a disease with no cure. I reckon it all must be a fate worse than death."

Ezekiel stared down at the pavement and blushed. He was so excited to hear tales about terrible monsters in the wasteland and the heroism required to drive them away. Never would he have thought those monsters were just unfortunate people. *Stupid story books,* he thought to himself as he ran his fingers through his long, dirty-brown hair.

Jack saw the boy, the look of shame on his face and reassured him. "Listen kid, you couldn't have known anything about them, you can't hold that against yourself too much. Is there something else you want to know about the outside world, or have you learned your fair share?"

Ez re-gathered his composure, assured Jack that he was fine, and insisted on continuing with the conversation.

"Hey, I think I have an idea."

"What would that be kid?"

"Instead of just answering questions one at a time, why don't you just help me figure all of it out in one fell swoop?"

"Oh? How exactly do you propose I do that?"

"Well, how about you just tell me the complete story of your trip from Phoenix to here, start to finish. If you let me know what happened, I think I could just put the pieces together myself. Sound good?"

"Yeah, sure Ez. I suppose it is a story worth repeating, after all. We shouldn't waste any time though, so you might as well sit back and relax, because this might take a while."

Chapter Two: The American Phoenix

You see little Ez, the first few years after the attack were…difficult on everybody in Phoenix. After the shock finally settled, a terrible plague of survivor's guilt set in amongst everyone in the colony. You were just barely born before all this happened, so you could never understand how painful it was to know your entire way of life could disappear in the course of an hour. People spent their whole lives planning ahead, but when they finally looked up from their schedules, the calendar was already cleared. Suicide rates skyrocketed all across the city. That was the first real plague to sweep the colony. Most people just couldn't find a reason to keep existing, so bodies piled up by the thousands. It's a dark truth, but there was a time when we couldn't go an hour without someone jumping off a building or putting a bullet in their head.

All the death drove many to leave the camp in search of a saner place to live. Entire families would walk out into the heavy fogs in the suburbs, and fade into nothing. Half of the population disappeared overnight, and by morning, Phoenix had practically become a ghost town. After all the dust had settled and the bodies were buried or scorched, there was only a lump sum of about thirty thousand of us left. Nobody really knows what happened to those folks who left. Some liked to think they made it to camps that didn't exist in Austin or Oklahoma City. Some say they walked into densely dowsed areas of the toxin and perished. I say they went and became the earliest raiders in the southwestern states.

At that time, people lived without aim or reason. We survived simply to survive, and just held out hope that someday we could find something to hope for. Funny enough, humanity has that weird way of finding itself again. After the year of darkness passed, we began to reform ourselves back to the point where we had society, or something resembling it anyway. We rebuilt roads, we renovated water treatment plants, we repaired power grids, we grew wheat and barley, we prospered. The whole town decided to set itself to the standard of human decency, which was a model that worked out surprisingly well. No dictator, no pseudo-popes, no crumbling factions. We were just people being there for other people. It almost felt like I found purpose again, but that was short-lived. Tending to crops and hammering fences could only keep my mind off of things for so long.

I originally went to visit my friend who lived in Phoenix for a weekend. It was a simple three-day trip. I boarded a plane from Massachusetts the morning before the attack. I arrived at the airport hours before everything went downhill, so my survival was a mere coincidence. My life was nothing more than a dice roll, little buddy. It was easy to feel guilty about that. Especially when every single human being around you was mourning over something. I thought I had come to terms with it all, their passing was water under the bridge, but deep down I still couldn't accept it. After I started crying over their pictures every night, I fell into a slump. I didn't care about improving Phoenix much anymore. I didn't talk much to neighbors or visitors. I didn't go to the trade carts. Most of my time was spent in a reclining chair, staring at the water-damage in a hotel ceiling. You know kid, sometimes, you work on something with a passion. You work and you work and you work and suddenly *bang*! One little thing comes along and ruins months of improvement and change. Living for each other suddenly didn't matter when the only 'each other' I cared about were likely dead in some ditch two-thousand miles from the elevator door. I kept a hand-filed machete in a dresser drawer in case I ever grew a pair. I waited to grow a pair for five months. Thankfully, the drought in town kept *anything* from growing, just barely long enough for things to change. That summer, a peculiar group of people arrived at our perimeter and gave me an offer I couldn't refuse.

One morning, I heard a what sounded like a parade roaring from downtown. Starved and exhausted, I lifted myself out of my chair. As I approached the window to investigate, I heard the revving of engines and the squeals of tires. Mechanical racket was rather rare in Phoenix, and also potentially dangerous. People didn't have the materials or reason to drive, so engines always meant one thing. Outsiders. The only other time I heard a vehicle in the past half of a decade was when a cluster of two-dozen looters rammed their way through our defenses and attempted to steal our supply of bottled water. Assuming the worst, I grabbed the machete. About a quarter mile away from my window was a long, somewhat thin line of people covered in worn clothing and rags. There were about one hundred of them in total, all grim and covered with dust, stretching all the way down the winding road to our main gate. Weary, but well equipped.

I left the room and walked into the area the city council deemed as the 'hub' to discuss why these strangers arrived. The hub was just our term for a small area near the courthouse downtown which had been cleaned and renovated with fresh wood and recycled steel. The street itself stood the test of time pretty well, so the vehicles and miscellaneous carts were able to cruise into the city with general ease. Three hundred of us stood and watched silently, waiting for the travelers to state their business. The whole place smelled like body odor and flies were swarming by the hundreds. After a few moments of uncomfortable silence, a darkly-tanned kid vaulted his foot on the wheel well of an old Jeep and stood atop its hood. He had a megaphone the size of a basketball in his hand. He was of normal stature, young, and he had a thick mop of dirty blond hair. He turned on the industrial size device with a terrible screech that startled the crowd, and cleared his throat.

"Hello, people of Phoenix. My name is Peter Adonis, and I am the conductor of the San Francisco to Boston survivor train. We are here to present an offer to any people who wish to join us on our journey to the east."

The guy had quite the speaking voice, I'll give him that. Everyone still thought he was insane though. It was unheard of to go much beyond the city limits, much less to a place as far as Massachusetts. Things like global travel were nothing but a pipe dream. After what we saw the first year after the apocalypse, nobody seemed too sweet to the idea. Peter saw the look of doubt on our faces and attempted to reassure us.

"I know this must be relatively hard to believe, considering the current state of things. However, through negotiation and discussion with traveling merchants, we managed to find a relatively safe route from coast to coast. Other reports have said there is a massive survivor camp in the heart of Boston. We have a reason to believe they have excessive amounts of food, water, housing, and most importantly, a fiercely-revered set of defenses to keep you safe. In about one year's time, we could venture from where you stand now to our destination, and still have enough time to take a two-week vacation on the Atlantic coast. However, I won't lie to you, it is a tough and trying way of life out there. It can definitely be conquered through teamwork and group effort."

He paused for a moment and gestured the audience should look at the group of nomads to his right.

"As the name suggests, we started out journey about one month ago in San Francisco, California and made it to here, without casualty. To those unaware, that is a lengthy venture of seven hundred and fifty miles that we survived by scavenging, hunting, and bartering with merchants. As I said before, nothing is impossible if we put our minds together and press on as a single unit. So, if you want to join us on our odyssey, you must speak to Franklin, our attendance manager, by tomorrow at eight o'clock in the morning, or we leave without you."

Peter pointed to Franklin in front of the Jeep, and hilariously enough, the man shared a few characteristics with Benjamin Franklin. He had slightly longer hair that looked quite a bit like a wig. He wore dorky glasses, at least twice as thick as any I've ever seen. The brown-fabric jacket wasn't doing him any favors either. The slim figure nodded and raised his hand as an introduction before Peter continued.

"I warn you, if you are to come with us, pack light. We don't have enough cars or space to carry any of your useless keepsakes, so it's for the best you bring what you need and scavenge for the rest. Lots of goodies still available on the streets, if you can believe it. We will wait by the main gate and rest there until morning. We hope to see some of you join us, because honestly, the more people you have out there, the safer it is for everyone involved."

Peter silenced the megaphone and handed it down to Franklin, who promptly placed it in the back seat of the Jeep. In unison, the entire 'Train' began their march and proceeded to circle the square with almost military cadence. Dust kicked up from the dry, desolate dirt beneath them, and in perfect synchronization, they sharply turned to exit back onto the main road. Most bystanders, unimpressed by the prospect, brushed off the offer and continued with their daily lives. Why would they leave that perfectly effective colony when they had everything they could ever need right there? It was the same contentedness that drove them for years to survive, now back simply to hold them to their chosen existence. I was different though. The offer somewhat intrigued and excited me in a way, because my family lived in eastern Massachusetts at the time I left for Phoenix. A massive survivor camp near my hometown could mean they made it through. If they weren't though, I would have risked it all and wasted my time, and maybe even threw away my life. My new life. I had quite a decision on my hands, and only twenty-four hours to make it.

~ * ~

Ezekiel grew somewhat impatient and cut off Jack. "Well, that's nice and all, but what's a conductor? How did they get out of San Francisco? How am I supposed to keep up if I have no idea what you are talking about?"

Jack glared at Ezekiel for a moment, and then cracked a fond little smile. "Ah, short tempered? It's funny, you kind of remind me of Delilah when she was just a toddler. Always ready to get up and do something without waiting for even a second. Your enthusiasm is a good thing kid, don't get me wrong, but you have to control it. Maybe take some notes or something. Just try and learn, one step at a time. I just need you to be really patient with me, okay?"

Ezekiel, while no fan of being compared to a toddler, saw Jack's point. He waved his hand and grabbed an old pen from his back pocket. Notes didn't sound like the worst idea, after all.

~ * ~

So Ez, I sat in my dingy room, staring at the thin, stained, brown carpet, wondering if this massive risk would be worth the reward. I would have to leave everything I worked so hard for in the past five years to have a one in a million chance of seeing my little girl and wife again. It doesn't take much brain power to see the issue I had with those odds. I mean, t hat sounds pretty crazy, right? But then I took a good look around me; the barren waste of my home. The streets traversed by people I didn't even know by name. The buildings and walls I had never closely examined before. Suddenly, the choice was as clear as the daylight. I had nothing there, I had nobody there, and they sure as hell wouldn't miss me if I were to disappear. So, without wasting another moment, I gathered up everything I owned.

I really didn't have anything highly practical, but I kept a surplus of the basics lying around. There were six canteens, all of which I filled with fresh water. The cupboards and fridge were... less than flattering, to say the least. Only four cans of fruit, three cans of mixed veggies, and trail mix. For weapons and equipment, I had the machete, two flashlights, a lighter, a compass, one sleeping bag, a quantity of different maps of the local area, and a pack of four disposable flares. That was a solid base to begin a journey with, all I needed at that point was a firearm of some sort. Sadly, there weren't many of those floating around for any price I could afford. My lack of food made me feel uneasy though, so I took every cent I had left in my wallet and went to the local market for one last purchase.

It was early autumn, and a refreshing breeze whistled through the cracks and alleyways of the city as I walked down to the old cannery. I elected to take the backroads to avoid foot traffic. Alleyways were dangerous, but I never really minded. Maybe I should have minded them, come to think of it. I'm sure you know what kind of people hang out in alleyways these days, Ez. As I went in between an advertising agency and an old law firm, some shrimpy-looking rat in a worn grey hoodie stepped out of the shadows and slowly paced his way over to me. He was a runt in every sense of the word. Short, thin, sickly, pale, unfocused. His teeth were rotting and falling out due to a mix of what seemed like chewing tobacco and years of total neglect. Out of his torn pocket, he pulled an old 9mm pistol and pointed it at my gut.

I looked the guy over thoroughly, chuckled and kept walking right toward him. He made a strange gesture, one I had never seen before, and began shouting.

"Hey, I see that money you got in your pocket there, so you better hand that shit over, pronto."

I never stopped coming at him. I think there was a stupid grin plastered on my face, too.

"What? You deaf, dumb and blind? I'll shoot you dead, don't doubt that old man. I ain't scared of you or nothing." His boney hands were shaking on the trigger. I walked right up in front of his barrel and looked him dead into the eyes. I reached over, grabbed his arm, and guided the end of his pistol into the center of my stomach. He exchanged a look of primal fear with me in that moment, but I maintained that animalistic domination the entire time.

"Go ahead, do it." I giggled.

~ * ~

Ezekiel was entirely puzzled, and decided to cut in. "Why would you do something so stupid? You just made a defining decision to your life. Did you just not really care?"

"Like I told you Ez, be patient with me and I'll explain everything to you in a little bit of time, alright? I can't rush my story any faster than it needs to go. You still want to learn about everything out there, don't you?"

Red in the face, Ez nodded, and Jack continued.

~ * ~

The kid started darting his eyes up and down from the iron sights. He was terrified, angry, and very confused. He was breathing heavily, and it smelled of garlic and stagnant water. I was sure he would cower out and back away from the confrontation. However, to my surprise, he closed his eyes real tight and pulled the trigger back. Nothing happened of course, and we stood in silence. He tried pushing me back before taking a look at the weapon's chamber. He yanked back on the trigger again and again, expecting something different to happen, wildfire in his eyes the entire time.

He uttered hopelessly under his breath. With that I put the runt up against the wall. I took the 9mm out of his hand and held it up by his face.

"Safety's on." I wrapped my thumb over the switch.

"Please don't shoot, man. I got things to live for."

I let him go, but kept the firearm. Before I walked away though, I turned to the pathetic little rat.

"People like you don't deserve things like this."

I arrived at the old cannery minutes later. I felt all the loose change and dollar bills in my pocket jingle around melodically, about thirty-five bucks total. I could feel the weight of the currency in my pocket. One quarter kept bouncing off my thigh with little jabs, pressured by the sack of dimes resting atop it. Not a bad problem to have. One of the few men I called a friend in the whole city, Jeremy Stallsville, met me at the gate with a warm smile and outstretched arms.

"Jack, it's good to see your face again, you son of a gun. You finally make it out of that slump you've been in?"

I gave a weak smile and shook his hand, glad to see him jolly and in high spirits. "Yeah, I think I'm out of it, Jeremy. I'm guessing I don't look like it though."

He let out a hearty chuckle and slapped my shoulder. "Well my friend, you definitely aren't wrong. Looking a little like hammered shit never hurt anyone. Come on in, its cooler inside than it is out here."

Jeremy was always a portly man. He had light brown hair, blue eyes, and heavy patches of freckles spread densely around his cheeks. However, he was most well-known for his beard. The thick mess of strands reached down close to his belly button. Jeremy had a heart to match the size of that beard as well. He was the proud owner of the gargantuan 'Stallsville Family Canned Goods Warehouse'. When everything fell apart, he provided enough food to the hungry and desperate to keep them on their feet until things got better, and for no charge as well. Some folk eventually came to call him *The Roundest Saint of Them All*. I personally believe he lived up to that name in every sense.

He led me inside and offered me a seat next to his front desk. The whole foyer was surprisingly cozy and comforting, considering all the wear and tear it received over the years. Jeremy went to the backroom and brought back a frosted pitcher of fresh water.

"Would you like a glass pal? You look like you haven't had

something to drink in days."

I accepted the beverage and sipped away at it in content silence.

"So, what can I do you for today, Jack? I still have a lot of corn, pears, peaches, beans, peas, and cherries. Any of that sound good to you?"

I reached into my pocket and pulled out my remaining fortunes. A few dimes rolled out of my fist and fell underneath a desk, but I wasn't one to count spare change. With a little thud, I slapped them down onto the counter and nodded my head.

"Yeah, I think I would be interested."

"Wow, that's quite a bit of change you're carrying around, isn't it?"

"It's not change Jeremy, it's all I got."

He looked somewhat concerned.

"Oh Jack, you aren't thinking about going with those rugged walking folks, are you? I mean, you have everything you need right here with us."

"Yeah, you got me. I'm heading out with them tomorrow, I just feel like there's something out there that I need to find closure for."

He looked very disapproving of my decision, but also accepting.

"That look in your eye is telling me there is no changing your mind at this point, so I guess there is nothing to do but have one final deal. How much money is that? How about this for a proposition. I take this, and you get whatever you want from the canned goods section from the very back of the warehouse. Sound good?"

"Well, I can't say that's a deal that I would ever turn down sober."

He guided me into the warehouse area and directed me to the canned goods. The supply depot had really shrunk since last time I had been there. Nearly two thirds of the products were now used or sold, and more were going every day. It was still about eighty cans wide by two hundred tall. The contents of the warehouse didn't have a lot of time left in them anyway, since most of the products were already rotten, or close to their expiration. Regardless of the lack of quality, I had never been so happy to see green beans in my whole life.

Jeremy turned to me and put his hand on my shoulder. His fingers were callused, and he always had a firm grip.

"Hey pal. You stay safe out there. I don't want to hear your body turned up twenty miles east of the border, alright?"

"Don't worry Jeremy. I think with all these people walking around at the same time we should be able to keep safe."

"Oh yeah, I'm sure. If you can make the trip someday, you should come back to Phoenix and tell me your stories over a cold beer or two. We could make it into a grand-old time. Hell, you can even bring me back a souvenir or something. Maybe a nice mug. I always love a good mug. I have some more people out front to take care of now, Jack, but best of luck. See you around sometime soon."

It was a hollow, but kind gesture.

"Yeah Jeremy, I'll see you later. Thanks for everything."

"No need to thank me. It's the same thing an old neighbor would do for another. Now get going, you have some prepping to do."

With that, the big guy waltzed his way back out to the front of the air-conditioned facility. I would never see him again.

After a few minutes, I left Jeremy's family warehouse with a respectable pile of tin treasures stuffed in my survival pack. As nightfall approached, I entered my residence for one last night of civilization before the trek began. What did I do with my remaining few hours of luxury, you ask? I drank, and when I say drank, I mean I cleared my liquor cabinet. I must have gone through a whole bottle of whiskey that night. I'm talking about the 'burns a hole straight through your intestine' kind people reach for when they want to forget their troubles. After reaching a state of boozed up Nirvana, I went to lie down in my queen-sized bed and went out like a light within a few minutes. The sheets were soft and comfortable. I never really realized how much I was going to miss warm sheets as I slept through my last pleasant night in Phoenix. Soon enough I'd learn to regret their absence.

Chapter Three: The First Few Steps

My alarm went off early the next morning, and the hangover I received upon waking was strong enough to split my head clean in two. Grumbling, I swiped at my alarm clock, effectively silencing it and shattering it against the bedside wall. I think it put a hole in the paneling. My hands shook as they held the sides of my head, my teeth clenched in pain and aggravation. It took some courage, but I managed to stand up and stumble my way to the bathroom. I promptly puked my guts out over the milky-white toilet seat. After about twenty minutes of pure discomfort, the migraine slightly subsided. I waddled over, rubbing my eyes, to the fully packed knapsack I set by the door. Everything was still there, and well organized at that. I applauded the organizational skills of my drunken self and promptly threw the felt strap over my shoulders. I turned at the doorframe and took one last look at the pale, brown walls and shitty, minimalistic artwork of room 107. I thought back and realized I made quite a run in there, but it was time for some change. The door was left ajar, and my short march to the central gate began in earnest.

It was relatively cool for an early morning. It was the kind of bliss only an early summer sunrise could give a man. A respite from the usual, blistering heat that was always prevalent in Phoenix. I walked down the busted sidewalks and atop the struggling brown grass, feeling completely prepared. As prepared as a guy in my shoes could be, anyway. Even though it would be my last chance to get a look at the city and say my goodbyes, I wasn't interested in stopping for any sentimental heartaches. Had no more seconds to spare for intangibles. Even when I passed by the church where I initially worshipped. That placed ended up burning after the reverend was found with more missing reserves of water and wine than scriptures.

I didn't even peak when I passed my old friend's apartment complex. Rest his soul. People used to tell him that experimenting around with purifying that water was a bad idea. A bunch of people, all smarter than him, had already tried and failed, but he was a stubborn thinker. Even I told him that boiling it and using iodine wouldn't be enough, but I was just the stupid security guard. Egghead. Do me a favor kid, never let that big brain of yours turn you arrogant. That's a one-way ticket on a speeding streetcar.

The gates at the edge of town we built were of thin wire strips. It actually held a decent resemblance to the one you have here, only much flimsier. It had meaning behind it though. The stories of thousands of hard-working, desperate men and women were the foundation of it, and their sweat sealed the cracks. I waved down the guard waiting in the tower, and with a push of a lever, the gears spun and the doors swung open with a thunderous screech. She gave me a quick wave and made good time slamming the gate behind me. I was out in the open world for the first time in years. Peter mentioned The Train set up camp a mile east of the city, which was unfortunate. East led me straight through the blighted suburbs. A place without regard for man or his sympathetic disposition.

I'm sure you've seen those rabid, delusional, frothing at the mouth, half-braindead creatures that nest outside contaminated areas, right little buddy? Phoenix's suburb communities had always been completely overrun by those things. Aggressive, frothy things with feathers or fur. Long time exposure victims. All of em' are vermin, but all the exterminators are a bit busy being dead to handle it. They grew fat on the corpses of the first families to abandon Phoenix, then picked at the suicides for dessert. At least they're only territorial, and not expansive. The only other time that they attack you is if you are alone, or seem to be an easy target. Ha.

I tiptoed through the concrete jungle to the outer limits, quiet as a church mouse. I could feel them all watching me with content silence from the telephone wires. It probably isn't that hard for you to believe Ez, but I knew when a feral beast was watching me. They were sneaky about it, but I felt the hairs on the back of my neck stand up. A cold, disconcerting experience in every sense.

I lost focus on what was in front of me while staring into the hordes of feathered freaks. There must have been dozens, maybe hundreds of blackbirds perched on their stoops, ready to dive bomb me as soon as I took one false step. Terrified, I reached into my backpack and pulled out my hand-filed machete and held it up as a guard. It wouldn't be able to stop the swarm by any means, but its sharp edge could buy me some time to run for cover. It's always good to have a backup plan, little buddy. Sadly, plans don't always account for one's own stupidity. An empty can of cola sitting on the tarmac made more noise than you would think. A size twelve boot against a tin husk made quite a crunch. I grimaced and began to hear the flapping of wings beat all around me. I stared back toward the sky, not to see the rising sun, but a cloud of ebony feathers, completely encircling me.

A kind of primal fear made my heart stop, but just for a moment. I regained control and checked my surroundings for something that might help fend the demons off. As I spun in a heightened sense of urgency, an old metal trashcan caught my eye. I broke into a sprint across the street. Every step I took, the louder the sound of the flapping became. There was a nagging sharp pain that erupted from my left ankle. Blunt, prickly jabs. They were going for my legs. Pretty smart for a bunch of crows with zero braincells left between them.

One of the grapefruit-sized beasts flew directly in front of me, and with a swing of the machete, I cleaved it in two. It let out a jarring screech as its body flopped to the pavement. I disregarded it, and instead continued to wildly shoo away the horde with the straight edge.

After a few moments, I stumbled over my own feet at the curb and fell face first next to the can. I took its metal lid and threw it to the side before raising the container over my head with a jerk. Without a second thought or moment or reasoning, I stuck myself into the center and forced the bin upside down. With gunk of a decade falling on top of my head and down my face, I slammed the lip of the open end into the ground. I took a deep breath, wiped the muck from my eyes, and braced for impact. For a few brief moments, I was enveloped in the sound of muffled wingbeats. White noise on a television screen, only inconsistent. Like it had a pulse. A heartbeat of unrefined savagery. The first bump came only moments later.

The next one followed a few seconds after, followed by another and another until the sheet metal rattled. The putrid smell of degrading plastic made me want to choke. The shrieks of the obnoxious little demons made my ears ache and my head throb in the way only high-pitched ringing can. The kind that echoes from one chamber of your skull to the next like a shark thrashes in water.

My thoughts were elsewhere though. They say your life flashes before your eyes when you are about to die. Mine didn't, but my dreams did. There was a big, luscious, green yard with a grill and a pool. A set of nice cars in a garage. Air conditioning. My wife stirring a pot of warm potato stew over the stove as I came home from work. Delilah drawing on the bathroom wall with crayon, then bringing me in to show me. A happy family. I thought of them, and I gritted my teeth.

After a minute the length of an eon passed, an eerie quiet set in. I let go of the walls of the bin and my arms fell limply to my sides. Flimsy as a piece of chewed gum. I was jarred, but still in control. It seemed I may just live another day. I lifted the metal shell up until it was just barely ajar, holding the hunting machete at my side, ready to be thrusted out at any stragglers. I heard nothing that squawked and saw nothing that moved, so I gathered my courage and tossed the can onto a driveway. Nothing could have prepared me for what met me in the light.

Corpses. Dozens of them, strewn about in little piles of feathers and flesh. Their dive at the can didn't have anything to do with that though. A result of carelessness. A lack of thinking. Most of the casualties seemed to be torn to ribbons by tiny little talons. Clawed to the bone from their backs. They must have been piling on top of one another to get their shot at me. Filthy animals, killing themselves senselessly like that. Maybe they weren't as smart as I gave them credit for. I turned back to see the garbage can that I threw. It was battered to a bent husk, with holes peppered all through it as if it had been shot to pieces by a rifle. I have no idea how something so flimsy held up, but I wasn't particularly interested with the science of miracles.

I looked down at the machete gripped tightly in my palm and saw a vague reflection in the steel. It was me, yes, but it definitely wasn't me. The garbage had done a good job tainting my skin from the dirty runoff. I think the veins in my face looked ready to pop out too. It kinda looked like a monster at first, with all the refuse on my forehead. Now I'm not so sure.

Maybe it was just the face of a survivor. I brushed some of the dirt and liquid from my eyes, threw the pack over my shoulder, and continued the march toward their campsite. The Train was going to leave soon, with or without me on it.

~ * ~

The suburbs were a desolate place. Besides the homicidal pigeons, there wasn't much left but the dusty cadavers of once-cozy family homes, and a small army of untouched picket fences. The sidewalks had been turned into concrete craters from years of rain and intense heat. The sound of chimes still hanging from declining eves gave the entire neighborhood an evil quality. It was a real ghost town. One probably filled with enough restless spirits to form a whole community. As I walked on, I liked to think about what that neighborhood was like before everything became so distraught. I imagined kids playing no-rule soccer with their friends in the front yard. I imagined the smell of ballpark franks and the Johnsons screaming over the hedges at the Myers for letting their cat wander around and mark its territory on their air conditioner. It was nice to imagine, but all that seemed impossible now, so I stopped daydreaming and started looking around for anything useful.

I'm glad I stopped where I did. There are goodies all over the uninhabited wastes, but it took some good timing to stumble upon something like I did. If I focused anywhere else, I wouldn't have spotted the pair of gorgeous field glasses in that bay window. The things were literally leaning up on a stack of books, beckoning to me. They were in surprisingly pristine condition, almost like they were fresh off a store shelf. You don't see things like that every day in Phoenix. I knew immediately that those binoculars would be handy, and since nobody would be missing them where they were, I decided to appropriate them.

The house they were kept in was not in such astounding conditions as the field glasses. I think it was supposed to be painted yellow, but the passage of time peeled it all off. The bay window was thoroughly smudged, but still clear enough to see through. I took a careful peak into the living room. The house wasn't much more photogenic on the inside. Dust covered every square inch of the dump from top to bottom. The far wall was completely covered with an unnerving collection of family photos. The bones of someone long-deceased remained next to them, slightly hunched at the back. An adult skeleton, thank God. I hated the sight of dead children. I took a step back and looked over to the front door. It seemed flimsy, and some of the hinges had already fallen off. It must have only been about three inches thick. I had my way in, but it was time for a little physical activity.

I took a few steps back and lowered my shoulder. With a short grunt and stiff push of my leg, I took off at breakneck speed. I was a human battering ram, and I was looking to make some splinters. Well, the wish granted to say the least. My shoulder slammed into the door with the force of a derailed streetcar, completely busting through the frame above the handle. The whole thing flew right off its screws. A total mission success, if I do say so myself. However, I may have forgotten to calculate what would happen after I went through the door. That momentum carried me straight through to the foyer. Before having a chance to slow down, I found myself having an intimate relationship with the far-side wall.

The floor was kind of sticky. Ew, yeah, it was definitely sticky. The bad news was that the migraine was back in full swing, but I could still walk, somewhat. The equipment was mine for the taking. I stumbled around the putrid shag covering to the windowsill. Some bugs skittered away in the darkness as I swayed along. Occasionally, I had to stop and hold onto furniture when the world caught some centrifugal force. Once, when the bay window was in arms reach, I tripped over my own feet and grabbed hold of one of the photos, taking it down with me. I regained my balance a second later, but opted to look at the photo whilst my body fully recuperated. I used the sleeve of my shirt to dust off the thick cloud of dust on the frame and took a long, hard look at the people inside it.

It was what you could consider the 'average family photo'. A mother, a father, a daughter, a dog. The father was a balding man in his mid-thirties, very physically fit with a tattoo on his right arm. The wife was slim and taller than most women, with very bright blond hair and vivid blue eyes. The daughter really took after her mother. She had the same blond hair, but shorter, same blue eyes, with a startlingly captivating smile that stretched across her face. She must have been no older than eight. I don't know why, but the image brought me some comfort. Maybe it was because it reminded me of my past. Maybe it inspired me to move toward the future. I got back up. The binoculars were swiftly snatched from their perch, and I triumphantly headed my way back out into the suburbs with a heavier load to bear than before. It was okay though, I had some strong shoulders.

~ * ~

The sun had risen, and with it came the usual scolding Arizona heat. I paused for a moment to check my watch to see if I was still on schedule to reach The Train before it departed. It was seven thirty, and I was only one tenth of a mile away from where the campsite was supposed to be. This was the furthest I had ever been from the heart of the city, and I hadn't even begun the trip yet. Being just outside my comfort zone was kind of a rush. Like an even cocktail of fear, excitement, and curiosity. It tasted kind of funny.

I made it to the outer limits of the suburbs without any more problems. The little fires in their camp were unimpressive, but numerous. I spotted them from a nearby hilltop and coasted my way down on my heels. No one really noticed me upon arrival. People didn't care much to talk or explain anything. They opted to sit around the fires drinking coffee and eating overcooked lentils instead. The air smelled of oil and melted rubber. Their faces were disturbingly blank, too. Maybe content, maybe a little dead on the inside. Like a bunch of department store mannequins decided to go on vacation to the Grand Canyon. It was relatively quiet, except for the crackling of the firewood and the squeaking of cheap wheelbarrow axels. I made my way toward the tent, but not before clumsily kicking some pots and pans stacked by a wheelbarrow.

A massive man with silt-colored skin towered over me by at least a head's length. I'm six feet Ez. Six feet. To him, I may as well have been Papa Smurf. He put his hand by his hips and took a close look at me.

"Hey short-stack, mind watching where you put those big-ass boots of yours, before I take them and place them somewhere else?"

I took a step back. "Yeah man, uh sir. I'm sorry. I'm from Phoenix and I was just looking around the place to get used to everything."

"Right. Another greenhorn from town. Sorry, I guessed I assumed you knew how things like common courtesy worked. Well anyway, you don't need to know my real name, but you can just call me by my nickname. People round' here call me Mountain."

I couldn't help but grin for a moment. Bad idea.

"What is it that you're smiling so much about, gnome?"

"Sorry Mountain...I just can't seem to tell how you could've gotten a nickname like that."

"Well, you should count your blessings, boy. I would have beaten the soul out of anyone who said that in this whole campground, but I'm having a real good day. That means today and today alone, I'll let it slide. Now what exactly should I be calling you, little buddy?"

"Well, I don't have a glorious nickname like MOUNTAIN or anything, but you could just call me Jack."

A wide, devilish grin grew on his face. If you could brace for the impact of a word, I was doing it right then and there.

"Jack huh? You know what that reminds me of? That old fairytale about the little squirt Jack and the magic beanstalk. So, instead of calling you Jack, I'm gonna call you beanstalk. You're just about as thin as one, anyway."

I honestly didn't care much for the nickname, but I knew he could be calling me something a lot worse. Instead of protesting it, I just took it with some good humor. I told Mountain I still had to sign in, and he directed me over to the main tent where Franklin was. I waved goodbye before rushing to sign in, wondering if I had just made my first friend on The Train by destroying his property.

The main tent was a dark burgundy color, but it had been beaten and battered by the desert just like everything else. Inside was a modest wooden desk filled up with miscellaneous paperwork, a battery powered lantern, a couple of cheap lawn chairs, and of course, Franklin. I stumbled in, took a seat, and waited as Franklin sorted through hundreds of files in a folder. After a minute or two, I realized he didn't notice me walk in. He was a real clumsy type, but even I underestimated how sporadically a scatterbrain can function. I cleared my throat with an exaggerated, gruff cough. He nearly jumped out of his socks when he finally saw me.

"Oh, sweet Christ. How long have you been sitting there?"

"It's fine, me waiting for a minute or two won't hurt anything. You said in town this was the place to sign in to take part of this?"

He nodded and pulled out a form with dozens of names on it. I didn't recognize any of them personally.

"Well then, mister uh…Jack. You are the twentieth person from town to join us on our little adventure. I must say I would never have guessed so many of you would decide to take our offer seriously."

"Paradise isn't all that it's cracked up to be. What's this column to the right supposed to be about?"

"We need to know what kind of gear everyone is packing so we can find a place to put you. Just go ahead and write down the best pieces of equipment you have so we can find a proper place for you."

I opened my pack to see what I could put to make myself seem more impressive. There wasn't much to be found. The only things of value that I owned were the pistol from the punk in the alleyway and the binoculars. It was a bunch of lightweight stuff. I didn't have extra rations to throw around, and no experience with heavy lifting. My skills were only par for the course as well. I guess what I'm getting at here was I wasn't too special.

I jotted down my equipment, slid the manila stock paper back over to Franklin's side of the desk, and tapped on it with my knuckles. He spun it around and gazed at my list with analytical flare.

"Well, it looks like you're packing pretty light, Jack. With a pair of binoculars, too. Well, it sounds to me like you will fit right in with the FCS."

"Is that, some kind of guard?"

"Well, not quite, but not all that far off either. The FCS stands for *First Contact Squad*. It's a type of…reconnaissance team that also acts as reinforcements for the guard of the conductor's car. That means if we make our way to a new destination or find ourselves in a bad place, it will be your job to let Peter know before all the unarmed folks get there. Do you have any objections to that?"

It sounded like a bit of a dangerous prospect to me, but I knew I was capable, and I swore I was getting aboard, so I nodded and was officially accepted. Franklin led me out of the main tent and promptly went back in to re-arrange his desk. I was to report to the east side of camp immediately and introduce myself to the other rugged survivalists who would serve as my team. It was seven fifty, which left me only ten minutes to chat. I took off to the east in a consistent jog, trampling rotted vines and crabgrass underfoot the whole way. Brushing past tents, people, fires, barrels, and anything else, I managed to carve a path straight through the heart of camp to the east in just three minutes. I took my first step into Recon camp completely breathless. I was really out of shape back then, the more I think of it. I made my introduction between heaving breaths.

~ * ~

There was just a small brigade of men there, I believe there were seven in total, myself included. Everyone was rather thin, lanky, and a bit shorter than me, mostly with strong legs. There was one named Jacques who had a small, patchy beard and a comb over. A bit classy for the apocalypse, but I am nobody to judge. Another was a Native American, with shoulder-length, greasy hair parted down the middle. Everyone just called him 'Adahy'. It seemed a bit…sectarian to me, but he seemed to take it in stride. He said it had meaning behind it, and that was enough of an explanation for me. There were two backwoods brothers there as well, named Jed and Hank, who looked almost to be twins with the exception of Hank having a sizeable scar on his nose. Both were practically skinheads. The guy they called Silent Bob was at camp as well. He was a quiet, stocky black man with a full beard and an eternal look of boredom on his mug. I never learned a damn thing about him except for his addiction to chain smoking. The only thing he loved more than lighting up was lighting up again five minutes later.

The oddball of the group was a somewhat elderly man with a stern face and a buzz cut. People told me he was a pyromaniac. Some people called him nuts, some called him eccentric, I called him my fearless leader. What you need to know about him now was he was cold, ruthless, efficient, and had the terribly non-threatening name of Todd. Legends said he felt no pain, except for in his lower back. He was an ace shot and could pick up a man twice his size. That old fart had some serious American grit. Finally, there was little old me. Average Joe with a pistol and fine binoculars, nothing too special about me, yet I was accepted just the same by everybody else immediately.

Besides looking like a group of frontiersmen, they were actually an outstanding group of guys. Within the first seven minutes I stepped foot into their campsite, each one of them introduced themselves, shook my hand, and sat me down with a warm cup of coffee. It was...pleasant. Sadly, it couldn't last. A blaring horn shot me up like a bottle rocket. It reminded me of a tornado siren. Long, smooth, and irritating as all hell. It definitely got your attention though, so it did its job.

"Well, looks like the meet and greet is over kiddos, better head out to the front and get this party started." Todd said, lobbing his remaining coffee into a nearby brush.

With military style efficiency, the small seven-man crew packed up the whole camp in the matter of a few moments. Hurling bags of equipment over their backs, they signaled me to follow them over to an old splintered cart that sat back in the middle of camp.

"That's the supply cart over there Jack. We put our spare supplies in there, and some of the heavy lifters carry it for us while we scout ahead."

The cart looked like it had been made in fifteen minutes. The tiny, vehicle-drawn wagon looked brittle, but when I pointed that out, the boys assured me the thing could survive a hurricane and still carry half a ton. As we talked, I helped to load any spare bags or luggage onto the shambling wooden box, carelessly throwing things over the side.

"Hey, watch where you put all that stuff. Show the lifters a little respect. We all have to use that gear for the next nine months. You ruin it, you make us a new one with your bare hands, got it?"

Todd seemed irritated. I looked over my shoulder to see an unreasonably massive pile of bags and boxes stacked on the right side. It looked ready to tip over.

"Wow, I didn't think about it. Yeah, I understand."

The frontlines were really nothing special, it was just a bunch of dead foliage and trees with bark falling off of their sides, which was something I hadn't seen in a long time, but held little interest in. One redeeming quality about the frontline is that it is very quiet and peaceful. You get to hear yourself think. Intimately. The air was also clean, which I never expected. Then again, I had been stuck in a cesspool for a quarter of my lifetime. I took a seat beneath a large oak tree and waited for something to happen. Everybody else in the core just stood around stretching, chewing tobacco, or lying down trying to rest their eyes. The sound of a revving engine in the distance snapped everyone back to reality.

They spit out their tobacco, stopped moving, and listened closely for a moment. It was a car alright, and that meant we would be taking point. I grabbed hold of the warm, rotting bark of the tree I rested under, and lifted myself off the ground. Just in front of an old hospital, we saw the Jeep, then the hordes of people, and the supply carts slowly pull down the main road. Jacques threw his survivor pack over his shoulder, looked at the rest of the crew, and nodded.

"Well, looks like it's time for us to take formation."

I watched on with intrigue as the six of them formed up into a partial 'V' formation, except for a missing person in the bottom right. I am no rocket scientist, but even I could figure that puzzle out. I jogged over to them and stood tall. I think I puffed my chest out a bit too. There was an air of professionalism about the group, so I did my best to match their machismo.

The conductor's car pulled up at a walking pace and crawled to a painful halt behind us. Peter stepped out of the driver's side door and trotted his way slowly over to us. Peter was your average prep school type. He was young, long flowing blond hair, and even wore a letterman's jacket occasionally, likely sentimentally. He handed Todd a map of what looked like the state of Arizona. He then patted Todd on the back and told him to "keep on trekking." Before going back a few paces to make a speech. It was always speeches with that guy.

"Alright FCS, you know what your job is at this point."

I had no idea what my job was supposed to be.

"Just keep six-hundred meters ahead of me and run back to alert us of any problems. Todd has the map with our current route displayed on it in his hands right now. We stop and set up camp at sundown. Good luck gentlemen."

He ended the directive, waved, and strolled back to the Jeep, where he went to make another announcement to the center. He sounded like a painfully falsified self-help guru. Words to live and prosper by, only three dollars and ninety-nine cents at Bookmart. That was it, the words to start of the most perilous journey I would ever undertake.

Adahy started triumphantly marching in front of the rest of us, and I took the first few steps. They were short, but also confident. I was ready, or at least I thought I was. Peril seemed like a distant relative, and I just wasn't expecting too many holiday visits. We kept going, leaving The Train a few yards further behind until it faded from sight. Once it disappeared completely, there was nowhere to look but forward. There was a suburb city ahead of us, little more than a few small businesses and residential homes. That would be the first place I would explore in the new world. Looking upon the strange and desolate sight of a new city filled me with determination. For the first time in what seemed like forever, I was excited to be alive.

Chapter Four: The Desert

The first few days were nothing special. On the cooler days, we would burn rubber for up to eighteen miles at a time. We used to fly back then. Walking was a real pain though. It's actually pretty funny little buddy. You walk all the time every day without thinking about it, but as soon as you don't get to choose when you stop, the world ends. I remember how many friction burns my toes got from giving my boots a thorough scrubbing every afternoon. Taking off my socks at night became an everyday bomb-defusal drill. I swear I had more blisters than feet left by the end of the first week.

More annoying news came around when some local merchants warned us of a dangerous raider group setting up camp directly east of Phoenix. Suddenly, we had to start taking our time. Worse off, they were directly in our path, which forced us to take a little detour. By 'little detour', I mean we had to cross a desert. I think it was the Sonoran, or at least that's what the maps said. Sadly, there wasn't much of an alternative unless we wanted to pick a fight with a group of well-armed savages. On our way heading south, we saw small town after small town, each with its nifty little shops and schools, each as quiet as death itself. We found our fair share of remains here and there though. Then again, we found remains pretty much everywhere. I'm not even affected by the sight of human bones anymore. It's easy to overcome a fear of them when the world is a closet filled with skeletons.

There were seven of us together in the FCS, and we seven got to experience the silence, the sadness, and the misery of small-town USA together. It met us at every store, every home, every chain burger joint. I saw a nursery once. It was dark, dusty, and lonely, just like the rest of Arizona. There were dozens of empty cradles completely filling the tiny establishment from corner to corner. Little accessories and bonnets were hanging on the walls by dented hooks, and the pink wallpaper behind them had peeled off in chunks due to water damage. The whole spectacle made my skin crawl.

Every night at sundown, the march stopped. Supply vehicles rolled up and delivered daily rations of canned food to us, regardless of how unappetizing they looked. Nobody was left to empty the pantries when all the inhabitants of the house spasmed to death. We would light a small bonfire if we could find dry kindling, or just sit around eating our rations in the darkness. We'd entertain each other now and then with tales of the past. Jacques told stories about coming to the United States from Canada and seeing the Statue of Liberty for the first time. Jed and Hank told stories about hunting trips with their father in the mountains of Washington State. Adahy told tales of life and tradition on the reserve he grew up on. Todd didn't really talk that much about anything, but when he did, it was about how damn hot it was. As you could probably expect, Bob didn't say much of anything. He preferred to puff up a thick cloud instead. The food was terrible, but the company was nice.

The days seemed to grow longer and longer the closer we drew to the desert. The sun was a toaster oven, and we were all the crumbs that get stuck at the bottom of it. The final town we passed was burned completely to the ground, from stores to homes to gas stations. That meant there were actual people who lived there. I'm not sure if I was happy, nervous, or excited about searching for them under the blazing dot in the sky. Regardless, I was on high alert. Trusting strangers in a world like this is an excellent way to enter an early grave. Adahy sent Jed back to base camp to alert the people of the carnage as the rest of us fanned out and searched.

~ * ~

Todd gave each of us a walkie talkie and passed on strict orders to look for two hours, then report back to city hall. I started walking toward the northern part of town to search the industrial section along with Jacques. The rest fanned out southward. We kept nice and quiet on the prowl. Whether they were raiders, cultists, murderers, or friends, we wanted to have the jump on them. We came across a massive manufacturing plant and a surrounding steelyard on the edge of town. We found the front gate with a massive gash cut into it, big enough for two or three men to fit through at once. Jacques inspected the tear in the aluminum wire and slid his hand across it.

"It's a clean cut, like by a circular saw."

That is never a good sign.

"We have to check it out Jack. Someone might need us out there."

I pulled the 9mm out of my pack and turned off the safety. The old factory was in shambles from top to bottom. The façade was cracked, and the windows were shattered. There were tipped over barrels and wooden pallets, opened containers, empty gas cans, and bullet holes. There was a strange odor in the air too. It smelled more...organic than usual. Maybe raw sewage. You get the point. Everything was covered in a thick coat of ash too, signs of a horrific fire. I took cover behind a storage container and tried to scope out the entrance while Jacques stood with his back to the double doors facing the loading docks. He slid a revolver out of a holster and slowly loaded it with shells one by one. He signaled that his side was safe before waving me over to take cover behind the other half o f the door. Whatever was waiting for us inside the plant, we would face it together.

I crept up and hit the wall with a gentle thud. Jacques snuck to the opposite side and went for the doorknob. He grabbed the handle and wiggled it. It wasn't locked, but not because someone used a key on it. Jacques put up three fingers. His whole hand was quivering a bit, and he couldn't help but breathe out of his mouth, but he had a hell of a lot more control than I did. He lowered one, so I raised my sights. He dropped another, and I steadied my grip. He dropped the final finger, and we breached the frame. Silently and methodically, we started our silent assault on the ashes of the warehouse.

I scanned the loading bay from top to bottom. There were spare steel beams, charcoal remains of storage crates, and a massive loading truck with its tires gashed. No people to be found, just that shit-ridden smell. There was an open doorway leading into the conveyer belts, so I signaled Jacques to follow me in. As I approached the entryway, I saw an unwelcome, alarming sign generously splattered across the wall. Blood, and no stingy amount of it. I stopped and gestured for Jacques to stay put as I examined the mess. The markings were relatively fresh. There had to be someone around, and I had the misfortune of having no idea where they were. Jacques eventually moved up and saw the artwork. He seemed to be familiar with the sight. At that time, he was a veteran survivor compared to me, a real new-world badass.

We kept up the search, row by row. I checked the catwalks over and over as Jacques searched the ground floor. All that time, the terrible odor just kept coming. It got to the point where my eyes began to water. It was like someone was splashing table salt right on my pupils.

"Jacques, you smelling what I'm smelling right now?"

"Yeah, I've been a lot of places, but I have never come across something this…potent. I think it's coming from the stock room."

I turned around to see a steel door by the corner. Flies were swarming from every crevasse, and from the looks of it, the whole thing had been dented outward. I turned back to Jacques and waved him off.

"I'll check it out. Try and find some useful supplies around here. Just be ready to back me up if there are any stragglers still lingering around."

"You sure?"

"Yeah, it can't be too bad."

He agreed and headed to the right into a room neatly labeled 'break' by a copper plate. I took a moment to assess the damages, but the door was still in perfect working order. It was almost like a barricade had been punched through, but the hinges kept uptight. It was the work of a battering ram. I grabbed hold of the metal handle. It was toasty to the touch, as if it had been heated and cooled over and over again by an oven. The whole door seemed so weighty. I ducked my head a bit and shoved the door wide open. I really wished I hadn't. With a rush of a thousand insects and disgusting fumes, I found the source of the terrible smell.

The best way I could describe the stock room was a massive human grave lying upon a cement floor. There were dozens upon dozens of bodies stacked up against the door into a massive pyre, probably something around thirty-six in total. Every single one of them was torched to a crisp, burned beyond recognition by gasoline. Behind the massive human pyre was a beige brick wall with some symbols painted on it. It was a crudely drawn eye with two lines forming a dark red cross behind it, making a 'Jolly Rodger' of sorts. There were five stars above it all, each one growing progressively larger from left to right. Everything was covered by maggots as well. The pyre, the walls, or anything else you could think of. If I can remember it correctly, which I'm not sure if I can, that was when one of the bodies fell from the pile on the door and landed on my feet.

I lost it a few seconds after that. Jacques told me he heard me screaming from across the factory floor. I frantically swiped the hordes of flies from my face. Apparently, I toppled over a gas can and fell onto my back. It was about then I realized what happened there. The door didn't fail because it wasn't being breached from the outside. It was being *barricaded* from the outside, so that nothing could get out. The door naturally swung closed again, but was left ajar when it snagged on someone's thigh. Jacques came sprinting out of the break room, carrying the scraps of a chewed-through bag of chips. I could barely control my movement, but managed to lift my finger slowly and pointed to stock room. He took a slow walk over to the handle, and gently opened it. Jacques did a double take in shock, stared into the mass grave for a moment or two, blankly, and shut it again.

"It's one of the raider clans from the east, that eye is their trademark symbol, no doubt about it." He reached down to the aged walkie talkie and pressed in the bright red button on top of it. "Hey, Todd, are you listening in? Jack and I just found something out here."

There was a pause before Todd's gruff voice echoed back out of small device.

"What is it Jacques? Are you fellas alright?"

"Sorry to say it, but I don't think we need to search for survivors anymore."

~ * ~

Little buddy, I think you could use an explanation on who the raiders are right about now. In my experience, there are dozens of raider hordes spread out across the nation, but the kingpins of them all were 'The Acolytes'. They had quite the impressive following for sure. Their membership was well into the hundreds at that time. Merchants we met on the trail set up routes explicitly to avoid their usual hotspots, but they would be miraculously found out anyway. Legend had it their leader knew all and saw all. A post-apocalyptic cult, but one that found undeniable success.

They are widely feared, not just because of their violent tendencies, but for their innovative uses for the human body. I heard tales from wanderers that claimed they knew one-hundred and six ways to grill an ear. Not the corn kind. Without condiments of course. They killed and ate and ravaged everything in their path, but their favorite method of destruction was salvaging vehicles and turning them into machines of death. I never saw savagery anywhere in the wasteland as brutal as the Acolytes, not even in feral animals. Honestly, that was the scariest part about them.

~ * ~

So anyway, I was bent over dry heaving, repressing the memory of that image only seconds after it occurred. Jacques noticed me curled over in the corner, so he jogged over and took a knee. Patting my shoulder, he said, "It's not a pretty sight Jack, then again, it never is. It will get easier to see eventually my friend. I need you to be strong enough to see it again and again and keep your head. Can you do that?"

I knew what he was trying to say. If I didn't toughen up, the world would chew me up and spit me out. He was right, but the hysteria wouldn't let me realize that for a while yet. With a grunt, I forced myself back onto my feet. Jacques took my pack and swung it over his back so it would be easier for me to walk. With his one free hand, he reached down and grabbed the walkie talkie.

"Hey Todd, we're headed back to the downtown now, eta twenty minutes. I will notify Peter that we can keep moving after Jack rests for a bit."

"Alright, but not for too long. What in the hell did you two find down there?"

"I'll just tell you when we get back."

Everything was shivering profusely from shock, and each step left a subtle burning sensation in my chest. Regardless of that, I kept moving, one foot in front of the other so long as my legs would carry me. The sun was setting and a gentle breeze had picked up. At least it wasn't so unbearable outside anymore. I never found the stomach to look back at that place once we got going. Something in my brain wouldn't let me twist my head that far. It just wanted me to take the one-way ticket, so I did.

After countless uncomfortable steps through the ashes of the tiny town, Jacques and I found ourselves back by the ruined city hall. I went to the collapsing steps and crashed onto my side. After maybe fifteen minutes, the rest of the FCS arrived and began speaking with Jacques.

I managed to catch bits and pieces of dialogue between my teammates as Jacques told the story. There were quite a few 'whats? wheres? and, how manys?' Mostly though, they were gossiping about the Acolytes. They were worried about the freshness of the fires around the factory and the body count. It was a subtle panic. You could see the fear in their eyes, but they still talked tranquilly as if nothing were wrong in the world. I suppose that's what real fear looks like. The kind you aren't even given the graces to show. Seeing everyone so distraught made me feel uneasy about the trip. Murderous psycho-cannibal fortune tellers were not something I signed up for. The Acolytes were certainly a point of interest to me, but I sincerely hoped to god I would never have to see one's face.

Jacques rushed off to inform Peter of the discovery and left the other six of us to stand around. Eventually, everyone came over to check up on my condition, except for Silent Bob that is. He decided to smoke up instead. Every time they asked me how I was, I promised that all was well. Even though I was shaken by the events of the afternoon, I had to try and hold together my somewhat-macho persona. There was still a little pride left in me after all, even if it was falsified. In the matter of a few minutes, Jacques returned and notified everybody that "Healthy or not, we move out in five." I managed to sit myself up and insisted that I was fine and ready to go. Thankfully, nobody called me on it. The FCS was always respectful in that way. Hank and Jed couldn't help but mock my hobble once we actually started moving though; I would have been concerned if those two clowns didn't have something to say.

The next morning, I awoke lying in a small patch of warm sand. Without realizing it, we made it to the edge of the desert. The same beige color stretched out for miles upon miles. Endless, timeless, but most importantly, scorching. I got up and stretched, letting out a yawn fit for a blue whale. There wasn't as much as a cloud in sight. It was almost ten o'clock in the morning, long after we usually began the march. I looked around the FCS campsite, but nobody was there, so I walked back toward the Center. 'The Center' was the term referred to the middle part of the Train, which consisted of unarmed or weak passengers, unskilled workers, scavengers, and food service volunteers. Followers, not leaders. Consider it a little bit like a herd of sheep that the FCS and caboose were sworn to protect.

As I made my way down, a lightly armored truck cruised by me. It was the color of a pine tree, with multi-colored waves painted onto the side of it. The windows were tinted a dark shade of grey, hiding the face of the middle aged black woman driving it. The most unusual characteristic of the vehicle however, was the large thirty caliber machine gun mounted on its bed. We called em' 'Hornets' because of how pesky they were. They stung just about as well as hornets do too. Besides the FCS and the backline, they were the only thing protecting The Center. The guns made up most of the pack behind our punch too, a real crescendo to our rolling tide. I casually waved at the man mounting the gun, who gave a serious nod in return. Riding in the Hornets were one of the most dangerous jobs you could have. Any raiders in the entire wasteland were going to put their sights on you immediately. They might as well have had a target branded to their foreheads. The stress must have been truly incredible, maybe unbearable. But hey, at least they didn't have to walk.

The Center was buzzing with activity that morning. Everyone seemed to be lugging around large jugs and canteens. They were trying to collect whatever extra water they could before making their way into the desert, which wasn't a bad idea. I checked the few bottles or canisters I packed with me back in Phoenix to find that only one full container remained. It wouldn't last, so I surveyed the camp to see where they were getting it from. It wasn't so hard to spot. There were about fifty people crowded in a mob around what looked like a diesel tanker. I walked up to the masses and tried to find a place to squeeze in. Not unlike a defensive line in football, they blocked me and occasionally even shoved me backwards, firmly placing me onto my rear end. I had to wait, but at least landing on the sand was soft.

I felt the breeze pass in between my feet and brush my face. It was pleasantly warm, like a thin blanket, and it almost made me want to fall back asleep where I stayed. I closed my eyes and imagined what my little girl looked like after eight long years. She was probably growing up nicely, nearly eleven years old. Probably tall with amber hair, and thin as a pole, just like me. I still remember what a beautiful shade of blue her eyes were, little sapphires. I hoped the world hadn't been too cruel to her. The thought of her smile made me want to smile too. I thought to myself for quite some time what I was going to say to her. I didn't want to just give some casual apology, but I didn't want to drag it out. The words just seemed to escape me. It might have been easier to say nothing at all.

~ * ~

My thoughts were quickly interrupted when an ungodly amount of sand was kicked into my face.

"Wakey wakey eggs and bakie, Beanstalk."

That was an unmistakable voice. I shot up, still hacking out a lung and wiping my eyes. I was in the shadow of a monolith, and I was ready to get up and start kicking his ass.

"What the Hell, Mountain? I was trying to think."

"Well I'm sorry princess. I will make sure to ask your royal permission next time, alright?"

I gave him a firm knuckle to the shin.

"Hey, Hey. Don't break any toes down there. Well your highness, you missed the water cart when you were 'thinking', so I got you this bottle for the road."

He passed me a glass bottle filled with clear water. No debris, no insects. It was some impeccable quality. Regardless of how angry I was at him, I couldn't help but thank him for the kindness. He offered out a hand, and I took it with whatever dignity I had left and quickly bid him farewell. I had little time to talk, because the Train was ready to move out, and as you know, it waits for nobody.

The afternoon passed quickly, and there was particularly little to report. There was nothing to see out there except for sand. I swear, the world was both dead and alive in that landscape. There was no life, but the cascading dunes seemed ready to swallow me whole at any given moment. A real uncanny valley, if you catch my drift. It was quite a refreshing break to see a cactus or something now and again. Monochrome was never really my style. At night, we set up camp near a road we found and drank unhealthy amounts of whiskey while staring at the stars. We were more exhausted than usual, so nobody cared to talk, especially not Silent Bob, who had partaken in a new 'advanced silence', where no noise irradiated from him except for a baritone cough every minute or two.

The next few days were more of the same. We walked, we sweated, we chit-chatted. Walking on uneven, grainy footing gets under your skin faster than you think. It crept its way under every article of clothing. Guaranteed. In my sleeves, under my hat, in my shoes, under my watch. I don't even know how sand can make its way into your trousers, but I can assure you it does, and it doesn't do any kindnesses to you when you walk all day. Honestly, by the fourth or so day of our little field trip into the heart of Egypt, all I wanted was a cold shower. Those were cursed thoughts though. Thinking too much about luxury made your knees weak.

It was estimated we were somewhat around the halfway point on our detour, and morale hit a new low. We were tired, we were thirsty, we were sweaty, but worse than all that, we were bored out of our minds. The endless cycle of sand and sunlight was enough to drive two pained souls in The Center to wander off into the abyss. No chasing them down in a place like that. I think everybody expected a little desertion now and then.

We started playing games to pass time. Not anything fancy, just something simple and repetitive. You know, so even idiots like Jed could jump in. My favorite was a challenge where the man in front of the formation would sing the first line of an old song, something obvious and easy to tune in to. The guy behind him on either side would sing the next line, and the song would continue bouncing from side to side of the formation until somebody forgot the words. Most of the time, it ended in the first few lines, but once, we made it the whole way through. There was a certain sense of pride we carried in finishing a song. Something intangible. No matter what the wasteland threw at us, nothing in this world could take away our memoires of singing a tune start to finish.

~ * ~

One night, I was restless. Sleep decided not to stop in for the evening. My consciousness got the better of me, so I wandered around for a while. The guards at the edge of camp were too busy seeing mirages to notice me slip out. There was a dune not far from base camp that I decided to scale, which was a mistake. The mound looked a lot smaller than it was from where I was standing. Physical activity initially seemed like a clever idea, too. I can't remember where that enthusiasm went halfway up the hill. My body was a block of lead by the time I was within reach of the peak. Sand slid beneath my feet by the half ton, and the dune decided to hit a ninety-degree angle fifteen feet from the top. In ten minutes or so, the task was done. I felt like I was on top of the world as I looked from side to side, seeing the majesty of the world from the view of a bird. The trip was worth it after all.

From eye level, the desert just looked like pile after pile of sand with no life whatsoever to be found. However, from this new godlike perspective, it held a certain beauty. The rolling dunes below me seemed to rise together in a single wave. The cacti and other surviving plants peppered the land below me, forming little clusters and patterns like a patch of inkblots. A natural Atlas, but I had no idea where it could have lead. The desert was an entity, and the sparse life fed off it and formed a community because of it. It wasn't void of life like I had once thought, but was blooming with the very essence of it. The greatest sight of all, was the line of thin, wilting tree trunks I noticed in the distance. We had successfully traversed one of the largest deserts in the nation, and did it in just over a week.

I more or less rolled down the hill back toward camp, eyes half closed and legs as weak as a pair of twigs. Finally, it was time for some rest. When I reached the bottom, I picked myself back up and stumbled in a kind of drunken stupor back to my sleeping bag. It was one of the best nights of sleep I have ever had to this day, no bed or pillow needed. The world and I come to terms sometimes, and when we do, everything is just peachy. You see little buddy, it's the little things like that, something as simple as a good night's sleep, that keeps you sane as you push onward out there. Without those precious little intangibles, you could never find joy in the legwork, or the journey.

The next morning came without incident. We began our journey at the usual time, and kept marching all the way into the early afternoon. However, when we passed by a patch of cacti, I noticed something alarming. It was a group of forty or so fire pits, all clumped together. Smashed wooden planks and a single set of human remains were hung from one of the plants like a coatrack. Amongst the litter in the camp, there was a small pile of hardened wax which had been shattered by a great impact. The camp wasn't buried by the sand yet, so that meant the occupants could have still been in the area. No doubt, it was an Acolyte camp, and we were most likely walking ourselves right into them. Frustrated, I turned and told Adahy to run back and tell Peter, and he sprinted off.

Honestly, I think Adahy had it the worst out of all of us in the Sonoran. He was a man who loved the forest, the solid ground, and all the life it offered. He was suffering in the grainy soup. The desert just didn't have anything to offer him.

We decided to sit around one of the fire pits and talk about the path we were traveling through.

"I think that we're too close together in the way we travel right now. At most, the two furthest wings of the 'V' are around thirty feet apart. If they see one of us, they see all of us, and if they see all of us, they will shoot all of us. I think we need to expand outward so the furthest wings are somewhere around one-hundred feet apart." Todd lectured whilst the rest of us sat there twiddling our thumbs.

Jed shrugged his shoulders and asked, "That sounds like an idea, but how are we going to communicate with each other if each of us are more than thirty feet apart?"

"I think they have a surplus of walkie talkies back in the supply cart," Todd said. "Maybe we could… commandeer a few of them so the far wings and the front can communicate."

I jumped into the conversation to give my input. "Yeah, I think I saw at least three in an old cardboard box earlier, there could be even more somewhere else."

As we set up camp that night, finally on the dividing line between the Sonoran and solid ground, Silent Bob and Jacques returned from the supply depot carrying a dusty old shoebox with three walkie talkies. They gently tossed them over to me, Todd, and Adahy. They looked like they were made of plastic, but to my surprise, they had a thick metallic coating.

"We have clearance to permanently use these three alone, so you guys better make them count."

The iron was warm. It was fortunate Peter planned on keeping tech like that in the shade. Maybe even wise. We would have ended up with a few useless ingots instead. That night, I toggled the station and volume on the device as it sat on my chest. It was incredible to think how far I had already come, and my journey had just begun. I didn't worry about what danger or challenge I would have to face next. The travel kept me content enough not to pay attention to it. I slept the full way through the night, but I didn't dream. I couldn't find a reason to dream when things beyond my imagination were surrounding me on all sides.

Chapter Five: Existing in a Place With No Name

I waved goodbye to Arizona four days later. The following week was a return to the usual. Find a town, scout the streets, loot the buildings, leave the town, repeat. Eventually, we gave a name to the whole process. We jumped our fair share of white fences on the trip. Probably one every residential mile. In the olden days, those little suburban homes with white fences and little yards were referred to as 'The American Dream'. So, we decided to name the pillaging of those little houses with pretty white fences *Dream Hopping*. It left a bitter taste in my mouth, yes. The number of goodies we got from it helped to rinse the feeling down.

If you could avoid the lingering scent of the neurotoxin and the decayed corpses, it was quite a lucrative business. If you can imagine a resource, those tiny suburban castles had it lying on a table. There were cans of fruit, bottled water, lighters, medicine, and my personal favorite, more rounds of nine-millimeter ammo. What a treasure trove. Well, at least they were for a while. When we got to another boondocks town close to Albuquerque, the pickings became slimmer. Scavenged to the bone by some manner of vulture. Even the city dumpsters were carefully torn through. We knew that if the outskirts of a tiny town were looted like that, it could only mean one thing. There had to be people.

The place wasn't shattered and torched to a crisp, so it was safe to say that the Acolytes hadn't stopped in. Our number one priority was to avoid them at all costs, so that was music to Peter's ears. That didn't mean we were in the clear though. Spread one hundred feet from edge to edge, our formation spanned across three streets, each one as typical as the next. Nothing went wrong initially, but something made me uneasy. Then I noticed a manhole cover sticking up in the near distance. I examined the strange object with my field glasses. They had gotten a few scars in the desert, but the handles were still smooth, and they still worked like magic.

The cover wasn't raised from the earth more than a couple of inches, but it was definitely tampered with. The rusted rim was completely flat, but elevated, and out of one side I saw a little green wire. I began to reason out what it was, but the universe decided not to let me finish that train of thought. It was derailed by the jarring sound of an explosion.

I don't remember a whole lot about what happened next, but I do remember it changed absolutely everything. I was sprinting through a backyard as fast as I could on a direct path to where the explosion came from. I tried to remember who was supposed to be the second spot on the left side. Adahy? No he was at the front. What about Silent Bob? No, he was in front of me. I kept going, brushing past trash cans, clothes lines, pools, from backyard to backyard until I got close. Up ahead, the yard was completely fenced in from side to side. I wasn't going to stop, especially for a few rotten pickets. The whole thing got blasted to chunks. It felt like I was cutting through warm butter. I made my way to the middle of the next street in a few heavy steps. It only took me a second to register what happened when I found what I was looking for.

There was a trashcan, or something that used to be a trashcan, splintered all around the neighborhood. There was shattered glass and other shrapnel from the sidewalks, to the roofs, to the above-ground pools. The whole place looked like it had survived a tornado. Next to the remaining heap of scorched and shredded metal, face down and peppered with flesh wounds, was Hank. Two metal chunks were visibly stuck in his forehead, while two others were jammed in his neck. He still had his map opened in the clutches of his cold dead hands. I rushed over to him, but I knew that he was long gone. He felt colder than a freezer-burned steak. Eyes were still open in shock too. I put my hand on his shoulder. I don't know why. Maybe I wanted to comfort him. Maybe I couldn't help but act like he was still alive. Honestly, I never got to know the guy well, but the look of terror painted on his face was more than enough to keep him in my thoughts for an eternity.

A few moments later, I heard a buzz coming from the intercom hooked around my belt. Adahy was panicking. He didn't really communicate well under pressure. I couldn't understand a word of it. Footsteps thundered behind me. Todd finally caught up from the rear flank, and sprinted over to us on the street corner. He knelt beside Hank and calmly searched for a pulse. It only took a few seconds for our fearless leader to give up completely as well. With a heavy, melancholic breath, Todd closed Hanks' eyes with two fingers. He reached down slowly and grabbed his intercom.

"Adahy, stop where you are and have the boys return to Baker Street. Don't let them touch anything, and keep them under control. We just lost a friend."

Todd turned to me and clipped the walkie talkie back to his belt.

"This can is loaded with sharpened metal and glass. It's a damn bomb lying in the middle of the street." From the smoldering pile, Todd ripped out some green wires.

"It looks pretty advanced for a shrapnel bomb. It's not triggered manually. The wires probably lead to a motion sensor of some kind." He tossed the burnt wires off to his side.

"Sorry Hank, looks like you drew the short straw this time."

Todd sat down and started stroking his hand over Hank's head, humming. It was strangely motherly in a way. It really could have been any of us, nobody could have suspected a lethal trap like that to be sitting in such a vacant neighborhood. Hell, it probably would have been me if it weren't for my gear. Survivor's guilt is a bitch, little buddy. You can improve yourself more and more and strengthen those around you all you want, but according to most folks out there, lady luck rules the land. Your day comes along, and you best have your bags packed. Roll high kid, if you can anyway. If not, the only thing you can do is trust your gut and take light steps.

Jed started screaming as he rushed over and threw himself to the ground right next to Hank. Hank and Jed were both around the age of thirty, and they had a brotherly bond stronger than any I had seen before. It was tough to watch him weep like that. Adahy, Jacques, and Silent Bob showed up a minute or two later. They saw Hank's corpse and a look of defeat fell upon their faces. After a minute or two, Todd told everyone he had to go back and tell Peter. I told him about the bomb I saw under the manhole cover, and he jotted it down in a notebook. Todd always had a knack for recording things on paper. He said he liked how solid it felt to keep an agenda, like nothing could change his plans once they were scribbled on a notepad. He jogged away somewhat casually, leaving the rest of us to listen to Jed's agonizing screams.

We set up camp that night on the street. Everyone was terrified to break any new ground when bombs could be anywhere. At sunset, I saw Jed digging in a patch of grass not far from a line of trees. Real stone faced. A man on a mission. Whenever somebody came up to comfort him, Jed would reach into his holster, grab his sawed-off, and look them in the eye. His usual, personable demeanor was understandably MIA for the night. He knew the can was a trap. He knew and he was furious. Whoever made that bomb, whatever man or woman that killed his kin, would pay with their lives. He helped to lower Hank down into his grave as darkness slowly spread over the tiny town without a name.

After the funeral, I returned to the comfort of my sleeping bag. The covers were thick and warm, but always uneven. Almost gave me a sense of security, until I realized it was just fabric. It sure wasn't any bed. Right when I was about to check out for the night, Peter stepped by the fire and took a seat by Jed's sleeping bag, looking diplomatic as usual. Jed wasn't in the mood to talk when he arrived. He wasn't leaving this town without blood on his hands. Peter stood up and began to pay his respects to Hank, but Jed wagged his finger and cut him off.

"Don't start Peter, his death was pointless, and he deserved better than an execution."

"We'll find them Jed, and they will pay for everything they've done, I promise. We can start searching for them at first light, and maybe clear some bombs along the way as well. We have to do this carefully, or we might lose somebody else."

Jed liked the idea of a manhunt, so he nodded enthusiastically in agreement.

Peter leaned down and put his hand on Jed's shoulder "Don't worry buddy, they don't stand a chance."

He turned to walk back toward the Center, but suddenly, a booming sound rocketed from the tree line. Peter hit the dirt hard, clawing at the hole in his letterman jacket as the sleeves turned scarlet. Everyone practically dove from their seats. I rolled over onto my gut and pulled out my flashlight. As I searched a patch of weeds and dried-up vines fifty meters away, I noticed a reflection. I reached into my pack and grabbed the 9mm, and within a few moments, I was firing wildly back at the rifleman. I saw him get up and begin sprinting toward the center of town. The medics arrived to begin treating Peter, while the FCS geared up for the hunt. Bob decided to stay behind to guard Peter. We couldn't be sure if any more snipers were lingering in the area. The five of us took off into the night. We were going to slaughter the bastard.

I didn't have time to tie my laces before everyone else took off. My boots were loose and flopping all over the joint as I tried to keep pace. There was a building not far ahead of us. It was a brown single-story box with a flat roof. It looked like a shack or small radio station, and the team stopped to investigate. It had ladder rungs attached to the wall, and the roof was covered in what looked to be loose garbage. It could easily have hidden one man in a camouflage vest. I leapt up onto the fourth rung, which promptly busted under my weight. The fifth rung remained sturdy though, and the rest of the climb was a bit more stable. After a few seconds of fumbling, I flung myself atop the roof. I felt my weight shift below me, just a little bit to the side, but I paid no attention to it. With the field glasses in hand, I started scanning the open downhill slope that sat on the station's front doorstep. At the bottom of the crest, I locked on to a dust trail. He was moving toward what looked like a cluster of small shops and houses. There was a tiny church smack dab in the middle of the town, too. It looked like the perfect place for a sniper's nest.

It wouldn't be long before he reached it. We had to get moving. I ran back toward the edge to deliver the news to Todd and the rest. Big mistake. I landed my first hard step and felt the entire world fall out from under me. A chasm the size of a sedan opened up on the flat surface and swallowed me whole. When the rubble and dust finally settled somewhere in the lobby, I regained focus. It felt like every bone in my torso had been bruised, but it would take more than that to kill me. I shifted my arms and legs around to make sure I was still able to move, and forced myself to get up.

I crawled my way to the glass double doors and looked to the outside, where I saw Adahy waiting with his thumb up. I nodded. Adahy pulled and pushed the door handles, but they were rusted in place. I shook my head at Adahy, who promptly signaled I should stand back. Taking out a hefty looking ballpeen hammer, he busted the glass open, swing by swing. The glass was nothing but particles within seconds. I forced myself through a narrow opening and toppled back onto solid soil.

That's when I felt something warm trickle down my arm. I looked down to find a shallow slash across my shoulder. With my bare hands, I applied pressure to it. Adahy saw the blood, and told me that I needed to go back to the medical cart. To my own surprise, I found myself insisting to continue. Finding the Rifleman was something I suddenly felt obligated to do. That or I just wanted to prove my bravado again. That's a stupid habit little buddy, don't indulge that if you go out there. I was willing to risk my health and well-being just so I didn't look like a wimp. That's the stupidest quirk you can have. I got momentary treatment with field dressings and bottled water before debriefing Todd and the rest about his pathing. I walked over to where the steep drop of the hill began and pointed to the church with the sniper's nest. Without pause, or another moment to breathe, Jed brushed off my report and sprinted off down the incline. Alone.

I chased after him shouting he needed to slow down or die. He didn't listen. My pack grew heavy, so I dropped it. Dropping weight was like a steroid to me. The barely-surviving greenery didn't do much to firm up the soil, so every step was taken loosely and clumsily. The distance between us had shortened significantly, but he was already approaching the bottom of the hill. I needed more speed. Holding my wound was slowing me down too, so I decided to let go of it. With both hands free, I began pumping both arms like an Olympic sprinter. The wound stung for a moment, but soon all feeling faded as I gained momentum. There was only one way that I was going to stop him.

I summoned what courage I had left in me and threw myself onto Jed's back. My wound collided with the dirt behind Jed's face, and I felt a streak of heat run straight down my back. I had a grasp on him. The backwoods avenger didn't like that very much. He shook and wiggled from my grip with every ounce of strength he had. Eventually, he wriggled free and firmly kicked me in the head before taking off again. I didn't give up though. I took off after him like a city bus behind schedule. My vision narrowed. I pumped my arms harder than before. My legs were stiffer, but also riled up with pent-up anger. With reserves of energy I never knew before, I caught up to Jed a second later and threw myself at him like a ragdoll in the wind. I guess I really had become stronger.

I landed cleanly on top of him and shifted my weight to the side. We took a little two-person spin atop some prickly weeds. When we stopped, Jed started to push and shove at me again. I held on tight, bracing myself each time he started to thrash and kick. The whole time I was trying to reason with him calmly and civilly. We both knew that would never work. I managed to somehow roll him over onto his back and held his arms down. I thought I had him for a second. That's when he forced his left arm free and grabbed a rock from the ground.

Rocks hurt a lot, little buddy. They are an effective natural weapon. You can find them anywhere. Oh, and from personal experience, I can tell you they knock the sense straight from your brain and out your earholes.

I felt nothing for a few seconds. By nothing, I mean I was numb. He did manage to shake a tooth loose, which pissed me off. I was fine, but he ignited a fire. A fire he didn't have the goods to put out. I raised my fist and brought it down as if god himself appeared to smite Jed where he laid flat. I remember that he tried to put his arm up to block it. Ha. I came right across his nose with a thundering crack, then I brought another one down on his right cheek. All the while, I screamed at him.

"How fucking dense are you? Do you want to die? Do you really want to die? I'll save you some time and finish you off right here if you want."

The tears rolling down his cheeks stopped me from swinging again. I loosened my grip on him.

"Look Jed, I know you want this guy dead, and so do I. Everyone does. But you can't go sprinting around a minefield and expect to come out with all limbs attached. We just lost Hank, we don't need to lose you. So get up. We're gonna get this guy the right way. Slowly and methodically."

I leant my hand to him, who was still stretched out helplessly across the ground, and lifted him up onto his feet. Adahy and the rest caught up to us a few moments later and checked my wound, which had gotten substantial amounts of dirt in it. Adahy and Todd took care of Jed, while

Jacques pulled out a cleaning rag and told me to close my eyes. Rubbing alcohol is a lifesaver kiddo, but it stings like a stubbed toe. I had to grit my teeth for a hot second, but I've always been a weenie when it comes to burning pains. You're probably tougher than me, kid. I'm sure you could handle it.

Anyway, I got stitched up on the spot by Jacques, who apparently used to volunteer at hospitals in Canada. Jed dusted himself off and felt the area where his gums had split. He then stood up, calm as ever. Todd tossed me the survival pack I dropped in pursuit.

"Never be caught stark naked in front of a bear," he said. What a guy.

I took my crack at being a leader and addressed the group. "That's where I think he will be, right on the second floor. Make sure to check for explosives and keep your sights up, or he'll pick us off one at a time."

The moon was centerstage and bright by the time we entered the town. There was a gate at the end of a dark alley ahead of us, but we could only see the vaguest outline of it due to a shadow cast by a nearby pawnshop. Each step we took was carefully planned and calculated. One mistake meant curtains for us all. The more I thought about it, something about that gate didn't make any sense to me. If the man was being chased by a crew of dangerous folks, why didn't he try to lock us out? I whispered for everybody to slow up, and looked around the ground for something to throw past it. If it were rigged to detect movement, an object being thrown should give us a big, flashy warning. That was the plan anyway. There was nothing on the ground or within my reach, so I opened my pack and began to search for anything I could sacrifice to the god of sulfur. When I reached the bottom, I noticed a spare can of peas I bought from Jeremy back in Phoenix. I blessed my lucky stars and sent it rolling down the pavement like a bowling ball.

It kept a steady, gritty beat as it slid from crack to crack until the lid entered the threshold of the iron bars. With a flash of light and a flame that spread all across the entryway, the can was blown from existence. I was blinded for a moment, and the heat from the blast nearly singed my eyebrows. Maybe shielding my face would have been a beneficial idea. The best thoughts always come along after they're useful, ya know what I mean, little buddy? Crumbled and bent metal was all that remained. I breathed a long sigh of relief. I made the right call, and what a call it was. With everyone still in one piece, we continued the march toward the church. We were lucky, but I guess we had some intuition too.

~ * ~

The can strategy seemed to work well the first time, so we kept it up. Everyone's personal rations quickly became gunpowder jockeys. We kicked em' ahead of themselves constantly, kind of like a bunch of soccer balls, while also scanning the rooftops and buildings for signs of the rifleman. It was nerve-racking work. Somebody had to guarantee the safety of the rest of the Train, and that somebody just happened to be us. I guess it always had to be us. Yep, it was always us brave boys up front. It's kind of hard to seem brave about it when you shit your pants at the sound of an explosion every three minutes.

Sometimes, I liked to keep track of the number of steps I took in between each explosion. It was therapeutic in a way. Each step was another day I get to live, and I had a lot of steps I needed to take. It was a stupid idea, but sometimes, stupid ideas pay off. If it weren't for the counting, I would never have noticed the pattern. One-hundred steps. That's the number I always reached before something got lit up. I wouldn't have thought much of it, but it was too consistent to ignore. It seemed like the Rifleman's methodical scheming finally come back to bite him, square on the ass.

I told Todd about the unlikely pattern, and he decided to test it himself. After the next minute or so of nervous pacing, we reached the next predicted site for the makeshift explosive. It held true as Jacques kicked a can of alphabet noodles and sauce toward a storm drain and it was launched straight to the moon. Everyone let out a chuckle in disbelief. The rifleman was a psychopath, but now we knew he was a methodical psychopath.

It became a kind of game. Each one hundred steps, we would stop, shot-call a target ahead, and throw something at it. If you picked the right object on the first try, you win. We didn't lose focus though. Even if we figured out his strategy on the rigged explosives, he was still as big of a threat as ever. I started to more thoroughly examine the windows of the buildings and shops as we passed by. He could have been anywhere, really. The shops were well decorated by stickers, banners, and posters of pumpkins, skeletons, and leaves. It was early September, and I found it both heartwarming and disturbing that the whole city was decorated in preparation for the season.

The small town wasn't really all that bad to tell you the truth, little buddy. Clean streets, family-owned shops, lots of character to it. What more could you ask for? I could kind of see myself living in one of those tiny homes. Maybe I would take a stroll down to the park with my daughter, go swimming at the community pool, then take her to an ice cream parlor and find some shade to fend off the summer heat. There was even a little diner called *Downtown Den* grill and family restaurant. The wooden sign was chipped and scratched, but you could still see it was made by hand, most likely by the owner. It looked like a place where everybody would know your name. I guess that's a pretty novel concept nowadays.

My thoughts were constantly interrupted by the blast of the motion sensor bombs. Annoying little traps. After one particularly big boom, we finally caught sight of our objective building. To my right, there was a ladder leading directly up to the roof of a hardware store, which would give me a better view of the second floor and the sniper's nest. I told everybody to keep their guard up as they proceeded and hopped onto the rung, which was thankfully strong enough to hold me. Below, I saw Jed and Jacques go to the sides to flank whilst Todd, Bob, and Adahy continued to approach him head on. I reached the top and took a quick look around. It was another flat roof, but this one felt sturdier. It had a satellite dish, some spare plywood, and a trap door leading up from inside the store. I could see pretty well from the perch. Todd and his crew were fast approaching the front door, and I saw Jacques take a position by a tree to the left of the main doors. I waited a moment and searched the right side, but Jed didn't show up. Suddenly, I heard something creak loudly behind me. My eyes were met with the picturesque view of the barrel of a .357 rifle, and an angry stranger gripping its trigger.

The shady figure, a man in a baseball cap with white hair and a beard smiled at me, shook his head, and gestured that I drop my weapon.

"Put em' up."

As you could probably expect, my guard was completely down. I dropped the 9mm and put my hands up above my head. The pistol made a loud clink, which I desperately hoped someone heard. He had a camouflage t-shirt and torn blue jeans. He was a real old-fashioned recreational hunter. The Rifleman was missing some teeth, and had quite a long scar across his face. It ran the full way down his cheek to his jaw line in one clean incision. Surgical precision. Something man-made. He looked like he belonged in an asylum, but he talked with a surprisingly pleasant southern accent. I would have guessed he was kind and courteous, if he hadn't already killed a man. The deepest recesses of my mind gathered together a plan on the spot, so I started talking. The only way that I was going to survive was if I could stall long enough for my team to notice he wasn't in the church.

"Who are you?" I started, hoping he would take some time to explain.

"Little ol' me? Well you can call me Bill, Sam, Isaac, Will, Robert, or anything else. Don't matter much."

"What do you mean it doesn't matter much?"

"Nobody been here for a long time, my friend. Things get easy to forget in times like these. Anyway, I didn't think you marauders cared much for small talk. I know y'all are more of the shoot-and-mutilate before asking questions kind of people."

It seemed like he was mixing us up with a band of raiders, but we didn't look anything like those filthy freaks.

"Wait now mister, we aren't here to hurt you, we just want to pass through, that's all."

He took pleasure in discounting my words with hushed chuckle.

"That's what you said last time too, wasn't it? Yeah, we just need to pass through cause' we're nomads, please let us in. The next thing you know, you disappear, and I am left sitting atop a pile of bodies. It's been a real empty place since you all passed through here, you know that? It's just been me sitting alone, doin' a lot of planning and not a lot of anything else. It gets lonely, but you wouldn't understand that. I made a lot of promises, you see. Promises to the people I used to care for a great deal. In fact, I believe I made a promise to little Jennifer that I would kill every last one of you, slowly, to make you pay for what you did."

"Look at me, right in the eye mister. Tell me that I look like a raider to you. Tell me what we have done to you to deserve this. We aren't looking to hurt you or make you suffer any more than you already have."

He began to hold his head, like he was in pain.

"Liar. Liars, all of you. My friends, my neighbors, my community, they all trusted you. My family trusted you. I trusted you. Everybody is gone now, and it's all your fault, you scum."

"Do I look like I am some ruthless killer to you? Look, I'm sorry for whatever the heathens did, but you have to realize your people are gone now. This place is deserted. You are all alone here. We just want to pass through this place. We will leave you alone. We are not like, and will never be like, *them*."

"You think this place is deserted? You don't get it, do you? They aren't all gone, in fact, I'm thinking they are all still right here next to me. They're always here to keep my spirits high when everything else drags low. Sometimes they whisper to me, give me advice, help me to stay happy and determined. Right now, they're telling me something *real* interesting."

He officially made the jump from murderer, to pure, unchecked sociopath.

"You know what, raider? I was going to put up some nice little ribbons and scarecrows along the old telephone wires and have a big Autumn celebration with my friends and family this month, but you ruined that. I was going to get a good sleep tonight at home after a hard day's work, but you ruined that too. So it looks like I have to get my hands dirty before I can get some rest, now don't I?"

I put my hands in front of me in a gesture trying to get him to stop and think. The quiet motion of something creeping amongst the shadows behind the rifleman caught my attention.

"You don't have to do this, this could all just end peacefully. We could just go our separate ways and this could all be done."

He snorted and spit on my boots. "Well that would be just dandy, now wouldn't it? Let's have that happy ending for you, let you walk back to your group of friends down there and laugh this all off as if it were some little joke. Wouldn't that just be fantastic.? No. You took that happy ending away from me a long time ago, and now I can never have one. So, the only thing you can do for me now, to make up for all the shit you did to us, is die."

There was a flash of light and the sound of a single shot echoed throughout the night. However, it wasn't the shot of a rifle. It was something... heavier.

The Rifleman was thrown onto his side, and pieces of his head were splattered all across the wall of the building next to us. Jed slung his sawed-off shotgun over his shoulder and walked over to the Rifleman's lifeless corpse, which now hung over the side of the hardware store. He kicked him and watched the body tumble down into the alleyway below.

"Scum."

We stared at the mutilated corpse for a while. It took the crew a second to realize what happened, so they showed up a minute or two late. Jacques says he saw a whole bunch of wires in the church, and in all likelihood, it would have taken out half a city block if they broke in. The Rifleman was a planner. He planned, and he planned, and he planned, but it was all on a goal that would bear no fruit. Preparation is fine kid, but if it isn't being utilized properly, all of that work holds no meaning. In the end, I couldn't help but pity the guy.

~ * ~

The sun rose an hour or two later, and I watched it from the rooftop along with everybody else. Glistening in newfound light and stained by everything from mud to blood to faded paint was the Rifleman's .357 rifle, still intact. I picked it up and walked out as the iridescent rays of light reflected off the ventilation ducts. We returned to camp not long after that and reported to Peter, who had gotten the bullet removed overnight.

Everyone paid their final respects to Hank's grave, which was marked by a simple plywood cross. The march continued that afternoon, and on our way, I got one last look at the small town. I would hope to forget about that place sooner rather than later, but life has a funny way of stapling memories like that to your forehead. I was happy to have the place behind me regardless. We had just lost a man for the first time, and everyone in the FCS was suddenly on a razor's edge. There was a lot of growing to be done for us. We just needed to look forward.

That night, I couldn't sleep at all. For the first time on the journey, I questioned if I was the good guy. The Rifleman was a man. Flawed like a man. Affected by the world, like a man. Capable of loss, like a man. Me and Jed, well, we killed a man. Is that right or wrong? Did he really deserve it? Did that make us no better than he was?

The line between good and evil is made entirely of questions, little buddy. I hate that line. That line sucks because it's constantly moving from side to side. Everyone wants to be the hero of their own story, but it's hard to see it that way when circumstances drag you into a grey area. I guess, when it all boils down, eventually I stopped caring about that line all together.

Chapter Six: Life Persists

It was a little past mid-day in Boston, and Jack was keeping Ezekiel's attention pretty well.

"Hey Jack, I have a question."

"Oh? What would that be little buddy?"

"It sounds like you had to go through a lot just from the start. Why didn't you quit after the factory, or the roof collapse, or the encounter with the Rifleman?"

"Well, I guess it would have been smarter to tuck my tail between my legs and get out of Dodge, but I've never been much of a quitter. There was still a chance my family was here in Boston. That kept me going, regardless of what I had to deal with. It's like I said a while ago Ez, everybody out there in the wasteland keeps pushing on for something, or someone. I kept pushing on for my family. That was more than enough for a guy like me."

"Yeah, I got that, but were there any redeeming qualities to the wasteland at all?"

"This is just my story Ez. Whatever you take out of it is what you take out of it. I certainly can't help you understand your own brain. That's your job."

"Yeah, I guess. You can keep going if you want to. I just have to start taking better notes."

"Alrighty, can do, Ez."

~ * ~

The next month was nice and simple. The only problem we encountered were a few local thugs that confronted the FCS and demanded our supplies. I think there were ten of them. I'm sure we could have taken them, but Todd demanded we sit around and pretend to negotiate. You should have seen the look on their faces when the rest of the Train pulled up behind us. I think the big fella up front pissed himself. They left not long after that.

We crossed from New Mexico into Colorado, then Colorado into Nebraska without a hitch. We had to avoid Texas like the plague though. People in the Center constantly talked about how the whole state still carried heavy doses of the toxin. They called it 'The Chemical Pit'. Not a lot happened in the FCS either that month. Jed began the long road to recovery after losing Hank. Jacques was starving after losing his food rations to the bomb, so he tried cooking a feral bird. Adahy immediately said it smelled like death. Bob still never said anything. Todd just kept complaining about how sore his knees were getting. The only thing that changed about me was I could feel my feet harden. Got so many calices down there I couldn't feel myself take steps anymore. People say you become a hardened veteran if you do something enough. I didn't know that could be taken a literal way. The dream hopping we got to do was always nice though. I found a solid, thick green long sleeve in a men's fashion store. Funny enough, the only time in my life that I could afford name brands was after brands stopped meaning anything.

Of course, that pleasant little pattern couldn't last forever. It ended when we reached the entrance to the forest. Reports said it was a safe haven from any trace of the neurotoxin. A miracle network of greenery that avoided the targeting of any of the missiles on the day of the calamity. I didn't believe it until I saw it. When you are out in the wasteland, there is always a scent in the air, almost like the musk of an old library book. That was a sign that very light concentrations of the toxin were still lingering. Nothing lethal or anything of that like, but still present. However, in the forest, you couldn't catch the first trace of it. The color was almost disorienting after staring at grey and brown for so long, too. I know the idea of seeing a bunch of pines doesn't sound all that exciting to a little adventurer like you Ez, but it was an incredible experience for an old man who hadn't seen them in eight long years.

I took a deep breath. The air was sharp and refreshing. Man, what a liberating feeling. Everybody in the FCS seemed pretty struck by the scenery as well, but our job wasn't to go sightseeing. No matter how gorgeous the place was, something could still go horribly wrong. We broke camp early in the morning and strolled into the thick foliage. There could have been anything in that forest, whether it was feral animals or the fountain of youth. Our duty was to keep everyone in the Center safe, plain and simple. No fern was going to stop us from fulfilling that duty.

It rained perpetually in that place. It was like the entire ecosystem was caught in a loop of constant flash-flooding. Sadly, I forgot my floaties back in Phoenix. Each drop landed on my head with a gentle thud and rolled down my face. I hadn't felt anything resembling a moderate rain since before everything fell apart. In the desolate survivor camp that was Phoenix, rain was something beyond a miracle. Any rainfall would put the whole town into a buzz like it was a holiday, and that would be all they talked about for weeks on end. In the forest, I could just hold out my canteen, and it would practically fill itself! It was safe to say I wasn't in Arizona anymore.

The greenery kept getting thicker the farther we progressed. The world was getting smothered by an abundant coat of ivy. I had to use my now well-worn machete to try to cut through all the vines and hedges. It didn't work too well. Sometimes, I had to spare five to ten minutes hacking and slashing at the same wall to make progress. Not being able to continue the march was demoralizing. Getting exhausted and not even walking was more demoralizing. Losing a fight to a bunch of plants was even more demoralizing. My reunion with natural life forms ended up being kind of bitter.

~ * ~

We made it to a grove of birch trees about two hours later. It was time for a break. I collapsed under the tallest, shadiest tree I could find and stuck my machete in the mud. It sunk in at least seven inches. The sound of falling rain always used to help me fall asleep, back when I had a bed to sleep in and a roof over my head. It becomes a bit harder to snooze when the thickest droplets are constantly slapping you in the face. Regardless of how big of a hassle traveling through this forest was, it was still an incredible ecosystem. I hadn't seen that many living things gathered in one place since the fall of western civilization. Hell, I could even hear a songbird above my head. It took me a second to realize that chirping meant that non-feral animals existed there too.

When I say that a bird was chirping, I mean that it was singing. It wasn't squawking, screeching, flapping, or trying to peck my eyes out. I opened my eyes slowly and looked into the tree branches to find a strong, young cardinal. It was a beautiful scarlet color Ez, kind of like those berries you've been carrying around. There were more of them on higher branches. In fact, a whole flock was practically nesting in the canopy. They swooped around in patterns and circles, at least two dozen in total. Eventually, they all glided their way into the infinite treetops and left me with the raindrops again.

I looked back down and saw my comrades collapsed under their own trees. Everyone except for Adahy that is, who was instead picking berries near the center of the grove. He put them one by one in a satchel and slid that into the front pocket of his flimsy cloth backpack. There were people in our group who knew the basics of survival very well, but nobody knew what they were doing more than Adahy. Adahy was a Native American who was born and raised on a Reservation in northern California. His family was filled to the brim with traditionalists. In other words, he spent a lot of time in the middle of the woods learning its do's and don'ts.

He knew what berries were poisonous and which were safe to eat. He knew what animal made what tracks and how long ago they made them. He knew the difference between every tree known to man, regardless if they looked the same to the bark. It was pretty obvious Adahy was miserable for the first month or two of the trip, going from desolate town to desert then back to desolate town, but he seemed happy there. Really in his element. Adahy moved through vines faster than the rest of the team combined, without any real effort too. He was like a forest specter. It was especially impressive since he was lugging around that heavy crossbow of his over his shoulder.

Adahy had always been a fan of hunting, even since he was a teen. He told me dozens of stories about trips he and his father had all around the nation to hunt big game like elk, moose, bears, and on one occasion, crocodiles. I don't even have the first guess on how Adahy could kill a crocodile with a crossbow, but I know he could. In fact, the only reason Adahy survived the calamity was his frequent hunting trips. Adahy loved to hunt deer and elk in the mountains of Montana, so he decided eight years ago, at the age of twenty-one, to make a solo trip. Good timing. One day, the radio told him about thousands of little metal rods striking the west coast, then everything went silent. He went to return home, but was stopped by a group of survivors that were crammed into an SUV. They told him horror stories of the west coast and the lethal toxin, and after careful thought and consideration, Adahy was forced to give up on his journey. He returned to the mountain cabin he was renting for the hunting trip, and alone, he hid from the world.

He must have struggled with being alone for that long. Seven years with no contact must have been tough. It was probably a really tempting idea to abandon the hut, walk into the mist and die, but he didn't. He outlasted it. While he looked at the pros and cons of breathing, Adahy lived off the land. He ate well, drank clean water, and got more than his fair share of fresh air. None of that helps with loneliness though. Gotta have company Ez. Going it out there alone will only make you crazy.

When he finally came to the full realization, he was by himself, Adahy began to figure out what his calling was. Adahy needed to find purpose, and wouldn't find it at the cabin. Eventually, he came to the conclusion to become a teacher. There are a lot of ways to survive out there Ez, but Adahy knew how to *live*. That kind of knowledge was worth sharing. After a short stint preparing words of wisdom, our native friend took off and headed south. Back down to California he went, not caring if he would die to the toxin. Luckily for nature's pedagogy, there was only a foul stench in the air, and nothing more. It dissipated over time into a thin, opaque fog. Harmless enough to travel through. Adahy could finally complete his journey back home, just seven years late too.

He found nothing there when he arrived but a few empty homes, and unmarked graves. His family was nowhere to be found, dead or alive. Adahy knew, deep within his heart, he expected to find nothing else. With a respectable amount of resolve, he overcame the discovery and continued with his quest to serve the people. If he could find any, that is. That's why he decided to head for a major city. Fate had him choose San Francisco. After a month or so of travel, he found his way to the Golden Gate Bridge. There were empty cars everywhere surrounding the area, but not too many human remains. Adahy began to think he was the last man on Earth, but before he was to give up, he would find a little camp inside a department store on the outskirts of town.

Their leader was an enthusiastic young man named Peter, and he welcomed Adahy with opened arms. He even showed enough hospitality to invite Adahy into their little survivor den. For weeks, Adahy met new friends and people who had all suffered just as he had, people like Jed and Jacques, Todd and Bob. He taught them about foraging and hunting, and in return they game him friendship. It was a fair trade. One day, Peter addressed everyone in the market and proposed a bold new idea, one that could provide all new opportunities for the survivors, or lead to their downfall. When he was asked about joining them on their journey, Adahy immediately agreed. More miles under his feet meant more people to be found. More people meant more students. Adahy really wanted more students. With that, he joined the most prodigious human project undertaken since the end of the world.

~ * ~

I got up and stretched my legs. They buckled a bit from stress. All part of the fun. I leant my hand out to Jacques and pulled him up onto his feet too. We heard the conductor's car and its muffled engine revving in close by. We had to make up ground, and fast. We rushed the next hundred meters, so the supply carts could have a path to travel through. The rest of a day crawled on at a snail's pace before coming to a complete halt in the late evening. We underestimated how strong mud could be, and you can believe me when I say it is one tough SOB when it wants to be. I can tell you that mud is strong enough to entomb a cart carrying one ton of equipment in ten inches of earth. The entire backline gave a crack at freeing the wheel, but no amount of manpower was going to save it. Not even the mighty ego of 'Mountain' could make the cart budge. There was no choice but to stop and set up camp while everyone tried to bring the cart back into working order. We abandoned it the next morning, spreading its contents evenly throughout the other seven vehicles, and to anyone who was willing to help carry it.

I took some spare bandages and stuffed them into my pack. It wasn't much really, but anything helped. The trudge continued soon after. We were supposed to reach the end in the matter of two days, but those two days felt like an eternity. The good news though was, by watching Adahy clearing pathways, I learned how to cut the vines. I never thought to search for the thinnest sinews like that. Even when Adahy wasn't teaching me, he was still teaching me. He was still way faster than me though. It was almost like he had lived there for his whole life, regardless if his stay was only for two days. I became frustrated over the ordeal, that stupid ego of mine again. The long and short of it is that I challenged the master at his own game. I like to call it my competitive spirit. My swings became heavier. My stride became longer. My movements became more fluid. Soon enough, I was carving through greenery like a bat out of hell. I even managed to catch up to Adahy, who noticed my pace increasing.

He took it as a challenge. I didn't expect anything else.

Adahy began to focus and took more precise swipes. Strength, accuracy, and speed, all in one bundle. My stupid pride wouldn't let me lose that easily though. Like a charging rhinoceros, I leveled whatever plant was unfortunate enough to be growing in my general direction. Dozens of yards behind me, I heard Todd calling for me and Adahy to slow down. At least I think he did. I wasn't paying attention. The race lasted a long while, but Adahy was always a few steps ahead of me. Past a patch of thorn bushes, I noticed an opening into a grove, and I sprinted to it. With all the energy I could gather, I threw myself through the gap and landed on the other side. I was on my stomach, face down, but I was happy that I managed to beat him here, wherever 'here' was.

Adahy stepped over to me and started chuckling. "What, you tired already Jack? I'm good for another mile or two if you are."

I turned myself onto my back and gasped for air between syllables. "Nah…you know what? You can go on ahead. I'll catch up."

"Overall, not bad, but your swings were sloppy and angled. The thorn bushes are still standing."

"Yeah, sure. I'll go fix that once I tell Todd about how I just beat you in a footrace."

"Beat is a strange word for a man to say when he is chin-deep in a mud-bath."

I shrugged him off. Just because he was right didn't mean I had to acknowledge it. After wiping off my machete and giving Adahy a solid slap on the shoulder, we went to rejoin the others. However, as we turned back to face the hole, we met a couple new friends. Two tiny balls of fur rolling around in the dirt, right by where the thorn bushes thinned out. Bear cubs. They were adorable, but any woodsman worth his weight knows one thing for sure. Cubs are never alone. I slowly turned my head to the right, and I saw a cave lying on the side of a hill, tidy and small. Definitely inhabited. There were cubs, there was a cave, and there was a big open space that a large creature could move through. That only left one thing that could be accounted for.

I reached into my torn pack and sorted through the endless bandages and meds. Of course, the 9mm would get lost right then, when I needed it most. There was some shaking deep within the tree line. I found my gear near the bottom and found a good grip on the barrel. I ripped it out of its entombment and loaded the magazine into it. Adahy loaded his crossbow and pulled out his knife, scanning the area of the cave and surrounding trees. I reached down to the ground and grabbed the old machete again, which had already been covered by the infinite pools of mud. It wouldn't be of much use, but I felt better having it with me anyway. The bear finally emerged as I fumbled with the safety. It made its appearance with a crack and a baritone grunt. I spun around and saw a massive black figure stomp down a bush with two massive paws the size of car tires.

It was a black bear, and it was not happy. The thing was practically frothing at the mouth. It was the biggest bear I ever saw, even before the end times. Bears usually don't exist in the plains states. It must have migrated from further up north. Just my luck. It probably didn't have any predators either, which explained the size. We stood our ground and started shouting and waving our hands in the air to look bigger. The plan was to look all massive and scary to spook the furry monster off. It wasn't really impressed with us though. The noise and show only seemed to aggravate the creature, so we put a pretty quick stop to it. It grunted and began to charge at us like a deranged bull, but we did not try to run away. Running away would just mean that I would die tired, and I was already tired. I took a good hold onto the handle of my pistol and finally managed to turn off the safety.

Adahy fired the first arrow out of his crossbow and it cleanly cut into the beast's neck, but the penetration was shallow. It didn't even slow the bear down, let alone kill it. I aimed my 9mm sights directly at her eyes and let out a shot. The round was low and to the left, so it collided with its massive jaw line, causing some teeth fragments to shatter into its throat. I should have known a pistol wouldn't do jack diddly to a bear, but panic makes you stupid. There wasn't much time to act before it would be on top of us. I let out two more shots which weren't quite so accurate, hitting her right leg and center mass. I might as well have been firing marshmallows at the thing. Adahy let off one more arrow which landed dead center on its chest. To our misfortune, all of the damage done wasn't crippling enough, and the furry monster reached Adahy with all limbs intact.

It stood up onto its hind legs and tried to swipe at Adahy's head. As its massive paw came swinging down, he dove to his right. The claw only missed by inches. Momma bear leaned over to take a bite out of him as he tried to roll away, but her railway-spike teeth only caught a strap of his knapsack. Two close calls in a row.

Sometimes, you just feel helpless. Like the world is the ocean and you are a pebble. That kind of helpless. A bear made me feel like that. A stupid, smelly animal. That feeling wasn't about to fly, not while I still had legs and arms to use. I was still exhausted from sprinting through the woods. Breathing was difficult, my head was pounding, and my stupid pistol was too weak to help. Yeah, I was practically useless too, but I was no coward. I had to do something. I raised my sights and started to bury shots into the beast's side, trying to divert its attention. I felt the recoil of each round until my hands grew sore. However, that little pea-shooter just didn't have enough kick, and the bear was still ignoring me. I had to try something else.

It began to claw at Adahy, tearing up his arms and back. It wanted to expose his face and neck. He dropped his bow and knife and covered his head in his hands. Even in all the panic of the moment, Adahy was still in control of himself. So was I. I dropped the 9mm and charged at the animal with my old machete. The bear started nudging at Adahy, trying to roll him onto his stomach. It bit into his shoulder. That got a scream out of him. I kept going, raising the old hunk of rusted metal over my head like it was a sledgehammer. As I got within a few feet of the brown mass of fur, I brought the blade down onto its neck. It sunk in pretty well for a dull, dirty blade, and it sure was an attention grabber. I even corrected the angle on it that time. It felt like a clean cut, maybe too clean. What I'm getting at here is the blade was in too deep to possibly retrieve.

It was frustrated, hurt, primal, and just about as pissed as an animal can get. I started putting some distance between the two of us. It took slow, heavy steps forward as I inched back, and I knew that it would be a matter of time before it started sprinting at me again. I decided to take that initiative before it did. Three steps later and I was in full stride. Momma bear's cave was sitting atop a nearby hill. It seemed to be my only option. That plan didn't last long though. As I picked up the pace, the bear started charging behind me at an incredible speed. For each step I took, the bear took two, and it was covering ground fast. There was no way that I was going to make it. In a split-second decision, I decided all I could do was divert the thing's attention. I ran straight into the branches and vines and bushes, not caring where I would go, so long as it was away from Adahy.

Running on uneven ground isn't easy, Ez. Balance is tough enough already, it's not comfortable, and you could break your ankle with just one bad step. Yet, I was still making good time. I heard the hefty steps of the bear following a few dozen yards behind me, but it seemed slower now that we weren't in the open. I put my arms in front of my face to block the tree limbs from hitting me, but sometimes they would still catch a piece of me. I felt hot welts from whipping branches sting my cheeks. I was far too afraid to be in pain. Momma bear thudded into the mud once every second or so, so I got an idea of its rate. Then I counted my own steps as grounds to judge distance. I was getting off about one and a half each second. That meant I was still losing ground. I tried to pick up the pace to outrun the bear, but my legs couldn't push any harder than they were. There was no energy left to burn. I felt myself slowing down at an alarmingly aggressive rate. My legs turned to mush. I stopped altogether a few moments later, huffing and puffing for air.

There was a big stick next to where I stopped. A fight seemed to be imminent, even though I knew exactly how that would go. I was too tired to carry on running, so my options were limited, but even in my panic, I still had my wits. If Adahy could keep his calm, so could I. In my final moments alone, I remembered the old survival trick you are supposed to use when a bear attacks. The stick flopped back into the earthy soup along with my body. My breathing hushed up real fast. Time to play cadaver. The low, toned crunches of the bears massive paws stroll up behind me and stop right next to my head. My hairs began to stand on end. *Just look like a corpse, Jack.* That's what I kept telling myself. Maybe, just maybe, she would lose interest and go elsewhere.

I felt its cold, wet snout run up my back all the way to the nape of my neck. Suppressing shivers isn't easy, but I managed it. Momma bear grunted and panted a hot, disgusting breath onto my exposed arms. I felt a gentle nudge under my stomach for a few seconds, and I let myself be rolled over onto my back. I held my breath, knowing well that one little sound would mean the end. Even though I put forth my best efforts to keep still, I began to feel my leg shake out of nervousness. After a moment or too, the bear noticed and trotted over to my right side. There was a tug on my pantleg, and my entire left side was slowly lifted up and shaken. It dragged me across the soil a few inches between shakes. The fabric began to tear and rip under the pressure, and soon enough, my exposed leg fell back to the ground. The thing had torn right through my jeans. Better yet, the dumb creature didn't even put a scratch on me.

I couldn't see the beast leaving me alone any time soon, so I decided to hold out and wait in hopes that it would walk just a few steps away, giving me the space I needed to book it. My thought was that a minute of inactivity would give me the energy necessary to escape the frothing fuzzball. A minute or so passed in a nervous silence. Nothing on the face of the earth moved except for her massive brown paws. They circled me endlessly. Momma bear was still bleeding from the mouth and neck, and I heard each and every drop hit the warm mud below its jaw. I listened for its steps to soften. Time slowed down. I laid with the back of my head deeply buried into the mud up to my ears. The sound was muffled, and I couldn't feel my face, but I could still pick up on the steps. Eventually, they grew quieter and less frequent. The bear was slowly inching away from me. That was all that I needed.

Right when I was about to take off like a fighter jet into sky, I heard a subtle noise coming from the shrubberies. It wasn't loud or clear, but I could still vaguely comprehend it. They were gentle whispers. It had to be my crew, there was no other possibility. The five of them would have little trouble taking the mama bear down with a combined effort. A sense of relief began to set in, and unwisely, I let it overtake me. I sighed. What an idiot, right? The stupid noise was loud and noticeable, and before another moment passed, I heard the animal making its way back over to me. Before I could regain my corpselike composure, the filthy wounded beast was standing right next to me, more suspicious than ever.

There was a series of little yelps and grunts, followed by what sounded like two of its paws leaving the ground. My little ruse had just fallen apart. I opened my eyes to see the giant wall of brown fur towering over me on its hind legs, ready to pounce down onto my stomach. I made like a paper towel and started rolling. The bear's massive weight shifted and crashed into the exposed earth. Her legs sank deep into the muck like a javelin in a grassy field. It seemed to struggle to pull them back out. As I continued to roll, I heard a volley of thundering claps and bangs fly overhead, and what seemed like a dozen bullets pierced into the chest and face of the animal. It twisted and recoiled, but it continued to give chase. Guess I'm just too likeable for my own good. I felt the thundering trot start again on my left side. There was no time to stand up, so I rolled toward the gunshots. That's when I heard the swishing of a liquid in a bottle soar over my head. I heard a crash and a low orange light gleam brightly over my shoulder.

I stopped my roll and sat up, looking at the source of the light. There were a few shards of broken glass and a fire blossoming like a flower that smothered the animal and the area surrounding it. Its fur ignited quickly, and a putrid smell began to fill the once perfectly clean air. Momma bear started wailing and running from tree to tree. She slammed her side against the trunks, hoping to smother the flames. For every one she put out, another doubled in size. The mighty giant whined and yipped as the flames consumed its body. Before long it rushed into the brushes, never to be seen again. Miracles do exist Ez. Their name is Todd.

Jacques lifted me onto my feet and threw my shoulder over his back. They had retrieved my pack from the clearing and brought it for me. I opened it up and found the spare painkillers and bandages laying on top of the rest of my supplies. I popped a few pills, regardless if I was fine or not, and put some gauze on some scrapes and cuts. Another day, another new, unpredictable experience under my belt.

~ * ~

Walking definitely wasn't an option. I was carried back to the medical carts, where a trained nurse named Vicky cleaned my wounds and replaced the bloody gauze. She told me that even in the biggest drunken stupor of her life, that she would never have been dumb enough to run up to a bear and hit it with a rusty piece of metal. Adahy was brought over moments later and was treated by the main physician. Though unsanitary, that sowing needle and fishing line did wonders for the gash on his back. I was ordered to sit on the medical cart and have an easy ride for a few days. Not really my style, but on this one occasion, I didn't really mind. Keeping yourself in working condition is an absolute necessity out there Ez. Don't forget that. Of course, I wanted to stay up front with the rest of my team, but there was no way that I would have been able to work in a condition like that.

Sitting around on a cart is a pain in the ass. Literally. The wood just wasn't comfortable at all. There was little to do and very few people to talk to, so mostly I just looked up at the clouds and daydreamed. I never really noticed how tall the trees were in the forest until I looked straight up at one. They seemed to stretch up and up infinitely, into the clouds, into the heavens, maybe places even beyond that. That's one way to make yourself feel insignificant. But hey, there is nothing wrong with being insignificant in the grand scheme of things, so long as you find your niche.

Within a day, I was feeling more energized. Each break we took, I got up and tried to do a couple of push-ups or jumping jacks to check my progress. Vicky reassured me I was healing well, and may be able to walk in as little as one day. That was a relief to hear honestly, because I felt the rest of The Train would think I was a leech if I relaxed for too long. Lesson learned. Ego aids recovery.

Every six hours or so I replaced the gauze on my leg and poured water onto the scrapes to clean them. At that point, I was pretty comfortable doing things in a cycle. Adahy came back to visit me once and a while to thank me again for leading the animal away, to which I would promptly respond "You would do the same for me." He was still fighting fatigue, and most of his days were spent keeping his fresh wounds away from anything that might get them infected. Things like infections were a death sentence. You know what they say, cleanliness is next to godliness.

Apparently, Adahy had gotten up around thirty seconds after I took off into the brush and went to find the others. Wounds and all. They immediately started to fan out and search for me. As they wandered toward the grove, I was playing dead in, they heard the footsteps of the bear. That's when they found me there, pretending to be dead, trying whatever cowardly tactic I could to fool the stupid creature. I would say they had some pretty fantastic timing, don't you think? Well, I guess a lot of things were avoided out there by sheer luck. One small slip along the way anywhere and I wouldn't have been here to tell you this story Ez, that's for sure. Without intuition, my luck would never have mattered either.

We reached the edge of the forest by the end of the next day. I noticed that afternoon the trees were becoming fewer and fewer by the hour. Any remaining animal life disappeared by the late afternoon. Eventually, the rain faded away, and the midday heat finally started beating down on us. It was a bittersweet reunion. When the ground dried out a bit, I decided to try my hand at walking again. The numbness and exhaustion in my legs were gone, and it felt as if I would be fine to rejoin the frontline, regardless of the doctor's orders. I slung the pack over my shoulder, feeling stiff from the past few days of total inactivity, and jogged back to my crew.

The Train was around a quarter mile long, and running through the forest, especially in my condition, took quite a while. After about fifteen minutes, I reached the front again to find my team swatting at the final group of bushes on the path until we were to reach an open field. They noticed me stumbling my way over and welcomed me back with open arms. Todd asked if I still had my machete. I told him that it had found a new home buried within about six inches of animal flesh, and he sighed.

"You gotta take better care of your equipment son. Your weapons and tools mean your life out here."

Todd reached into his pocket and pulled out a fancy looking switchblade. Close to four inches long and vivacious blue. It felt lighter than air. It was no machete, but it was sharp and easy to carry, so it was good enough for me. I thanked him, and tested its durability by sawing away at a low hanging branch.

It took some time, but eventually we managed to clear our way through the remaining weeds and tree branches. I was already tired and sweating from the little work that I did, but I managed to hold my own. The desolate wasteland welcomed us back with glee. Long live the dusty soil. The sun was setting, and a strong breeze was sweeping across the dry earthy surface, kicking up debris clouds. The crabgrass, while prickly and stiff, was a relief to feel. Solid ground had eluded us for some time, but it really wasn't worth the cost. The pure air we were breathing had slowly been tainted, and the same old musty stench of the toxin had returned. Ever since that moment, I have never had another breath of truly fresh air. All good things have to come to an end at some point though, right Ez?

~ * ~

Ez had been taking notes on his arm with a pen the whole time. *Health first, never go it alone, watch structures, raiders aren't only the bad guys, there are no such things as bad guys.* He had already learned a lot. Now it was time for a question.

"What is it little buddy?"

"Do you ever wonder why you took this whole journey? Have you ever regretted it?"

"Yeah, but just once, for a minute or two, that's about all. You can't let a silly thing like regret slow you down little buddy. Stress and tension build up like a stack of bricks that you have to carry on your shoulders at all times. If they ever get too heavy, you are liable to collapse."

Ez sat back on his bags and smiled. Clicking his pen again and opening his palm, Ez jotted down another note.

"Thanks Jack, you can keep going now."

Chapter Seven: Where Time Forgot to Alter

It took three more days to finally ditch Nebraska. The small towns became even smaller. Post offices became open weed-tundras. I was never really a big fan of barns, farms, or silos, so the scenery didn't do much for me. Not all was grim though. The land was flat and there was no storm or heat wave to make things miserable. Iowa was lucky during the apocalypse in the way that it avoided total destruction. There weren't many non-feral beings present, but some of the grass was still fighting for their right to exist. It was nothing in comparison to the forest, but any pigmentation other than grey gave me comfort. It wasn't quite paradise either though. Rain had continued to plague us, and our food supply had finally begun to falter. My pack grew lighter, my stomach smaller, and my energy non-existent. Some folks in the Center resorted to eating the remaining grass for sustenance. They looked like cattle. Starving cattle. Okay, we were all starving.

Three days in, Adahy, as vigilant as he was, caught sight of something off the beaten path. In a field behind a gas station, there was an industrial-sized farm. The soil looked fresh and tended to, and there were symmetric rows lined to the hilt with leafy stalks as tall as I was. We had stumbled across corn, and a whole crop of it. My instincts kicked in. We covered the distance of the open field faster than Todd could call for us to slow down. I ripped ears from their stalks like a deprived chimpanzee reaching for a banana. The outer husks were softer than silk. Adahy told us that meant they were ripe, but I don't know if he really meant that. We never even thought to question who grew the stuff. The growling in our guts tuned out anything coming from the backs of our heads.

By the end of it, I must have had a dozen ears stuffed deep into the pockets of my pack. They were oddly heavy, and the insides stuck to me like wallpaper glue, but starving was starving. Walking back to camp with the good news, The FCS got a quick spring in their step. News about something as simple as a vegetable would probably send the Center into a total frenzy. Jed in particular was looking forward to seeing who'd froth at the mouth first. He kept calling it *people rabies*. It was around the time of our arrival back at camp when the big question finally hit me. *Where did it come from*? After visiting the small town where Hank died just two months ago, I couldn't shake the idea that all survivors were evil, not just the Acolytes. It's cruel to make assumptions like that, but I would rather be cruel than dead.

I knew Peter would stand strong about his policy of inviting people to join us, so worrying was kind of pointless anyway. His gunshot wound was still healing, but Peter was still willing to speak to the next survivors he met, no questions asked. He just loved the sound of his own voice that much. Out came the megaphone, up went Peter to the hood of the vehicle, on came his siren. The megaphone got quite a bit of wear and tear in the desert, but the siren was still kicking pretty well. That's a pity, because I hated the sound of that siren. It was so high pitched that one blast could bleed a dog's ears dry. Anyway, Peter used it to get the attention of the already irritable Center and began his usual rants.

"Listen up people," He began. "Our scouts have reported there is a cornfield not more than a half mile from where we stand. That obviously means that somebody around here grew that corn, and maybe willing to trade with us. Hopefully, they are cooperative, and we can communicate civilly. It is even possible that more survivors will be joining us on the long walk. In saying that, I want all of you to keep your weapons holstered and sheathed. Try and make a decent impression. However, if this whole thing goes south, I trust you will do whatever is necessary. We will probably reach whatever settlement they have by mid-morning tomorrow, so just keep your guard up tonight and put forth a pleasant demeanor for when we arrive. If we do this right, I don't think hunger will be a worry for us any longer."

The thought of not being hungry was motivating. The many scowls of the folks in the Center gave way to excited chatter. Like office drama, but about not dying of hunger instead of who keeps stealing all the staples. My crew headed back out into the front of The Train to set up our tents and build a fire. I remember it was a calm night. Clear as a polished mirror. I think I could even see every star in the Big Dipper, which was a treat.

It was just about as comfortable as I had been since this whole trip started, yet I couldn't manage to sleep. Something was keeping me up. I swear I could feel every hair on my arm stand, but when I sat up and looked around with my light, we were entirely alone. I retired back to my pillow graced only by the sound of a gentle hum constantly ringing in my ears. I fell asleep a few minutes later, but the low humming sound never stopped.

~ * ~

It felt like I woke up as soon as I shut my eyes. I snapped awake with a cold sweat on my back and blurred vision. Nightmares plagued my sleep. Not any usual nightmare either, it was one of those dreams that grabs you by the ankle and drags itself into reality. To put it kindly, I was in a world of hurt. Arms limp, stomach queasy, stiff legs, sore back, I was a real hospital case. It seemed that mind really was over matter, at least in my case. I didn't remember much about the dream after the first time I had it, but what I did remember at that point was that I was alone, more alone than I have ever been in my whole life.

With whatever effort I could dredge up, I dragged myself out of the sleeping bag and balanced myself upside the bark of a dead oak. I kept a strong grip on a sturdy branch and propped my weakened legs on its roots, using them as momentary braces. My immediate thought was that the starvation was still picking at my brain and leaving me disoriented. I reached into my bag and grabbed an ear of the miracle corn. Before taking my first bite, a rather interesting thought stuck to the roof of my mouth. I hadn't felt sick like that from starvation for days before, so why would it start then, when I actually had grub in my gullet. I amended my original thought. Something I ate caused the sickness, and I had only eaten one thing in a long time.

People had once told me that the symptoms of the chemical affected people from the inside out, starting with the core. You would go numb there first. Then it would boil like hot lead, choking you and burning your digestive track like loose rubber. I felt a twinge of that in the corn, the evil root of the toxin. In all likelihood, the soil wasn't that clean after all. The only food I had seen in weeks just happened to be poison.

After putting some thought into it, I took another bite from a fresh ear. I decided that hunger was a more dreadful experience than sickness. Hunger made you weak and desperate, the other just made you weak. So the mutant corn became a cross that I was willing to bear. Calculated risks are essential to survival out there Ez, if you don't take risks, you never make progress. Remember that.

~ * ~

Half an hour later, we packed up and left camp. We tried to keep our guard up while looking non-threatening. It was no simple task. The paths were made of stones and dirt, almost like it was hand paved. It was a pleasant change of pace for me to walk on a flat surface instead of sand, mud, or degrading structures. However, the march through Iowa had become tedious and paranoiac. Looking for a threat without being able to act upon the threat can get frustrating quickly.

There were some posts sticking out of the ground here and there along the path as well. Maybe they were up to my waist, possibly a bit higher. I was impressed with them, because they had lights wired to each stake. Todd called for us to investigate before continuing. One thing was for sure, these people were civilized. As Todd followed the wires through the grass, I checked the lights for any signs of explosives. We had learned our lesson. Right about when I was done with my inspection, I was caught completely off guard by someone shouting, "Hello there," right over my shoulder. I spun around like a top and stared straight into the middle of about twenty lightly armed men and women coming out from the fields of produce.

I kept my hand as far away from the 9mm as possible. One false move and this entire day would turn red faster than a cigar burn. Instead, I put on what some experts would refer to as "a smile." I'm sure it wasn't a convincing grin. Strike that, I'm sure I looked like a serial killer. The crowd didn't seem to mind though. A big fella in a thick red flannel stepped out in front of the mob and introduced himself.

"Welcome travelers. The name is Saul, I'm the mayor here in our little community of Parkersville."

Saul had to be at least two hundred and eighty pounds of pure muscle. He had a thick brown beard and a surprisingly well-tamed comb over. He was a lumberjack on steroids and protein powder. After I took a good look at him, I motioned for Jacques to act as our ambassador, and he gladly stepped up to the plate.

"Hello Mr...Saul was it? My name is Jacques, and our little band here are representatives of our larger group."

Jacques was immediately cut off by the big man, who seemed awfully annoyed all the sudden.

"Oh, not you insufferable little bastards again."

He took a stainless-steel carving knife from a holster and pointed at Jacques. Things hadn't gotten off to a good start. Jacques flinched, but thankfully, he recovered his posture.

"Sir, I think you may have confused us for somebody else. We have never as much as seen you before once in our travels. We represent the San-Francisco to Boston Survivor Train, and we were looking to trade you for enough food to make it there without losing anyone to starvation."

He loosened his grip on the handle. "My apologies buddy, we've just been having some troubles with a small group of riff raff. They said they were here representing someone too. Didn't care much to listen. I don't know why I thought you were them, you dress nothing like those lunatics."

"I'm glad to see someone still has the ability to reason out here," Adahy whispered

"So, how many people are on your, uh...what did you call it again?"

"Train."

He nodded. "Oh yeah, of course. What, are there twenty, thirty, forty of ya?"

"Actually, I think that we are something around the lines of one hundred nowadays."

His eyes grew to the size of saucers.

"One hundred? Well then, I guess I can thank my lucky stars you aren't like that other riff-raff. I hope we have enough to trade with you so you can make your way along. Where are the rest of you?"

"About a quarter mile back by now, they should be here in something like ten minutes."

Saul nodded and gestured for us to continue down the road. "You should come across a brick post office about two hundred feet past that hill. All of you except for Jacques can go get something warm to eat, just say that Saul sent you. I just need one guy up here so we can identify your group as they show up."

Yeah, we may have left Jacques alone with the group for a bit, but he was a competent negotiator. He would do just fine. We were also starving, so any offer of food trumped any bond of friendship. Especially warm food. Bob lead the way for once, which did a good job of surprising Todd. I guess an empty tank can even drag introverts out of their shells a little bit.

Just as Saul said, once we reached the top of a small hill, we could see their entire, blossoming village. What a view. We saw kids running around on a playground, men and women grilling corn cobs and beef, and a beautiful red-brick building. An American flag flying over top of it too, which was a nice touch. There was a quaint little painted sign hanging from what looked like an old mailbox. It was made of a pallet covered by canvas, and there was a curving and twisting red border. In a central, bold black text, there was a message saying, 'Welcome to Parkersville, the last little town on earth.' It was...well, what's the word for it? Nostalgic? Unique? Homely? I think I'll just go with *impossible*.

The people were pretty friendly as well. They were obviously confused as to who we were, but once Todd said the word Saul, they seemed at ease. He must have had some impact on those people. Without as much as saying a word, they guided us over to where they were grilling and got us a plate of warm food. The strange taste and feeling was consistent in the corn, but I could already feel its effect dulling on me. It was awfully exciting to meet some folks out in the wastes that didn't want to cut my head off. A real relief. For the first time in nearly eight years, not only had I found a group of friendly outsiders, but also experienced hospitality. I started to think that maybe the corn killed me, and Parkersville was the afterlife they sent me to. A spoonful of their mashed potatoes almost made me cry.

Not long after we finished the warm meal, I heard the oh-so familiar sound of the Conductor's car rolling down the hill. The brakes were squealing a lot more than I remembered. I sat back on my bench and relaxed while Peter gave a speech not at all different than the one he gave back in Phoenix. With his booming voice and strong linguistics, Peter did his best to persuade the city to trade supplies or even join us on our journey to the east. He honestly looked broken with the bandage wrapped tightly around his shoulder. Like a baby bird that accidentally fell from the nest and snapped a wing. Not very imposing. However, he still spoke with the same fervor and gusto that he always had, and by briefly looking around I could see that the villagers were agreeing with what he said. Yeah, Peter is obnoxious, but he always did his job.

After he finished his great speech, our resident Julius Caesar stepped off the dirtied black hood of his vehicle and went out to greet the people. I watched him shake their hands and laugh amongst them. Maybe he was the world's last great politician, maybe he was just full of shit. Didn't matter much to me. I found an empty trash can and dumped the remains of the toxic meal into it before I went on to mingle with the townsfolk, along with Jacques. There were about fifty of them and one hundred of us. The public area was barely big enough to fit everyone. We were sardines lined from building to building. I forced my way through the crowd, giving friendly greeting after friendly greeting until I found myself staring straight up at Saul.

"Hello there. You were one of those scouts we met up with earlier right? How have the people and food been treating you?"

"The best time I've had in months."

I made the poor mistake of going in for a handshake afterward. It felt like I placed my right hand under a moving steam roller. After about four seconds, I managed to rip my fingers from the Jaws of Life.

"That's one hell of a handshake you have there." I said rubbing my now red and trembling pinkie finger. "How strong are you?"

"Well, some people say I'm the strongest man left on Earth, and nobody has come around to prove me wrong. Hopefully that helps answer your question."

A lightbulb suddenly went off above my head. It was time for some entertainment. Maybe Saul was the strongest man left alive. Saul was a big guy. In fact, I'd say he was almost as big as a mountain.

"What's up with that silly grin on your face, do you think you can take me on?"

"Not me, but I do have a friend I want you to meet."

~ * ~

Following at my heels, Mountain kept tapping my shoulder.

"Hey Beanstalk! Where are you taking me exactly? I do have a job I should be doing right now. Peter is gonna get pretty peeved if he sees me away from my cart. We can't trust all these folks yet."

"You'll see Mountain, we'll be there in just a minute. I just need you to help me put a guy in his place."

"Yeah sure little buddy, I got your back. What bug are you looking for me to squash today?"

"Oh, just some local punk that thinks he is the strongest man in the world."

Mountain rotated his shoulder and stretched. "That's all? Sounds like a snap. Ain't nobody wandering around the wasteland with as much raw strength as yours truly."

I walked through three or four more people and the crowd opened up to a large, grassy circle with nothing but a school desk, two chairs, and Saul sitting in the middle of it.

"There's the little bug Mountain, now squish him."

He took a moment to look Saul over and sighed. "Alright, I'll see what I can do."

Mountain made his way to the flimsy school desk and said something to Saul. The two, while giants in their own rights, looked just about as different as night and day. Saul was tan, and very clean cut. No dirt, no scrapes, no bruises. On the other hand, Mountain's typically dark skin had grown even darker from months of writhing in dust, sand, and dirt. He had heavy purple bags under his eyes, and there were bruises all along his arms. Regardless of his less than flattering appearance, I knew Mountain was still awake, alert, and as strong as ever. They took their seats and lent their right arms across the table and gripped them tightly. It was gonna be a real dogfight.

A local walked up to the desk and held their hands together. It was a portly white woman in a big hat, probably one of the farmers. She began reading the obligatory ground rules to an arm wrestling match.

"Keep your hands locked, your elbows on the table, and keep your dirty tricks to yourselves".

There was a slow count up to three. You could see the mix of confidence and nerve in each of em'. More so in Saul than Mountain. I'm convinced Saul forgot there were other massive people like him out there in the wasteland. It was time for a reminder. As the portly lady let the word slip from her mouth, both Mountain and Saul put forth a sudden explosive effort, yanking and twisting at each other's hands.

Their muscles strained and tightened, and veins were visible on their biceps. Each one tried to rotate the other's wrist, but neither would as much as budge. Not a centimeter. Mountain's bald head shined with sweat. Slowly, his hand began to slowly fall back. Saul finally got his angle, and he drove down hard to the plastic. Mountain closed his eyes and pushed back, but it looked like he just couldn't find the strength. Saul began to smirk in-between breaths and grunts.

"Not bad, nobody has put up a challenge like that for years."

Saul's confidence was obvious, but it was premature and misplaced. Yes, he had Mountain at the cusp of defeat, but that was where Mountain wanted to be. No matter how much force Saul put down, Mountain's elbow held firm. The job just couldn't be done. Mountain's face grew into a ridiculous grin and he calmly stared up at Saul.

"You haven't done a whole lot of heavy lifting lately, have you?"
"What?"

"You are running out of gas pretty quick there, you aren't even half as strong as when we started. It's like you have no endurance at all."

Saul replied with a swift "shut up."

Yet slowly but surely, Mountain lifted his hand back up and turned the tides of the fight. Saul kept pushing harder and harder, but he had no more steam. After another moment or two, his hand tapped, and a new champion was crowned.

Saul wiped the sweat from his forehead and rubbed his aching wrist. "Where in the hell did you find the strength to pull something like that?"

"Simple. I have to lug around three hundred pounds of cooking gear on a glorified wheelbarrow for six hours every day. That kind of weight sticks in your arms real good."

"Three hundred pounds. Ha, and to think the work I did around here was tough."

Mountain lent out his fist. Saul picked up on the message and gave it a satisfying tap with his knuckles. They turned and faced the cheering crowds and took a sarcastic bow. Mountain wasn't much of a personable guy. He was never a people person. Hell, he was barely social. However, when it came to diplomatic relations, I guess even he could find a useful part to play. Even if it involves embarrassing the town's leader in front of a roaring crowd.

~ * ~

Nightfall came shortly after that, and our campfires lit up the sky like a thousand matches on a beach. I sat on a bench along with the rest of the FCS and drank warm coffee from a Styrofoam cup.

"Well gents, I could not be happier that you all showed up. This is the most fun I've had in a long time. Some of our residents here are looking to follow you guys to Boston," Saul said to a toast.

Todd took a sip of coffee and turned over to the bearded giant. "Are you one of those people?"

"Nah, I would love to, but I have so many blessings here that I could never give it up. Not in a million years. So as long as it stays, I stay."

It was a respectable decision. I don't think anyone expected anything different, and there was no reason trying to sell our plan further. Instead, we sat in silence and took slow sips, until Saul slapped himself upside the head.

"Jesus Christ, I forgot to tell Tinker that it's past sunset."

We gave him a collective puzzled look as he jumped to his feet.

"We have an old man in town who helps to fix equipment and provides power to the city. During his free time, he even brings machines back from the junkyard to patch them back into working shape."

Adahy leaned forward on his seat. "Alright, but what's the big issue?"

Saul turned to look at Adahy. "He works in a little shack on the outskirts of Parkersville that has no natural light, so he needs someone to let him know when the day ends, or he will keep working until the next morning."

"You are telling me that there is a man around here that knows how to fix things? I feel obligated to meet him then. Tinkering is kind of a passion of mine," Todd said with legitimate enthusiasm.

Jed stood up and brushed off his pants "Well, if Todd is going, I say that we all go and meet this nerd as a community."

~ * ~

The moon illuminated the cracked and decaying pavement of a once prominent Main Street. Saul took the time to give us the quick synopsis of his settlement, starting with the day it all fell apart. Parkersville saw the rockets carrying toxin soaring above them by the thousands. They saw wildlife from all over pour into their village and take shelter there for years until they began to expand again. Apparently, that caused a wolf problem to arrive, so a hunting party was formed to drive them out. There was a lengthy period of peace and prosperity until about one month before our arrival, when that little group of thugs showed up and started threatening civilians. When he mentioned that, I remembered I wanted to ask him what they looked like, but he brushed me off. Soon enough, Tinker's little shack was in sight.

I'll just say that Saul wasn't exaggerating when he said the Tinker lived in a shack. The place looked like it was made out of roof tiles and sheet metal. It couldn't have been more than twenty by ten, and the front yard was covered by rusty aluminum. It looked like a landfill had a baby with a scrapyard. However, when we drew closer to its entrance, I noticed something alarming about the shady little structure. The humming starting vibrating in my ear again.

The slim rusted iron door had seemingly been bashed in by

something, like the butt of a gun. That had never been a good sign, so I immediately upped the pace toward the door. The rest of the group kept at my ankles, and we got to the welcome mat in unison. I jiggled the handle and gave it a gentle push, but it would not budge. With everyone not but a few steps behind me, I threw myself though and fell head first into the interior. I was hoping that Tinker was just a slob, but funny little coincidences like that don't happen in the wasteland. I saw what I knew I was gonna see.

Chunks of metal were tossed to the floor without care, and what did remain in place was covered in blood. On the cold cement floor, an elderly man with goggles on his forehead was stretched out with a long slash wound across his back, and an arm missing. The wound was fresh, and on the sheet metal wall sanding behind him atop of a makeshift workbench was a pained eye. As the others entered and assessed the damage, I turned to face Saul. He seemed shaken by the sight.

"What...What was the name of the local thugs that kept threatening your town Saul?"

"I dunno...they only mentioned it once, and there were just a few of them. All I remember is them screaming up to the sky that they were gonna make *good use* of us. They wouldn't trade, they wouldn't join us, they wouldn't leave us alone. They just told us to burn. Real freaks. I think they called themselves...umm...well...Oh, right, they called themselves..."

"Acolytes?"

"Yeah, that's it."

Chapter Eight: The Acolytes

Somewhere in the far distance, I saw the pits of hell open, and fire rose from the soil.

Todd leaned over and grabbed Saul's shirt collar. "You said they were small group of thugs, not the kingpin raiders of the whole fucking wasteland."

Saul was in a state of total shock. "How could they...? They were just a couple punks. I scared em' off myself, I swear. Was it all a trap or something?"

Todd let go of his collar and turned to the rest of us. "Must have been a welcoming party. We need to get our asses moving back there. All hands required. Load up now, this whole scene is gonna be pretty spicy as soon as one of those sociopaths catches a whiff of us."

I loaded a full clip and cleaned off my knife. Saul picked up an aluminum baseball bat wrapped in what looked like barbed wire off the wall. It must have been one of Tinker's contraptions. Saul carelessly slung it over his shoulder and made his way out of the shack.

"Well, I screwed this up pretty badly boys, no excuses acceptable. I'm not going to let all of my friends and family die because of me. I'm going to kill every one of them by myself if I need to. Can I count on your help?"

The question needed no reply. Next thing I knew, we were charging toward a thick cloud of smoke. Into the jaws of death.

~ * ~

When we got a bit closer, I diverged from the pack and grabbed my field glasses. I stopped atop a steep incline and dug into the weeds and dirt. Through the lenses, I caught a solid glimpse of town square, or what used to be town square. Everything was ablaze. A group of townsfolk were taking cover behind barrels and overturned benches by the post office. From the windows and front steps, I got my first glimpse of the Acolyte warriors. The wax masks they wore were melting due to heat exposure, but the freaks refused to take them off. I'm sure the material was scolding their entire faces, but they preferred to keep em' on anyway. Although the masks were meant to make the raiders seem uniform, the melting deformities made each one a unique mutant. The warriors carried anything from assault rifles to handguns to strange looking spears made from sticks and glass shards. There were about ten of them, and about six villagers were fighting them in the town square. I had to do something fast, or else they would be overwhelmed. It was time to make use of some new gear.

The tripod of the Rifleman's .357 stuck perfectly into a patch of loose dirt. It took a few jiggles, but the roots did an excellent job of steadying the barrel. My breathing became calmed and controlled, almost rhythmic. I got a firm grip on the stock, a perfect angle on the bottom-left side. One Acolyte was by the flagpole nearest the base of the steps spraying clip after clip of handgun ammo into the overturned benches. I held my breath and began to count my heartbeats. The crosshairs steadied on the center of the mask. I took a slow, deep exhale. A flash of light obscured my vision, and the kick rocked against my shoulder like a morning tide. It had a good line, fair bearings, and little wind resistance. A perfect bullseye. The marauder flew backwards and hit the floor like a sack of rocks. One down. I chambered the rifle and gazed down range to pick my next target.

In the front door with his back hugging the mantle was an elephant of a man with plaid overalls. He was carrying an old hunting rifle with iron sights. I took a deep breath and let another shot fly. It lodged deep into his shoulder. A crippling blow, but not a lethal one. He wasn't about to get away with a little graze though. Another well placed shot to the chest was enough to stop his squirming. They finally took notice of me, and one or two of them started to peak around corners, trying to get a beat on where I was hiding.

I stayed quiet or a moment or two, trying to understand their pattern. Once every five or so seconds, one would peek out for a moment from behind an old post box. I started counting along with him, and as I reached to four, I pulled the trigger. It missed by only a quarter of a second, so the bullet just ricocheted off the steps instead. I sat back and waited another four seconds and tried again. The Acolyte wasn't bright enough to change his pattern after the near miss. Hiss loss. He got clocked right on his nose. Wax, pulpy flesh, and bones vaporized after spraying on the grass. It was a real gruesome sight, which was a good thing. The Acolytes were finally starting to get nervous.

Their cover became thorough, and it was rare for me to find even the slightest opportunity to pick one of them off. However, as they began to cower and retreat, the villagers pushed them back from their positions deep into the heart the office. I couldn't even see them anymore through the rising smoke, but I did see some movement just outside an open window. The shady figure of Todd slowly crept up to the open pane of glass and reached into a strange silk bag. He retrieved what seemed to be a bottle with a rag sticking out of it. After igniting the rag with Silent Bobs old silver lighter, Todd lobbed it inside, over his shoulder. Like a superstitious aunt chucking salt behind her back. Massive flames rose from the inside of the facility and spread like a fresh plague. Within a minute or two, panicked raiders fled out of the front door. Tragically for them, a volley of small arms fire from the villagers met them on the welcome mat. None of them even made it down the steps.

I chambered the rifle again and raced down to Saul and Todd, who were helping the wounded reach safety. As I sprinted to them, I came across one of the village survivors holding a small handgun. I believe it was the same model I was packing. He couldn't have been more than twenty years old with long, greasy black hair and a thin mustache on his upper lip. He was shot in the shoulder and side, but he was still breathing. I lifted him up over my shoulder and lugged him over to a nearby field where doctors from the Train had set up. As I gently set him down onto a gurney, he reached down into his belt and drew the pistol out. He could barely breathe, let alone speak, but I could tell what he was saying. I took the pistol and holstered in in my belt. He definitely wouldn't be needing it in his condition. In a field not far from where I was, I saw a group of Hornets kicking up dirt and firing their mounted guns toward a group hiding behind a crashed truck. I thanked the boy and took off, back into the fight.

~ * ~

The stranded fighters were grouped up real tight, so a direct approach would be suicide. My only option was to circle around back through the corn and flank them. I stopped to survey the area with my field glasses before sneaking in for the kill. It was difficult to see through the stalks, but I was still able to count out thirteen of them from my low perch. That's when I felt a hand touch my back. I just about leapt out of my own skin. I whipped the barrel of my pistol around and pointed it directly in the face of a crouching Silent Bob. He had an assault rifle pointed directly at my lower back.

"Where in the hell did you find that?"

He met my question with a shrug of his shoulders. I sighed in frustration and handed him the binoculars.

"There are at least a dozen out there right now, and the Hornets can't make it past them and get into the fight until we clear them out. If we play our cards right though, we could kill a third of them before they even realize we snuck up on them."

Bob seemed worried, but I could tell he knew as well as I that this was our only option. I signaled to make our way to their backline. We kept on all fours and crawled through the fallen plants like ghosts in the putrid smog.

The Hornets were still shooting at the raiders, so there was a nearly deafening volley of explosions coming from the mounted gun barrels at all times. Every once in a while, you would hear a new sound, instead of the usual 'bullet eating dirt' kind of thud. Sometimes it was more like a crunch or a crack, followed by a grunt or scream, then came the thud. The Hornets were our deadliest weapon for a reason. The fallen cornstalks thinned, and I eventually came face to face with a pair of bloody boots. Point blank range. I drew out Todd's blue-handled switchblade and flipped it open. The boots belonged to what looked to be a middle aged white woman with short blonde hair. She stood near the cornstalks and shot an ancient-looking revolver. I got up and tiptoed my way to her back, and as she began to turn around, I lunged and drove the blade into her throat.

Her sputtering drew their attention. The other Acolytes turned to find their dead cohort sprawled out on the ground, but before they could aim their sights my way, I felt a hail of fire coming from directly behind me. Silent Bob unloaded every shot he had into them, rocking back and forth as each round left the chamber. I think six toppled over in the first two seconds. I drew out the two handguns from my belt and started letting bullets fly at anything that still stood. They all fell in a shower of brass and lead. None of the Acolytes even got a shot off. More good planning, with a little side dish of good fortune. With the slaughter finished, I jumped over the cover and waved the Hornets onward, signaling everything was clear. They roared down the stretch of dirt and dust into downtown, cheering and hollering the whole way. It was a close call, but we were okay. The only violent explosions and gunfire left were coming from the field to the west. Bob and I threw whatever spare ammo and equipment we could into our packs. I only had ten total bullets left, and if I were to make it through, I would have to conserve every one of them.

Bob threw his assault rifle to the ground and pulled out a crowbar caked in rust and other signs of old age. We crept back into the tall grass and fallen cornstalks and made our way toward the action. There was an odd, gritty surface smothering the fields from top to bottom, like sand, only coarser. A foul odor, totally unlike that of the lingering toxin, suddenly set my nose on fire. Sulfur and diesel for sure. I raised my head from its grassy tomb to see a massive metal monstrosity rolling down the field we just abandoned. I stopped in my tracks to get a better view of the machine as it passed through the light of the brushfires. Now, my pops always used to read me Frankenstein as a kid, Ez. He told me man has always been known to make monsters now and then, but I had never heard of any beast like this come from a laboratory.

It had eighteen wheels, like the big-rigs from the old world, but much crueler. On the front bumper of its giant grey chassis was a thick row of barbed wire, and pikes made of rusted iron. There was a cloud of black smoke bellowing from its massive exhaust pipe. The windows were tinted, and through the wall of dark grey glass, you could see the figure of a large man hunched over the steering wheel. There was a long white trailer attached to the vehicle. It was covered in stains of god-knows-what. The sound of the engine shook the soil, and the machine accelerated forward like a passenger jet. When Silent Bob saw the death machine, he dropped his half-smoked Marlboro into the muck and stared at it in total awe.

That machine was a juggernaut. No matter how many tires I could shoot out, it would always have enough left to carry on. The side was armored, and the driver was moving too fast to have a clear shot at. There was no logical plan of action to take. It was simply too strong for any kind of rational planning. So instead of thinking, I decided to just act. With a grunt, I leapt onto my feet and started to shoot at the windshield with my 9mm. I shouted and hollered and begged for the beast's attention. The truck deviated from its course heading to the west field and made a sharp right. I felt a great worry lift from my shoulders, and I took a moment to let out a sigh of relief. This, however, was short lived. Bob gestured for me to take a closer look, and I found the truck accelerating right at us at ramming speeds.

I told Bob to spread out at a wide angle. That way, it could only go for one of us at a time. The truck was rolling over cornstalks like diner straws. It was closing in fast. I kept my guns by my side. There couldn't have been more than a few bullets left, so I had to wait until the truck was right on top of me if there was any hope to stop it. As it approached, I saw the wax of the driver's mask through the tinted windshield. Pristine and smooth. Blank. Seventy feet, sixty feet, fifty feet, I raised my gun to the right side of the window. It took two shots to finally shatter the plexiglass, but when it did, the man behind it never stood a chance. With a third bullet, his upper chest slumped over the horn. It blared like a fog siren as the chassis continued flying at me. The machine was slowing down, but not nearly fast enough.

There was no time to dodge to the side, so I just followed my instinct and hit the dirt. The wire and pikes passed right over me, along with the trailer. I held my breath and closed my eyes as the spinning alternator deafened my ears and the putrid sludge from the exhaust smothered me. The odor wasn't any more pleasant up close. The final tires rolled right past me, and I was whipped by an artificial breeze. Dirt, mud, and oil covered every inch of me from head to toe, and the chemical cocktail felt like it was eating at my skin. Bob, who was now lying prone a couple dozen feet away jumped to his feet and rushed over as I wallowed in the dirt. He waved his hand in front of my face, but I was too dazed and confused to think, let alone say anything. He grabbed me by my newly-ruined shirt's crew neck and shook me. That worsened my headache for sure, but at least he brought me back to reality.

Bob practically threw me over his back to get me on my feet. He poured some water from his canteen so I could open my eyes again. I checked my two 9mm pistols, which were now covered in gunk. In conditions like those, the guns would most likely misfire or jam, so I threw them into my backpack and pulled out my blade instead. I wiped some of the grime and soot from my arms and spit. I couldn't get the taste of the sludge out of my mouth. It was thick, like spoiled beef stew. I could barely breathe, but there was no rest until this fight was over. Bob took a moment to gather himself before we launched ourselves at the final wave, so I decided to sit down and sharpen my blade on a rock. However, before the first scrape was made, the back end of the truck's trailer rocked due to an immense impact.

I leapt to my feet again, dropping the rock into a patch of thick slush. I wiped my blade off on my shirt and inched my way over to the wreckage. Silent Bob heard the noise as well, and he sidestepped his way over to the backdoor. It was barred from the outside by a plank of oak and a cable tie. It looked secure enough at a distance, but as we drew closer, we noticed the wood was bent, and the cable tie was snapped. It was only hanging by a thread from the hatch. I took the limp hanging wire from its perch and threw it into the ankle-deep muck. I examined the plank, and after seeing the massive black crack stretching from one side to the other, I signaled for Bob to get away from the door. A lock that flimsy sure as hell wouldn't hold anything in there for too long. Bob didn't listen, and as I hauled ass away, I heard another thud against the door. The oak plank fell to the earth in two pieces, and the white door slowly opened with a series of harsh screeching noises. I stared into the darkness of the trailer, and saw nothing inside except for a large slab of rusted steel peeking into the subtle amber glow.

A tattered pair of brown boots slammed onto the metal bed of the trailer and lifted the slab. The hunk of steel kinda looked like an old door, like one of the gates you would find in a county prison. Out of the shadow appeared a massive man, towering at least six inches above me or Bob. He had his arm shoved through a fabric strap in the back of the metal door and the other firmly grasping a weighty wooden club. The club was a pasty white color, and it seemed to be whittled into the shape of a cone. The end of the blunt stick looks as if it were the size of my head, and it was wrapped in a metal casing with several little bolts firmly drilled into it. He wore a large suit made of thick armor plates and a particularly dense facemask. The behemoth lifted and held the shield like a man carries a bag of groceries. It was a monster hidden within a monster.

His eyes poked through the slits in the mask like a blazing cattle prod. Dead. Grey. Lifeless. His body was loosely hunched over. It looked like his spine had been ripped from his flesh. He brought the door down, burrowing it firmly into the ground. It stuck straight up. He sloshed his way through the mud toward me. He looked like he had the intent to kill in his eye. I guess every Acolyte had that look. Silent Bob, who was still hiding behind the truck, snuck up behind the behemoth and rose the crowbar to the sky. He brought it down with a blunt force, and it collided with the monster's head with a riveting clang. The face mask got caught by the bent end of the bar, and with a strong tug, Bob ripped it off completely. The Acolyte didn't seem to be affected at all. In fact, I saw a little smile grow on his face. He turned to face Bob, who threw another haymaker at him, landing the end of his crowbar into the shoulder of the giant with a disgusting crunch. Another smile. Bob tried to tear the rusted metal out, and with one slow and powerful movement, the freak grabbed hold of Silent Bob's wrist.

There was a tremendous crack. Unpleasant, boney, the sound of something permanent. With a massive twist, the behemoth had broken Bob's entire arm. Although in terrible pain, Bob wasn't prepared to throw in the towel. He dropped the crowbar out of one hand and picked it up with the other before bringing the flat end swinging up. It caught the giant on his chin. This only gave him more sick pleasure. I think he cherished the suffering. I swear he did. In fact, it seemed to give him strength. He brought the massive chunk of wood and metal above his shoulder and swiped it across his chest, colliding with Bob's broken arm with a shattering force. I heard a cracking noise, and Silent Bob shouted and kicked and screamed until the giant decided to throw him to the side. Bob's arm was barely attached by the time he landed.

The behemoth started trotting my way. Blood was spilling from his shoulder, but he still seemed content. It was like he was on a Sunday cruise for him or something. I flipped my blade around nervously. There was no way I could harm something that size with a knife. I started to search for a weak point in the armor, but he was too close for me to take a good look. Instead, I hovered just outside his reach to buy myself more time. He lunged at me to grab hold of my arm, just like he did to Bob, but I was too fast for him. He got frustrated quickly, the big oaf. He started to charge, swinging the club wildly from side to side. The whooshing sounds in the air tickled my eardrums with every pass. I kept inching backward, ducking and diving to avoid the bone-shattering impacts.

Eventually, the behemoth reached his breaking point. He raised the club up to the heavens and brought it down on top of me. I threw myself to the side, just in time. I landed in a thick patch of muck that covered me to my shoulder blades. I looked up to see the behemoth tugging and ripping away at the partially-submerged handle of his weapon. He couldn't seem to pull it from its earthly tomb. I wiped some of the mud off my face and looked at it. I remembered the forest. That was when I realized his weakness. Between his size, the club, and his armor, he was too heavy to operate. After finally tugging the weapon from the ground, the behemoth walked back slowly toward the truck and picked up the cast iron shield. He clanged the two together, goading me to charge at him. The smoke in the air from the brushfires began to grow thicker and denser. He disappeared into the tainted mist. It's like a chemical fog rolled in, and it left me completely blind. The contaminants were unbreathable. After a moment or two, my lungs became desperate. I ran blindly through the smog, hoping to find Bob somewhere in the mist. We had to get out of there, our chances of beating the behemoth were scarce, and we were already needed elsewhere. We needed a tactical retreat. I busted out of the wall of smoke, ready to flee. Unfortunately, I found myself staring straight into the face of the giant, holding his shield across his chest, prepared to swing it like a left hook.

The steel was actually pretty cold. You wouldn't expect something sitting in a dark, dank trailer like that to be that way, but the behemoth managed to keep it icy. There was no pain at first, only shock. The ground beneath me passed by like the yellow lines of a paved road. I felt the blue pocket knife slide out of my hand and fall to the ground. It propped up against a twig back near the pit of muck we encountered by the truck. I splashed into the sludge a moment later. A surging pain slowly grew more severe. I think my nerves were completely fried, all in one shot. The giant chuckled wildly, swinging his club over his head. He was mocking me.

I couldn't beat him in close quarters, and I knew that. A calculated risk had to be taken if I wanted to stand a chance. Reaching into my burlap back pack, which now had a new rip from sliding across a sharp stone, I found the muddy handle of my 9mm and yanked it out, along with much of the pack's remaining contents. One shot was all I needed. With my good arm, I put my sights on the one part of his body that was left unprotected. His ankles.

I pressed down hard, and with a slow slide, a familiar flash of light ignited from the barrel. The blessed sound of lead cracking bone rang in my eardrums. I had to grin at a noise that crisp. The giant stumbled for a moment, but he didn't fall as I hoped. In fact, he was still moving at full speed, only with uneven steps. I tried the trigger again, but my luck had run out. The gunk kept my chamber well stuck in place. I took a knee and tried to get up, but as soon as I began to move, the Acolyte took to a sprint. I braced for impact, but as the steps got closer and closer, I heard a distinct clanging noise, and he stopped. Bob was behind him again, prying at the back of his head with the sharp end of the crowbar. One of Bob's arms limply hung down by his side, but the other was alive and enraged. He twisted and ripped at the behemoth's skull like he was splitting a melon.

The Acolyte turned around, taking a quick hit to the eye. The Behemoth finally recoiled. His club was by his side, and with one harsh swing, he brought it flying upward with the strength of twenty men. Silent Bob was caught squarely under his chin. My comrade was lobbed into the air like a sack of rice. As he fell onto his back, I saw the extent of the damage. His arm and neck were twisted in ways that looked almost inhuman. He twitched, helplessly like the bodies of the birds I encountered outside Phoenix. I knew there was no coming back from something like that.

Bob was gone.

Enraged. A simple term that creates extraordinary outcomes. I don't know if you have ever felt your blood boil Ez, but when you do, it feels like you can shoot fire from your fingertips. A fire you can't control, but a fire nonetheless. The behemoth crossed a line, and he was gonna pay for it. With one stiff movement, I reached over to the twig and grabbed the handle of my blade. As the giant dropped his shield and reached for his eye, I launched myself like rocket toward him and leaped into the sky. He saw me coming, but he was weak from the head wounds, tired from bearing the heavy equipment, and slow due to the thick patch of mud. A giant was too weak to stop an ant. I landed onto his back and griped tightly around his neck, digging my nails in deep to keep from getting flung off. I raised the knife over my shoulder, and with the blood-red rage, I took it to his neck.

He desperately tried to shake me off, but I stayed strong. I tore the sharp edge out and drove it back in on the other side. The second impact shifted him off balance. The freak swayed like a mechanical bull in a cheap bar, but I wouldn't be chucked off so easily. My grip was stronger than death itself. Again and again, I dug the edge into his neck and shook it around. The sound of the Acolyte choking on his own insides reassured me that the fight was over. I tore the blade out of the right side of his neck and leapt off, landing in my side. The behemoth choked and fell, face first into the muck.

One of his eyes remained peeking out of the mud after he stopped breathing. It seemed to stare at me, eternally. Like it wanted another shot at me, or to just shoot me. I don't know which, and I don't care. I kicked it back under the muck and limped over to Bob's corpse, helpless once again. The funny thing about death is that it is nearly undefeated Ez, once it has someone, it has them for keeps. We as people can't do anything but watch as it does its good work. Maybe we can move on. We have to move on. There was a half-smoked pack of cigarettes poking out of his worn black raincoat. I took it and slid it deep into the pockets of my torn survival pack.

The adrenaline from the carnage had slowly worn off. The pain and the exhaustion returned, a couple of old friends for the road. I limped toward the westernmost field. Although there was no way for me to fight any longer, I wanted to see the outcome of the battle with my own two eyes. I felt my legs buckle under my own weight once I reached the top of the steep incline where the battle began. I was just within sight of the final act. I fell flat onto my backside, senses dulled and head pounding. The carnage was absolutely brilliant. It was a struggle to keep my eyes open, but I wouldn't have dared to look away from the incredible sight, even for a second. In that moment, atop that little hill in a little town in a lonely world, I got to witness something resembling a miracle.

Racing across the field at a break-neck pace, a half dozen Hornets were chasing down hordes of Acolytes as they retreated on foot. The mounted guns lit up the sky. The field was a graveyard of Acolyte vehicles. Motorcycles, armored cars, trucks, they had all been disabled. The freak s literally had to turn tail and book it out on their own heels! Amongst the crowds of reveling survivors, I saw Todd, Jacques. Adahy, Jed, and Saul firing shots from the Acolytes' own hunting rifles into the air, hollering and laughing like madmen. The significance of it all finally began to sink in once the last volleys were launched by the survivors. I had taken part in the largest armed effort since the beginning of the apocalypse, and against all odds, overcame the overwhelming size and power of the mo st savage group of human beings left on the Earth. I remember fading from consciousness not long after that.

Honestly Ez, my arm still gets a slow burning sensation once in a while. It's another grim reminder of the dangers I encountered on my journey that will burden my body and my mind for the rest of my life, but the pain has meaning. It will always remind me of the Acolytes, and a miracle of a victory we had over them. It will always remind me of little Parkersville and Saul, and all the suffering that they had to endure and overcome. Greatest of them all, this little wound will always remind me of Silent Bob. His friendship, his social ineptitude, the smell of old cigarettes, and one hell of a valiant last stand. He gave me another chance at life, Ez. I got a little glimpse of what good was still left in humanity from him. Seeing that selfless act, that little glimpse of decency, it gave me hope. After all, it's hope like that which makes carrying burdens and scars possible. Without that hope, I would likely collapse where I stand under the weight of it all.

Chapter Nine: Campfire Stories

"Hey Jack, I have a question for you. It's probably pretty dumb, but I just wanna know."

Ezekiel had been contently listening to Jack all afternoon. Pen marks now stretched all the way up his arm. Aphorisms of the wasteland wanderer were scribbled at every angle and every size. Ezekiel had to switch arms soon, but he had never been good at writing with his left hand. He just hoped the notes would turn out okay.

"Yeah, sure Ez, you've been patient. What is it pal?"

"Mother always told me never to talk much with strangers. She says they are no good, dirty, and probably want something from me."

"Well, I'm flattered."

"Oh, don't mind her, she broke into her personal cabinet before she said that. I just want to know, how do you put trust in people you don't know? How could you be sure The Train wasn't a slaver caravan? Those have been getting real popular recently. I mean, you were practically surrounded by people you didn't know a moment before joining them and you still find yourself sharing food with them, surviving with them, and even falling asleep next to them. Did that make you paranoid? Is it okay to be paranoid?"

"Yeah kid. It's fine to paranoid, but you have to keep that in check. Fear only slows you down out there. Be confident in the fact there is decency in people, but also be cautious enough to make sure you can escape a shady situation."

"Oh, alright. More about finding balance. Got it."

"What, am I sounding like a broken record to you?"

"No, of course not."

"Okay, fine Ez. I'll give you a bit more substance for this one. Just keep jotting stuff down on your hands."

Jack took a swig of water from his plastic canteen and took a deep breath. "During the first few weeks of travel, I slept with my handgun tucked tightly under my sleeping bag. I was ready to kill the first dirty nomad rat to lay a finger on me. I couldn't get much shuteye the first few days either. It was bad enough that I didn't have a bed. For a while, I didn't think I could trust any of them at all, but that changed after Hank died. As I busted through the fence and saw Hank stretched across the street, torn to ribbons, I realized. We were all survivors. We were scared. We were vulnerable.

"Later on, Jed came sprinting in, and Todd and Jacques came to comfort him by the fires. That's not something strangers do. That's something family does. I came to terms with my situation, and the people who came with it. In the matter of a month or two, The FCS became the best friends I ever had, before or after the end of the world."

Ez sat up from his slouching position. "There had to be more than just that. Trust is tough to earn."

"True, true, my little cynic. Real trust was built on the walk. We didn't just travel in silence. We were supposed to, under Peter's orders, but eight-hour stretches of silence are impossible. Talking is natural. Especially when there isn't anything to look at besides dead flora and fauna. We took quite a bit of time every day to joke around and make small talk. For morale, of course. Even after the walk was over, we would keep chatting around the bonfire every night. That's when all the good stuff found its way to the table."

"Really? A campfire? What did you guys talk about?"

"Well, I guess we talked a little bit about everything from the old world and the new world. But mostly, there were stories."

Ez always loved stories. Bedtime stories had always been the fondest part of his childhood, when his mother was in a condition to read, of course.

"Awesome, tell me about them."

~ * ~

Alright Ez, I'll let you in on a few of them. One evening,

somewhere between the desert and the Rifleman, we set up camp in a patch of dead brambles. We made a pit of rubble fallen from awnings and rooftops. They were surprisingly abundant, and they made a decent firepit. We dropped our packs and scavenged supplies onto a cart as always. Bob already had a fire going by the time we got back. He stood next to the kindling with his arms crossed. He looked pleased with himself. We planted our asses on the dry, dusty earth and kicked back. Most of us were still working on clearing sand from our earholes, and the air was still like steel mesh on the lungs, but we were happy to take a seat anyway.

Our little detour through the Sonoran took more out of me than I thought. I felt kind of lightheaded from dehydration. I think I got a nasty rash on my chest from sand-friction as well. Of all the enemies we faced out there, the environment was always the craftiest of the bunch. Thankfully, the other guys appeared to be in much higher spirits. They passed around a pot of black coffee, whistled, and mocked off Jed for getting dysentery. Dysentery usually isn't funny, but Jed was a special case. Jed always had a knack for calling everyone else in the crew weak or stupid. One time, he tried to lift and carry Jacques for half a day because he twisted his ankle on a pothole. Apparently, Jacques 'lost his walking privileges, because French boys don't know how to move their feet, they only know how to surrender'.

We started to chat about our families while Jed took another break to explore a rotting stump.

"Yeah, my parents were just about as strict as they come." Todd chuckled. "My dad was a marine and my mother had served as a nurse in the Vietnam War, so it doesn't take a whole lot of brains to determine what I was gonna be when I grew up. There was a wakeup call every morning at six on weekdays and seven on weekends at home, no exceptions. My pop used to play catch with me in the backyard, but every time I missed a ball I had to drop and give him five pushups."

Hank laughed. "Sounds like a blast. No wonder you run us so damn hard on these marches."

"Nah, it's not like that, Hank. My parents raised me to be tough, spit in the face of the world, and that type of go get em' attitude really helped me in military school. I excelled at everything we did, and I put ten times the effort into our lessons and drills than everybody else combined. That came back to bite me in the ass though."

"Bit you in the ass?" Jacques butted in, taking a sip of water out of a small tin cup.

"Well, about five years into my enrollment, a couple of the bums who never worked at anything began to have problems with me. One in particular, a boy named Rodrick, really didn't care for my gung-ho attitude. He wanted to prove himself to be the bigger man. One evening, after hours of classes and drills and exercises, Rodrick and two of his cronies approached me in a corridor of the barracks. As we crossed paths, one of his buddies took a sucker punch at me, and it caught me square in the jaw. Them three just started wailing on me. I was on the ground in fifteen seconds flat. They laughed and high fived each other before spitting on me and leaving. I can't remember another time I was that mad. These were supposed to my peers, and honorable military men in training, not thugs. I got myself back up and quietly trailed them all the way across campus. My patience paid off, because as they approached a fork in the cement walkway, the two henchmen headed to the left, while Rodrick had to go the opposite way.

I continued to follow the scrawny blonde prick down the sidewalk, ducking and hiding from tree to tree until I knew he was alone. Once everything went quiet, I took off in a sprint right at him, and as he turned to face the loud footsteps roaring behind him, I slammed my shoulder into him. I dug into his side, hard. We took an express flight right into the dirt. Our collision kicked up dust. That was good, because nobody got to see what I did to that brat's arm. He was still dazed and confused from the hit, so it just took a simple twist and yank to do the job. He started screaming like a little kid on the playground. Snot and tears were all over his face. It was a real pathetic scene.

I got the revenge I wanted on the kid, but I felt even angrier than before. Soon after, that anger turned to shame. I had taken a cheap shot at a punk and sunk down to his level. The whole night had been a failure of my own god damn standards. I thought I deserved some discipline, and I didn't have to wait too long before I got it. The day after, both me and Rodrick were called to the headmaster's office. We were personally expelled and sent home on the spot. With tears in my eyes and bruises all over my face, I turned my back on the academy, and never looked back. I never really knew what happened Rodrick after that whole fiasco. Some say he went to college and became a lawyer, some say he killed himself, but in all the stories I heard one single similarity. That similarity was that whatever I did to his arm never healed."

~ * ~

That night I learned Todd had quite the dark side, but then again, it's not very difficult to learn things like that when you are as bored as we were. I came to respect him, and if you can believe it, fear him a bit more after that. Another time, we were sitting ankle deep into the mud of the forest. Adahy was looking to the clouds for about an hour straight. Looked like he was in a trance or something.

"What in the hell is up with you?" Jed asked while chewing a large chunk of tobacco from a plastic pouch.

"Ah, nothing Jed, this forest is just reminding me of a hunting trip I took with my father."

"What made this trip so special compared to the ten thousand other ones you took? You find your spirit animal or something?"

"Well, it was special...since it was the first hunt I ever went on."

Everybody looked up at Adahy with a certain intrigue.

"Well, I guess I have to tell the whole thing now..."

"Go for it man, anything to distract me from this forsaken downpour." Jacques said, with a chuckle.

"Well, I was just a boy, no older than nine, and my father decided it was time I started to become a man. One Sunday morning, he woke me and set a brand-new crossbow at my feet. He simply told me to 'get ready'. Still half-drunk from slumber, I stumbled around my home, gathering water and equipment. No more than fifteen minutes later, I was pulled to the edge of the village. We were about to enter what my family called *The Proving Grounds*. It was a place forbidden to boys and children, and until that morning, I had never as much as touched a single tree. It was time for me to face a trial. Each of my three older siblings had taken the trial already, and conquered it. It always ended with their entry into manhood. I was going to be *a man*.

An hour or two passed as my father and I wandered aimlessly through the brush. Each new tree a giant lumbering over my head was a higher power, one that I could never hope to comprehend. I lived on the doorstep of this wondrous place my whole life, yet I never had the privilege of seeing any of it until that moment. It felt as though I belonged there. As we hiked deeper and deeper into the heart of the forest, my father kept joking to me that I would be a real outdoorsman one day, even better than he was. I've never been a prideful man, but those words stuck to me. I couldn't even keep my mind off of them until we set up camp near some branching tree roots at sundown. He said that the place would do nicely as a hunting blind, and he was sure by tomorrow morning we would see our first deer.

He patted me on the head and smiled. "Tomorrow is going to be a busy day, you should get some rest now son."

Saying that the forest is an entity is a cliché, but that night, I swear I could feel it breathe. The leaves were rustling in unison and the bullfrogs croaked in volleys and the sound of a nearby stream made the ground seem like it was shifting. Pure excitement kept me awake for a while, but eventually, the day's exhaustions got the better of me.

When I woke, the sun was just barely peeking over the tree line. Birds were chirping, and there was a sweet aroma tickling at my nose. It was like a grove of lilacs had sprung up on the spot overnight. Grabbing my crossbow tightly, I rolled onto my stomach and look around at a neatly tucked-away cove that sat at the end of a nearby brook. There, drinking from the natural spring, a six...no...an eight-point buck stood regally in the dawn. My father still asleep next to me, I allowed my hunters instinct to take over. My sights aimed expertly at its heart, I fired one arrow with incredible precision and struck it down where it stood. After that I shook my napping father and show him my new prize. He was so proud of me. We carried the buck back to the village to great applause. I was accepted as a man instead of a boy, and my life had never known greater satisfaction.

But then I woke up.

Well, the next morning arrived in the form of a light drizzle. The sky was grey and the clouds were thick. I slowly sat up and looked around our camp to find my father was already awake, looking down upon the cove with a very serious expression on his face. I crawled my way over to him while looking around for the eight-point buck I saw in my dreams. Not only was there no buck, but there were no animals whatsoever. The whole morning passed in silence, and soon enough, I began to lose hope I would find anything to bring back to the village at all.

As the afternoon arrived and the clouds finally broke, we finally saw another living creature, but it wasn't what I imagined the night before. Passing through a cluster of tall oak trees, I saw the bright eyes and bushy tail of a doe, and walking closely behind her were two of her younglings, no more than three months old.

My father watched on, nudging me in the arm to get my attention. Shifting my chin out of the dirt, I turned to look him in the eye. He placed a hand on my shoulder and pointed down the slope to the young family. Looking up at him with a heavy stare of disapproval on my face, I managed to gather the courage to shake my head in protest. He shot a stern look at me, and his cold brown eyes cut straight to my gut. Terrified, I averted my eyes back on the deer. The children still showed the wobbling-clumsiness of newborns. Maybe they weren't three months old after all.

With a deep breath, I set the sight on the doe's heart. My hands began to shake. My shoulders felt heavy. My head began to ache and my breathing became faster. I kept telling myself what I was doing was unforgivable. I was about to kill the mother and leave the babies alone in a forest to die. My father leaned over and whispered in my ear.

"What are you fumbling your hands for, boy? Take the shot." I could he was growing impatient, so I forced myself to look back down the sights. It hadn't moved since I lost focus. Still innocent, just as I left it.

Should I pull the little black trigger and end the doe's life to please my father? Should I let the deer live to give myself closure? Was there anything I could do that would make everybody happy? No, there never is. I made a choice. Feeling the chilling gaze of my father rattling my very soul, I lifted the sights up only a few inches. Pulling the trigger, I watched the green fletching of the arrow soar through the air with a calming whistle. There was a crack and rustling of leaves as the tip entered the bark of tree a foot or so above the mother's head. Panicking, she and the children clumsily darted back into the brush with a rustle, never to be seen again. I sat up, feeling more relieved than I had ever been in my whole life. It was probably the best decision that I have ever made."

"Well what happened after that? Did your dad beat you for dishonoring tradition?" Jed mocked.

"No, I think child abuse is meant for inbred trash, but you already knew that."

Jed got real red in the face after that one.

"My father let out a sigh of frustration and jumped up onto his feet. Without as much as saying a word, he headed back in the direction we came. The day passed in a tense silence, but nothing was going to destroy the joy I received from my victory. My father didn't say a single word to me that day or the next, and when he did start speaking to me again, it was coldly and professionally. He knew I flubbed the shot on purpose. Throughout the remainder of my childhood I tried to repair my relationship with my father, and as I grew into a man, the memory of my disappointment faded from his mind. However, as his mind changed with time, I remained the same."

~ * ~

Jack snapped his fingers and pointed at Ez, who was thoroughly entranced. "If that doesn't help explain how I got to trust them, I have one more. This fire took place only a couple days before we arrived in Parkersville. The air was only slightly tainted, and we actually found a patch of grass to sit on. We set up a shaky but effective pit out of old cans and boxes for our campsite. Since the traveling was so easy in the plains, we all had some energy to spare, so we stood around the fire and talked about our favorite material thing from the old world that we had to leave behind. Todd mentioned an old family heirloom. Jed mentioned a king-sized mattress. Bob and Adahy kept to themselves, but I think Adahy just couldn't think of an answer. To make up for the awkward boycotts, Jacques stepped up to the plate that night and gave us a little look into his life before all this ever happened.

Standing over the fire lighting a cigarette, Jacques dug the toe of his boot into the dry sod.

"Well, that's an easy one for me."

"Yeah, and why's that?" Todd asked, while gesturing a flask in his direction.

"Well, there was just one thing from my life that I left behind. It's still sitting around collecting dust in my New York apartment. I went to visit an old friend from San Francisco, and while I was there, I heard that the whole world had crumbled. I didn't believe it at first, until all the lights went out, and the riots started breaking out. It was soon after I realized, I wasn't going back for it anytime soon. Everything there was as good as dust."

"I guess I'll ask again Jacques. Why is this object so special to you? Is it a family heirloom like mine?

"Well, not exactly. I guess I have to do some explaining now. You see my friends, I grew up a poor boy in a farming community in Quebec. My father was a stern man of tradition, so most of my childhood took place out in the field or in the presence of a Bible. He grew carrots, lettuce, and other common produce. He worked very hard from sunrise to sunset to take good care of his crop. Father took pride in his work, but he never gloated about the menial success that his farm found. He was an honest-to-god working man. We went to church on Sunday morning then tended to the eastern half of the carrot patch until he was too tired to continue working. It was a simple existence, but my father couldn't have been happier with it. I think he relished in its simplicity.

"Always by his side was my beautiful mother, Anne. She was thin, but far stronger than he was. She had jet-black hair that was always kept short and curly. It was tough being a first-generation French immigrant, but Anne pulled it off seamlessly. Independence was always her strong suit. As a child, she would tell me stories before I went to sleep at night about the most incredible things. She would tell me about the beautiful and mesmerizing lights of Paris, the winding roadways, the tourists, the high-rises, the adorable shops, all of it. Sometimes, Anne would talk about the incredible culture the city held. The food sounded exquisite, and the music she used to play on her CD's were fascinating. The times we talked about art were my favorite though. Something about creating standalone works from your own hands and beating heart really appealed to me."

Off to the side, you could clearly hear Jed pretending to vomit and gag while punching Bob in the arm to measure his reaction. Bob never really gave a reaction.

"Well, her words stuck with me all throughout my childhood, and as the years went by, I yearned more and more to create art. To speak my piece without ever opening my mouth. However, my day to day dream came to a sudden halt one dreary afternoon. As I returned from my daily duty on the fields, I found my mother on the ground, struggling to breathe. Anne had fallen severely ill. She was bed-ridden for months, fragile as a pane of glass. We drove her to the hospital many times in those months, but the doctors there were unable to even identify, much less cure, her ailment.

"Winter came faster than a crack of thunder, and it arrived with a vengeance. It wasn't uncommon for us to get completely snowed into our tiny home, and whenever we did get snowed in, there was very little for us to do. In my boredom, I took a cheap lead pencil and some copy paper and brought them to my room. I would spend hours at a time drawing whatever came into my mind, from my mother to my school house to interpretations of paintings Anne described to me before. At first, as you can most likely imagine, the artwork wasn't anything to look at twice, or once for that matter. They lacked uniform style and grace."

At this point Jed was chuckling to himself loudly, and Todd grew tired of the obnoxious noises. One quick kick to Jed's shin turned the giggling to a grunting, curse-fueled rant.

"However, as time went on, and the months passed by, I found myself becoming better and better at what I did. The strange lines finally began to take shape into something original, unique, and strangely mesmerizing. I loved my newfound hobby, but still felt that there was something missing from my work. Not long after I began to show my mother, our final Christmas as a family arrived. I never really got much for Christmas, given our circumstances, but that year I received something truly special. Wrapped in thin red tissue paper covered with decorative green dots was a simple spotter brush with my mother's name engraved into the side of it."

"Your mother's name? I thought you said it wasn't an heirloom?" I asked.

"Well, I wouldn't consider it an heirloom quite yet. I'll wait until I give it to my grandkids before I start calling it that. I had never gotten a real brush before, so I was ecstatic. Also under the tree, I found a sampler of different paints and a package of canvases. Even though my father disapproved of me leaving the farming business, he still decided to support my dreams. I was never happier than in that simple, joyous moment. Something so small managed to have more gravity than the rest of the entire planet.

"Not long after the holidays, my mother's condition grew more severe. She lost whatever independence she had left. She was feeble and weak, but she kept her motherly charm about her. I tried my best to keep her comfortable. I gave her fresh water and fluffed her pillow. The simple stuff. It was hard to watch as a growing boy. I had just barely begun to abandon my childhood to find a dark reality on my doorstep. One night, a coughing fit left her gasping for air that she couldn't seem to find. She passed away sometime that March, and I couldn't tell if I was miserable because she was gone, or relieved because all of it was finally over. My father and I buried her in an old cemetery back on the family farm, in a plot next to her grandmother.

"The next year was hard for me and my father to get through. The once lively and happy farm house had fallen into an eerie silence. A lonely silence. The work in the fields became more mundane, and I soon became sick of the repetition. Waking up became a chore. Getting up became a chore. Chores became living hells. I developed an unhealthy tendency to avoid all my responsibilities. And I mean all of them. For a while I didn't know where to turn or what to do to make the situation any better. During that time of struggle, the only thing that seemed to keep me sane was painting. It helped to relieve my stress and kept me decently level headed from day to day until the situation finally improved. After that year finally came to pass, my father and I learned to move on, and things finally began to look up. My father's crop was large that year, so we hired a couple more farm hands, and I even got to send a portrait of my mother to a national competition for youth artists.

More good news rolled around a few months later when my painted portrait came back with a ribbon pinned to the corner, and a four-figure check. My father had grown quiet ever since Anne passed away, but even he found himself in spirits high enough to congratulate me on the achievement. I found the one thing that my art needed. Meaning. Without meaning it all lacks purpose, and without purpose, there is no reason for art to exist. My works became well known in my hometown and surrounding cities, and eventually, I was offered a sizeable scholarship to attend a school of visual arts in New York City. I knew this was a chance to follow my dream and develop my skills, so I jumped at the opportunity immediately.

Months later, I bid my father a fond farewell and caught a plane. A new life, a new beginning. Everywhere I went, every class I took, every painting I created, I took and used my engraved brush. I kept it as a reminder of my mother, of my family, and of my childhood. I would do anything to get that brush back now, and since we are traveling toward New York on our route, I plan on making a stop to retrieve it. So for now, I would say the brush is the thing I miss the most from the old world, but I don't intend to keep it that way."

~ * ~

Ez, intrigued by the stories, looked at Jack with a befuddled expression on his face.

"You still confused little buddy? Well, I guess I can't blame you. You weren't there to experience it yourself. You see Ez, hearing the life stories of these guys, kind of getting to know them inside and out...it really helps. It signifies trust in one another, and helps each and every one of us to bury the hatchet and smother anxieties about one another. So to clearly answer your question, at first I couldn't trust them any more than a pack of bandits. However, as time went on, we experienced more hardship, and we learned each other's quirks. It just became easier. Eventually, I put so much confidence in those folks there was no situation where I wouldn't put my life in their hands. Understanding is key to coexistence. Coexistence is only one step away from camaraderie. Camaraderie is only one step behind friendship."

"So…" Ez bellowed out slowly, as the pitch of his voice rose slightly. "What you are saying…is that it doesn't matter if you don't know someone, even out there. You just have to take a leap of faith, and learn to trust them. Eventually you will come to terms with the idea?"

Jack reached out his arm and patted Ez on his left shoulder with a wide smile on his face. "You know what Ez…I don't think I could have said it better myself."

Chapter Ten: Over Troubled Waters

"Okay little buddy, where were we?"
"Well, I think you just drove off the raiders."

~ * ~

Oh yes, of course. With most of their vehicles disabled, they had no choice but to turn tail on foot. A real kick to their ego. I didn't get off scott-free though. When I woke up however many hours later, my arms were beat red up to the shoulders and pulsed with aches. I couldn't even move them anymore, along with my legs. I may have been awake, but there was no way in hell I would have been able to pick myself up. It almost felt like I had been attached to the earth by a chain, and anyone else besides me had the key to unlock it.

An hour or so later, I felt a gentle tap hit my side. It felt like a light kick, or tap from a stick. Reluctantly, I forced my eyes to drift open. A bright light left me disoriented for a brief moment. The wound on my arm had opened up since I collapsed, and I was lying in a puddle of my own blood. A hand grabbed hold of the back of my collar and yanked me up. I forced myself to lean on the person's shoulder like a crutch, throwing my arm around their neck like a loose noose. The Good Samaritan wiped dirt from under my eyes with a wet rag, which helped to restore my vision. At least a little bit. I caught a single glimpse of them as they wiped gravel from a cut in my head. The person was short, maybe five foot seven at most with a head of log, curly, black hair. At first, I mistook them for Bob, but I knew better than to imagine him like that. His hair wasn't that long. I was being carried by a woman, and one with extensive willpower. Not many people could carry some one hundred and fifty pound nobody across a field with one arm, but she could.

116

A lingering smog only served to suffocate me as I was hauled back to town by the mysterious Samaritan. I was placed laying with my back on a long bench, where the Samaritan abandoned me. Soon enough, my eyes were closed again, but before I could even think about sleeping, I heard a blank, monotone voice beckon to me. I opened my eyes again and was face to face with Silent Bob, who was standing over while me holding his crowbar and smoking a cigarette. I asked him what he was still doing here. He didn't give me an answer. I couldn't have expected more. He disappeared as soon as I blinked.

Small fires still crackled and glowed from the insides of the post office, revealing dozens of corpses sprawled on the front steps. They were carried back to the town square by a group of unharmed locals. The once lush and green fields had been burnt to ashes. Only a quarter of a field remained untouched. Grabbing hold of my aching sides, I forced myself to stand. I had to find my crew, or what was left of them. I made my way back west. If they were anywhere, it would be on the battlefield.

Walking made me hellishly queasy. I almost slipped a dozen times on empty bullet casings. They were scattered at every corner of Parkersvillle, and in no small number. Amongst the dust, I spotted Jed and Adahy looting anything useful from the dead. They took guns, ammo, cans, water, all the essentials. Strike that, anything that they could get their hands on. Todd sat on the trunk of a fallen tree, cleaning his face with some ripped cloth and water from his flask. Jacques leaned up against a truck and wrapped his knee, which bled profusely as he applied a heavy gauss bandage. It seems that one of those glass spears nicked him by the joint. I hobbled my way over to Todd and took a seat a few feet from him.

"Hey, you made it," he drawled.

"Yeah, half-dead, but I guess I made it."

Todd spit into a nearby bush and set down his flask. "Well, then there was one hell of a fight down here Jack. Vehicles flying by every which way, dozens of them freaks shouting about purging us and roasting our livers on a spit. I even saw a few of em' running around on fire. In all that chaos, I saw everybody here fighting right by my side. Everyone that is, except for you and Bob. Where the hell were you Jack, and where is Bob?"

I was shocked by the shift in tone. Never before on my journey had Todd ever accused me of being a *coward*.

"We came across a transport truck, eighteen wheels and a trailer. We had to try and stop it. We succeeded and I managed to make it to the field by the end of the fight, but Bob...he wasn't so lucky."

"You trying to say he dropped dead?"

I nodded my head while cold sweat rolled down my back.

"Well then Jack, you best take me to him. He deserves a proper burial, just like Hank had."

Together, we limped our way back up the hill to the site of the transport vehicle and I showed him Silent Bob, who now rested peacefully in the soil. Todd looked down at our comrade, then back to the behemoth of rusty metal that sat inactive only a few yards away, then to the giant wallowing in the mud, then back to me.

"You two stopped this by yourselves?"

I nodded again. I had no words left to share, or spare breath to share them with. He lifted Bob's body and carried him back to camp on his own, and as we passed by the others, we were met by stares of surprise and helplessness. We buried him under a makeshift gravestone on the edge of the western field.

Silent Bob's funeral service was private, quiet, and straight to the point. Kind of like the man it was honoring. The FCS took a kneel over his gravesite in a bitter silence. Not a tear was shed over our comrade, but it is hard to imagine another time that we felt more broken as a team. Jed, who was the closest to Bob out of all of us, left without saying a word. The next morning arrived without anyone grasping a single, sweet moment of slumber. We were drained and weary on all fronts. We sat like lobotomy patients in the town square until the conductor's car pulled in front of the Post office later the next day. The Jeep, which now flaunted three new bullet holes and a shattered window, came to an agonizingly slow halt.

Saul, looking as exhausted as anyone else in the village, limped his way out of the back seat. He was cut, bruised, and shaken up to all hell, but he still held that headstrong look on his face. Peter, who was left relatively unharmed, stepped up onto the hood as usual, before clearing his throat and giving a speech. It was always speeches with that guy.

The crowd remained a horde of lifeless expressions while Peter spoke with his usual charisma. He spoke of how five-dozen Acolytes were killed in comparison to our twenty casualties. He spoke of how we eliminated one third of the largest raider clan in the entire nation, and he said it in pride. However, he also spoke of how the fields were decimated by oil, blood, and tire tracks. No crop would likely grow there again for generations. This all lead to the final announcement. An important one. With Saul by his side, Peter announced that the entire village would join us on our journey. They had nothing left to lose in Parkersville. We had won, but at a severe cost. Now, just as always, we were left with one option.

Keep moving forward.

~ * ~

My off-and-on slumbering in town was continually haunted by the reoccurring nightmare. The world around me was covered by a deep, all-consuming blackness. My body was withered, and a stern feeling of sickness swelled in my stomach. I couldn't find the will to move my legs anymore, yet I couldn't find the will to give up and close my eyes either. A sense of dread and perfect loneliness caused my head to spin. Every time I shifted my weight, the feeling of weakness grew stronger. I thought about how it wasn't worth the effort to move at all. Maybe I was just tired. Anyway, if I moved, I'd just be standing in the same blackness, only in a different spot. So I stood there in the agonizing solitude of the darkness until I finally snapped back awake.

For the remainder of the day, as well as the following night, whenever I dared to close my eyes, the dream was waiting for me. Eventually, I gave up on sleeping entirely and stared at the sky instead. For the first time I could recollect, I didn't think of my family, or my friends, or the Acolytes. I only thought about a soft pillow. Maybe some warm sheets. The thought of a comfortable queen-sized bed and a roof over my head almost drove me mad. I would do anything to get one good night's sleep on that thing, and I meant literally anything. The rest of the evening crawled along with the imaginary smell of detergent.

~ * ~

We skipped town the next morning. The exhaustion from the battle was still fresh on everyone's faces. The march began slowly and disorganized, compared to our usual schedule anyway. It took a day or two for the people of Parkersville to become acclimated. Our lifestyle wasn't an easy one. Most of our new passengers wound up in the Center. More to protect, more to feed, less supplies for the rest of us. It caused some tension between Parkersville folks and others aboard. Mountain almost killed one of them when we encountered a slaver caravan. One of the loud mouth farmers offered to sell Mountain for two weeks of rations, and in response, Mountain smashed a rock on his nose. Nobody really talks to Mountain now, but he insists that it was the right thing to do. I agree with him.

Eventually, the Parkersville folks came to take on menial tasks like cooking and carrying supplies. Not very glorious jobs, but they were necessary. At least they were doing something. Sadly, nobody from town joined the FCS. Most people just said that they "didn't have what it takes", but the real reason was obvious. We had the highest death rate of any part of The Train, by a long shot. People were just scared of the responsibility. I mean we were scared too, but at least we bit our tongues and did our jobs, like we were supposed to. If the FCS didn't handle that paranoia, that cross would become everyone's to bare.

The next few weeks brought us the familiar sight of cozy, backwoods towns. Everyone began to dream hop again. The supplies were welcomed and very much appreciated, but I had to take a stab at my morals again. Even if the people were all dead, stealing from abandoned homes never got easier for me. Cornflakes were cornflakes though. We cut a path from Parkersville straight through Iowa, Illinois, and Indiana into western Ohio. Soon enough, we came across the massive wreckage and ruin that was Columbus. We ditched the dream hopping strategy and took to the highways. Our days were dreary, but efficient. Traveling was simpler when there is only a straight line to walk on. The scenery never changed, which was a real bummer. You can only look at so many abandoned offices before you've seen them all. I secretly missed the sight of the fresh greenery in the forest and Parkersburg. At least things were different there. My only consolation was the presence of shriveled vines, crabgrass, and the pungent odor of the lingering chemical weapon.

We were warned that there may still be dangerous pockets of the neurotoxin persisting in parts of the cities, especially in moist, humid buildings, or by any open water source. As a safety precaution, all survivors were given rags and facemasks to keep us from inhaling it in, but it was a hassle to continually hold a towel to my face, so most of the time I didn't use it. Maybe I was just gaining an immunity to it, but the denser air didn't bother me too much. I felt tingly, sure, but no major symptoms of poisoning were slowing me down.

Since the situation was so dull and mundane, I passed the time by smashing the windows of any red car that we walked by with a brick. Psychotic, right? The others thought I had gone crazy at first, but eventually, they picked up on the idea and started joining in. Jed chose silver. Jacques went with blue. Adahy chose white. Todd smashed any windows in sight, regardless of color. When asked what all the commotion was that evening by Peter, Todd said that we were just scaring off a few feral birds.

We waved goodbye to the bleak city in the matter of a day. Ohio was hit especially hard by the initial attack, and the lingering chemical was so dense we couldn't manage to find any living plant life, not even the weeds. I had never seen a place more desolate before, nor would I see one again. Maybe that place was just cursed. It was easier to just think about it that way.

~ * ~

Eventually, we came across a factory that mass-produced cigarettes. We looted the place completely. No product would go to waste. We knew some of the passengers back in the Center were almost powered by nicotine, and they would be elated to hear the morons out front found thousands of packs in a factory and brought them back. It was a good day to be a hero.

"I personally think we'll be lifted up on their shoulders and carried all the rest of the way from here to Boston." Jacques said with a smile on his face.

He carried a trash bag over his shoulder that was nearly filled to the brim.

"Yeah, somebody's gonna get laid tonight boys," Jed shouted with an overbearing tone of joy in his voice.

"Don't get your hopes up Jed, the people in the Center probably want to fuck you as much as they want to fuck an exhaust pipe," Todd replied with his usual sarcasm.

A short, awkward silence passed.

"Bob would have loved it here."

Adahy dropped his trash bag of cigs and patted me on the back. "Yeah, this would have been a paradise for him. We'll smoke one for him later when we set up camp."

And so, we did.

Later that evening, we arrived at the Center and presented the crowd with our thinly-rolled gold. They cheered and clapped as we handed out packs to them. The smell of tobacco and smiles spread faster than wildfire. As we threw the last of the plastic boxes into the crowd, we were pulled in. I would have given Jacques about two to twenty odds, but he was right. We were lifted on their shoulders. Think about it Ez, just some slips of paper rolled around tobacco was enough to send the masses into a frenzy. Later on, when the crowd dissipated, Mountain walked over to me and put out his hand for a low-five. I swung down and made a solid, crisp smack.

"Hey Beanstalk, how the hell have you been man? It's been a long time since I got to see your scrawny ass. How are things up front?"

"It's been alright for me lately, getting some solid legwork in as always. You?"

"Well, I overdid it and pulled my shoulder a week or so ago, so no lifting carts for *this* guy. It's been real smooth sailing aside from that though. I gotta say, I'm getting a little paranoid lately."

"You afraid that someone's gonna sell you off again while you sleep?"

"Don't give me that. I've just been hearing some stuff at night sometimes, that's all."

"What kind of *stuff*?"

"Oh, not much. Some nights, I hear some subtle humming, like an engine. It's incredibly faint, and you can barely hear it on a calm night, but it is there. I'm sure it's there."

I remembered what I heard the night before the Acolytes attacked and felt a little shiver.

"Huh, that's odd. It might just be your imagination." I mumbled, trying to avoid any unnecessary hysteria.

"Yeah, you're probably right. I'm just hearing things. Thanks for listening anyway."

I bid him a farewell not long after and returned to camp. The Acolytes had to be gone. They had to have learned their lesson after what we just did to them.

~ * ~

Things took a turn for the worse a week or so later. It's actually pretty funny, after walking around two thousand miles, I finally took a bad step on solid concrete. Man, did I feel like a deer getting hit by oncoming traffic. My ankle was numb after the fall, and it inflated like a balloon by sunset. Each step was pins and needles, and the constant movement never let the wound heal. The constant drenching of toxic rainfall wasn't helping my mood either. I'd say the sky opened up for three weeks straight in that stretch, judging by the prunes that developed on my toes. You know what they say about when it rains, Ez. All those aphorisms are more than true.

As we approached the northeastern edge of the state, we found ourselves walking along a rather large river which flowed with a fury thanks to all of the consistent storming. The water was a murky brown, and massive rapids formed in clusters. Every crossing and bridge we found had decayed and fallen into a state of total disrepair. Most of them were missing whole sections, or had already collapsed entirely. There was simply no place where we could safely cross on foot due to the current. It seemed like we were stuck along the waterfront, that is, until we noticed the rope bridge. Jacques found it dangling over the thinnest part of the river, but given that it was our only option, we took a while to inspect it. If we managed to get all the people across safe and sound, then the vehicles could really open up their engines and find a different route in no time.

It was made almost entirely of plywood. The rain had completely soaked the planks, leaving them splintered. It stretched from one cement walkway to an iron base which was drilled into the dirt on the other side. It must have been ten feet wide and one hundred feet long from base to base. The bridge seemed to be in a stable condition, but we weren't the type of people to take a risk on it, so we confronted Peter with the idea first before we took a single step. Seeing little alternative at the time, he reluctantly agreed to send a man over to test its strength, preferably a good swimmer.

Everyone in the FCS gathered at the base of the bridge to devise a proper way to decide which of us would be the one to take the risk. Using all of our logic and reason, our scientific minds decided that drawing straws would be the most effective method to choose our sacrifice. Todd was the first one to choose. He grabbed the straw furthest to the left of Adahy's hand. He didn't seem nervous at all, then again, he never was. It was the size of a pencil, no shorter than eight inches. Todd was safe. Next was Jacques, who quickly grabbed the furthest straw to the right and ripped it out of Adahy's hand. Another pencil-length drinking straw. Adahy moved on to Jed, who attempted to look as macho as possible while his quivering hand slid out another long straw. I was getting nervous. Adahy offered out the remaining two straws to me and gestured for me to grab one.

I took a deep breath and took a firm hold of the straw to the left. Slowly sliding it out inch by inch, I grimaced. Every moment, I thought that the straw would come to an early end, and I would become the lab rat. I was already sopping wet, Ez. One little dunk in the river might finally snap those final straws of sanity I had in the whole haystack. Luckily for me, the straw never cut short, in either case. I gave a great sigh of relief. Adahy had a nervous laughter radiating from him, but he managed to keep his cool.

"Well, I guess that's just my luck, isn't it?"

Adahy was a rather thin man, only about one hundred and fifty pounds total, not including gear. His steps were naturally light and his strides were long. He floated step by step until he was halfway through his walk. The bridge swung slightly lower there, and his steps became even lighter. Everyone in the crowd held their breath as Adahy finally made his escape from the low swooping center and found his way to the other side. The act drew applause from the waiting crowd. It was like some kind of staple circus act to them. Wiping the rainwater from his forehead, Adahy turned and beckoned the rest of the FCS to join him. Gladly, we obliged. My friends began to perform the death defying act themselves, one by one. The bridge seemed to do a good job of remaining steady, but still, something was bothering me about that swooping center.

Todd, Jacques, and Jed all tiptoed their way delicately across. As Jed took the last step onto the solid iron block on the other side, I took my first step onto one of the slippery planks. The floor beneath me felt weak, but it had carried Todd, who was heavier than me, so I figured here was nothing to fear. Each step along the glossy dark surface gave me more and more confidence, and soon enough I found myself taking firm steps at my full stride. I kept rolling until I reached the low hanging swoop, the winding serpent of oak and fiber. Shifting my weight on a specific board shook me pretty good, considering the crack I heard. Noise like that was never a good sign. I had to stop moving completely and wait it out, but judging from the increase in pitch of the creaking, I was pretty sure that it wasn't working. Stuck at the center of the bridge, I could only think to grab hold of the thick rope handrails and hope. I heard the crowd of spectators begin to gasp, and nervous clamoring soon drifted on the breeze.

I looked down cautiously at my mud-soaked boots, which for the moment, remained on solid ground. As I maintained my pose on my uneasy post, the cracking finally grew silent, and you could feel the palpable tension in the air dissipate. I didn't want to breathe. My mind was telling me to stay where I was, but my nervous heart was telling me to rush forward. Feeling the desperate need to finish this hellish walk, I finally lifted my left foot. It was a poor decision.

I felt an absolute break in the wood under my feet, like an earthquake was occurring right underneath my shoe soles. From the cliff top where most of the Center sat, I heard a chorus of screams and shouting. They shrieked and yelled and beckoned for me to run. They didn't need to tell me. I took off like a flash of light across the midway. The bridge shook and swayed and crumbled, progressively collapsing as I made my escape from the swooping low point. The handrails snapped and fell limp amongst the maelstrom of falling support beams, and balancing upon the broken path became an exercise in futility. I broke out into a full sprint toward the other side, but my ankle slowed my pace to that of a fast jog. One extremely loud crack busted half of the planks, and with it, the bridge fell. About three quarters of the way across the platform, I lost whatever I was standing on and felt myself plunge into the rushing white-water torrent below me.

I smacked the water like a smooth stone, and sank deep beneath the current of putrid brown water. I hit the sediment on the bottom of the river and tumbled like a ragdoll. It was a struggle to determine which direction was up and what was down. My backpack, which was still tightly strapped around my shoulders, caught hold of a sharp rock during the tumble. I was yanked back from my own momentum and sat, ensnared by the current. The next few seconds took years to pass. My lungs began to burn from the deprivation of oxygen, so I struggled and thrashed to untangle myself. Eventually, the movement worked out, and I felt a gentle jerk. I turned back to see that there was another gash in the fabric of my pack. A few items tumbled out and became victims of the current. They were washed away in an instant. The momentum of the water started carrying me again.

Running out of strength and air to work with, I forced myself to swim up. As I approached the surface, I felt myself choking on the river water. Bouncing off the sediment of the riverbank, I breached the rushing foam and muddy brine that covered the surface. Coughing uncontrollably and spitting out large quantities of vile liquid, I fought to keep my head within reach of daylight. The mighty riptide tore me from side to side like I was being towed along by a vehicle. Whenever I could find an opportunity or calm moment, I would swim closer to the shoreline and scan the cliffs for a search party. However, whenever I looked upon the hillsides and the lifeless plains, there wasn't a soul to be found. A few minutes passed in the merciless grip, and I had barely made any progress making it back to solid ground. I decided if I was going to do something to save myself, it would have to be right then. Managing to use the current to my advantage, I swam along the sudsy gallons of racing water until I finally came within arm's reach of the shoreline.

Still moving at a break-neck pace, I threw my arm onto the earth and grabbed onto a patch of dead reeds. After pulling myself closer to dry land, I dragged my other arm out of the depths and clawed my fingers into the dirt. After minutes of effort, I crawled out of the rapids onto the earthy terrain and squirmed back to higher ground. My lungs were filled with the infected waters of the river, so I did my best to cough up and spit out as much of the toxic liquid as I could before collapsing onto my back. There I remained, motionless as a rock. My damaged pack slung weakly at my side, I forced myself to sit up against a boulder. I already felt the faint remnants of the poison drifting inside me, parasites floating in the recesses of my bloodstream. There was a gentle numbness that grew in my core. With somewhat blank eyes I stared down at the river which had taken me, and I thought to myself. *How in the hell did I manage to make it through something like that?*

Chapter Eleven: Alone in the World

Ez enjoyed listening to his newfound friend and learning about the wasteland, but something had been bothering him. As Jack talked about being washed away in the dark, impure waters of the river, Ez was building up his confidence. He wanted to know more about the roamers. Jack said that he had seen them personally before, but they hadn't even been mentioned. After a moment of awkward silence, Ez went to speak up, but Jack beat him to the punch.

"Hmm, you feeling okay little buddy? You look like you're getting sick or something…"

Ez continued to glance at Jack with nervous eyes. He remembered how reluctant Jack was to talk about them earlier, and Ez was sure bringing the subject up again would make things worse, but he still felt compelled to ask.

"I want to know more."

Jack leaned forward. "You want to learn more? More about what?"

Ez cleared his throat and went to speak again. "You said that you had seen the monsters out there, in the wasteland, but you haven't even as much as mentioned them yet. Did you really see any of them during your trip, or was that just a way to get my attention?"

"Haven't you learned yet, Ez?"

"Learned what?"

"I don't know how many times I told you this by this point, but you have to be patient. If you really want to understand what's going on out there, you have to let the details come naturally. Just hold your horses kiddo, I promise that the roamers will come up pretty soon."

There was a sigh of relief and a little snicker.

"And what are you laughing at kid?"

"Hold your what?" Ez held back a snicker.

"You meaning to tell me that you have never heard of horses before?"

Ezekiel shook his head. He thought they only existed in cowboy stories.

"Wow kid, you really have never left this city, have you?"

"My mother always told me that it was dangerous to go out into the wild. She even hated the idea of me scavenging the outskirts for valuables. "

"Well, I guess she isn't wrong. However, for your information young man, horses are tall and strong creatures that stand on four legs and people used to ride back in the good ol' days."

"You mean like a big dog?"

Jack cracked up and leaned back in his seat, breathing between each chuckle.

"Hey, don't laugh at me old timer. I've never seen one before."

"Well little buddy, imagine a dog with short hair, a weird looking tail, and a long snout. That's more like a horse."

"Oooooh, I can see it now."

Jack sat back and ran his hand through his hair. He hadn't realized how sheltered the boy had been throughout his life. Then again, Jack hadn't seen many animals in the city either, with the exception of the slaughterhouses for hogs and cattle. It wasn't entirely impossible that horses went extinct around these parts, but the thought of something as important as horses fading from memory made Jack feel uneasy. Jack began to wonder what other words he had introduced to Ez since he started blabbing. Maybe he was teaching the boy more than he first thought.

~ * ~

Well, anyway Ez, I sat by the riverside for a few minutes until I could feel my arms again, and decided to check what had fallen out of my pack when it tore on that sharp rock. I dumped the remnants onto the hillside and took an inventory of everything that had been washed away. One of the handguns, my spare rifle ammo, and most devastating, my canned food, were all taken into the depths. I still had one handgun, a knife, soaked cigarette lighters, clean canteen water, and luckily, my field glasses.

My map of the Train's intended route was heavily damaged, and the colors on the page had nearly blended, but I could still see the intended route. Franklin may have been a dork, but he was a dork that labeled in permanent marker. The group was making a pass through a shopping district close to the PA border to search for supplies. My estimate was that they would reach the city in two days. There was no reason to turn and walk back to the bridge to find them at that point. Hell, I must have been miles from where I fell. I was certain they carried on, just as the Train always has, with or without me. My best bet was to try and rejoin them when they came for the supplies.

I turned back to take inventory of my remaining medical supplies to find that my rifle had taken considerable damage from the fall. Its scope had fallen off its mount. Large shards of the sights had completely shattered. After further inspection, I realized that the filthy water had flooded every crevasse of its design. The barrel was even bent due to the initial impact with the sediment. The frame was cracked. The weapon was useless. With a heavy heart, I let go of the loose weight by tossing it back into the depths. The Rifleman's legacy slowly sunk beneath the foam of the rapids.

I knew I had to make good time if I was to meet up with them, so I marched onward. The effects of the dirty water began taking their toll not long after that. The toxin is a sneaky killer, Ez. It starts by creeping under your skin a bit, like a snake. It squirms around, making your muscles twitch and shake until it makes its way to your stomach. There, it rests, and slowly starts to numb your body from its core. I was officially on the clock.

The high concentration of the toxin in the air had still kept most remaining life out of the area, so I was left alone with my thoughts. There were no words of symbolism or wisdom, courage or strength, hope or willpower to be found in me. My twinging forearm was hogging too much attention for me to do any thinking. I began to wonder if this is what everyone else felt like before they rolled over dead. What an unpleasant way to go. Not because I was in a lot of pain or anything, but because it feels like you are strangling yourself from the insides. You barely feel like your body is yours anymore.

~ * ~

As the day progressed, my body continued to shiver from time to time, but my legs remained strong. I thanked my lucky stars for that. Moving was essential to survival. My northeastern path led me straight through a rotted forest to a cluster of small towns surrounding the PA border. My number one priority was finding a means to stop the progression of the toxin, so I decided to go on a pharmacy run. There wasn't much to be found there initially, but after an afternoon spent exploring, I found a dollar drug-mart on a secluded street corner. It seemed like I finally caught a break. The building itself had fallen into the same ugly state of decay as everything else in the wasteland, but for once, I didn't mind. I checked the sliding glass door to find it entirely sealed shut by an iron-bar barricade and a pile of store shelves. Someone had locked themselves in, and probably never made it out. I stood back and looked for an alternate way in. Fortunately for me, there was a shattered window, only a few inches beyond my grasp too. That was workable. With some ingenuity and a wet piece of rope, I found myself laying face-down on the store's main floor.

I was ecstatic to make it inside, but my joy was immediately cut off by the sight of human remains. It was a long dead body of a rather large man. The bits and parts of a broken gas mask were sitting next to him. On the walls, there were tally marks cut deep into the brick. There must have been hundreds of them stabbed in the mold. There was a note hanging limply from his decaying hand, so I slowly reached down and snatched it. The writing was shoddy, but still somewhat legible. I could tell that the paper had been there for quite some time.

~ * ~

Well, this looks like the end of the line. Woke up today nice and early to find that one of the windows was cracked. Bad news bears. I went to grab my mask, but in a panic, I managed to step on it. What a genius. There are so many useless things in this store, but luckily for me, none of them have the parts I need to fix it. I can't really risk going out either. That smog will put me down in the matter of a minute or two without my gear.

Guess that means there's nowhere left to run. In case anyone ever busts into the shop and finds my little den, I ought to let you know that the keys to this joint are hidden under the doormat. Have fun with what could have been my best hope for making it through this. I'd say that I have about a day left until this stuff in the air gets to me. Still, I can't say that five hundred and twenty days wasn't a bad run for one guy who had no idea what was going on most of the time. It isn't all bad anyways. I will be able to see my wife soon, so at least I get to look forward to that right? Hell, maybe I'll even be able to eat something other than saltine crackers. What a life. Anyways, good luck asshole.

   -Your buddy Mickey

   I slid the note into the damaged front flap of my pack and made my way through the store, raiding it completely for anything usable until I found my way behind the pharmacy counter. Just as Mickey said, the shiny brass key was sitting right under the welcome mat. I found countless bottles and containers of prescription medications of every size and shape. After a minute or two of thrashing through the meds, I found a strangely named pill roughly the size of a quarter that claimed to combat tingling and numbness. Busting open the child lock, I popped two of the yacht-sized pills into my mouth. A little lukewarm flask water did wonders to get them down. I stuffed two more bottles into my newly filled pack and promptly climbed back through the window. After half an hour of intense discomfort, the tingling subsided. The mammoth medication seemed to do the trick.

~ * ~

   Nightfall arrived shortly after I passed the first rusted green signs welcoming me to the keystone state. Another day, another state traversed on foot. All around me were quaint brick houses with large yards and paved concrete driveways. Probably a real snooty neighborhood at some point. The open streets only helped the gurgling screeches of feral birds to travel great distances both far and wide. They were the first signs of life I had picked up on since the collapse. The border must have avoided the worst of the attack. That always seemed to be the case, but I couldn't hazard a guess as to why. I had to start keeping my guard up. Large packs of feral beasts could be anywhere, or even worse, hostile survivors. Brushing the thought off, I took shelter on one of the porches and set my head on the hardwood. I figured The Train had probably set up camp an hour before me, so I had made up some ground. If I woke up early, I would likely make it to my destination with a day to spare.

Forcing myself to sleep wasn't easy. There was a constant, humid moisture that brushed against my forehead. I had to wipe it off every minute or so, or I felt like I was drowning. Eventually, I became frustrated and threw my pack under my head like a pillow. Out of sheer boredom, I began to count sheep. It never worked for me as a kid, but things were different. Back then, I *wanted* to sleep. On that doorstep in the middle of nowhere, I *needed* to sleep. Honestly, boring myself was the only strategy I could think of. Funny enough, it seemed to have an effect on me. Moments later, I was completely out of it.

I found myself standing in the oh-so familiar darkness that had become my recurring nightmare. The same looming feeling of loneliness. The same cold. The same exhaustion. The same malaise. It seemed as if I had no legs or arms, yet I stood upon my two legs and felt a strange tingling in my fingertips. It was always the same, and that infuriated me. I had come to despise the dream and how it's process never changed. I lamented how *my* process never changed. Refusing its rules started sounding pretty good. I felt my blood boil to a fever pitch, and for the first time, something shifted.

My mind was still helpless in the iron grip of the dream, but my body became strong. The weakness that had burdened my legs shattered like a pane of glass. The chains of complacency fell to the ground at my feet. I was bored with the conceited thoughts. It was pathetic. I am not pathetic. Yeah, I would probably find the same thing over there as I had found where I was, but it's not like I had anything better to do. A liberating breeze brushed against my back. It motivated my legs to inch forward until I felt my boot leave the ground. In the trance of the shade surrounding me, I felt the bottom of my feet touch new ground, and it felt like nothing I had ever experienced before.

~ * ~

Suddenly, there was a blinding flash of light, and I snapped back into reality, and all of its unpleasantness. I propped myself onto an old rocking chair on the porch and sighed. It felt like a dagger had dislodged itself from my heart. Everything almost seemed at peace.

There was no time to celebrate my victory though. As I sat back to think about what it had all meant, I heard a multitude of subtle footsteps pattering their way to the doorstep. Light, but consistent, and numerous. My eyes met the glaring reflection of yellowed flashing teeth. I slid the remaining 9mm from the deepest chasm of my pack and stood directly in the face of a pack of vicious feral dogs.

They clamped their jaws together and snarled while thick white foam seeped slowly from their gums. Of course, I was terrified, but with my newfound confidence, I was certain that I could make it past them. That weapon had been with me since Phoenix. Or maybe it was the other one. I don't remember which of the two identical pistols had fallen to the river. It didn't matter. It was the trigger-finger that mattered. The snarling rose to a fever pitch, and one of the bone-thin followers leapt onto the top step. The trigger slid in with a pleasant ease, and the resulting kick was sturdy. The beast flopped over with all the momentum carrying it forward. The violent clap of the bullet sent the other three into a blind fury, thrashing and lunging all around me.

Thinking fast, I threw myself over the side rail, which broke into splinters under the weight of my vault. My backside landed in a soft pile of weeds before I rolled back onto my stomach. There was no time to take a breath. I launched myself back onto my feet and darted across the front yard toward the road. I heard the taps of paws on the pavement behind me, and in a hurried and inaccurate attempt, I whipped around and fired three shots at the closest bag of fur. Two of them collided with the pavement, and only managed to kick up dust upon impact, but the final shot landed square on the smallest dog's forehead. The mangey freak tumbled over itself. Another one down. Shifting my sights onto the final two frenzied monsters, I pulled down on the cold steel again to put an end to the chase.

Click. What a disheartening sound. I could have sworn I had two shots left in the magazine, but somehow, I must have miscounted. I've never been good at math. There was no other option for me but to fight my final pursuers hand to snout. I wasn't feeling particularly lucky. Turning tail again, I took off down the highway. My ankle still ached and stumbled, but I wasn't gonna let it slow me down again, not after last time. My rotting boots crushed loose stone under my feet and kicked chunks of it up behind me. Ahead was steady downhill stretch of pavement leading to a small group of mom and pop shops. I decided if I was going to stop and fight, that would be the place. When I crossed a shattered window of a diner, I finally slowed down. The pocket knife came out, still dull from after the fight in Parkersburg. Feeling the flat edge, I returned it to my pocket. Instead, I got a good grip on a sharp wedge of window glass and broke it off. The thunderbolt edge gave my palm a little nick.

The dogs caught up to me in the matter of a few seconds. One held a distinctly shimmering brown coat of fur, which had been scarred all over. They looked like teeth marks. One of its ears was also mangled to shreds like a loose rag. The other animal was a slim, muscular beast with a large, pointed snout and jaws. It was the only dog from the pack that didn't look underfed. The animal's strong legs were covered in a completely jet-black fur. It was natural camouflage, perfect for a dark night. Unfortunately for me, it was a dark night. Its snout was long like that of a Doberman Pincher, and it had one narrow scar, thin enough to be made by a knife, stretching up toward its grey, emotionless eyes. The foam dripped from their mouths in a hungry, frothy stream. Feral animals lose all sense of compassion and thought, Ez. They are only meant to hunt, kill, and eat. This lot was no different.

I held the shard of glass so tightly that the nick opened up a bit. Blood dripped to my wrist.

The sight of the crimson liquid sent the hounds into a fit of rage. The remaining underling of the pack gurgled and snarled before leaping its way toward my throat. The creature's front paws collided with my chest, forcing me to the ground. I kept my throat covered with my right hand and held the monstrosity back with the other. It snapped those glowing white teeth open and closed over my guard, spitting saliva onto my face. Through the barking and growling, I heard the strange squeal of tires behind my head. Disregarding the noise, I let go of the mound of fur and drove the glass pane I held on to deep into his heart. After a few seconds of heavy panting, the mutt collapsed on top of me. I shoved the lump of flesh and enamel off my chest and shot back onto my feet. The pack leader had disappeared. I brushed the blood and drool from my shirt and face and began to wrap my wounded hand in a makeshift cloth bandage. My senses were heightened by the fight, so any noise that whimpered on my earlobe sent me spiraling to find the source. A super power, but one with a major flaw.

I heard the sound of squeaking brakes coming from a nearby side street, but as I turned to face it, I nearly overlooked the slim torso of the pack leader darting at me from the shadows. There was barely any time to react, but with the menial seconds that I did have, I raised my arms up to my face. The aggressive canine's snout collided with my wrist, and its razor-sharp fangs sealed on thin air centimeters from my skin. Seizing the opportunity, I drove my elbow deep into its ribs and knocked the dog into the pavement. It slid through the asphalt on its stomach, but quickly recovered. It patiently planned its next charge. The wind rustled a pile of plastic bags that floated about on the street corners. One collided with the dog's snout. It snapped its jaws and spun in circles as the shopping bag obscured its sight and smell. The thin material didn't last long. A tear in the plastic was followed by a tear in its mental fabric, followed by a tear across the pavement. It had the same kinetic ferocity as the mother bear in the forest, only sleeker. I raised the steel of my blade up to my chest and waited patiently to drive it through the mutt's neck, but after its paws left the ground, there was a deafening blast from beside me that completely split my ears.

The mongrel was lifted from its stance and flew through the air before landing as a pile of meat a few yards away. I gripped my head firmly in my hands in a desperate attempt to stop the ringing in my ears. My brain was rattling. When double vision became one-and-a-half vision, I looked to my right to find the business end of a twin barrel looking me right in the eyes. Startled, I fell back onto my side and looked up to the shady figure of a young man in the glow of a dusty green lantern.

He was no older than thirty, with a face still young and clean cut. He had a somewhat cumbersome pair of thick rimmed glasses that hung tightly to his face. He had short blond hair that formed a raised curve over his forehead. It's like he found a discount salon among the ruins and got a full treatment. While on the shorter side, the guy looked like he had been bodybuilding since the cradle. Stretching across his head was a thick red, white, and blue bandana that had almost as many rips on it as there were stripes.

"I still have one shot left," he said, while gently waving the barrel of the gun. "I wouldn't try my luck."

"Okay buddy, I'm really not looking for any of this shit right now."

"Can't say I expected that. Okay. I'll bite. What exactly is it that you're looking for then?"

"I'm just passing through, not really looking for anything in particular. However, if you keep pointing that at my face, I might start looking to break it over your head."

"Nice bravado, I can appreciate that."

He took a step back, but kept the 12 gauge pointing in my direction, just in case. I casually brushed the dust off of my clothes and looked back at the stranger. He had a tendency to look down on me, like I was no threat to him whatsoever. I knew he was being cautious, deep down anyway. Maybe the bravado was entirely surface level. Whatever the case, he hid his fear very well.

"Listen pal, I have a deadline to meet here, and I need to safely make my way east. If I don't get there in a day and a half, I'm up shit's creek."

"You said east? Well, that sucks."

"What do you mean *sucks*? Is there danger east of here?"

"There's danger everywhere man, but going east is just making it worse for yourself. Going the most direct route means that you have to sneak past those freaks."

Still concerned about his incoherent babble, I kept pestering the survivor for whatever information I could about these so called 'freaks'.

"What, the freaks?" he said, expecting me to already understand what he was saying. "They are these weird, zombie-looking things.

Disgusting, pale, and too curious for their own good. A real pain in the ass. They don't bother you unless you bother them though, so I guess that's a good thing."

"Zombies?" I said, in total disbelief.

"Go ahead, believe me or not, I really can't say that I care at all what happens to you. If you aren't going to listen to me though, at least make sure that you are armed so you can defend yourself if they spot you."

He was a madman. He had to be, with all that talk of zombies out in the wasteland, but he was right about one thing. I was terribly unarmed.

"Fine, do you have any 9mm ammo that you could trade for something?"

He gestured that I should walk over to the flimsy and brittle trunk of his compact car, so I followed.

"You have food, old man?"

"Yeah, but I'm not old." I replied, showing all the boxed crackers and canned soup I found while raiding the store.

"Good, then I have just what you need."

He flipped open the frail covering of his trunk to reveal a large black box containing thousands of rounds of ammunition. There was a small pocket that held a couple dozen shining yellow casings. Absolutely perfect for my weapon. Loading them into a brand-new magazine, I gladly handed over half of the food I gathered. In an uneasy silence, the young man trotted his way back up into the driver's seat and plopped down into the sunken fabric.

"Thanks for doing business, and good luck doing whatever it is that you're doing."

Before he had a chance to roll up his window, I came to a quick conclusion. "Hey, I'm actually looking for a group of survivors heading east to a massive safe-haven in Boston. Lots of good company to be had. Maybe some mediocre food, too. You would be more than welcome to join us on the rest of the trip, if that sounds appealing."

"Boston? Hell no. I kind of prefer working around here with my crew. I've kind of gotten a taste for surviving like this, you know, scavenging day to day. I honestly think that I would be bored doing anything else. Being told what I can and can't do when there is nobody around to enforce it doesn't sit too well with me. Thanks for the offer though."

Before he pulled away into the night, I managed to stop him one last time.

"Hey, I almost forgot to thank you for saving me back there, it has become a rarity to see any kindness like that these days. What is your name?"

He tapped his hands on the cracked plastic of the dashboard. "It's no problem, I'd do it any time. As for my name, I can't see why you need it. You'll never see me again, I'll never see you. We'll live our happy little existences, separately of course. In the end, all you need to remember is what I did, if you even remember that much. Sound like a reasonable deal?"

With that, the beaten little car pulled away and roared into the distance, into the infinite landscape of empty places where families belong. The mysterious stranger was cryptic, maybe pretentious, but I could appreciate his desire to carve out his own path. Exhausted from the day's events, I limped my way over to a nearby bar. Putting pressure on my leg made my whole right-side twitch and buckle. Shuffling through a wooden door that had been left ajar, I dropped into the shredded and frayed material of a booth. It wasn't any bed, but the thick white fabric was still cushiony and supple, so it would do. I didn't even have my sleeping bag. All of my luxuries were probably still in the FCS cart. If they hadn't been auctioned off, of course. Still paranoid from the thought of wild animals and confused from the bizarre talk of zombie-creatures, I left the safety of my 9mm off and set it down behind my head. I fell into a shallow and insecure sleep. As I rested my head on the old lopsided seat, for the first time in months, the dream did not haunt my thoughts.

The room was warm and humid, but the smell of rotting wood was a less than pleasant sensation to wake up to. The lacquer must not have held up very well. With a rock of menial momentum, my torso went upright. I figure I must have slept hard on that booth. When I got up, there was a deep imprint of my head on the inside corner. When I looked out the window, the sun was just barely hanging over the skyline, no more than a few feet, so it must have been midmorning. Time to move out.

Not everything was sunshine and rainbows. The neurotoxin had returned in force, this time reaching my shoulders and upper arms, as well as my gut. It was reaching closer to the lethal stages of the poisoning, and I was still weary and queasy from sickness and the past weeks insomnia, but I still managed to force down one of the massive tablets with the help of a spare bottle of forty-year-old whiskey. It's amazing what you can scavenge if you are willing to look around every corner.

I estimated that there was ten hours of daylight left for me to work with. If everything went smoothly that day, I figured I would end up on the outskirts of my destination. There was a fierce wind blowing from the east. Cascades of leaves and garbage whipped by in waves. It was a cold breeze, an autumn special. I forgot how little tolerance I had for the cold anymore, way too thin for that chilly bullshit. Eventually, my path deviated off of the highway across a wide, open field. The strangest thing about the setting though, was the return of pigment to the grass under my feet. Most of the greenery I saw out there were branching weeds and vines, but for the first time in a while, natural grass almost seemed alive. I got all giddy, like a child in a toy store. However, being in an open field like that only served to remind me just how alone I was.

The typical ominous silence that unnerved me while traveling with The Train was grim enough, but without any companionship whatsoever, it was unbearable. The only companions within miles were families of feral rats that watched me from underground nests. I decided meditation wasn't for me, so I started to make some noise. I began to whistle the first thing that came to my mind. Funny enough, that first thing ended up being a company jingle. I think it was for a candy bar. It was obnoxious back when it played on commercials, but I came to miss the campy creativity. *Why yes, I think I could use a caramel crunch, thank you.*

As I approached the end of the grassy plateau, a little spec of white caught my eye. Taking a knee, I slowly shoveled my hand into the earth and lifted a heavy mound of dirt up to my eyes. Proudly sprouting out of the tormented soil was the beginnings of a beautiful white flower. It wasn't very large, but it was still one of the few wild flowers I saw outside of the forest that had survived. Its tiny green stem stood straight and defiant. It was as if the little plant was spitting in the face of the world, and I loved the idea of that. I took a moment and placed the little survivalist inside an empty soup can that I left sitting in my pack, taking care to give it a spot where it could get some sun as I walked.

The rest of the morning was spent crossing the immense rolling hills that stood between me and the city. As I reached the top of each slope, I would take a brief moment to stop and view landscape. While it really wasn't anything too exceptional compared to the other places where I had been, there was something that felt different about those fields. It was strangely calming to look at the untouched scene and the few brown plants that hung limply from their stems.

Ahead of me was the final hillside before reaching the city where the 'zombies' were supposed to live. This hill was steep in comparison to the size of its peers. It wasn't an easy climb, but for once, I was well rested. My feet tended to slide on patches of loose pasture, which was annoying. In order to keep my footing, I dug the toe of my boot deep into the soil. A little substance to balance on did wonders. After a few exhausting minutes of scaling the colossal ridge, I set foot back onto a piece of even terrain.

I had clear vision in almost every direction for miles around. Not even a tenth of a mile east, there was a small shredded wire fence covered with vines. Behind that barricade sat the crumbling remains of a wooden home. Excited to finally see some measurable progress, I confidently marched toward the fence. As I heavily stamped down my boot onto the plateau, I felt a certain shift under my feet. I stopped moving and looked down between my feet to see a large crushed stem and yellow petals under my soles. Maybe crushing my soul in return. It was such a stupid mistake. Such a careless blunder. I could have just killed the first fully-grown flower in the wasteland because I couldn't have bothered to watch my feet. To be honest, stamping on the flower made me feel more like a murderer than ever I did killing the Acolytes.

In my pointless frustration, I took a knee on top of the soft earth and felt the stem of the dead flower in the palms of my hands. It was snapped and uneven, yet smooth. The petals were softer than velvet, and vibrant like neon paint. It was like the entire organism had been painted by hand. My vision fixed on the deep mustard center that held on to each individual petal. Taking the tip of my index finger and poking it, I felt the pollen rub off onto my skin. It left a light orange stain on my fingertips. Feeling remorseful for my inattention, I took the tiny wildflower I had found earlier in the hills and gently returned it to the earth, directly next to the corpse of its counterpart. As I slowly patted down soil underneath its tiny roots, another patch of white resonated in the corner of my left eye.

Standing up and brushing the dry dirt from my pant legs, I gazed at the vibrant color that caught my attention to find a miracle of God. Dozens, no, hundreds of tall wild flowers sprouted from every crevasse of the earth. Blues as deep as the sea, reds as light as berries, violets as vibrant as the most flawless amethyst, and oranges that mimicked the color of the mid-afternoon sun. Nature's finest collection of daughters and sons. Call me a softie, but I never thought that such a thing as a field of flowers could exist anymore. The world was supposed to be dead, or at least gasping for air. Death and desolation were supposed to be all that remained for us. But a silly little plateau in the middle of nowhere defied god, defied death, and defied expectation. It grew. It made new life from fallen, failed ancestors. It survived, Ez.

If a bunch of plants could manage all this and put the pieces of their existence back together, then I couldn't find an excuse not to do the same. All of this. The attack, the toxin, the empty wasteland, it doesn't mean that this is the end. It was never meant to be. We may have been beaten and driven to the furthest corners of existence, but nothing will ever put us down for good. Life is annoyingly persistent that way. Always has been. Heck, I guess that makes us the most annoying of common weeds. Not even the chemicals can shrivel us up enough to remove us from the garden. I think I can eventually be proud of that comparison. Can you, Ez?

Chapter Twelve: A Colony

There was no more time for me to stand around and look at porch decorations. I decided to shuffle my feet across the remainder of the field. No more wildflowers would be stomped on my accord. Scraping my feet on the soil made this grody, crumbling sound. Not entirely unpleasant compared to the usual thumps of marching. The graininess reminded me of playground mulch. The cheap, manila kind. It brought back memories of me taking Delilah to the park. The big plastic slides were always her favorites. The metal ones always got too hot and burned her legs, but the plastic ones were just right. My baby girl slid and turned on the whole way down until she came to a delicate stop on the level lip at the bottom. She laughed and smiled and laughed some more. Her giggling was infectious. Eventually, her face would get all red, and she would have to stop just to take a breather. Pure joy. That's how I remembered her. No better motivation than that.

I reached the hole in the barbed wire fence after a few minutes. The gap was relatively thin, but it was just wide enough for a man to fit through. It looked as though the fence had been separated violently by hand into thin strips. Drooping weakly from a piece of severed iron was the cloth of a flannel shirt. The color was faded and sun-bleached. Whoever tore the fence did it a long time before I showed up. Attentively, I put my first foot through the tear, rattling the fence and scratching the rubber toe of my boot. Sliding my back along the rounded metal slivers, I pushed the rest of my body through the fissure.

~ * ~

There was a hillside path leading into the heart of the city. The entire route was covered by live saplings. They were likely mutated, like the corn, but they looked as happy and healthy as any other plant I had ever seen. There was a makeshift hunting blind in a thicket of them outskirts of town. Only one man could fit inside, and the roof was covered in dry leaves and netting. The whole area was littered with cans and boxes of snack crackers. I couldn't even begin to guess why it was there. The blind presented me with an excellent opportunity to look around though, so I wasn't about to complain. The field glasses had seen quite a substantial bit of wear and tear in the months they traveled with me. The once sleek and untouched jet-black casing had been degraded from the sand, water, dirt, and stone. However, as I placed the lenses up to my eyes, I was met by the crystal-clear vision downrange. It seemed like the outside world couldn't destroy everything after all.

The street signs and ancient advertisements became clear. The road had accumulated quite a few pot holes, so the pavement looked more like a minefield than a path that cars could travel through. Everything down there seemed pretty dead to me. Dense silence on all fronts too. I was pretty sure it was a ghost town, but there was one thing I spotted that kept me on my toes. Along the road, there were dozens of mounds. Panes of glass, jewelry, light bulbs, trinkets, hood ornaments. If it shined, it could be found there. I'm not talking little anthills either Ez. These were at least up to my neck, and they were numerous. No doubt that was manmade, unless the prairie rats were trying their hand at creating a metropolis.

I was confused by the...unreasonable sights. I kept my head and continued to scan the display windows. There had to be somebody left alive down there to do all of that. Piles of valuables don't pop into existence for no reason. Leaning on the tent flap, I weighed my options. If there were somebody down there, what exactly should I do about it? It wasn't really like I could just go up to the guy and shake hands. He was making mounds of shiny objects along the street and kept a hunting blind tucked in the far corner of the city. That wouldn't be made by anyone sane. I mean, what if he had traps, just like the Rifleman? If I walked out there carelessly, I would be throwing my whole life away. The situation needed to be waited out. Handled real delicately. Not really my specialty, but I made do. By nightfall, I would move from my perch and sneak through the buildings. Hopefully, twilight would keep me hidden long enough to make my escape.

~ * ~

The rest of the afternoon was wasteful. I knew that I was burning precious time, but I had to take my surroundings in carefully, especially in a place as potentially hostile as a shady little village. Going around the city would take more time than I had, and it would leave me exhausted, so that was out of the question. Not to mention my ankle still firmly whooping my ass every now and then. Waiting was the way to go, like a snake in the grass.

The sun fell from above my head to the tree line, then sunk into the earth. The city found itself shaded in a scarlet tint. It was my time to slither and strike. The remainder of the path was treaded with silent steps. I crossed into a gravel parking lot, and my paces grew even shorter. My 9mm was firmly grasped in my right hand, so tightly that it numbed my fingers. There was a sign that creaked and swayed in the gentle gusts of wind. It helped to camouflage whatever little noise I was still making. Through the decimated and rotted pine, I could still vaguely read what once was artistic calligraphy. Though most of the letters were lost to blight, the words 'Funeral Home' remained pretty legible. How appropriate.

I swung open a heavy, steel gate enough for my body to slide through. Every inch that the thick bars moved was met by an orchestra of creaks. A nice, agonizing slow-burn. Oddly enough, I started to catch the gentlest scent of neurotoxin in the air as I proceeded through. I finally placed my left foot back on solid concrete, and I felt a little wave of relief wash over me. Maybe I was just allowing myself to fall victim to fear. It's always easy to lose your nerve out there, but I hadn't even seen anything yet. Oh, and the only pre-existing threat I knew about for this dingy little neighborhood were zombies. Zombies. What kind of idiot did that guy take me for anyway? But as I was lost in self-righteous encouragement, I heard something rustle and tumble onto the pavement.

Startled, I whipped my head around to see an old mug that had fallen from its perch atop a pile of valuables. The handle had shattered into fragments of ceramic, and the cup itself splintered in half. I was both relieved and frustrated at the sudden sound being a number one best dad cup, but my attitude quickly changed when I saw a pasty white figure shamble into the street and kneel down beside it. I can assume my eyes grew to the size of saucers right about then. In a panic, I took a careless step back into a pothole. My feet stumbled over themselves, plummeting me down to the concrete. I placed my hand in a position to break the fall, but it slid off of a small pile of dinner-plate shards. One wedge drove itself into my forearm, making me involuntarily grunt. Catching myself on my uneasy descent, I lowered the rest of my body to the ground quietly.

The creature must have been hiding inside the shop all day. My guess was that, based on that pale skin, the roamers didn't care much for sunlight. Its figure was disturbingly slender and morphed. Uneven shoulders, legs were shriveled and bent, a real chiropractic mess. There were only a few shreds of hair still left sitting atop its head. There were tears and cuts all over the creature's flesh, too. Judging by how they picked at their skin, I assumed they were all self-inflicted. Slowly, I forced myself back onto my feet, now holding the gash in my arm like a tourniquet. My breath grew heavy and drawn out, but I tried to make silence my ally. Step by step, I crept my way out onto the yellow pavement lines and inched away to a four-way intersection. My eyes were locked on the creature, who was now limply clawing at the ground where the mug had fallen. With my laser focus on other…more pressing matters, I let an old habit get the best of me. Another pane of broken glass that sat perfectly in my awkward path.

I stood in that spot for a moment, hoping whatever that freak was didn't catch on to my blunder. A hollow hope. Hope loves to be hollow. I felt oddly hopeless because of my inattention, like whatever would happen next was completely my fault. The same feeling I got when I encountered the birds on the outskirts of Phoenix. The very first mistake of my journey had come back to haunt me. With a certain sinister movement, the nearly-bald head of the pale figure slowly shifted from the shattered mug over to me.

Its face was just as terrifying as the body it belonged to. There were very few teeth left inside its putrid jaw. The monster's tongue somewhat awkwardly stuck out of the left side of the mouth. Its lips were cracked in spots, and they were strangely thick. They reminded me of leather a little bit. The abnormal freak had no eyebrows or eyelashes either. However, the most dreadful feature were the eyes. The reason that the eyes were so disturbing was the fact that they were normal, just like yours or mine. It was a bright azure. Ocean skyline color. They still had a soul in them, but that soul was trapped behind…their cadaver of a body. The type of eyes that cut deep into your heart and make you feel remorse. The kind that could only be human.

It examined me like a physician checking a patient. I really wasn't looking for an appointment. It crept along the ground gingerly, while sputtering and coughing up a strange grey liquid. From what I had gathered from the initial sight of the beast, I could tell that it was a man, or at least he was a long time ago. He shook and quivered as the frail remains of his body dragged along the dirt. I heard the echoes of the stranger's voice in my head.

What, the freaks? They are these weird zombie-looking things. They don't bother you unless you bother them though, so I guess that's an improvement.

Well, I had officially bothered them. Instinct immediately overcame reason, and I pointed the barrel of the pistol directly at his chest. I only wanted him to stay away. That was all I needed.

Seeing the metal of my weapon reflecting the moonlight only seemed to intrigue the creature, so the man began to casually limp faster at me. I took a few steps back, being very careful not to trip over any more loose objects on the road. For every foot I retreated, he advanced two more toward me. It shambled more than it walked. Empty threats escaped my lips. You know, the average *stay backs* and *not another steps*. My messages didn't seem to slow it down at all. In fact, it seemed to get the creature excited. It picked up its shambling walk into an unnatural run.

First, his arms reached down and let his fingertips touch concrete. His legs propelled him nearly by the knee. Spine bent, arms loose, it was a monster alright. Primal, like some kind of long-extinct spider. Whatever the movement was, it was making him fly across the shattered glass and spare stones with almost inhuman speed. I knew I wouldn't likely outrun it, so I brought the chipped metal ring of my iron sights and let off a quick, inaccurate shot. There was a sudden crunching sound, followed by the familiar whine of lead ricocheting off of the ground. The creature was still coming, with a bright red blotch on his elbow that dripped blood and puss. There was no space left between us, no more time to fire. I went to pull the trigger again, but before I could line up the shot, he had lunged for my arm.

With a firm grasp on my wrist and the surprising force of a small car smashing into my chest, the wild monstrosity threw the both of us to the ground. It thrashed and gripped my weapon like a deranged animal, crying out with an incoherent howl. I kept my arms stiff and tried to regain control of the situation by throwing the slender creature off my chest. I shifted my weight into a rocking motion and whipped his narrow figure back and forth. My plan was to make like a pendulum and build enough force to knock him off, if only for a second. Its bony white fingers began to slip from their stronghold on my wrist, and I was almost ready to make my move. Just as I went for the finishing shove, it repositioned its bony hands and found a grip in the gash in my forearm. I felt the little tongue-depressor sized appendages dig in and rip around. I suddenly felt weak from the shock and pain. I couldn't even find the strength to scream.

The effort was stopped dead in its tracks. I was left to stare into those eyes again. They looked concerned yet intrigued, terrified yet excited, dead, yet still alive. In my helpless, vegetated state, I felt my blood run cold. Tenseness and rage took over the captain's chair a second later. I didn't understand why the creature was after me, why it was here, or how it came to be. There was so much I didn't understand, and no way for me to come to an understanding. I stopped caring a second later. I just wanted to see it die.

The half-living corpse let loose its grip of my wound and grabbed hold of the hand that held my pistol. It slowly dragged the bloodstained weapon above his head, aggravating the gash again. My fingers still wrapped around the handle and trigger, the roamer intently stared at its newfound treasure with an innocent intrigue. It was almost like a child looking at a snow globe for the first time. Maybe it hadn't seen a gun before. I didn't care. It lifted the barrel up and down as if he were trying to get a feel for its weight. All the while, I felt the gentle drops of blood coming from the roamers shoulder wound drip onto my waist line. It was pulpy, thick, and coagulated on contact with open air. I sat waiting patiently for any opportunity to end the beast's life, maybe even put it down like a dog. My helplessness had turned into frustration and bloodlust. I felt my rational mind fade into a sea of red, and my strength came back to me tenfold.

Ripping my arm from the creatures weakened grip, I took a firm hold of the trigger again. The steel handle struck the creature across the face, forcing it to recoil back into a perfectly straight posture. It continued to groan and squeal with that same ear piercing, devilish noise it made before. It covered the part of its cheek that I struck, but I doubt it was in pain. With a quick jolt, my arm swung to the left, bringing the tip of the sights directly under the monster's jaw.

Chunks of flesh and clusters of broken jaw fragments sprayed all over my face. My arm remained rigidly extended outward whilst the gun remained tightly wrapped in my cold, raw fingers. The fresh wound began to rock my body again as I snapped back from the brink. The roamer was nothing but meat. I was too far gone to even realize I shot the thing.

I no longer had control over my actions. Fear and confusion overpowered anger and reason. My magma-fueled rage had iced over. Survival was the only thing on my mind. I pulled the trigger again, hearing another satisfying explosion rocket from my fingertips. It made me feel safer. Another flash, then another, followed by three more. Each as satisfying as the last. Breathing heavily and holding the side of my head, I looked down to see my good work. A pile of ligaments riddled with holes and shiny lead rounds, a proper end for something like that.

The roamer was dead, yet I could not feel safe in its presence. Though he no longer moved, his haunting eyes stayed open. It was a look of misunderstanding. It was a look of confusion. It was only then that I realized how scared it…how scared he, probably was. I wanted to run away, and leave those eyes to rot and become food for the feral animals, but for some reason, I couldn't look away. A crunch of loose stone finally drew my attention, only to look up and find dozens more glaring at me from the darkness. More pale skin, more torn ligaments. They were all similar in figure compared to the creature I just slaughtered, but each one remained fundamentally unique.

One had long hair that fell in cluttered strands to the side of its face, its eyes were a light brown. Some were tall and hunched, while others were short and crippled by nonfunctioning legs. Some didn't even take notice of me, and instead found pleasure in staring at the piles of shiny trinkets, or the radiant stars over their heads. However, a silent few watched me from a distance. They seemed almost angry. One even found the audacity to waddle on all fours into the open. It was a girl I think, not very old, yet still as decrepit as all the others. Her arms were clawed raw by something, maybe herself. I guess that doesn't matter.

She hunched over the fallen roamer and placed her hand atop the remains of his forehead. It rubbed back and forth in a brushing motion slowly. She was caressing him. The others slowly wandered off onto different streets after a few minutes, but not her. I remained still until the female roamer lifted her head and looked right at me. Her eyes were a pale green color, still very animated and spirited. A puppet on a frayed string. They showed no fear, no anger, no curiosity. Just frustration and disappointment. Looking back into them was death. I forced myself to turn and run away from the whole scene, leaving the little girl and the thing I killed behind me forever.

~ * ~

I used strength that my body didn't have to offer to escape the city. As I bolted down alleys and courtyards, I felt their piercing eyes stab through me like a thousand syringes full of acid and rock salt. Occasionally, one would trail me for a minute or two, then give up and shamble into a nearby building. There must have been hundreds of them. My legs grew numb and ran on their own rhythm, much more like a machine than something of flesh and blood. On my way out, I noticed a large, rod-like structure sticking out of a dollar store. That's when I noticed the musty poison smell growing stronger. It was slender and bent terribly, but it still held a coherent shape. The rod looked as though it had crashed there a long time ago. For some reason, the entire shaft hadn't detonated. It's easy to wonder how long it had been there, as well as what it had done.

Well, anyway, my legs managed to carry my barely functioning husk of a body to the outer edge of the city before collapsing. I tumbled into a patch of crabgrass and laid flat onto my back. I held my throat tightly and gasped desperately for any air I could find. Eventually, the gasping turned into coughing and coughing turned into vomiting. An hour or so of complete bodily hell passed before all the pain and revolting illness subsided completely. Eventually, I managed to prop myself onto a guardrail along the highway. A lucky third leg for someone who didn't have one left to sparc.

I thought back to my blind cynicism I gave to the traveler. What an idiot. I should have just believed him and taken the detour. My choice was lazy, dangerous, and damn well could have gotten me killed. My frustrations almost made me miss the fact I made it to my destination. The paint was worn and impossible to read, but judging from my damaged maps, it was exactly where I needed to be. Frustration turned to laughter, then to somber silence. After a few more minutes, I picked myself up and went on for the last leg of my lonely journey.

I traveled along the main road, which was packed with broken-down cars and SUVs. All filled with remains. Evacuation wasn't the golden option they thought it would be. They created a virtual obstacle course for me to navigate over the course of the next few hours. Vines and stubborn weeds had sprawled around all the vehicles, making a thick natural camouflage for each chassis. Fresh grass began to show itself again, marking my exit from the affected area of the toxin and, with it, came all of the sounds of feral animals scavenging in the brush. I saw a bird picking away at a squirrel on the side of the road. Kill or be killed. It was always the rabid-animal mantra.

I was jumpy, to say the least. Every loose paper rolling about and each squawk from the telephone wires startled me. My memory of the previous hours had been fuzzed significantly, but I decided that was for the best at the time. Only later would I recollect the events of my atrocity in the colony, safe and sound within the perimeter of The Train. Hindsight is easy to look at when you are tucked in some nice, warm covers after a full meal.

I marched my way into the hub of the town. My maps said that The Train would arrive in the shopping district within a matter of hours. It seemed that my scheduling and routing was right on the money. Stepping into the rubble, I was met by a scene that was entirely unexpected and unwelcomed.

All of the buildings were busted into chunks of raw materials, and bullet casings smothered the ground in a copper haze. The only structures to survive whatever chaos occurred were an old movie theatre, with neon lights that had long since fallen into the parking lot, and a massive complex further down the road. A shopping mall. There was graffiti everywhere as well. In white and yellow spray paint, there were symbols and words painted across the brick and solid grey stone that spoke of revolution. Some of my favorites were "We end the oppression NOW", "Bring me liberty and bring them death", and "hunger stops when you slaughter the pigs."

Upon further investigation of the city, I found a plethora of bodies hanging from light posts and rooftops. Many of them wore signs around their broken necks that read simply 'traitor'. I didn't know what happened, but whatever it was, it must have devolved into all-out war. Homemade pipe bombs were still scattered amongst the bones, unused after all that time. Some of the cars were even jerry rigged to have armor. A few of the larger specimens were covered in dangerous materials such as plow blades. It was all incredibly strange. I progressed down to the mall, figuring that it would be a good vantage point to spot The Train as dawn arrived.

The revolving door at the front entrance no longer had any glass left. There were still dozens of bullet casings covering the parking lot. The fighting seemed to make its way there as well. Cars were smashed along the eastern wall, almost as if they were trying to breach their way in. Although there were massive diagonal cracks along the solid surface of the mall, there was no clean hole punched through it anywhere. The sidewalk immediately adjacent to an old clothing shop was littered with bones. I'm not sure if they were human, but given what the rest of the city looked like, I could at least entertain the idea. I had to keep my guard up. After stumbling over a few charred remains, I made my way deep into the mall complex.

There was only more desolation inside. The carpet of the mall was torched to a deep grey color. There must have been one hell of a fire in there. I had to really pick up my feet to avoid shuffling through empty rifle magazines and cartridges. With lingering anxieties, I crept along the pitch-dark corridors and scanned everywhere for signs of life. There was nothing with a heartbeat to be found. There was a terrible stench too. A very familiar stench. At times I considered turning back and leaving the building, but a certain curiosity kept me searching further. Soon enough, I found my way at the atrium, and it harbored what was to be the most gruesome sight in the war-torn hellscape.

A hall of the dead the size of a monument took form in front of my flashlight. Dozens...no... hundreds of people piled atop of each other like a pillar of the damned. A gentle moonlight illuminated the upper quarter of the monument just enough to outline the figure's entire structure. I immediately stumbled backward and shifted my sight away from it all. Flashbacks to the factory beat against the side of my head like a hammer to nails. The blood, the bodies, and the horrible scent, all of it.

Even though this new gruesome sight was more massive in scale, I didn't feel the need to dry heave or panic as I had done before. It took only moments for me to collect my calm, rational mind and further examine the situation. It was like I had become desensitized to the sight of bodies. Maybe I was less moral than I thought I was, even back in Phoenix, when everything was put into question. The jury's still out on that one.

Beside me, laying atop an empty green crate, was what looked like a journal. Torn, light grey, thin. I opened the binding and skimmed through the slim contents. Mostly doodles, some numbers being jotted down, and the occasional catch-phrase underlined four times in pen. Finally came the last page. The ink was a dark blue, and the handwriting was barely legible at best. I shined my light closely onto the manuscript, trying to decode what the strange scribbles were trying to say. After some time translating the slaughtered English, I got what I was looking for.

~ * ~

We got our first bite to eat in two weeks yesterday. It was a real good bite too. Paul gathered us all up by the old theater and got himself twelve barrels of diesel from the Petrol Plant. It was a good bonfire. A real good bonfire. Got some portions cooking on the skillet once the sun finally dropped. Thick portions, and with the slow-cooking, they came out juicy and tender. I think Marge's kids woulda keeled over if they waited another fifteen minutes. We all would have. We don't got to worry none about things like that anymore.

The last of them government pricks turned heel two days ago, and they left us a heaping helping of useless shit to sort through. Uniform kissers even took the good water, so all we got was material. We got lots of material. Paul said to us that we still got the better of em though. Said we snatched the lights right out from under em. All the candles and lighters and such. Paul says we have all the vision left in the world now, and it's our duty to make use of it. Says a higher power wants it that way, and he'll keep us safe so we can do so. Guess it's gonna be that way whether we like it or not. Seems kind of crazy to me, but the calories don't lie. My Mama always used to say a full gut never lies.

I'm just happy to still be breathing. According to Paul, we will be more than just breathing soon enough. We're looking to expand. Little villages around here have had it rough too, so it looks like as good a time as any to come together. They won't mind if we flash some meat their way. More folks mean more food consumed, but also more food acquired. Paul says we need them people. Says strength is in the calculations. I calculate that we already have hundreds of folks with a taste for this stuff already, but I've never been the best at math.

There just isn't enough land here to keep us plump anymore. If we stay, we starve. So with or without them, we are hitting the trail. Our only chance now is to show the world what we got, and what we got is a lot of good weapons, transportation, and gas. All useful things for gathering a good morsel here or there. The armor trucks will be ready to move at dawn. I think I'm just gonna leave this crummy diary here. I never make good use of it anyway. It'd only slow me down. Anyway, Paul said to pack light, and that there would be food anywhere we went. The higher power wants it that way. I sure hope he's right. After that feast at the bonfire, I've really been looking forward to my next chance to grab some leg meat.

I gingerly set the note back down on top of the pale green army crate. That place, where I stood amongst the silent bodies of the dead, was where my greatest enemy had been born. I got up off of my right knee and began to shine my flashlight along the glass windows of the closed down shops. Eventually, I turned back to face the pile of bodies to find a detail that I hadn't noticed before. Near the bottom of the pile, not far above eye level, there was a large white banner made of a sturdy cardstock. Splattered on it with a thick black paint was that sickening symbol that had grown all too familiar to me.

Chapter Thirteen: Returning to Something Resembling Home

I fled from the body pile, carrying whatever limited ammo and supplies I found in the atrium. There was an ominous yet promising place to set up camp in a corridor that connected two discount clothing stores. The entrances were thin. They were easily barricaded by rubble and overturned benches. Another key reason to stay was the relative luxury of a crack in the boarded windows. By peeking through, I could keep my eyes on the road, in case The Train arrived early. It was secure enough for me, but it was a loose satisfaction. I could rest easy, at least for a while.

Seeing something other than darkness in my dreams was a long-forgotten luxury. I must have been hung up on a movie that night, because my imagination was stuck on a silver screen. Every frame of my adventure was on display in 70mm. The only thing I was missing was a bucket of popcorn with too much salt and not enough butter. I gotta say, I may have had a good shot at being one of those big-wig directors at some point if the world hadn't…you know, died. Whatever memories I had projected to myself were awful entertaining, and just a bit too dramatized for my own taste. The bird scene outside Phoenix was my favorite. It was shot from the point of the view of the birds, and it ended with a cascade of feathers that disintegrated to dust. Real artsy stuff. Action, adventure, my life could have been a blockbuster in the old world. Just my luck that there was nobody to really share it with. I guess that really doesn't matter to me. It made for one hell of a story. I had one hell of a story to tell.

When I woke, I was feeling pretty well rested. I stretched my back and retrieved my pack from the stained tiles. I took a moment to stare out the crack in the board, finding nothing but the glowing red light of the dawn. Another incredible thing to come out of the situation was the full sensitivity that had returned to my hands. My core was feeling nice and sturdy, and the tingling sensation in my toes but expectations don't mean much outside these scrap iron barricades. I had never heard of anyone survive an encounter with the toxin like that, not in years. I was amazed by my dumb luck, then stopped, and thanked myself for working so well under pressure.

As I searched for some breakfast in my pack, I heard the sounds of bullet casings shifting. Consistent, heavy, drawn out. Someone was rolling their feet over them, and by the sound of it, there was more than one person. I launched out of my seat and laid myself up against my jerry-rigged barricade. Reaching quietly into my pack, I drew my handgun from the drooping front pocket and pointed it into the main hallway.

The crunches and shifting crackles amongst the debris grew louder. I was exhausted, far too exhausted to combat another pack of vicious dogs or drooling freaks. However, from the rhythmic sound of the movement, I came to doubt it was either of those. These guys were organized. I knew I would have to strap on the boxing gloves one last time before my comrades arrived, but it was a coin toss if I could outlast whatever new enemy was lingering in the abyss. I began to hear faint whispers in the darkness, but they were still fuzzy. Once in a while, I could catch a word or two echoing down from the atrium.

"Holy shit, what happened in here?" one voice rang out.

"Look at the symbol on that paper. Acolyte work."

"Hey, take a look at this."

"What? it's just a pill bottle."

"Yeah, but I think that is the only thing in this place that isn't covered in blood, guts, dust, shit, or all four."

"And?"

"It means something's still alive in here."

This was met with a dull sounding "Oh."

They kept real quiet after that. Total radio silence. I kept relatively still, only taking small movements to pan across the hallway. Any noise they made became incredibly subtle, but not inaudible. They were hunting me, a pack of wolves searching for the elk.

I cupped one hand over my mouth to suppress my breaths, rubbing it across my growing beard for a moment. Guess I grew a beard at some point. Easy to forget stuff like that on the road. It was bristly, like the pricks on a cactus. Not exactly high fashion. I began to see flashlights shining down my corridor and reflecting off of shattered window panes. My head was still peaking over the top of the barrier, so I forced my chin down to leave myself invisible. The steps became clear and vivid. It seemed as though they were only yards away from my position. After a long pause, I saw a light poking over the barricade. It scanned from side to side, from kiosk to kiosk, and eventually it fell upon the bench where I rested, emptied food cans and all. The guy caught on fast and started peaking corners. Eventually, the light tilted downward right on top me, but before anything else could happen, I launched into action.

Grabbing the man's arm, I dragged his whole body forward. The stranger's front end flipped over the barricade, head first. I dragged him out of sight toward the kiosks and held him down. He grunted and struggled like an angry dog, ripping and tearing at my grip with all his might before I managed to bring my gun up to his chin. He attempted to bring up a long stick of some sort to my forehead, but stopped when I got the advantage. He sighed and sat waiting for a moment while the other shadowy figures came running from all directions.

"Okay buddy, you made it this far, now what are you going to do?" the man said with a tone of total annoyance in his voice. That drawl was instantly recognizable. I loosened my grip for a moment and pointed the 9mm away from his jaw.

"Todd?"

"How did you...? Who are you?" He uttered.

I picked up the light that I had swatted from his hand and shined it in his face. Just as I expected, it was the old man firmly grasping the handle of his hatchet.

"Oh, thank Christ."

Todd lifted up an old hatchet and grabbed hold of the shoulder I had pulled on.

"Don't you fuck with me. You died a couple days ago. Dropped straight in a river infected with that toxin. Nobody survives that. Nobody."

I turned the flashlight back onto my own face.

"What can I say? I took some extra strength antacid and things resolved themselves."

After closely examining my face for a moment or two, Todd took a few steps back.

"No, no, no, no, I'm going crazy or something. There is no way in hell. So if you would kindly stop haunting me, that would be just peachy."

The others arrived a moment later, shining an annoying barrage of LED lights onto me and pointing their various weapons at my chest.

"Hey fellas, you won't believe the week I've had."

After a moment or two, Jacques leaped over the broken wooden planks and brick shards and sprinted over to me. Unexpectedly, I was met by a strong fist digging deep into my gut.

"What the hell?" I gasped after inhaling a hefty amount of disgusting air.

"Sorry Jack..." he replied. "I had to make sure that you were real."

"Aww gee thanks for that, Floyd Mayweather. Next time just pinch me on the arm or something. Alright?"

~ * ~

We left the mall after dawn and worked our way back to the Center. By midmorning, I came face to face with Franklin, Peter, Mountain, and the rest of my companions. As I took my first few steps back into camp, I was met by stares as blank as a slate by a majority of the survivors. I'm not sure whether they had forgotten me already, or just didn't care enough to even try to seem surprised. My money is on the former. Most travelers preferred instead to swig dirty water from their flasks. At least Mountain noticed me out of the corner of his eye and actually had enough courtesy to greet me as I walked past.

"Beanstalk," he called with innocent sincerity as he shoved aside a few smaller folks. "Hey pal, when the hell did you get back? How have you been? Looks like I've been better than you. You kind of look like hammered shit."

Well, I definitely couldn't say that he was wrong.

"What can I say? I thought taking a little vacation would have been a better idea than it was. Has The Train built their monument to my sacrifice yet, or do they need more time?"

"Ha, I guess that whatever happened to you couldn't have been too bad. You still have that stale sarcasm."

"Nothing could ever change that."

"You should head over to the medical cart to treat all those cuts and gashes. Don't want those dainty little arms of yours getting amputated due to infection. Anyway, I'm sure they've never seen a dead man walking before."

I felt the still open gash in my arm and realized how poorly I had taken care of it. It'd been marinating in dirt and dust for Christ sake. If it wasn't treated right that moment, it was sure to get infected. Stupid. I was so damn stupid. Don't be like me Ez, it'll keep you alive longer. At least a bit longer.

I ditched my friends in the Center and rushed over to the splintered abomination that served as our mobile hospital. It was no more than a few used stretchers and an old cart being pulled by a pickup truck. I had used the cart before, on the edge of the forest, but I never required any real medical attention. That kind of worried me. The stretchers were hardly sanitary, and the supplies weren't any better. One of the assistants told me to lay down on one. To my disgust, I followed their orders. It was sticky. After a minute or two, I was met by the gaze of doctor Rick Ranford. They were calm, yet masked in an aura of stress. I call it controlled chaos. He hunched over me like the limbs of an old willow.

~ * ~

Rick was one of the few remaining medical practitioners on the planet, and it was no stretch to say that he was incredible at his work. He had performed dozens of life-saving surgeries in the few short months he traveled on the Train. That's even more impressive when you realized how little equipment he had. Once, it was said that he removed a bullet from a man's heart using nothing but anesthetic, a kitchen knife, and a pair of toenail clippers. Those are just stories, but I believe them. Legends like that are nice to stake a claim in.

The doc had his dark side though. In doing these 'spare parts' surgeries, often you could hear the screams of the patients. They didn't always get anesthetic. Another disturbing thing about Rick was his total disregard for the agony of his patients. His ideology included a rough and rowdy 'if you survive, then it was all worth it' attitude. He was just, useful, but also cruel. I suppose that was what he needed to be to do his job. Nobody else on The Train could have lacked that much sympathy. Most of the people came to call him "Stoneface." You know, for the blank facial expressions he gave while cutting you into jerky strips. It never really caught on for me though.

After gazing at my arm for a few seconds, he immediately reached for a smudged glass bottle filled with thick, maple-brown liquid. Rick adjusted his oversized glasses and gestured with an old sewing needle.

"You best drink up. That wound looks pretty ripe."

I picked up the crystallized container and swished its contents around for a moment.

"You're going to need at least a few good swigs for what I'm about to do," he said grimly.

With that foreboding message, I quickly began to chug the stuff straight from the cap. When I'm scared, I don't screw around. When the drink first hit my lips, I realized the stuff was thicker than syrup. After a second or two, I realized there was something else mixed into it causing a strange consistency too. Something grainy. Grounded-up painkillers. I set the bottle down with a loud clang and began to cough profusely, leaning over the side of my stretcher.

Regardless of the unpleasant aftertaste, the serum more than did its job. It was easy to tell the magic was happening when I saw four mirror images of the Doc reaching for a pair of pliers and rubbing alcohol. Did I mention how happy I was to get knocked out before that? In practically no time, I hit a wall. I could tell I was as still as a rock in my sleep as well, because when I woke up nearly twenty hours later, my body was stiff.

~ * ~

I sat up and stared at the rising sun for a moment and realized I was back in my sleeping bag. I tried stretching myself out to relieve the strain. This was a terrible idea, because as I extended my arms outward, a massive rush of heat and pain radiated all along the left side of my body. I looked down to see my arm gripped tightly by a wrap of beige medical tape. A dark brown stain was clearly visible atop my forearm. I must have been a real mess.

The other members of the FCS were either still asleep or drowsily wandering around our campsite. Jacques noticed me squirm and turned to look down at me.

"Good, the drugs finally wore off. How are you feeling?"

I managed to fit my shirt over the wound without stretching it. "I feel somewhat dazed and hung-over, but I'll be alright. What time is it?"

"Sun is just barely peeking over the trees now, so about six or so. You sure that you can travel up front this soon after the surgery?"

"Yeah." I said after a moment's pause. "So long as it doesn't involve any lifting."

~ * ~

Not long after that, I decided to search around for Peter, so I could have a thorough chat with him about what I had seen back in the colony. The whole camp was silent except for a few night guards chatting between each other. On the north side of our camp, the Jeep sat parked by a ditch. A few feet from the rear left tire was a dirty tent. At one point, it was a vivid scarlet color. That night, it resembled the same dusty brown that shrouded the rest of the equipment. Sitting right next to it was a tiny structure, too pitiful to be called a shelter. Maybe a child's tent. That was where Franklin usually slept. I marched over to the more sizable tent and opened the flap. Sitting at a makeshift desk that once was a filing cabinet, Peter was reviewing maps and documents. He always did that in the morning. Say what you want about his cut and dry personality, but Peter was a damn dedicated leader.

"Hey Peter, can I talk to you?" I asked quietly. For some reason, there was a hint of awkward fear hidden within it.

"Well isn't it our resident specter? Yeah Jack, I think I could spare a minute or two. What's up?"

I prepared to be laughed out of the tent. "When I was alone after being washed downstream, I came across some sealed off area. There were…these creatures that inhabited the abandoned buildings. Really strange and decayed looking characters with pale flesh. I have never seen anything like them in my life. They were like zombies, only some of them tended to just…stare."

"Huh, we haven't seen any of those in a quite a while…"

"What do you mean in a while? There are more of those things out there or something?"

"Those creatures you saw aren't all that uncommon where I come from. Near San Francisco, there are whole pocket cities that have fallen victim to long term exposure. It eventually kills off their nervous system, day by day, and all color is eventually flushed away from their skin. Along with their physical bodies, their minds slowly deteriorate as well. They are left with the most basic human senses and functions, and little more. So long as you don't mess with them, they should remain pretty harmless."

I touched the bandage that was now cutting all circulation from my biceps and chuckled.

"Well, I'm not so sure about that part."

As Peter continued to thoroughly explain and describe his experiences with the monstrous creatures, I found myself gazing down at a report sitting atop of his desk. It was thoroughly labeled with bullet points lining the left side and crude handwriting stuffed in the margins. It was yesterday's events list. Usually, it was the same five or ten scheduled events that occurred daily around The Train, morning siren, formation check, lunch service, water collection. However, that day, there was one bullet point at the very end written in bold and underlined several times. *SCOUT STILL MISSING (DAY 3) PRESUMED DEAD*. Well, I guess I couldn't blame him.

I looked back up and resumed listening to Peter's lengthy synopsis on the roamers. From what he was saying, it could be assumed he was just finishing up some personal anecdote from before he led the survivors.

"Well, we made it out of the supermarket, but just by the skin of our teeth."

I nodded, attempting to radiate attentiveness and conscientiousness.

"Well anyway Jack, I think what you encountered was most likely just an aggressive variant of the creatures who live by San Francisco, nothing we really have to worry about."

"Thanks for the reassurance."

~ * ~

When I got back to camp, Jacques was still up. He was tending to a small fire and making low-quality coffee in a tin. I took a seat on a rotted log and thought about my missing report. Three days, that was when my death sentence came along. Even though I was close brothers-in arms with all of the scouts and some folks in the Center, I had still been forgotten. It only took three days, Ez. It was a humble reminder that, out in the wasteland, things love to be temporary.

When I woke up the second time, the sun had finally risen up visibly to the east. Camp was actually buzzing with activity. Still weary from my long isolation, I groggily wandered around for a minute, regaining my senses before grabbing a plate of porridge. The light brown slop made my mouth water, regardless of how watery it was. This was the first real meal, let alone first hot meal, I had eaten since the accident at the bridge. I took a few moments to savor the warm slop before tossing my empty plate to the side.

I returned to my team, who now sat impatiently atop of high rising rocks. Jed picked up chain smoking, and he was surrounded by the remains of cigarettes. Down to the stubs. I expected more comments about my miraculous recovery from the collapse, but I was met with total disinterest. They kept to themselves as if nothing happened in the first place. Honestly, I was relieved everything was normal again. I have never really been a person who cared for attention or drama, and they knew that. At the end of the day, the most considerate thing they could have done for me was ignore my injuries and let the status quo take control. I climbed onto one of the rocky formations while gingerly using my healing forearm to keep my balance.

As I reached the top, I hunched over and looked down at the boots which served me through a majority of my journey. They had decayed so much they resembled loose rags more than they did footwear. Most of the remains were left limply hanging off of the side of my feet and dragged along the tarmac. No wonder my ankle hadn't healed yet. The Train must have gone at least one thousand miles since I joined them, and only now had I noticed all the damages. Tapping the useless halves of the footwear against each other, I came to what I believed was a reasonable decision. I would leave them where I sat and walk barefoot until I could scavenge a new pair. The dragging textiles were only slowing me down by catching rainwater and getting snagged along roots. My feet could have really used the freedom anyway.

When the siren went off alerting us to take formation, I left the scraps baking in the sun and strolled across the surprisingly vibrant grass in my bare feet. Each slick blade skid across my skin like the gentle tickle of a feather. The sharp pains on my bicep had finally subsided, and for a moment, I did not feel fatigued. I had almost forgotten what it felt like to feel normal. My comrades took a leisurely stroll about one third of a mile ahead of everybody else and patiently waited to hear the second siren. There was a loud, pulsating noise in the distance. The siren I had come to both hate, and silently appreciate. Back on the road once again. As soon as we started, Jed decided to beam Adahy in the side of the head with a ball of mud. Adahy almost shot him for that. It was nice to have company traveling by my side again. Boston was only a few months away at that point, and with my crew by my side, I knew that we had a real chance of making it there in one piece.

Chapter Fourteen: Needle in a Haystack

It took quite a few weeks, but eventually, I melted into the strict daily schedule. Back to the basics. The more distance we put between the back of The Train and the towns by eastern Pennsylvania, the fewer living beings we spotted. Since we had significant numbers, any remaining flocks or wolfpacks shied away from us and kept to their shady hiding places. They always loved to stare at us as we limped along en masse. I suppose it's like window shopping at a diamond store to them. Eventually, even those pathetic groupings of desensitized annoyances vanished. It took a week for half of all vegetation to wither. Within a month, there was nothing but grey skies and the musty scent of poison stinging our lungs.

The eastern edge of the state was especially dreary. For such an uninhabited area, those towns took quite a dose of gas. No safe water, constant pockets of lethal remnants, no life to be seen. The sanitary masks were distributed for weeks at a time. They were about as useful as torn napkins. The only redeeming quality of that whole leg of the journey was the afternoon that I found a new pair of footwear, still in perfect box condition. A basic grey pair of hiking boots that were heavier than sandbags. Just my style. They were a perfect fit as well, so I was feeling pretty damn good about myself.

Ezekiel did a double take to find that those boots were still on Jack's feet, albeit in rougher condition.

~ * ~

A day or so after that, we crossed through what looked like a turn pike checkpoint and entered New York. The last state we had to cross before making it to Massachusetts. If we could make it through the empire state, the rest of the trip would be a snap. Unfortunately, the first signs of winter became clear as we progressed. The air held a certain chill, the sky kept a consistent shade of aged grey, and people started puffing streams of vapor without any nicotine once the thermometers hit twenty. It began to snow during our third day, and the temperatures only continued to drop. The powdery white omen smothered the grass and pavement, leaving a perfect and untouched layer of white fluff blanketing the entire county. Yeah, it was eye candy, but the hindrances it put on travel really weren't worth the view.

Freezing rain was another unexpected obstacle that poisoned our momentum. It was heavy, thick, and never seemed to give us any time to dry off. It was so devilishly consistent, and worst of all, it soaked right through your clothing. Anyone caught out too long came down with a fever, violent coughs, constant shivering, and more often than anything, frostbite. Frostbite means unsalvageable limbs, Ez. The medical cart became part clinic, part butcher shop. Water ran scarce about two hundred miles across the border, and with fevers still running amok, some folks never stood a chance. Six died, but not before giving the tingly death sentence of a cold to Nicole, the head nurse. Poor Doc Ranford looked like he was about to have an aneurism for a week straight. Trying times. All times were trying, but those times were trying to *kill* us.

Our march turned into a crawl. There were a lot of quick stops made for funerals to honor some nobodies in the Center that decided to abandon our ranks once their symptoms became too far developed. Went right off into a blizzard, curled up in a ball, and died. It was suicide, but in the most heroic manner, so it became worth honoring. At least that's what Peter went with. I'm just glad they didn't decide to stay around. The buck needed to stop, so they stopped it. Our numbers couldn't stand that kind of strain for long.

We were lucky to make it a measly three miles per day. Setting up camp took painful hours of scouting decimated businesses since sleeping outside became…less than optimal. Although the journey had become a tedious operation and one hell of a mess, we still managed to find our way into New York City after a solid month of travel. Incredibly, the largest city in the nation managed to avoid total chemical annihilation. It was bad, yes, but the area wasn't still saturated like Austen or Atlanta reportedly were.

The missiles did the job on the day of the calamity, yet it didn't have the gas to stick around long. Literally. We saw our first blackbird pecking at some telephone wire two miles outside city limits.

~ * ~

All of the extra free time that was accumulating weighed heavily on my patience. I was bored out of my mind, Ez. Sitting around on an iced-over curbside and shivering was not compatible with my personality. Having the hairs on my arms stiffen up into stalagmites wasn't really my style either. I was no porcupine, dammit. One particularity bone-chilling day, I decided that sitting around wasn't doing me any good. That afternoon, as the sun tried to peek in and say hello behind a cavalcade of cumulous, I marched my way through ankle-high snow to the tent where our assigned cooks were serving warm soup to the ill. It was just about as cheery as it sounds. Miserable, pale faces enveloped the kitchen like a dirty eggshell. All hunched over, those people looked pathetic and defeated. I shoved my way through the horde and managed to make it up to the counter whilst being beaten over the head by empty bowls. People began to boo and sneer at me as if I had just shot a puppy in front of them. The head cook of the operation, Jen, marched over quickly to settle the uproar.

"Hey," Her voice was shrill and commanding. "Everybody relax out here or I dump the soup right on your heads."

She then sized me up as I stood awkward and aggravated in the middle of the sick populace. Jen was a little fireball of a woman. Only standing at around five feet, she was one hundred pounds of pure attitude. Jen had dark brown hair and mint green eyes that I am convinced were capable of taking X-rays if hooked up to the proper equipment. She came from Phoenix, just like me. She had really made a name for herself near the back of the Train as an efficient cook. Practically started the community cafeteria all by herself. She had one hell of a time cooking for one-hundred greedy little snots like us, until the men and women from Parkersville joined that is, and some of the extra survivors were given jobs as chef's aides. The kitchen ran real smooth for a while after that, but then the sickness hit us like a freight car.

"Jen, looks like this has all gotten out of hand a little bit."

"Yeah, glad to see you have eyes." She replied. "Who in the hell do you think that you are? Barging in front of all of these sick people like that. You better start explaining yourself before I have you thrown out."

"The name is Jack. I'm not here to eat anything, but I was about to volunteer to help you and your staff for a couple hours with…this. Unless you have the situation under control, of course."

"Jack huh... Oh, you are the one who fell off the bridge. Nice footwork. How you made it back still beats the hell out of me."

She paused for a minute, weighing her options and deciding if I were worthy enough to handle a ladle and some warm broth. After a second, she nodded and waved for me to enter the four-pole bistro.

~ * ~

There were a few small fires and portable stoves floating about the kitchen. All were kept at full capacity to meet the growing need of our friends. Caked in rust, go figure. Jen didn't say much else to me after I stepped inside. The exception to this was a brief set of very unhelpful instructions about how much soup each bowl gets. One and a half ladles, that's all. She said that it was enough to keep everyone alive and satisfied, but little more. She then lobbed the old metal tool to me with a certain grace and went back to serving. Peter may have been our commander, but Jen was a strong leader in her own right. I got to work on the simple and mind-numbing task of digging the rounded hemisphere into the light brown liquid and pouring it into paper bowls. The conditions weren't exactly sanitary, and the food wasn't flattering, but the masses still looked at the whole operation as if it were giving away free vacations to the Caribbean.

The rest of the afternoon was spent in solitude, filling bowl after bowl with the bitter mixture until the crowd finally dissipated. The workers in the tent were very friendly to each other, but the same kindness wasn't even remotely given to an outsider like me. That was just the way of life aboard The Train. You kept your group closer than a belt buckle, and everyone else was practically extraterrestrial. It was the same with the FCS. We were brothers in our travels at this point, but with the exception of

Mountain, I never really spoke to passengers anywhere else. Learning everybody's name was already unnecessary, but making friends with them, well that just seemed ridiculous. However, my social isolation was ended not long after the day's work had slowed down. Jen returned and took a seat on the ground next to me. She wiped off what looked like spare soup from her right cheek and tugged on my shirt sleeve.

"Hey Jack, I have a question for you, if you don't mind answering."

I nodded and set my ladle down into an empty bowl. "Yeah, sure. What's bugging you?"

"When you fell into the water weeks ago, did you drink any of it?"

She knew the answer already. I guess she just wanted to hear it coming for me.

"Well, yeah. Of course I did, I practically drowned out there. Smelled like bleach. Didn't taste much better."

When I looked back over at Jen, she seemed to be incredibly deep in thought. One of her soup-stained fingers twirled her thin hair.

"I think that you were supposed to laugh at that."

"It's just...strange, that's all."

"What do you mean strange?"

"Well Jack, you know just as well as anyone else what that stuff does to you when it's inside your system."

I nodded. Drinking infected water was an infamous form of suicide after the initial calamity struck. Folks with nothing to lose would sprint down to a nearby river that had been overrun by the toxin and throw themselves in, like a frothy baptism. They would drink, and drink, and drink some more until a passerby would drag them out. A few minutes later, the toxin would poison their whole system. They would convulse, vomit, shake, cease up, and drop to the earth like a falling tree trunk. It wasn't a pleasant way to go.

"Well, back then, everybody died from taking just a few sips of the stuff, but you, you somehow consumed whole pints of it and walked dozens of miles to meet up with us, all in just a few days. I know you're one tough SOB. I remember dragging you back from the battle in Parkersburg with all them bruises and contusions, but even so, it seems impossible. I guess I am just stuck firmly on the question of how. You a demon or something?"

I laughed a bit at that one. I should have figured she was the one strong enough to lift and carry all my dead weight across a pasture like that.

"Well Jen, I may be a demon, but that's totally unrelated. To be honest, I have no idea how I made it out. All it took to fight off the poison were some meds I found in a pharmacy."

A sudden look of melancholy grew on her face. "Listen, the toxic water...it has taken quite a lot from me. Things that can never be replaced or mended. About five years ago, I had a daughter named Vivi. She was no older than four, in fact, she was born only a couple days before the calamity. Way back then, there was no food, no water, no order, nothing but the purest variety of chaos. She fought through that with me, even as a tot. Then the dry year came around. Poor Vivi, one hot and miserable afternoon, broke down and drank whatever water she could find. That stream water she sipped from ended up being highly concentrated. The stuff might as well have been drain cleaner. She died one day later, just from a few sips, Jack. It only took two lousy gulps to take my whole world away from me."

I remembered the dry year like it was yesterday. Three rainfalls. That's all we got for the entire summer. Heat was so much that even the toxic waste dumps we called rivers dried up. People shriveled up like raisins once the heat wave started chafing skin. It was the worst, driest kind of heat too. The kind that sucks the moisture right from your mouth when you breathe. I only made it through because my friend was a marathon runner that always stocked his apartment with bottled water and Gatorade. I figure if he didn't give up and die like that, I would have been left without a drop on my tongue.

"Yeah, the dry year was the worst of it."

"Ya don't need to tell me that. Anyways, what I was thinking was, that since you had managed to keep all that down without stiffening up like a board, it can only mean one thing."

"What would that be?"

"The water has to be filtering it out, Jack. After all these years, its finally filtering that shit out."

"Maybe one day it will disappear completely, and we could start to rebuild everything from the ground up." I added.

"Yeah, someday. I would really like to see that happen during my lifetime. I reckon I would like to see that more than just about anything."

"Just keep living Jen, and I'm sure you will get your wish."

~ * ~

Later that day, as I marched along the eastern side of our makeshift camp with a silly smile plastered firmly onto my face, I found myself face to face with Jed and Jacques. Jacques seemed very eager about something.

"What has got you in such a good mood?" Jed asked with a giddy look on his face.

"It looks like I should be asking you the same thing."

Jacques stepped in front of Jed and wrapped his arm around the back of my neck. His coat was chilling to the touch, and a second of exposure or two sent my body into a total shiver.

"Well, we're in New York now. Land of the free, and the land that housed me. Currently, we're only a mile or two away from my old apartment complex, and I'm pretty excited. I'm sure you can guess why."

I grinned.

"You know what is sitting on top of an old oak chest in that complex, Jack?"

"I think I have an idea."

"Then you know what I'm about to say next."

Jacques put a foot onto the curb of a gas station and pointed north. I couldn't help but let out a frustrated sigh. I knew he promised to himself one day he was gonna grab the brush, but under the current conditions, it would be a big risk. Frostbite, feral animals, survivors, there were a million ways for Jacques to get his stupid art supplies shoved down his throat out there. I wanted to support him on his journey, but I had to at least warn him of the danger.

"Alone?" I began. "You know leaving The Train in a place like this is suicide, right?"

"Ah, come on Jack. A little death never hurt anyone. I feel like it will be all worth it in the end. Anyways, if I'm gone for two days or something, the Train will probably have moved a mile given our current…unimpressive pace. Hell, we may not even move at all if the weather gets any worse than it is right now."

I couldn't argue with him on that.

"Well Jacques, regardless of our lack of progress, I'm not going to let you go alone. That's too careless, even for me. I'll head along with you in case something shady happens."

"This whole place is a trap. You two can wander out there and get your nuts frozen off if you want, but I'm staying here and getting into a close relationship with a fleece blanket," Jed added.

~ * ~

We started a slow trot out of the kitchen area toward the far edges of camp later that day. We gathered our basic supplies from our sleeping bags and planned a route. The path to his apartment would be a day's travel. We said our momentary goodbyes to Adahy, who had been bed-ridden by what the doctors could only assume was pneumonia, and a harsh case of it.

It was midday when we snuck out of The Train's outer perimeter, narrowly avoiding the sight of our happy-go-lucky sentinel Josh. Josh was a young black man from Phoenix with big dreams and a can-do attitude. This made him a crowd favorite among the desperate and wistful residence of our little traveling band. He was fast for his tiny stature, and he had eyes like a hawk. There were stories he spotted the attack by The Acolytes in Parkersville minutes before the rest of the guards. His precise and inescapable vision helped us to prepare just in time to fight off the first wave of cultists. He was a hero, a friendly guy, and from what I heard, a real Casanova. He had caught the attention of almost every girl and woman on The Train. Regardless of his incredible sight and unbelievable track record, Josh was often found goofing off and talking to his fans every afternoon at one pm like clockwork.

Jacques and I managed to dash into the ruins of an old boutique. I found a hilarious pair of John Lennon style sunglasses inside. They were perfect for a quick gag, so I took them. Jacques told me that, "The look suited me pretty well".

I decided he was right, so I kept the glasses on for the remainder of the excursion. The majority of the afternoon was spent wandering through back alleys and crossing destroyed buildings. It may have prolonged our travel, but we figured anything would be better than walking out in the open. Being human target practice didn't appeal to either of us. We were in the largest city in the nation, and even if it were hit by the chemical, there were bound to be survivors, or so we thought anyway.

The interiors of each building tended to be clones of the last. Dusty, quiet, infested with feral rats, and worst of all, smothered with pockets of the toxin. We had to move quick from shop to shop if we didn't want to get sick. Then again, we couldn't really leave the shops either, because Mother Nature never slows down for the weary. The unbearable winter ate right through my heavy gear like they were made of Paper Mache. Going building to building was our only bet for avoiding the loss of sensation in our fingers and toes.

The late evening crept up on us faster than we thought. According to our schedule, we should have already reached the front step, but the complex wasn't even in sight. Knowing Jacques, he may have…underestimated the distance a bit. The sidewalk we were on was shattered into rock fragments and gravel. It was like the street had recently been hit by a bomb. We twisted and turned around the corkscrew of a rout for seven hours at that point. While rounding a corner by a collapsed light post, Jacques grabbed my shoulder and jerked it back. The sudden momentum forced me to lose my balance atop a pack of thin ice. I tumbled to the ground with an overbearing thump followed by a medley of…strong and unique language.

After the furious screaming came to a close, Jacques was finally able to put in a word edgewise.

"Wait, wait, wait a minute Jack. I didn't intend to make you fall or anything. I only wanted to draw your attention to the skyline. Look above that old department store. You can see my home towering right over it."

I rubbed my back and let some of the vibrant red coloring escape my face. As I peeked over the edifice of the destroyed *Buy-It-Mart* in all of its faded glory, I caught sight of an old neon sign. It was a disgusting yellow-green color, but it sure was noticeable. Stretching down a respectable amount of the twenty-story high-rise read the words *Midtown*

Ridge. It was in a pretentious cursive font. Just Jacques' style. However, the reason the building was so recognizable wasn't only an old sign. As we jogged our way around the supermarket, we noticed a foreboding tear in the structure. Much like a tower of Jenga, Midtown Ridge was almost ready to collapse due to a sizeable hole punched through the bottom floors.

"Jacques, I'm not so sure this is a good idea anymore."

It must have been three times the size of a bus. Whatever made the impact really managed to dig deep as well. There was a crater underneath the lobby. Another thing that was immediately noticeable upon reaching the courtyard was an increasingly potent stench of death and chemicals. There had to be a pocket airborne toxin still lingering around there. The stakes had just gotten a whole lot higher.

"No way, you aren't talking me out of this when I am this close to getting what I came for." Jacques told me with a tone of absolute determination, whilst throwing his pack to the ground.

"Hey Jacques, what in the hell are you throwing your gear down for? We aren't camping out in the open, are we?"

He unclipped the front of his solid green hiking pack and reached into the right side, fumbling and shifting dozens of metallic goods under the sea of lime-shaded fabric. After a moment or two of unorganized rustling, Jacques tore a pair of goofy looking masks out.

"Are those...gas masks?"

"You guessed it."

I took a few steps toward him and helped to separate the masks before dangling one in the air to get a full view of it. It was a basic model, but even the basic models were extremely rare. Plain charcoal grey, plastic air filter, and a Plexiglas face covering. Even though they were as standard and travel weary as they come, gas masks were particularly valuable to find in the barren wastes. While the neurotoxin was particularly lethal and effective in shutting down a human body, it still needed to pass through an airway to have any serious effect. Usually, a gas mask could keep high concentrations of the stuff at bay, but only for a short time. The nickname they gave the masks were *Rent-A-Coffins*. Usually, if you were desperate enough to put one on, your goose had already been cooked.

~ * ~

Ez heard of the masks before. He even saw some of the guards use them whenever riots broke out downtown. They would put them on and send something white flying into the crowd. His mother said the white stuff burned people's eyes. He never knew the masks had a purpose like that. He just thought they were just there to scare people.

"Jack, if the gas masks could keep someone alive in bad areas for so long, why didn't people use them?"

"I wish things were that easy."

Ez raised an eyebrow at the remark.

"Little buddy, they tried their hardest to get gas masks out to as many people as possible when the calamity first began. That may sound like a solid plan of action, but the attack occurred within a matter of half an hour. When the remains of the government ran out to the cities and towns, all they found were bodies. It was just...too quick to stop with such conventional means. Those who did get the masks in time either fled their homes in search of safe zones or died after the hour of protection expired. Maybe if we had more time, or maybe if some more of the missiles had been stopped before they hit, or anything at all happened differently, maybe things wouldn't have been so bad."

Jack held a look of regret and remorse on his face. Ez saw it all in his eyes, so he immediately dropped the subject and insisted that he continued on with the story.

"Thanks kid."

~ * ~

Well anyway Ez, I awkwardly tightened and fitted the protective equipment onto my face while Jacques continued to dig for treasures in the bag. He managed to pull out a couple of weak flashlights that were designed to fit in a front pocket, a flare, and one large air horn, which Jacques claimed could scare away the feral dogs. I thought there was little point in having the horn, but my buddy insisted it was necessary. The only thing I could see it accomplishing was it leading a bunch of local thugs right to us.

We embarked across the courtyard with all the basic gear we could need for a ridiculous nighttime climb through a crumbling building. A slope submerging from a wide, unnatural trench in an eight-lane roadway led us directly to the front step. The front door no longer existed, and in its place was a pile of brass and concrete.

We stepped through the annihilated stone wall into a large, bland room with a shattered desk and a non-working snack machine. There were still a few candy bars stuffed inside, but it was safe to say that I wasn't going to eat them. Strange, thick particles, the color of dandruff kept floating onto my shirt and sticking. They almost seemed spore-like. I powered up the pocket light and turned to meet a large structure sticking out of the back wall. Through my mask and the less than efficient lighting, I noticed what looked like a pipeline ejecting out of a large set of filing cabinets. It was large and rusted beyond all recognition, but its tubular shape was still easily definable.

"Holy crap Jacques, I think that your home got hit by one of the bombs." I said, waving him over so he could get a closer look at the metal monstrosity. The end that collided with the cabinets was crushed and shriveled up like a ball of tin foil, but a jumble of foreign words could still be identified on the fuselage.

"I wish I was made of whatever material these filing cabinets were. There is barely a scratch on them," Jacques joked while taking a very close look at the thrusters.

"Hey man, I wouldn't get that close. You don't know if that thing's still leaking the toxin, and I don't want to drag you out of here while you choke on your kidney."

"I guess you're right, we should really get moving. I'll take point."

He got up and took a few quiet steps over to the door labeled 'stairs'.

The stairs were sturdy, stone, but a bit thin for someone with my shoe size. The crack in the guardrails didn't do wonders for me either. Jacques crept up on all fours until he determined the flights were structurally sound. Once he was halfway up the first flight, he turned and impatiently waved for me to follow. I took a moment to size up the thin incline before trotting happily up to the second-floor landing, two steps at a time.

We began to increase our pace after each passing floor. I had gotten into pretty decent shape over the thousands of miles I walked in the FCS, but running stairs was different. Using mildly different muscles made me feel like I hadn't exercised for two years straight. By floor nine I was profusely sweating. By floor ten I had lost any running composure I had and began to slouch and move on all fours. When I saw a corroded sign that read 'Floor 16' I stopped completely, just as Jacques tuckered out and took a seat on a bottom step. It felt like my throat was being clamped shut by a rubber band. I realized while hyperventilating on chilled air the mask made it impossible to breath at a normal rate. That was likely what was slowing me down, or at least it was keeping me down. What a day for the elevator to be out.

"Hey pal...you doing alright over there?" I asked between heavy breaths.

"I...don't know...I can't see straight."

I forced myself to stand up again and I wandered over to him, taking a seat right by his side. "It will be fine, we should still have forty minutes or so until the masks lose any of their effectiveness. What floor did you say that you lived on again?"

He shook his head and held his heart. "Twenty-seventy floor, apartment 2721."

There was really something disheartening about the way he said that. It was a mix of disbelief and hopelessness, and there was a blank expression on his face apart from the heavy breathing. It looked like he was too exhausted to make it in time. By the looks of things, it would take him a few minutes to muster what he needed to get up, let alone climb one hundred and fifty more steps with no oxygen. I was barely up myself, but there was still a measurable gap between our conditions. I looked down at Jacques as he choked on his tongue and patted his mask. It was time for some heroics.

"Hey buddy, look at me. There is no way that you are making up the rest of these steps, and at this point, the hour will pass while we're still on the stairwell. I can keep going. I swear I can, but I need you to give me your flare. If you pass it to me, I will go up there, get the brush, and bring it back with time to spare. Can you do that for me?"

He looked as though he were half dead, but he nodded, and passed the small red cylinder from his right pocket over to my outstretched hand. I nodded and took off on a slower jog up the rest of the steps.

~ * ~

The mask began to fog up as my assent continued. I could feel the oxygen deprivation slowly strain my eyes and stress my shoulders. It's one of those rare feelings of discomfort that puts pain to shame. I could feel myself sweat profusely, and a solid stain slowly grew on the front of my sweater. The already narrow grey and white striped cement walls seemed to close around me like a prison cell. It was difficult to tell if the building was finally falling apart, or if it was just a cruel practical joke being played by my frontal lobe.

I reached floor twenty-three when the fatigue hit a devastating high. Not only did my heart burn and swell, but my legs had begun to tighten as well. Things weren't looking so good, so I took a moment to stop. I was unsure I could get up again once I sat down, but I had no more air to breathe. Funny enough, lounging around only managed to make the situation more dire. The climbing may have been beating me to a sweaty pulp, yes, but the true enemy was sneaky. It hid behind my life support. My rent-a-coffin was doing its job alright.

I had to do something drastic right then, or else there was no hope of getting our objective. To tell you the truth, dying for a friend may sound all poetic and shit, but there was no way that I was going to throw in the towel when I was that close. Especially not for some stupid paint brush. But then again, I had drunk the toxin before and came out with only some stomach pain and blurred vision, so how bad could the air be? It took a few seconds, but I managed to loosen all the safety clasps. With a subtle click, the straps and plastic fell to my side and dangled next to my pockets. I took a few long and deep breaths, and let my body return to a normal, functioning state. The atrocious aroma typical to the toxin had amplified many times over, and the smell quickly overwhelmed my senses. However, in the following moments when my muscles were supposed to begin to freeze up, I felt nothing but a subtle numbness in my fingertips.

I had finally regained my composure and got enough air into me to continue my trek, so I re-applied my gear and waited for the tingling to cease. Soon enough, I was charging back up the steps like a raging bull. During my dead sprint, I caught sight of a small brown figure scurrying across the floor and through the crack at the bottom of the door of the twenty-seventh floor. I stopped to grasp the doorframe for a moment and let the palpitations slow down. I thought about the foolish decision I made moments ago and shook my head. It was an incredibly dangerous stunt. I really should have died there. The whole experience posed more questions than there were answers to. The gas seemed to still have some effect on me, but it wasn't really lethal anymore. Not like it was during the calamity. A civilization-ending virus just gave a little tickle in my fingers and dissipated a minute later. What a joke. Either I was invincible, which was not likely, or all the rumors about the gas becoming less potent were more than true.

I shook the handle of the thin metal door to find that it was locked. Par for the course. I could have searched a while for the key and found it laying around on a hat rack, but as you might remember, I have a violent history with weak doors. I honestly took a lot of pride in my no-loss record as a human battering ram, and I sure as hell wouldn't blow what was potentially my last shot to bust one down before we made it to Boston. I took a few steps back and lined my heels against the wall. A small leak in the ceiling dripped onto the hinges and rusted them to a brittle state, and the door itself was relatively flimsy. Just like I did on the first day of my journey, I flew at Mach speed toward the helpless hunk of tin with a certain ferocity. It never stood a chance.

I stumbled through the newly emptied frame to face a nearly pitch-black corridor. I controlled myself for once, so I didn't quite fall flat on my face due to momentum. For someone who never finished college, I was still capable of learning things now and then. As I stood with a stupid smile of petty victory plastered on my face, something skittered across the top of my boot and flew into the hallway. Before I had time to react to the first set of tiny feet passing over me, a dozen more brushed past by. In the panic and confusion that came with the darkness, I desperately reached into my jean pocket and drew out the flare. In a moment, the whole hall was illuminated by a pleasant jade glow. Avoiding the light like a plague, hundreds of feral mice swarmed out of the premises and flew into different crevasses. They evacuated and trampled over each other, making sounds like a newly installed smoke detector through the whole ordeal.

When the tiny-footed stampede finally come to an uneasy end, I took my first steps onto the shaggy green and white flower-patterned carpet that covered all of the twenty-seventh floor. It couldn't have looked any more like a cheap motel. There weren't many rooms in the corridor, but the massive distance between fragile wooden doors seemed to stretch out the whole building. There were sets of artsy sketches and minimalistic paintings from wall to wall. There was even a few cheaply-made plastic statues made by little known artists set on nightstands between armchairs. It was certainly a unique design for an apartment complex, but I'm still not sure if I mean that in a good or bad way. Regardless of its peculiar design, there were still standardized brass room plates loosely bolted to the top of each doorframe. The room which sat directly next to me had a label which had rusted to a pale brown and read '2711'.

I remembered that Jacques had gasped out the room number 2721 on the stairwell, so my only rational thought was to follow the odd numbered doors down the hallway until I found it. I slowly jogged my way through the overturned furniture and mouse corpses until I was met by the last door on my right. '2719'. I kicked over the doormat and knocked over a vase. No time for nonsense when the air is trying to hit the off switch in your brain. I frantically paced up and down the hallway again, rechecking my steps for some obvious mistake. Regardless of how many times I wandered across the ugly carpet and mouse droppings, there was nothing new to discover. There was no way I made a mistake.

Beyond the final rooms on the floor there was a sign marking the laundry room for the upper floors. In desperation, I stepped onto the bland white tile floor in search of another room packed away in the corner. It was a long rectangular space with about one dozen washers and dryers lining the far wall. Sure enough, sticking out of the far-left corner was a thick maintenance closet with the blessed number '2721' pinned onto its frame by a thumbtack.

I reached down to the frail looking handle expecting for it to be locked up. Honestly, that would have been perfectly fine with me, because

I would have another excuse to buckle some bolts. To my surprise, it was completely open. I guess if anyone was going to leave an apartment unlocked during a weeklong trip to San Francisco, it would be Jacques. The room itself, as you probably could have guesses, wasn't too impressive. The whole apartment was practically one room, with a bed, microwave, television, couch, refrigerator, nightstand, and a small space in the center of the room that served as a studio. The whole flat was illuminated by the light of one single bay window. If it were cloudy outside that night, I would have been blind. I strolled over to the nightstand and found the brush right where Jacques said he left it.

The brush was almost a perfect match to Jacques description at the campfire. Engraved, solid wood with a coat of thick black paint engulfing its handle. Real good condition, too. I was sure Jacques would be happy about that. I turned to leave the tiny compacted flat, but out of the corner of my eye, I spotted a pattern of lights along the cityscape. I jogged over to the window and slid it open. After examining the situation a little better, I could tell there was something massive settled only a few miles from the Midtown Ridge. I set down my pack and dug into its main flap. Sliding out a small black box I found back in my travels alone on the countryside, I drew out the still pristine lenses of my field glasses. Time for a little sightseeing. I changed their setting to 20x zoom and steadied them on the windowsill.

The small blots of light turned out to be campfires. Dozens of them lined the streets and a nearby parking garage. Next to the fire pit closest to our location, I recognized Peter's Jeep, parked on an angle in the middle of an intersection. It was The Train, still in absolute immobility from where we had left it. You could even see some of the many survivors walking around in heavy coats and wool scarves, looking discontent as any other Thursday. I couldn't believe how far my gaze branched from the twenty-seventh floor. I swear, I could look ahead ten miles if my eyes weren't so fuzzy from oxygen deprivation. I'm still counting my lucky stars I could see so far like that. Otherwise, I probably wouldn't have noticed the *other* camp. There were more lights there than in ours, and they were far larger. Whatever I was looking at, it was bigger than we were.

I zoomed in further, upped the field glasses limit of 25x

enhancement, and looked back at the incredibly large etching of lights. It sat only a few miles from our base camp. Darkness finally set on me, which meant that I only had fifteen minutes until the gas masks began to fail, but I had to figure out what I was looking at before I left.

There was a great deal of foot traffic in the mystery camp. They all seemed to be bustling around, preparing for something. Hundreds of people, all in one place. Shadowy figures skirted in and out of sight behind the veil of their oversized pyres. There was an old and beaten down truck parked on the outskirts of the gathering. It looked awful beaten up but, seeing something in mint condition wouldn't have been any stranger. There were stacks of something in the bed that rose up five or six feet, and under further investigation, I found what I assumed I was looking for the entire time.

Blank eyes. The cold, empty, lifeless eyeholes of wax masks stared back at me from their post atop the flatbed. Each one, mocking me for my pathetic belief all evil eventually dies. Every hair on my air stuck up like an antenna searching for a signal. I threw the field glasses carelessly into my pack and took off sprinting out of the room like a flash of light. We had to get back to the Train as fast as our legs could carry us. For at that moment, every single life aboard our caravan was in the gravest danger. They were in my hands alone. It was nearly time for the Acolytes to finally enact their revenge. It was time for a final stand.

Chapter Fifteen: Convincing an Old Friend

The door to Jacques' apartment was left wide open on my way out. With my full stride, I could cover the whole hallway in the matter of fifteen steps. By grabbing the handrails, I flung myself down a flight of steps in two bounds. My foot slipped off one of the middle steps on the twenty-second floor, but after a quick tumble, I bounded right back up. I was far too preoccupied to notice the fresh bruises along my ribs.

After hitting the landing deck for the nineteenth floor, I caught sight of Jacques impatiently leaning against the railing.

"Whoa there buddy, what's the big hurry about? I think we still have fifteen minutes before the masks wear off."

I grabbed him by the shoulder and yanked him toward the next flight. "We need to get back right now, there's no time to explain."

"Hey, hold the action-movie bullshit for a minute. Tell me what's going on," Jacques said, standing his ground firmly on the top step.

"Look Jacques, I saw an Acolyte camp from outside your window. They were awfully close to The Train, and I don't know if anyone noticed it. If they didn't, everyone is probably gonna die. That enough action-movie bullshit for you?"

~ * ~

Jacques seemed doubtful, but as soon as I flashed the paintbrush at him, he was content enough to follow me. While coughing up my upper intestines due to the limited air, I made it back to the lobby, and in record time. We flew past the corpse of the missile and barged our way through the hole in the wall. I took off the gas mask in the middle of the courtyard and tossed it back to Jacques. He struggled to keep with my pace, but I had no intention of slowing down. We passed though the same boutiques and small cafes we broke into before, but never checked the streets for threats. There was no time for caution.

Paranoia started screwing with my head when we were about a quarter of the way back. Everything started sounding like gunshots. Even Jacques' breathing started to sound like an engine shifting gears. We had to go faster. I figured we were already unsafe, so we decided to go the whole nine yards and skipped the shops entirely. The open roads were still bitterly cold, but at least they were faster. I'm lucky The Train conditioned us so well, or the return trip could have taken all night. We only had to stop once on our whole transit, when Jacques managed to trip over a curbside and scrape his arm.

However, every passing mile delayed our pace. Slowly, methodically, consistently. Lungs aren't built to last forever, ya know? Eventually, the adrenaline of the situation began to subside. I finally had some room in my head to think for a second. I began to ponder what I would say to Peter when we reached base camp. The gravity of me telling our leader about a cultist gang on a revenge quest set in on me pretty quick. That was a tall order for anyone, and I'm not much of a storyteller. It wasn't likely that he would believe me at all.

~ * ~

"I mean, would you believe me Ez? If I told you the band of murderous sociopaths which had all supposedly perished months previous had tracked us for hundreds of miles seeking revenge? Wouldn't you think that I was insane?"

Ez shook his head with honesty. "Maybe not insane, just seeing things."

"Well kiddo, at least you were honest with me. Stranger things happen outside those walls. If you want to explore the world someday, you have to realize anything is possible. If you refuse to accept the impossible, you won't be able to believe it when it comes up and socks you on the chin."

Ez took time to mark that one on the back of his right hand. He really liked the way it sounded.

"But Jack, why wouldn't Peter or your friends believe you? Weren't you reliable? Weren't you trustworthy?"

"Yeah, I suppose I was, but not THAT trustworthy." His face grew an expression both amused and quizzical. "Hey Ez, you have quite a big vocabulary for a kid your age. How did you learn to speak like that?"

Ez shrugged his shoulders. "Whenever I get bored around here, I pick up and read a bunch of old books. People just leave them around everywhere, if they don't use them as kindling first. My mother says reading is a waste of time, but I don't think like that. I like how anything can happen. It's not boring, like everything around here."

"Huh, well that's awfully impressive. I can't say I know too many bookworms nowadays."

Ez glowed vibrantly from the half-hearted compliment. He never usually liked being called a worm, but something about adding a book before anything made it sound more regal.

~ * ~

Well anyway Ez, I thought long and hard about it, but came to the conclusion the only way I could speak to Peter was blatant and straightforward. Maybe he would take it seriously. It wasn't likely, but it was at least possible. It must have been three in the morning by the time we made our return. I was just relieved to see the place wasn't up in flames by the time we got back. We made the mistake of making some noises and shouts on our way back into camp, and one moment after breaking the threshold, we were met by the barrels of military grade submachine guns. The faces of the guards were nothing but silhouettes on a lighted backdrop, and identifying individuals by face was impossible. I recognized the higher tone of voice that belonged to Josh amongst them and instantly tried to explain myself.

"Josh, Josh, put the gun down. We have some urgent news for Peter, and we have to get to him immediately."

He began to lower his gun, then pointed it back at my chest. "That's fine and all man, but why was it that you were sneaking out of camp and wandering around like you were?"

That arrogance got to me. Everyone's life was in the gravest danger, and he was trying to have a dick-measuring contest with me. I was up for it. I put on a brave face, and filled with absurd amounts of impatience, prepared to do something risky and dangerous for the third time that day.

I pulled the barrel of his submachine gun into my gut and I drew my face only an inch away from his.

"Listen. If you want to bullshit with me when I say that something crucial and important has occurred, well then you may as well just pull the trigger right now and save me some legwork."

Maybe I had just gotten good at pointing guns at myself, because after a moment of tense staring, he lowered his weapon and waved me and Jacques back onto the campgrounds. I quickly raced over to the conductor's Jeep with the exhausted Jacques limping at my side. The only reason he hadn't rolled over from cardiovascular failure was the brush still meekly poking out of my back strap. What can I say? I know how to motivate.

To be courteous, typically we waited for Peter to step out of the vehicle before speaking, but I wasn't feeling the urge to be courteous. I threw open the unlocked doors and shook Peter's foot as he slept in the backseat. He was out like a light, and his head was entirely covered in a blanket of maps and schedules. After slapping his leg with whatever strength I could muster, Peter shot up like a rocket, spewing paper and empty energy-drink cans all over the leather seats. He hit his head on the roof and mumbled something completely incoherent as he forced himself angrily out the side door.

"You better have a really good reason for doing that, Jack."

"Peter, Jacques and I traveled into the heart of the city yesterday, and from a vantage point atop an apartment complex, I spotted a massive series of campfires just a few miles west of here."

Peter was holding his forehead on the spot which struck the roof and looked very unimpressed. A large, pulsating, beet-red lump had already begun to form on the spot.

"You mean...oh I don't know...us?" He seemed unusually pissed.

"No Peter, not us."

"Well then Jack, who was it? What boogeyman is creeping around our camp three hours before first light? What other camp could possibly be making their way in the same direction as us, at the same time, without any guards noticing them?"

I shook off any remaining nerve and just said it flat out. "The Acolytes, Peter, they have an idle camp resting practically on our doorstep."

He shook his head and groaned. That wasn't a good sign.

"Damn it Jack, do you even know what you're saying? We put an end to those lunatics a thousand miles back, don't you remember?"

"Look Peter, I know that this all sounds insane, but I swear on my life that I saw the masks that they wear through my field glasses. They are here, practically on top of us. They might have tracked us to this point, looking for another fight."

"You think they are going on some sort of revenge quest? I really thought that you were bright Jack, but now you're really making me question myself."

"You have to believe me. Why would I lie about something like this unless there was a legitimate reason behind it?"

"I think you are hallucinating Jack, that's all. Maybe sleep deprivation, exhaustion, PTSD, something like that. You probably just need some sleep or a cup of coffee, maybe a day or two off. Here, how about I schedule you for one-day travel on the medical cart so you can rest your head?"

I took a step forward, ready to take a swing at him for being so arrogant, but I felt the firm hand of Jacques grip tightly onto my shoulder blade. I'd rest my head alright, right on his gut as I picked the squirt up and threw him over the hood.

"You are smarter than this Peter, I know you are. Why would you even take the risk if preparing for it wouldn't impede our progress? We are moving at one mile per day. If we skip a day and arm ourselves properly, we will only miss out on about an hour of travel. So please, for the sake of everyone who has traveled these hundreds of miles under your lead, don't let them all die at the last second because of your poor decision."

Peter leaned against the side of the jeep and shook his head. "Look Jack, I think throwing everyone into a false sense of panic would do us unfathomable harm. It could potentially be a complete collapse of trust in our leadership. Everything would fall to chaos, and The Train would completely disintegrate into fragmented groups of tiny, unstable survivors. Most of them would likely die to small bands of raiders, sickness, hunger, the animals, or anything in between. I can't make questionable choices like that without some kind of physical proof, can't you understand? We just can't be spreading ghost stories without reason."

I felt myself lose focus, and moments later, I wandered away from the tent without uttering another word. The sleepless days and constant rigorous movement hit me all at once. Stumbling awkwardly for a minute or two, I managed to limp my way back to the FCS camp. It kind of felt like the world was spinning. We were placed in the middle of a parking garage with little going for it besides the overhead protection from the annoying snowfall. Our only source of warmth was a rusted oil barrel stuffed with newspaper and sticks. We managed to start a small blaze with it, but it didn't do much to warm our aching bodies.

My legs fell limp as I approached my comrades, and I toppled over mere feet from my sleeping bag. I wiggled and writhed on the floor for a moment, trying to scoot myself onto my worn bedding. I soon gave up on the idea, since the bag was so far away. At least the concrete was flat.

There had to be a way to prove it to Peter. There had to be some telltale sign or marker that I was missing. I didn't even want to sleep, because when I opened my eyes, I'm sure the world would be consumed by fire. Utterly decimated. Incinerated. Turned to ash. Ash and dust and smoke. That's when I noticed the thin lines of smoke drifting upward from the barrel in little wisps. I had found my answer.

~ * ~

With a turn of my hip, I shifted myself onto my stomach. From there, it was easier to get back up to my knees. I grasped the solid surface of a concrete mound and pulled myself up onto my feet. People used to tell me that not sleeping for a certain amount of time made you drunk, but I never believed it. I do now. I had to constantly shift from wall to wall to keep from falling back into the snow. When I reached the open streets near the heart of camp, there was no more wall to lean on. After taking my first steps into the Hornet operator's camp, I fell face first into a pile of rusted pots and plastic soup containers. I felt the blunt force on my nose, but I can't remember if it bled or not. Behind me, I heard a very familiar tone of voice angrily call out with vengeance on his tongue.

"What the hell runt? You know how long those take to stack? Beanstalk?"

An irritable Mountain stood right over me and lent a hand down. I didn't have the energy to reach up and grab it, so instead he lifted me up by the collar

"What's wrong with you, chief? Somebody attack you or something? Oh Christ, you look rough. You need some stitches or something?"

"No. Peter...Peter...get me to him."

"Peter? What could he do? You need medical help."

I grabbed the collar of his black sweatshirt with my left hand and looked him in the eye. Mountain always had a way of communicating without words when he needed to, so I was sure the message would get across. He helped me waddle my way through the rest of the camp until we stumbled upon the hill where the beaten Jeep still sat.

Mountain sat me up straight on a trashcan and wandered back over to the rear right door of Peter's vehicle. Mountain did not mess around and never had time to be correct, so after a moment of peeking through the tinted glass, he slung the door open and tapped Peter on the knee. Peter shot up like a light and banged his head on the roof again. He seemed more openly agitated that time. He climbed out of the backseat for the second time that night and stood in front of Mountain. Peter tried to puff out his chest, to look somewhat commanding. It was kind of cute, really. In comparison to Mountain, he looked like a child throwing a fit in the supermarket. After a momentary standoff, Mountain said something quietly and pointed over to me.

Peter shooed Mountain away, and Mountain took pleasure in casually flipping Peter off as he strolled back to the center of camp.

"What now Jack? Why are you bleeding?" Peter said.

Maybe I was bleeding.

I gave no answer to his questions, and instead wiped the blood from my nose and pointed to the sky.

"What are you doing?"

"The smoke...from the fires. They are going to rise at dawn. You're going to see it clear as day Peter, and they are going to see us as well. Hope you give everyone enough time to prepare."

The paranoid look in his eyes made me realize what I said before clawed its way into his head after all. I should've figured. Peter was always a solid actor. He looked confused and doubtful, but I knew he would at least check. Judging by the size of the enormous pyres that the Acolytes had built, I knew that the smoke would be easily visible to him at first light.

"Alright Jack, I'll play your game."

He turned and shouted back toward the conductor's car, "Franklin, get up, we have a job to do."

In a tiny burgundy tent small enough for a child to sleep in, I saw a flashlight turn on. Franklin, covered in large pajamas and two blankets, popped his head out of the flaps.

"What did you say Peter? We have to do something? Oh, what ungodly hour is it?"

The trip certainly hadn't been kind to Franklin. His glasses were cracked, and his already tiny frame was more compact than ever.

"Yeah Frank, we have to spread some news around the camp before dawn arrives."

"Alright, but I'm sure the sleeping refugees won't take kindly to me waking them hours before we are scheduled to mobilize."

"Well Franklin, that's the thing we need to talk about..."

~ * ~

"WHAT?" Franklin shouted in a surprisingly high tone, after the situation was explained. "That's impossible, we drove those sand heathens away months ago. How do you know they are back in action so soon? Oh, this is just our luck."

"Hey, hey." Peter said in a comforting tone. "We don't know if they are really here yet or not, Frank. We need to wait until first light to check for smoke stacks. If we see anything, we will know they're close. So for now, I just need you to alert everyone that we are staying put for tomorrow. Oh, and tell them to arm themselves. In fact, tell anyone on the street to move indoors and hide our equipment, just in case."

Franklin hesitated and prepared to produce a counter argument, but one stern glare from Peter sent him reeling back. "Alright Peter, whatever you wish. I don't like this one bit though, and if it were up to me, we would already be running away."

"I probably could have guessed, old friend. Now hop to it, we need to get the message spread."

I sat on the brink of collapse against the snowbank as Peter gave orders to one of his couriers. Before Peter could get someone to carry me back, a few pairs of faint footsteps crept up behind me. Like a hot air balloon had strapped onto my torso, I was lifted into the air under the support of six hands. I was met by the smiling and familiar faces of all my FCS crew members. Jacques must have seen me wander off and came after me. I'm sure he filled in the rest of the crew on the way as well, which was probably for the best. Even if I was crazy, at least the FCS could be insane together, and with a plan of action too.

"You morons actually went all that way for a paintbrush? Yeesh, and you say I'm the dumb one," Jed mocked.

"If I ever see you too scramming off for such a stupid reason again, I will personally shove my boot up your ass," Todd threatened.

It felt good to be carried by friendly arms.

We passed up the medic cart, which was inconveniently crammed into an old coffee shop, and I caught a quick glimpse of Adahy resting atop a booth. The effort to hide equipment had spread tremendously quickly, and by the time we reached our sleeping bags in the parking garage, the streets were completely clear of any sign of The Train. My crew set me down on top of my surprisingly warm bedding. I didn't remember the covers being that soft. We shared a few quick laughs about our current dire situation, regardless of how serious the threat was. Jacques made jokes about his air horn scaring the thugs back to whatever hole they came from. It was a good joke, I promise. I just can't remember it too well. As everything quickly faded into a dreary silence, Jacques promised to get us all up bright and early so we could eat breakfast before everyone got shot.

Jed replied, *I ain't dying before I get my oatmeal.*

~ * ~

The radiant pink backdrop of a new dawn painted its way across the open skyline like a brush on a canvas. I rested peacefully without interruption, attempting to re-gather whatever strength I could for the impending rapture. I didn't think about what this battle would ultimately decide, or what I might lose in the carnage. I just dreamt about a promise I made before leaving for Phoenix. On my way out the door, I promised my wife I would get her a souvenir. Something small, and inexpensive. She loved gardening, so I said I would get her a cactus, straight from the desert. She laughed at that one, but I thought it was a good idea. She called me a 'prick' right as I closed the door. That was it. Those were the last words she said to me before I headed out. I guess not all promises are meant to be fulfilled, Ez.

Groggy, sore, and in a daze, I sat up and adjusted my eyes to the light whilst Jed took a knee beside my sleeping bag. He tapped me on the shoulder as soon as I opened my eyes.

"You were right buddy."

I rolled onto my stomach and pushed myself up using the frigid concrete. The artificially paled surface almost glued to my skin on contact. Shivering, I hobbled over to the waist-high cement barrier of the second floor and looked at the skyline. Dozens of noticeable towers of grey hovered above the rooftops. They were there alright, and estimating by the number of fires that they lit the previous night, they had us well outnumbered.

"Well, I can't say I expected to see anything else." I replied

He took a seat on a box of food rations and lit a cigarette. "I'm getting real tired of dealing with this shit."

Todd was up as well, but he decided to spend his remaining prep time in the solitude of his tent, and he insisted everyone leave him alone. I spent my time talking tactics with Jed and Jacques to prepare for any possible scenario during the raid. We discussed what to do with our weapons and ammo in the case one of us died in the middle of the fight.

We decided where the best vantage points would be in the case we got a jump on them. Most importantly, we described where to meet up in the case this was the end for The Train. It was decided that if everything was to go to hell, which was very possible, we would meet up in Albany within two weeks. It was far enough away to the point where any Acolytes would give up the chase on survivors, but not long enough to the point where we would all be killed by feral animals or smaller factions of raiders. It wasn't much of a plan, but it was all we had time to come up with.

~ * ~

Ez grew almost insulted by what Jack was saying.

"Hey, you aren't telling me t you would be willing to give up on The Train, on all of your friends, in the case of one fight going downhill?"

Jack grew serious for a moment. "Listen real close to me Ez, this is very important and I am not going to repeat it. You live and die out there by your own decisions. You have to look out for number one, first and foremost. Friendship is necessary out there, don't get me wrong, but in the end, you are out there because of you. So only you can save your own ass. If you decide to be a white knight out there, you will die a white knight. You gotta be strong enough to save your own skin before you can ever hope to save someone else's."

Ez understood well enough, but that didn't save him from the feeling of being absolutely crushed. There had to be a way to show heart and grit while still being a hero, he knew it. It's what all the books said. Somebody has to come along some day and put themselves before others, right? He refused to believe the world was that cruel. The wasteland sounded like a harsh and unforgiving place, yes, but one filled with hope as well. So, while biting his tongue, Ez laid back onto his ruffled bag, nodded, and gestured for Jack to keep going. He didn't write anything down on his arm.

~ * ~

Well Ez, our little team meeting was interrupted a short while later as Franklin and Peter visited our site bringing a few new...guests. Their footsteps were accompanied by the gentle purr of mufflers, and soon enough, we caught sight of the signature armaments of our Hornets. They looked strong, as always, but definitely worse for wear compared to what they used to be. Two of our five remaining combat vehicles parked a few dozen feet away from the ledge of the second floor and sat quietly. Peter finally made his way over to us and grinned. Jed wasted no time in asking him why he was 'so goddamn smug'. Peter pointed down at the street below us and answered simply 'that's why.'

"You see fellas, we are most likely outnumbered by two dozen or so people, and most definitely out gunned. Hell, half of our current population doesn't have a single round of ammunition to spare. Sounds desperate, right? Well, we are, but we do have one advantage still leaning onto our side. The element of surprise. Now, if I can direct your attention down to the end of this street, I can show you exactly what crazy idea Franklin and I concocted earlier."

On my left, there were dozens of my friends and fellow passengers lining the windows and roofs of apartment complexes and convenience stores, holding anything from small handguns and hunting rifles to bricks and bottles. On the other end of the street, there was a small barricade of angled cars and stacked crates, completely clogging the roadway. Waiting impatiently behind those boxes and vehicles were the big guns.

I saw Mountain amongst the ten or so well armed fighters waiting eagerly behind cover. He was smoking a cigarette and slugging around heavy caliber handgun along with a pump-action shotgun. Those around him were carrying around automatic rifles, sub-machine guns, military-grade explosives, and ballistic vests. I never knew the Train packed that much of a punch before, especially since everyone else could barely scrounge up a couple of 9mm shells. It didn't take a lot of tactical knowledge to realize this was going to be an ambush. We would launch it right over the Acolytes' heads. But it was risky. Immobilizing the Hornets would leave them vulnerable, but if timed right, the trucks could change the tide of the entire fight.

"We have received reports from the folks on the rooftops that Acolyte forces are following our breadcrumbs directly in this direction."

Peter seemed eerily cocky for such a quickly concocted plan.

"What's our job, oh fearless captain?" Jed asked, whilst lazily chewing on a toothpick.

"The FCS has a very simple job during the brawl." He pointed over to the two manned hornets parked in the center of the lot. "You keep them safe at all costs. Without them, there is no way we are going to kill enough of those brutes to force them away again. They'll try to break in and dismantle our big guns. Hold them at the incline, and we should be fine." He pointed over to the small slope leading up to the second floor. It was a pretty solid angle. We would have the high ground in any engagement we got into.

"I know you all are capable of handling this. I mean it's not like you have ever let me down before." He turned away with Franklin a step or two behind and began a casual walk back out of the garage. "Oh, and gentlemen, one more thing. I will be on the rooftops directing this whole operation, but the plan still requires one last piece of equipment to guarantee that this moves smoothly. We need a surefire way to signal the beginning of the ambush, but the megaphone has been broken for weeks. We also can't afford to waste any ammo. We have an estimated one hour before they are on top of us. Anyone have any brilliant ideas?"

Jacques lit up like a bulb.

~ * ~

They left with the airhorn minutes later. Jacques would never let me forget how he managed to make that thing useful, but hey, it worked, so I'm sure as hell not gonna complain about it. I congratulated him on his stroke of dumb luck and proceeded to load my handgun. Luckily, the ammo I traded with the stranger for back in Pennsylvania was still abundant, and I had four magazines worth of ammo for my one remaining pistol. Todd finally emerged from his hibernation, holding a bunch of bent cans. He did not throw them to us, but instead handed each one out, one at a time, gingerly. I guess you could say they needed to be handled with care. As I inspected the soup can more thoroughly, I noticed a pin sticking out of the top of it. Having seen them in action once before, I realized Todd experimented all morning and made a handful of shrapnel bombs. He carried one bomb of his own, alongside a Molotov cocktail, to the wall separating the second floor from the incline. I crept over to the side rail with my bomb, handgun, and multipurpose pocket knife. All that was left for us, was the waiting.

I tried to keep my cool during the waiting period. That didn't work out. Not even the cold air could stop me from sweating. I only peaked my head over the side to the point where I could see, and no further. If I were to be spotted, the Acolytes would be alerted, and it would all be over. Peter made a brilliant plan, but it required precision. Sleepless nights weighed heavily on my eyelids, but my mind would never allow me to doze off. I tried to shake off the fatigue by splashing some fresh fallen snow onto my face. The shock from the change in temperature seemed to do the trick, at least for a while.

After forty-five agonizing minutes, we began to hear sounds of muffled engines and mixed footsteps. I checked my ammo one last time before ducking below the barrier, completely hiding me from the watchful eyes of the approaching cultists. *Wait for the airhorn.* Their footsteps grew louder each second, and the sounds of their voices muffled by the wax masks became clear enough to listen to. *Wait for the airhorn.* One with an incredibly low tone mumbled on about how they were going to 'get a spit roast ready'. Another replied with 'Yeah, I'm going to scalp the first one I see'. Another reminded the group 'not to waste a morsel'. This was followed by an orchestra of mixed agreements and applause. *Wait for the airhorn.* They seemed almost like a choir, if choirs were so hungry that they wanted to sauté someone's liver. I felt my pistol-hand shake, scraping metal against the concrete. I quickly placed the shrapnel bomb by my feet and steadied the quivering fingers with my free hand. *Wait for the airhorn.*

I heard the steps gently come to a halt.

"It's just another dead-end, Paul. How should we proceed?" one with a high pitched voice shouted. He was then followed by a booming, energetic voice.

"Another? This is ridiculous. Knock them down, quickly. Those heathens are probably getting away as we sit here twiddling our thumbs."

There was a bitter sound of cold breaths and shifting bodies that clouded the whole area. The herd stopped. From the sounds of it, every last member of their crew had bottlenecked right where they were supposed to be. The Acolytes managed to walk right into us, blind. Yeah, the Acolytes were strong, but they weren't smart or careful. They didn't even have an advance warning group. I suddenly felt validated as a scout.

It seemed like time had paused right there and then. The whole world had drawn to a temporary close. I thought of my wife and daughter waiting for me in Boston, sitting in a small apartment together doing a puzzle or listening to an old CD. I would walk in and my daughter would recognize me in an instant, shoot up off of the couch like a firework into the nighttime sky and wrap her arms around me. I would lift her up and tell her about how much I missed her and how big she had grown in all those years of my absence and all the other absentee father lines. I owed her that much. After that, my beautiful wife would greet me with a kiss on the cheek and gently whisper "Welcome home, Jack." We would sit by a fire in the hearth with a warm meal and tell stories of our past and our futures together. Later that night, I would wash my face in a running sink and sleep in a beautiful bed, big enough for two. Big enough for three. There, I could finally rest.

The air horn erupted from above my head like a stick dynamite in my eardrums.

Chapter Sixteen: The Last Stand

I leapt onto my feet and let out a few shots before I even knew what I was looking at. To my pleasant surprise, the street was packed like a can of sardines. They were everywhere, two-hundred at least, with the same vehicles we saw in Parkersville bringing up the rear of their caravan. The Hornets drifted against the wall of the complex, smashing their sides against the guard rails. The two gunners immediately let loose, killing countless cultists as they attempted escape to the safety of the buildings and alleyways. Our other vehicles blocked off the last few openings before a single one of them made it out. They were completely trapped.

Ten seconds into the fight, I heard the first wave of people crash against the street-side barricade. I took a few more pot shots at fleeing enemies, pegging one of them square in the back. I saw one of the hornets on the north end of the road go up in flames, but another pulled up to take its place before they could evacuate. I heard another slam against the barrels through all the chaotic gunfire. The structure was weakening. I left my post at the window and took cover behind a large stone support beam and readied my jerry-rigged bomb. You could still hear the hollers and cries of agony pouring from the wounded below, but I tried not to focus on it. A few seconds later, I heard the bins finally topple, and a stampede of footsteps battered their way into our makeshift firing range.

Todd, Jacques, and Jed had all taken cover in their own tactical locations surrounding the entrance. Jacques and Jed kept the sights of their pistols and shotguns on the ramp while Todd prepared a lighter for his cocktail behind a barrier. Three or four younger-looking men and women poured in through the gate, most of them armed with nothing more than knives or pistols. As soon as they broke from the side wall of the incline, they were met by a volley of small caliber rounds. All but one were blown away instantly. The last of them charged Todd with a large hunting knife.

I had never seen such desperation before. The guy didn't even make it within arm's reach. He took a few steps back from a close-range blast before tumbling back down the incline. We were safe for the moment.

~ * ~

"Now, you have to understand these scenes weren't pretty or artfully describable in any fathomable way, Ez. I need you to answer me honestly, do you think that you can handle all of the...gruesome details?"

Ezekiel promised himself when the story started, he would listen to absolutely everything. He had lessons painted up both arms, and visons of lands barely imaginable flooding every crevasse of his brain. He had to face the bitter music sometime.

"Well, we're this far in already, so why stop now?"

Jack nodded and gave Ez a small dig in the arm. "You will grow up to be a real man someday Ezekiel. I know it."

Ezekiel smiled at that one.

~ * ~

We didn't get more than a second to catch our breath after the first wave. Before you could tie your shoes, we heard another pattern of thumps jolting back at us. Re-gathering ourselves and taking aim back at the ramp, the four of us just managed to get our ducks in a row before five more rampaging sociopaths made their way back into our sights. Armed with small handguns and handmade spears, this group managed to put up more of a fight. They ran toward a pair of broken-down smart cars and dove behind their husks. We managed to graze one in the back of the leg, but that was by no means a killing blow. We exchanged gunfire for a minute or so, each side nervously poking their head around corners every few moments and taking inaccurate shots. The incredibly loud blast of the hornet's mounted guns finally claimed my hearing. All I could pick up was ringing and vibrations.

Things in the fight weren't going so well either. I downed a clip every twenty seconds, and I didn't have that kind of brass to spend. Most of my shots were taken with extreme inefficiency. They mostly just punched holes in the passenger doors of the two passenger electric hybrids and vanished into white powder. It seemed for a moment that we were seriously being outgunned, but we had even numbers. That kind of math didn't hold up. As we fumbled around with our limited supply of lead, I noticed Todd waiting behind his guard rail carefully holding a lighter and one of his firebombs. That's when I realized Todd wasn't even using his gun.

One of the Acolytes, in a strangely box shaped mask and thick leather jacket, drew out an older looking handgun with a long barrel and took a carefully placed shot at my exposed head. It drew to the left and narrowly avoided my flesh. Instead it caught the very edge of my pillar, exploding on the hard surface and sending large chunks of sediment flying at my face. A small cloud of dust and pebbles jetted into my eyes. Each piece of the shrapnel stung like a wasp, and the smoke left me hacking up clusters of debris. I rubbed the dirt out of my corneas using my tattered sweater and hugged the wall. Another mistake like that meant death. One of the larger rocks scraped past my face and narrowly avoided putting my left eye out, too. A gnarly cheek scar was all I had to cope with instead.

The leather jacket Acolyte took two more shots from his hand cannon, landing directly in the center of my cover. His remaining three allies decided to follow his lead and hammered my position with dozens of small caliber rounds. Jed took advantage of this situation and took down the Leather Jacket with a shot to the shoulder. Jed stood out in the open now, but at least he lessened the death grip they had on me. The injured cultist tumbled and rolled back down behind a powder-blue smart car. One of the remaining three Acolytes turned to face Jed and threw a spear made of a wooden broomstick and sharpened stone. It was painfully inaccurate, but somehow managed to stick in his calf. It looked like the sharpened tip sunk in slow, too. Realizing his obvious mistake, Jed limped back to cover and assessed his gashed leg. With their attention split, Todd decided it was time to jump into action, and from behind my column, I saw him light the rag sticking out of a large green whiskey bottle. He took aim at two scrawny old men tucked behind a van. Todd leaned back and lobbed the fire bomb onto the vehicle's hood, igniting a violent blaze right under their bootstraps.

Large strains of dead vines under the chassis helped to spread the blaze in the matter of seconds.

They had no choice but to run into the open, and as soon as they broke from their hiding spot, we put them down. After that duo was out of the picture, our combined effort was more than enough to overwhelm the remaining Acolyte. The four of us lit up the smart car that the now unarmed Acolyte was desperately hiding behind. His spear was a dozen feet away at Jed's feet, and it seemed as though he was completely out of ammo. After making a dash for the exit, Todd connected two shots which blew a chunk of flesh from his ribcage. We sighed deeply at the sudden calm. The war raged on outside our window, with the sounds of small arms firing, glass shattering, and the sounds of bullets breaking skin. With only two shots remaining, my current clip wasn't worth keeping. The cartridge was flung carelessly out the window as I did a recount on my final batched magazine. I elected to pass some spare shells to Jed, who was now pouring blood from the deep cut in his thigh. He was lucky the stick didn't strike him a few inches higher. I'm sure he would have bled out on the spot.

There wasn't another wave sprinting, so I took a moment to tend to his wound. I ripped a piece of cloth from one of the dead Acolytes shirts and wrapped the wound tightly around the affected area. The yellow-striped flannel was quickly bled through, but the cotton was all we had to work with. Jed leaned on a broken SUV and screamed he would be alright over the roar of machine gun fire. Jed wasn't the brightest person you would ever meet, but he was one tough bastard. I didn't argue the point with him, and instead took cover right next to the ramp. Maybe taking the fight to them could spice things up.

~ * ~

The garage was suddenly rocked by what felt like an earthquake. Fumbling my shrapnel bomb, I shuffled my way over to the sound of the explosion to find one of our Hornets shredded by a rocket. The corpse of our gunner flew a few feet back, and the driver was killed on impact. We only had two hornets left. Without them, the Acolytes would have a chance to turn the tide of the fight.

In a window of an abandoned insurance agency across the street, there was one rather beefy Acolyte with a cracked mask holding a rocket launcher. That piece of military hardware was more advanced than any other weapon we saw in our travels. It had to be dealt with. The driver of the Hornet next to me shouted out of the now shattered window. "Someone, mount that gun." Re-evaluating the damage done to the first Hornet, I realized the machine gun was still intact. Before I could say a word, Jed hobbled over to the charred truck bed and took up the role of temporary gunner. Like I said, Jed was tough as nails when it came down to it. He held the trigger down with his full grip and completely decimated the floor of the building where the Acolyte stood reloading. Every window was vaporized with great attention to detail. No sign of living inhabitants remained after Jed was finished with it. Down at the entrance to the garage, I noticed three people in what looked to be heavy armor and cast-iron masks marching up from the first floor. Likely unloaded from the transport trucks.

I re-established my position at the ramp and signaled for everyone to get ready for the next fight. Before another moment passed, I caught hold of the heavy, clunky pattering of our last three combatants climbing the ramp onto the second floor. I drew out the rusted can bomb from my pack and pulled the pin. After hearing their footsteps echo right on the other side of the cement wall, I lobbed it over. There was a gasp, like that of a child, followed by a chain of successive clashes and the sound of something heavy falling over. That had to be at least one of them dead. Most of my comrades followed suit and bombed the hell out of the entryway. Smoke billowed from the incline like we were sitting directly on top of a power plant. I couldn't see ten feet in front of myself anymore. I thought we were safe after that, but then a small cylindrical object bounced up the steps and rolled right in front of me. It wasn't anything homemade. We were talking professional grade explosive here. There was a small spark that ignited inside the container, and everything went white.

My eyes burned for a short time, but after covering them with water that I carried in my flask, I regained vision on the garage. The two remaining heavies had stormed forward and lit up Todd's barrier. There were holes peppered in the stone from top to bottom. Empty shells rained from their rifles like a gunpowder-stained waterfall. Todd fell to the ground, tightly gripping his forearm and shoulder while spitting bloody saliva onto the ground next to his fallen weapon. Close range wounds. He winced at every ginger movement, like a deer after being struck by a car. One of the thugs emptied his clip on the spot. His gun rattled and shook like a loose ladder as the stream of copper and lead dug into the concrete.

Jacques attracted the attention of one brute after ineffectively trying to put a chink in his armor. I think he put three good shots through the guys upper back, but his Kevlar was thick. It seemed to do a good job of pissing him off though. In return, the brute generously spent time and ammunition putting as many holes into the guardrail Jacques hid behind as possible. The other, however, kept going for Todd with his rifle drawn. With both of them distracted, I prepared to launch an unexpected attack from behind. However, as I prepared to leap into action, I noticed how light and unburdened my right hand felt. There was something important that belongs in that hand. Something important that I managed to drop in the flash. What an idiot.

I immediately began to brush aside a rather large pile of cement chunks and ammo casings searching for my handgun. Any second now, the Acolyte would be right on top of the old man, and in his current situation, he didn't stand a chance. My left foot slipped on a handful of loose pebbles, forcing my heel to collide with a something strangely dense. Recognizing the shift in substance, I whipped myself around and caught sight of it, covered by gritty cement. I picked it up and shook off the dust before turning to face the unsuspecting enemy. He was a mere foot or two from Todd's cover, so there was no more chance for a sneak attack. All I could do was draw his attention until Todd could get a hold of his weapon again. I burst from cover, putting half a dozen shots into the armor padding on the cultist's back. He dropped to a knee, but quickly turned around and pointed the rickety old barrel of his assault rifle at my gut.

He reached for a trigger with a good shot at my chest. Instant regret. I expected to die there, Ez. I really did. Up to that point, my skills and planning had done enough for me to make ends meet. Experience is meant to help you do that. No amount of experience could have saved me there. Maybe it was my destiny to make it through the brawl, maybe it was all dumb luck. Whatever higher power vested itself in that garage decided the Acolyte's weapon would jam, right there and then. The tables turned in my favor one last time. After landing three more shots into the center mass of his armor, I ran in close to finish the job. The heavy threw his gun at me and turned to run back down the ramp, but it was far too late.

I chased him across the garage while ducking the crossfire between Jacques and the other heavy. Looking for some weakness or chink in his ridiculous armor wasn't easy, but I found he had left two spots unguarded, his neck and his heels. Since he was running away, his neck wasn't a viable option. That left me with one simple options, and I like simple options. I'm kind of a simple man. As we played cat and mouse for the next thirty meters, I continually poked at his ankles with low caliber rounds until he finally slowed down. He wavered and leaned on every object he passed, throwing off his boots and socks near the entrance of the garage before finally falling face first into a mound of slush. His arms were stretched when he landed. I still wonder what he was trying to embrace as he dropped.

I finally caught up to him and rolled him onto his back, revealing the crudely made cast-iron mask, now covered with frost. You could see his pale brown eyes through the slender square in the visor. They were dilating and darting back and forth. The rounds that entered his chest plate had still cut into his flesh. He was pathetically weak. The Acolyte lifted one of his padded arms and nudged my weapon to the side. Kind of like a child trying to beat away an older sibling. I closed my eyes and leaned down, pointing the gun under his mask. He grabbed hold of my arm and mumbled something through the chaos. I'll never know what those words were. I put an end to the struggle a moment later. His hands fell from my forearm and rested on the soiled snowbank. The mask hung loosely from his face. It served as a hollow reminder of what it meant to be an Acolyte. You kill until you are killed, and that was your entire purpose. I removed the freezing hunk of metal from his face and set it next to him on top of the pile of slush. I could at least do that much.

The man was nearly bald with the exception of two thin patches on both sides of his head. He had a thick, bushy, and untamed mustache of a light red color that seemed to puff out of his face. Some patches of the facial hair had frozen together after enduring the bitter harshness of winter. A long cut stretched from his left cheek to his ear. The scar was recently made, no more than a couple of months ago at most. It was made by a tool or blade. Sleek and straight. He must have gotten that during the fight in Parkersville. I almost grew the nerve to chuckle at what he must have been through. He got cut to ribbons hundreds of miles back in the middle of jack-nowhere to a group of absolute nobodies. After suffering that total embarrassment, he must have marched angrily for months upon months with no end, only to get caught off guard by the same people. To top all of that off, he gets run down by some skinny asshole with a peashooter in some dirty parking garage. I mean, how bad of a day can you have?

My ironic little thought caused me to lose focus, and before I could tell which direction was up, a few of the remaining Acolytes blindly fired shots from behind dumpsters in a nearby alley. Some flew over my head, some hit the ground fifteen feet from my ankles, and thankfully, none took my head off. I dove onto the slush and crawled my way inch by inch, all the way back into the safety and shelter of the first floor. One Acolyte chased the rabbit and came charging at me with a spear across the roadway. He must have wanted me bad. Maybe he would have gotten me if half of The Train didn't have their sights on him.

I rejoined my team soon after, who promptly dealt with the remaining Acolyte. Four bullet holes were engraved into the forehead of his mask. Todd was wheezing and pouring alcohol from an unused Molotov directly onto his wounds. Jacques received a nasty few cuts on his face, but nothing too severe, given the circumstances. I brushed some of the dirt off of my sweater before wandering back behind my pillar again. It was pure instinct. Like I was still preparing for the next wave to show up and kick our asses. Jacques sat nervously in position. He had run completely dry by now. If any spare Acolyte made their way up the ramp, we would have to bring them down with our bare hands. No ammo, no explosives, limited vision, and little hope left in the tank. Together, we sat and listened to the remaining pitter patter of footsteps get snuffed out entirely.

~ * ~

Eventually, the team with all the heavy gear crept from cover and swept the streets. They didn't find much left to put down. Three Acolytes that hid behind a dumpster tried to launch a counterattack once they realized they couldn't climb the wall. They didn't last long. A while after, the air horn was blasted from a far rooftop. The whole saga of the once-feared raiders and cultists, the entire legacy of The Acolytes, had finally come to an end. All by the hands of a hundred o r so simple bumpkins who had walked a little too far for their own good. It was an excellent day.

Jacques was the first one to start cheering. The people on the rooftops were quick to follow, and it was louder than a finale at a fireworks show. The Train had a habit of celebrating miracles by that point. Jed stumbled down from the truck bed, holding his gashed thigh, covered in gunpowder and with eyes as wide as frisbees. He made his way over to me and used my shoulder as a crutch. A large grin snuck its way onto his face as well. I'm sure our cheering could be heard on every street corner and bar and discount grocery store from New York to Albany. Jacques trotted over to us and dug the palm of his hand into my upper back. I was in no shape for a slap like that, but I appreciated the sentiment. He slung Jed's arm around his other shoulder, and together, we walked him over to Todd. Even the old man had a smirk to give, behind all the scrapes and bullet holes of course.

"I don't think I can hear anymore." Jed said as he wheezed in his gravelly southern accent.

Jacques lifted his free hand and cupped it around his left earlobe. "What did he say?"

My eyes began to water from the thick s mog. The stuff did a good job of choking up the entire situation. The second floor of the garage had a bronze tint to it due to all the sandy vapor from all of the explosions and concussive blasts. If there's one color I hate more than grey, it would be beige. Just as boring, just less consistent. I used my free sleeve to wipe a variety of debris from my eyes and joined in the banter.

"I don't know Jacques, but I think it was something about swimming in the family gene pool."

A moment later I felt a steady palm clap against the back of my head like a bag of falling bricks. I probably deserved it. Our entire three-man stretcher almost hit the pavement.

"Hey asshole, I ain't looking to land on this leg five minutes after a sociopath cut me up with a broomstick. So if you would be so kind as to keep your footing like a man instead of prancing around like a gazelle, I would appreciate it an awful lot."

"I mean it makes sense. Us gazelle are naturally attuned to skitter away when we smell chewing tobacco and unwashed socks." I replied.

"You just wait until I get this leg patched up Jack, then I'll give that prissy little attitude you have a reason to scurr..."

A blaze of fluorescent yellow light pierced through the fog and startled everyone with the shrieking sound of gunpowder igniting. A large caliber bullet whistled for what must have been less than a second, and all three of the standing FCS members were thrown to the floor with a sudden, violent jerk. I landed on sharp pieces of rock and rolled onto my gut. I couldn't let a little back pain slow me down at that point. Jacques quickly recovered from the fall and drew out his knife, knowing his handgun had finally run dry. With half a clip still loaded, I drew my weapon from my side holster and shoot back at the source of the light.

We exchanged a few inaccurate rounds before I realized how close to dry I was as well. All of those wasted shots were finally catching up with me. I decided I needed to wait out the smoke and pick my last few attempts carefully, or I may just lose it all after the fighting ended. The large caliber pistol continued to go off for the next ten or fifteen seconds, splintering concrete pillars and tearing holes through car chassis. In fact, there seemed to be a pattern to his firing. Then again, there was always a pattern with lunatics. One, two, three, bang. One, two, three, bang. He was conserving ammo just as I was, but even if he slowed down his consumption even more than he was now, he would run out well before the smoke cleared. The flash grew further and further away from us, and the gap grew from three to five to ten seconds. He made the mistake of trying for one more hit and run on the FCS. The penalty for that was death. After a few short moments, I knew in the pit of my gut he was out of shells.

I broke from behind cover and sprinted blindly toward his position.

Even if he had some spare shells, he wouldn't have a chance in hell of hitting me. It felt like I was trapped in the middle of a sandstorm. As soon as a new object came into sight, something else would vanish into the mist. I scanned around every few seconds for the Acolyte, but there was nothing to be discovered except for the empty casings fired from the hand cannon. Following the breadcrumb trail made the tracking a bit easier. The floating dust particles clogged up my lungs though, so I eventually called off the search and went for a breath of fresh air by an opening in the wall facing the street. I couldn't chase him if I couldn't breathe. I spit down onto the sidewalk, clearing the grit from my mouth. Jacques called out to me from somewhere in the garage.

"Jack, where are you? Did you find him?"

"Not yet, just keep checking the vehicles."

Fatigue was really doing a number on me during the final ascent, but I managed. Trying not to get shot was the only thing keeping me up, and that kind of motivation doesn't do wonders for your nerves. Keeping by the innermost wall of the parking deck gave me better visibility and cover, so I hugged the barriers. Fortunately, as I moved further and further away from where the hornets parked, the debris seemed to clear up. Things were almost normal by the time I reached the end of the next incline. Almost immediately, I caught sight of a reddish-black trail dripping along the white pavement lines. It led straight to the top floor, no tricks, no roundabouts. He was hurt and he was running. It would be my pleasure to put him down.

Usually, I grew unsettled at the thought of killing somebody, but in this case, I almost felt gratified. Anyone as low down and no good as an Acolyte who would ambush three wounded men after a fight was less than capable of receiving a single drop of my pity. I was angry, panicked, frustrated, and full of bloodlust. This was a dangerously unstable cocktail of emotions. As I approached the third-floor landing, I noticed something reflective on the ground. It was his handgun, completely empty and purposely ruined by a jam so it couldn't be salvaged. He even took time to dismantle the loading mechanism. Looks like he didn't plan on making it out.

I left the gun in place and continued to follow the blood trail up to the faint light of day. Nowhere left to hide. I quieted my footsteps and peaked over the railing. The open air was bitter and impure. It tasted like chalk and cigarette ashes. The thick grey and white clouds which had ominously hung about all morning finally broke, but snow still fell in light, fluffy particulates. There was a reflective, rectangular tube that engulfed half of the top floor like an incomplete spider's web. It was an extensive system of fumigation vents. Judging from the cotton-like density of the ashes on the lower floors, there were doubts that they still worked.

The blood trail disappearing behind them was easy to spot.

Another thing I noticed whilst four stories up was a crowd of a few shadowy figures which hung over the ledge of a nearby bistro. Some big commotion on an elevated patio. A bunch of folks were shoving away tables and closing frozen-shut umbrellas. The figures huddled around something in an awkward semicircle facing away from me. It almost looked like they built a campfire, and were sitting around it for warmth. As I peered over the roofs edge further to get a closer look, I realized they were survivors from the Train, gathering around what seemed to be another survivor. They were flat on their backs. Only one conclusion to draw from that. For the first time since the battle had ended, I really began to think how many of my friends bit the bullet.

I couldn't even tell you if long days without sleep or the feeling of concussion were to blame for me carelessly forgetting my objective. Whichever it was, the culprit knew exactly how to push my buttons. Hell, I wasn't even looking at the blood trail anymore. They say idiots are always gluttons for punishment. Boy were they right. A loud grunting sound drew my attention from the bleak situation. A lowered shoulder was about to flatten me like a roller on some pastry.

I raised my sights and tried to put him down before he had the chance to reach me, but I pulled the trigger early, and the bullet instead clashed with an old circuit breaker. At least I got my feet square and balanced before I got launched into the stratosphere. I think he lifted my entire body over his uninjured shoulder and careened us toward the edge.

If he could've lifted me a touch more, yours truly would be mystery pavement meat.

The pistol went flying from my hand and took the four-story drop. I nearly flipped over the aged-mustard guardrail, but I manage to get a grip on it with my heel at the last second, keeping myself from tumbling. I thrashed my leg at the guy, and a full size twelve cracked him square in the chest. When I regained my ground, I saw the signature jet black leather and the shoulder wound that matched the Acolyte who had blinded me before. He reached into a thin pocket near his right breast and pulled out a switchblade. It was a pale green, serrated like a saw, and tightly connected to the handle by thick screws. So I guess it was more of a saw than a knife. My own switchblade had dulled a bit, but luckily for me, it would still do the job. Looks like I had to get my hands dirty, just one more time.

We circled around for a few moments, sizing up each other and looking for an obvious weakness to exploit. For him, it was the open wound. One love-tap there would be enough to bring him down. His strange, five-point mask was cracked in three places, but it was still together, so hitting the face wouldn't do much. While the injury left him griping in pain and limited the use of his arm, he was still well rested and spry, unlike my sorry state. If I noticed this, I was sure he did too. My only chance was to end the fight early, before I slowed down enough for him to catch me off guard. The other problem on my hands was the complete disorientation. Dust, slush, and bright lights had left me reeling three separate times in the last hour. The world around me tended to grow dim when I blinked. This normally could be bearable, but I didn't want to take my eyes off him, even for half a second.

The bastard decided it was a good time to start to start taunting me. It started with him flipping his weapon from hand to hand. That was when he started giggling. Next, he flipped his mask up and stuck his tongue out at me. I was half expecting him to shoot a spitball at me. I mean, it was like I was fighting a child. My patience grew real thin. I took a run at him as he tried to readjust his headgear.

"Ooh, a little angry, are we?"

He mocked as my first slash was dodged by a quick duck. I lunged at him, driving my knife towards his injured shoulder. He was quick though, and before my blade could even touch the frayed material on his jacket, he had juked to the right.

"Don't you know when to quit? Your friends are dead. Your cause is dead. Your organization is nothing more than crow food now. What's gonna make you realize there is no good ending for you?" I slighted at him, trying to get him to lose his cool. "I mean, what are you going to do now, you disgusting little peon?"

He went low and slashed at my thigh, but I drew it back far enough that the only thing he hit was some loose cloth from my second pair of jeans. Realizing my opportunity, I swung my fist not carrying the blade across the nose. The mask got a few new cracks. He stumbled back and grabbed hold of a nearby vent to steady himself.

"What am I gonna do? Well, I figure I should start by gutting you like a fish. Maybe next, I go downstairs and garret your boyfriend's neck with some shoestrings. Anything can come next asshole. The world's my oyster. Who knows? I could always go out into the wastes, find some desperate slut or roadside beggar, and recruit them. People are hungry and scared nowadays. They'd love a little candle to hold. They'd love some warm food. They'd love a good prophecy. A good god to follow. If you think you put an end to us here, boy do I have some Sunday-morning news for you."

I wiped some wax fragments from my knuckles and readied myself for the next round. He ran at me that time, swinging the serrated blade in a zigzag. I stepped backward, rolling back to the left and right to dodge his flurry. When I backed myself into the railing he decided to lunge straight for my throat, but luckily, I had enough room to narrowly avoid the strike. With a quick move and some pressure, I pinned the knife hand in place with an elbow.

"I got you now, you little punk." I said, ready to plunge my knife into his side.

Suddenly, in a last-ditch effort, he ripped the mask off of his face and swung it at my head. Before I could raise my arm to block it, the accessory shattered across my cheek, splintering pieces of cold wax all over my face. I fell onto my back holding my stinging and irritable eyes. My blade slipped from my hands during the fall too. He hit me right where he needed to.

"Want to say that again, geezer? I think the mask was clogging my ears a bit. Ah, it's fine. Pigs aren't supposed to talk anyway."

Between the flashes and dark spots, I could see that the young, bearded man in the leather jacket was standing over me with the saw right over my head. His face was youthful, and almost well kept. It seemed like he was a murderer by choice, a savvy savage. The lunatic chuckled and kissed his blade before loudly proclaiming for me to "Die."

As he went to take the plunge, Jacques came flying into my field of vision and threw himself into the cultist with his full weight. Both slammed into the guardrail with a massive clang so loud, that it alerted the survivors atop the restaurant. They struggled and wrestled along the edge, trading punches and blows until the Acolyte managed to push Jacques away. With his attention separated from me, I recovered from the dizzying blow and grabbed my switchblade. He reached down to pick up his own weapon as well, but I was faster. Driving my arm upward, I dug the tip of the steel edge into his gunshot wound. He screamed and hung over the railing mumbling something between groans. I yanked the knife out and placed it underneath his stretched neck. He was hemorrhaging from his shoulder now, and his eyes grew red and bloodshot. Although he was finally beaten, the Acolyte smiled anyway.

"What's so funny?"

"Me? Oh nothing. It's just that we're the ones with all the bad press. Murderers, psychopaths, raiders, all the good stuff. I just got my first look at exactly what you did out there. Pretty impressive if I do say so myself. Go ahead pal, take a little peek at it. Any good artist always examines his own work after all. Maybe you and I are closer than I thought."

"Shut up. We are nothing like you and we will never be like you."

"I don't know about that. How many of us have you personally killed? Five, ten, twenty, more? Most of us haven't even killed that many people. We were just hungry folks. Just like you. We just had different ways we went about things, that's all. But no, no, no. Gotta pin the blame on the guy in the mask. Makes it easier for you, doesn't it? You have quite a few skeletons in your closet, don't you, mister bone-collector? Yeah, I was wrong alright. We aren't even alike. We're two of a kind."

After peering over the edge, I returned my icy gaze to the young man. Watching him try to squirm out of my grasp. After a moment's thought, I shoved the edge deeper into his throat.

"You know what Acolyte... I think you may just be right."

With that, I pushed him over the edge. He tumbled down the side and bounced off the third-floor landing. His thick jacket wavered like a parachute, but he fell like a sack of rocks. The Acolyte was dead by the time he hit the ground, and to be honest, I lost track of his corpse pretty quickly in the mountain of bodies that WE, The Train, created.

Chapter Seventeen: Boston

Ez couldn't draw a single word from his expansive vocabulary to give to his friend. He thought for a moment that Jack may have been insane after all. Calling himself an Acolyte was the one thing Ez never expected to hear from Jack. It became hard for the child explorer to look the nomad in the eyes. Jack was the type to keep things straight to the point, but the point was stranger than fiction. Ez was sure he meant that as bluntly as he put it. When it came down to it, The Train was willing to kill just as easily as the cultists, they just needed a better excuse. The boy wasn't about to accept such a moral though. Jack was a teacher by nature, whether he would admit it or not, and there was more to that message than met the eye. Ez decided he would figure out what it all meant when he got older. Years passed before the light of the situation finally shined on the right spot.

Jack seemed distant after recounting the battle. Ez noticed the unfocused glare on his friend's face, and rushed over to wake him. After shaking him by the shoulders for a few seconds, Jack seemed to snap out of it.

"Hey hey, what's with the physical activity Ez? You lookin' to learn how to fight or something?"

"No. You're just acting weird."

"Weird?"

"You keep zoning out."

"Oh, sorry kid. That happens sometimes. Just keep batting me around whenever I fade out."

"I think I can manage that. Keep going with the story. You're almost there."

~ * ~

Okay Ez, whatever you want. After the leather jacket Acolyte met his demise, I rushed over to help Jacques, who had fallen over a segment of metal tubing. I dragged him up to his feet and wiped some of the blood off his grey trench coat. His nose was broken from a punch he took during the struggle, but besides that, he seemed to be alive and well. I, on the other hand, was ungodly exhausted and beaten to a bloody pulp. My face was cut in six different places, and I couldn't open my eyes the whole way. Couldn't hear worth shit either. I was ready to lay down and die on the spot, but before I had the chance, Jacques gasped and started running back toward the ramp.

"Jacques, what's going on?"

No answer. There had to be a reason. Jacques had a level head. The kind made for precision. He wasn't oblivious. He wasn't an idiot. He wouldn't just blindly barge away from a wounded friend unless...

Jed.

I leapt up and started running toward the ramp. How could I have been so stupid? If one of us was hit by the shot from the Acolyte's revolver, knocking us all down, and it wasn't me or Jacques... It could mean only one thing. Jacques busted through a locked service door on the stairwell that lead us right back to where our defensive position was. The dust and debris in the air finally cleared up enough for Jacques to see. I did my best to follow his blurry figure. Jacques slowed down and halted in front of the ramp. I caught up to him a few seconds later, hoping and fearing what he stopped to see wasn't what I thought it was. Then again, what else could it have been? A pot of gold? Gold doesn't twitch like that.

I rushed over to him, pushing aside one of the hornet gunners who was trying to put pressure on a large hole in his stomach. I took her place, holding an alcohol-soaked rag down on the hemorrhaging wound. Jed was still alive when I arrived, but he was less than an entire man by that point. His hands were shaking violently, and he couldn't lift up his arm more than a couple inches. He coughed and shook his head whilst he mumbled something incomprehensible under his breath. I turned to the gunner of the remaining hornet and sternly demanded to know what the words were. A relatively young farm girl with flowing blonde locks adjusted her baseball cap.

"Well, he just keeps saying that it's gonna be okay."

I looked back down at my dying friend and did what I could to comfort him. "Yeah Jed, things are going to be just fine, just keep focused on me, and don't close your eyes."

We tended to him for the next few minutes, doing anything and everything that we could to improve his condition. Fresh rags, adrenaline injections, a pillow to raise his head, the whole nine yards. We knew nothing would work by that point though. The bleeding continued at a lethal rate, and no amount of pressure or bandaging could ever hope to stop it. Eventually, Jed's mumbling stopped completely and his hands ceased to shake. He began to close his eyes, but I tapped him on the cheek and forced him to stay awake.

"Come on Jed, don't you even *think* about it. We are so fucking close. If you ditch me now, Todd's gonna make *me* the whipping boy of the group for the rest of the trip. You just can't do that to a guy. So just keep trying, as long as you can manage. Okay?"

Maybe my words did have some effect on him, because he held on for another minute or two before fading again. Nobody, not even Jed, could shake those wounds. He let out one final breath and tensed up. There was nothing more to do. I let go of the hole in his gut and walked over to his sleeping bag. Inside was a set of feathery camouflage covers that he used to use on cold nights. After it was placed over his head, I turned to Jacques and the Hornet operators and gestured for us to leave him in peace where he was. I washed my hands off in the bitter baptism of a slush pile.

Jacques and the gunner walked over and picked up Todd, who was also bleeding profusely from his hands and upper arms, and made their way to the exit. Infection was still a very serious threat on his life, but he at least had some kick left in him. Todd was too stubborn to die of anything.

I was finally alone, but I had one more thing I had to do before turning tail and joining the rest of The Train. I kneeled over the body of my old friend one last time and whispered to him through the sheets.

"You did pretty good, Jed. You did good."

With that I turned, picked up my pack, and made my way back out into the street, leaving Jed to rest. I could never find the strength to take a peak back at the garage as I entered back to the corpse-ridden street. I feel like I was too afraid to, maybe I was smart enough not to. You can never look back Ez. Looking back is the worst thing you could do.

~ * ~

Ezekiel could see the blank stare growing back into Jack's eyes, but he seemed to keep himself in check, even if it was only by a thread.

"Jack, what exactly happened after everything stopped? Who was still alive? Where did you all go from there?"

Jack seemed a bit distant, but the sudden slew of new questions seemed to draw his attention away from the subject of Jed.

~ * ~

Oh, right. Sorry kid. Well anyway, there were thousands upon thousands of empty casings and hastily made weapons lining the street and sidewalks. Amongst all of the decay, I saw my handgun, which fell from the roof sitting atop a patch of fresh, white snow. One of the last ones on the street. I picked it up and stuffed it into its usual place in my burlap sack. Hell, it was incredible I managed to find the damn thing.

Their few remaining vehicles met fates similar to their operators. Their hoods had been crushed in by falling rocks, bricks, sandbags, bottles, and other heavy supplies. Their hulls had been riddled and torn apart by heavy machinegun fire and high caliber rounds. Small gas fires were spreading at an alarming rate from their armored vehicles and transportation trucks. Their supply depot was up in flames within minutes. One vehicle to the next, the blaze consumed all. Their medical equipment, their food, their water, everything. A fitting end for people like them. Some frantic passengers scrambled around the vehicles and carts in a desperate search for supplies. One of our crew got too close and found themselves feet away from a fuel tanker that decided to explode. They didn't make it out. Peter ordered an evacuation of the street minutes later. The whole situation could still draw all types of unwanted attention from feral animals and other raiders.

While we killed at least three quarters of the Acolytes that morning, we had also lost twenty-five of our own, including Jed and four of our

Hornet operator teams. Amongst the dead was Josh, our prolific guardsman, fifteen people from the Center, and worst of all, Saul from Parkersville. In fact, Saul was the body in the center of the huddle on the rooftops. Apparently some Acolytes pushed their way to the top floor of the building and picked him off before anybody even noticed them. It seemed like half of The Train mourned his death. He was always popular, but I didn't care enough to attend his funeral for more than a few minutes. Instead, I took Jacques over to the medical tent to visit Todd and Adahy, who were still fighting to keep alive through their own severe circumstances. On a barstool, we lit a small candle inside an old tin of spearmints and sat in silence. I'm sure everyone there wanted to say something about Jed, but nobody had the gut to bring his name up. Not even Todd. He was too busy rubbing at his bandaged forearm.

The evening went on and the group began to talk again. Adahy's condition had grown worse from having to walk between buildings, so he retired back to his stretcher. He stumbled over a collapsed stretcher on the way back, and required the assistance of Doc Ranford to make it to the beds. Poor guy really needed some rest. Jacques and I started asking Todd about his shoulder's condition, to which he would reply. "It wasn't my head, so I think it will be just fine." The look in his eyes were telling us something entirely different. We continued to pester him on the issue until he grew frustrated and finally broke down.

"Look, I can't feel my one arm alright? That's all. It doesn't hurt anywhere but the shoulder."

I took a close examination of the now bandaged area on his lower arm and encircling the point of entry was a black and purple cloud of flesh. The thing practically stretched all the way up to his biceps. I wasn't sure if it was a bruise or something more serious, but I wasn't willing to test his patience any more than I already had. The bacteria would have to sort it out for us.

"Well, we're finally in the home stretch now." Jacques awkwardly mumbled. "How long do you two think it will take for us to finally arrive at Boston?"

Todd stuffed a large wad of chewing tobacco into his upper lip. "Well, I hate to say it, but I don't think that we are going anywhere any time soon."

"What do you mean by that?" Jacques replied.

"Well, take a look at it this way, Jacques. We just lost twenty-five people, and there are dozens more injured just like I am. How do you think that this precise and fluid machine will flow and function with a quarter of its workers temporarily or permanently out of commission?"

"You're too pessimistic, old man. I think we can still operate more or less functionally with three quarters of our crew still alive and well. I bet we make it long before the last snowstorm of the season hits."

To be honest, I had to agree with Todd on the subject. We had already been crawling mile by mile the past month due to sickness and weather alone. Now with an army of wounded and dead that needed tending to, I knew we couldn't make much progress. It would be a bloody crawl to the finish.

"End of winter? Cocky. I wouldn't even give us a shot to move at all until spring hits. At that time, we might get a bit of breathing room to travel, and we may just be able to scoot ourselves there on our last legs."

"You're just crochety, old man."

"And you are clueless."

The two were on the brink of an argument, so I decided to break it all up by suggesting we all get some shuteye. I personally hadn't slept well in three days. Those two bickering could have finally made me snap. You know, the straw that broke the camel's back.

~ * ~

Jacques and I took our leave. On the way back to our lonely campsite for two, Jacques and I came across Mountain, who was sitting atop a busted vehicle with his head in his hands. There were some kind of smudges all over his cheeks. I didn't want to ask what they were. In any case, I was relieved. For a second, I thought he was one of the few who didn't make it out. I probably should have known better. Mountain is the strongest guy I know, after all.

"Hey, Mountain, good to see you still alive and well."

"..."

"Are you feeling alright man? Usually you have more spunk than this."

"…"

"Come on buddy, what's your deal?" I said, giving him a little dig in the arm.

He finally looked up at me and nodded. "Yeah, I'm fine Beanstalk. Just a little shaken up that's all." His voice was bitter, and his face was more stern than usual.

"I don't believe that."

"What did you say?" he said, cupping his right ear and leaning toward me.

I cleared my throat and tried again.

"I said I don't believe that."

"Well, you should. I just can't hear so well anymore. Things got pretty loud down on the frontline, and not long after everything started, I couldn't hear nothin' but ringing. To tell you the truth, that's still all I'm hearing."

"I feel your pain Mountain. I still can't see too well from what happened to my eyes earlier. I got kaleidoscope vision or something."

"Yeah, I can tell. Your whole face looks pretty fucked up to me."

I was glad to see Mountain was okay after all.

We had a laugh about his slighting little remark, but it wasn't too long before things came to a standstill. Jacques, who was still steaming over his argument with Todd, wanted to jump into the conversation.

"Hey, uhh...Mountain was it? How long do think it's going to take for us to get to Boston?"

Mountain had surprisingly never spoken to Jacques before, and you could tell that the tall, strong, bearded black man wasn't impressed by this tiny French-Canadian with a busted nose.

"It doesn't make a difference to me anymore. If it takes us a week, great. If it takes us a year, great. To be honest, I'm not even sure why I'm going to Boston anymore."

"What do you mean you don't know? Why in the hell did you board The Train in the first place?"

"I guess I joined because I thought it would be safe in Boston. But now? Now I just think I won't be able to adjust to simple colony life anymore, and things will grow too damn boring for my own taste. It would let me think too much."

"You are absolutely insane."

"Come a little closer and I can show you just how insane I am."

Jacques backed off while taking his hands out of his trench coat pocket and holding them up.

"Okay big man, I'm not looking for a fight right now, I just had a simple question. Jack, I'm heading back to start a fire. You should swing by camp and get some rest after you are done talking to...this thing."

After making that remark, Jacques picked up the pace into a fast walk and sped away with his legs buckling underneath him.

"Lil' bitch," Mountain mocked as Jacques made his great escape.

"Come on Mountain, he didn't mean to aggravate you like that. Just let him off on a warning this time for me, will you?" I asked with my freezing hands dug deep into my coat pockets.

"Alright, fine. If I ever see that scrawny midget ever again, I will put my boot so far up his back end that they'll find a shoelace during his next prostate exam."

I stared down at his massive size thirteen snowshoes and nodded. "You got it."

"Well, he does have one thing right. You need sleep, Beanstalk. Even the bags under your eyes have bags."

~ * ~

The wear and tear in my calves kicked it up a notch when he mentioned that. Sudden-death point of collapse. I agreed and took off immediately, bidding Mountain adieu before slugging my way over to the campsite one heavy step at a time.

My head barely touched the fluff of a pillow before I was out like a light. Camp had been relocated into the lobby of some dusty old law firm. The weather was still cold and grim, but at least it was warm enough to rest by an open window without getting frostbite. The evening was quiet, and my imagination started getting the better of me. Ever since my solitude in

Pennsylvania, I hadn't had the dream anymore. Instead, I had this wonky vision of an escalator that lead to nothing.

If I remember correctly, I slept through breakfast the next morning. No way I could stomach anything after the previous day's events. Just imagining the warm, buttery smell of cornmeal made me want to vomit. The extra two hours of dozing off helped get my strength up though. Sleet was covering my eyes in layers by the time I got up. A welcome nuisance. We got moving shortly after.

In the end, Todd was right about our timeline. Jacques finally admitted he was wrong about the one-month estimate about fifty days in. By that time, we hadn't even made it halfway there from New York City. There were too many wounded, too many sick, too many hungry, too many cold. There were too many 'too manys' for us to find our footing. An outbreak of the flu stopped us dead in our tracks on the thirtieth day. It was one of those nasty little bugs that snuck up on you overnight, then took a week to sweat, cough, groan, and sleep it out. Soup isn't strong enough medicine for every ailment, Ez, and even that remedy was in scarce supply.

Peter eventually decided we would have to make camp until our condition grew better. So, in a suburb in western New York, we embedded ourselves. Another shoddy suburban utopia. Each decaying front door managed to keep the wind at bay. Each shingle in shambles did enough to keep the snow off our noggins. The only real problem we had was removing the…previous tenants. Apparently, Mountain found a pile of bones that got canned on the can. People started calling him 'John on the John' after that. It raised morale a bit, but I still thought the joke was sick. We looted the whole city for anything useful, water, food, meds, weapons, kindling, entertainment, you name it. The shops had a surplus of the extravagant goods for us to snatch. We helped ourselves to anything from old movies with DVD players, to pharmacies packed with countless untouched prescriptions, to cream-filled puffs and sugary snacks from the local gas station. We had just carved ourselves out a little slice of paradise.

~ * ~

If I'm being honest with you Ez, there really wasn't anything to do while we stayed in the community. We didn't have to hunt or scavenge. We didn't have to stay on the move. We didn't even have to boil our own water. All there was to do was sit and stay warm. It was a perfect situation for us, so perfect some survivors protested that we should just start our own colony there. However, people like myself who had things in Boston we needed to seek out protested the movement and quickly brought an end to the discussion. Jacques, myself, and Adahy, who finally overcome his illness, moved into a small twelve hundred square foot ranch style home on the same street as everybody else and stuck our claim there. Three bedrooms, two baths, and a gourmet kitchen. A fuckin' gourmet kitchen, and it worked too. You should see Adahy try and sauté something sometime, it's a real show. The crowning achievement of the whole place though, was the immaculate, still-working latrine. Jacques made a joke one evening that Jed would probably have called it 'shit-gri la'. He definitely would have.

Three weeks of twiddling our thumbs and reading old magazines passed by without a single noteworthy event. I took quite a liking to sitting on a dusty old recliner. Kicking my legs up for more than two minutes made my knees jitter. Oh, and I stuffed my face on the regular as well. Beef Jerky, frozen bottles of name brand cola's, stale crackers and chips, I munched down my weight in snacks every day. After a few weeks of the 'junk food treatment' I was no longer able to see my leg bones pressing against my skin in the mirror. Heh, I guess I might have even looked healthy for a second. Unconditioned and flabby, mind you, but not bone-thin either.

The good news kept rolling in too, because by the next week, Todd was cleared to leave Doc Ranford's care. I remember waking up late that morning, maybe around midday due to an annoying beam of light that snuck its way in through my window blinds. I stumbled out into the kitchen to make a cup of coffee atop the gasping gas-powered stove. As I poured myself a fresh cup, a strange noise rocked the front door. It wasn't a distinct knock or bang, like Mountain usually did. I guess it was more of a prolonged scratch. I expected it to be Jacques, who had left an orange sticky note on the refrigerator door explaining how he was going to visit some friends for the day. Seeing that Adahy was currently out wandering as well, I went to answer the door by myself.

I got my first glance at a drastically different figure from the man I once knew through a dirty bug screen. Todd's grey hairs had fallen out in patches, and it looked like he lost ten pounds. I'm not talking about the weight he lost when they amputated his arm. The doc said his chances of making it through without going under the knife were slim, but for some reason I still held hope that Todd would luck out. I guess he was lucky enough to get a prosthetic when they were in such short supply. It was thick and clunky and ended in a mounded semicircle, so eventually everyone in the group came to call it his 'peg leg'. He seemed bitter and brutally sober, but we were happy to have him back nonetheless. When Adahy and Jacques returned later that day, we held a celebration. However, something had permanently changed inside Todd. He was quiet, introverted, and often in a haze. We couldn't get him to utter more than a few sentences during the whole party. He's remained sour and reclusive like that to this very day. Whatever our fearless captain lost in that arm, he never got back.

~ * ~

I started volunteering at the medical cart as an assistant, in hopes that having more people healthy could get us moving faster. I helped some girl from the Center give birth in that time. It was the first instance in a while where the number of travelers on The Train actually went up. Who knows what possessed that couple to have a baby in the middle of all this. The kid probably died before hitting Boston. Nah, I shouldn't say that. *Maybe* the kid died before getting here. Anyways, one glance made me understand just where they were coming from, at least a little bit. The look in the mother's eyes, the moment she wrapped the child in a towel, those were special. Real special. Making life in a world of desolation must be a pretty unbeatable experience. The kid cried all through the night too, the cry of a champion.

~ * ~

March finally slogged its way to our doorstep. One morning, Peter decided to jump on top of the Jeep and rattle our lifestyle to its core again.

"Everyone, I think our stay in this little town has finally grown unwelcome. Its resources are dried, its streets filled with garbage, and its hospitality has been overdrawn. That is why I have authorized the final push to be made, starting in six hours. Pack what you need and nothing more, we can always scavenge for the rest. If we hustle, Boston can be made in four weeks of travel, maybe less if we push to sundown every day. You're all rested enough for the job anyway. I believe that our journey has finally drawn to a close. Let's finish it."

His speech drew a mix of uninspired applause and hesitant silence. Nobody per say *wanted* to leave such a paradise, but in their hearts, everyone knew what their goal originally was. Peter was also right about the supplies. All the stockpiles in the dingy, dusty broom closets in the forgotten gas stations had finally been cleared out. We were lucky they lasted that long. By the late afternoon, everyone abandoned their couches and their beds, their roofs and their fireplaces, their neighborhood, and their homes. It was a good day to hit the pavement.

~ * ~

The reconditioning back to a nomadic lifestyle was grittier than I expected. I tried not to pay attention to how my socks were constantly rubbing against my boots and burning my heels. Walking on concrete never really helped anything either. I couldn't stretch my leg out all the way by the end of the week without recoiling from soreness. The ball of my left foot was a solid red by the end of day two. Little aches were still commonplace for me though. What was really getting under my skin involved stomach cramps and heavy breathing. Nine months of walking managed to go down the drain in eight weeks, Ez. The world is cruel like that.

The springtime weather made resettling into schedule a bit more bearable though. The air was cool and refreshing. It was the kind of breeze where you could feel the moisture brush your face if you turn the right way. Not shivering constantly kept our energy up, so our usual ten-miles-per-day routine finally became viable again. That didn't stop us from excessively sweating and taking breaks to rest or drink extra fluids though.

Progress was progress. and in a desperate push for glory, we made our way there one step at a time.

The men and women who were injured in the last stand against the Acolytes had been reassigned to cozy jobs in the Center, including Todd. He seemed reluctant to give up on his friends in the FCS, but he also knew that a one-armed man would be a hinderance more than a help. He had that kind of intuition. After that, we kind of fell into a slump. Three men traveling nervously along together felt much lonelier than five or seven. Nobody was left up front to make jokes, or berate someone for making jokes, or pretend to not hear jokes anymore. The F in FCS suddenly stood for fragmented. However, regardless of our stupor, we did what the scouts do best, and never looked behind us.

Good omens finally started rolling in a week or two after that. Green omens. The air cleared up by the time we reached the heart of the state, and the animals started looking a bit more...alive by the time we reached the seaboard. Jacques found a bike shop and dragged out a Schwinn with red rims and a purple chassis. He said his feet were sore, but judging by how many times he rung the bell on the handlebars, I couldn't help but be suspicious of an ulterior motive.

~ * ~

We finally caught sight of Boston from the top of a freeway overpass. The skyline just barely peaked over the branching chain links of the fences. Jacques judged the distance to be something around the lines of five miles, or one day of careful travel. With great excitement and energy, the collective trio that was now the FCS sprinted back to Peter and shouted the news straight up to the heavens. We got the confirmation it was a survivor colony that night, when some flares shot up in patterns over the city. Someone told me that signifies curfew around here. I'm still gonna call it a good omen. The Train celebrated with our remaining food rations and a good night's rest. As you might guess Ez, we have never been good at throwing parties. Funny enough, Peter was right on the money when he spoke to us back in Phoenix. We were going to make it there on schedule after all, and we even had time for a little vacation.

At the end of the fourth week out of NYC, we reached your scrap-metal wall at the edge of the city. A few homeless beggars looked at us like an alien species as we wandered around the perimeter. Maybe they thought we were raiders. We didn't look quite mean enough to be marauders though. Half the folks in the Center were staring up at that thing for hours like a bunch of tourists. Franklin even found the nerve to pull out a disposable camera and took a few photos. Whatever merchants mentioned Boston to Peter knew what they were talking about when they said Boston was a safe place.

~ * ~

"That's all the scrap metal from the ship yards, we built it about two years back to deter bandits and animals." Ez interjected.

"Yeah, I figured as much. How many ships did you have to scrap to make that?"

"All of them."

"Well, that's a damn shame Ez. Those might have been useful one day."

"Yeah, maybe, but they were useful back then, too."

"Guess I can't argue with you about that, kid."

~ * ~

Your guards were pretty impressive as well Ez. By impressive, I mean there were a bunch of them and they all had guns pointed at us. They seemed really interested in who we were, judging by the amount of times they shouted for us to identify ourselves. There were about twenty people on that section of the wall, but one in specific, an Irishman who was at least three hundred pounds with a face redder than a cherry tomato, tended to do all the shouting. His voice was grave and baritone, commanding and stern. We all put down our weapons collectively, put our hands to the sky, and waited patiently for them to speak with Peter.

Sadly, almost three uneasy hours passed before one of your leaders finally met with us. She was thin and short, maybe five feet at her tallest, with long brown pigtails shooting down to her lower back. You could tell just by looking that she was a fireball. She stepped out of the gates in a denim jacket and jeans, all accompanied by a pair of thick rimmed sunglasses. The Train had collectively forgotten what civilization looked like, so someone in a matching outfit was almost enough to blow our minds right out our earholes. She walked into the middle of our crowd with a burly bodyguard and spoke with a dominance.

"Which of you do I have the absolute pleasure of speaking with?"

Obviously, Peter stood up and raised his right hand to wave at the strange woman. Peter was ready for that call. Too ready. He went for it a little too eagerly. The bodyguard assumed the fast movement was a trap and pointed his rifle at Peter's, head. It was a hot moment for sure, and I could tell a few loyal followers of Peter were about to jump into action. This included a tall, black haired woman who was kneeling next to me. I could tell that she was slowly reaching for a small caliber handgun next to her, so before she could cause a scene, I reached down and grabbed her wrist. She nearly slapped me on the spot, but I managed to get her under control.

"Don't do anything stupid."

The crisis was narrowly averted once Peter stood up and showed he was unarmed. Before long, the lady in the denim jacket lead Peter inside the gate to discuss our…-immigration. Everyone knew Peter was a good orator and negotiator, but that didn't do much to quell everyone's nerves. I mean the guy just stepped into a potential lion's den. You people could still have been cannibals for all we knew. We all sat about, drinking watered down beers and complaining about the humidity while the guards only managed to grow in number. They had to strip search our vehicles and carts as well, one at a time. They certainly didn't trust us, but they didn't have to. All they needed to do was let us in.

~ * ~

Nobody on The Train had the first idea of how long Peter would be gone. Hours passed by without any word on where he was or what they were doing to him. Nightfall arrived without an apprehensive word escaping from anyone's lips. We weren't allowed to build fires per command of the fat guardsman, so we had to shelter ourselves in artificial glows of lanterns instead. Moths crawled at your floodlights by the thousands. Trust wore thin under that pale glow. Many began to hatch schemes, hidden beneath the white noise of normal conversation. Some believed that the worst had already occurred, and Peter may already be dead or captured. Some even believed that the guards would turn on us and kill us all as soon as we shut our eyes. Thankfully, there were peacekeepers in the crowd that managed to quell any talk of a riot. Everybody was insecure and afraid, but thanks to the efforts of the calm headed people amongst us, we made it until dawn without terrible incident.

As the sun finally began to rise over the skyscrapers to the east, we were greeted by the familiar figure of the short denim-woman, carrying a handheld megaphone. She was alone, and seemed mildly irritated. This fanned the flames of doubt that Peter was still alive and well. Before the crowd grew restless, she went on to speak.

"Good morning to you all. My name is Isabella Wright, and I am the head of refugee affairs here at the New Boston colony. I have spoken overnight with your director, and after hours of debate and conversation, we have negotiated a deal for all of you. Everybody present in the crowd will be allowed passage into our camp on the condition that any firearms or explosives be given to our weapons department for permanent storage. You all must understand our concern with well-armed strangers walking amongst us, and we hope you will cooperate with us on this simple term. We will now open the gate and allow you all to enter in a single file, neat, and orderly line. From the bottom of all of our hearts, the community of New Boston welcomes you."

She spoke just like Peter.

The rusty gate swung open with a loud piercing noise. Nails scraping a chalkboard. Seeing my opportunity to jump ahead in line, I shoved my way through the crowd up to the front to be checked in first. By the doorway were two black men in navy-blue tee shirts sitting at a desk with a notebook and half a dozen pens.

"Name, sir?" The one on the left asked me.

"Jack Fitzgerald"

~ * ~

Ez shot up like a rocket. "Your last name is Fitzgerald?"

Jack, taken aback, answered. "Yes, my last name is Fitzgerald. Its long, and unnecessary, and it's kind of a pain to spell, so I never use it much."

"Is that why you told me the people don't use names out there?"

"No, that's entirely true. I just can't speak for every lunatic out there. That's all."

Jack's face developed a rosy tint.

"Fair enough, but you should still know, I think Fitzgerald is a fitting last name for you." Ez mocked.

Jack smiled back. "Thanks, Ez."

~ * ~

Well anyway, they searched through my pack and confirmed my identity with Peter, who stood safe and well next to the table with a cigarette in his mouth. I knew everybody was going to be happy to see him. It took about five minutes for me alone to pass security, but after clarifying a few things that thoroughly frustrated the guards, I was cleared to explore. Before I left, I asked for a few directions.

"Hey, where can I find the residents list of this place?"

One of the two guards stood up and pointed to a rather large and clean building that looked like a city hall.

"That's the archive. Any information you need is there. Names, locations, ages, any records."

With my open backpack swaying behind me by a thread, I leapt up the steps of the dome-roofed monolith three at a time. Moment of truth. Inside the hall was an expansive library of old and new works of scholarly literature and maps. Everything was still arranged by the Dewey decimal system, and the oak shelves looked like they had just been waxed. It was all very impressive.

There was a single man, maybe seventy years of age, with a large handlebar mustache sitting behind a service desk at the far end of the library. I trotted my way over to him whilst taking in the whole environment.

"Excuse me, sir. Do you know where the records are for current residents?"

He took a moment to adjust an embarrassingly large pair of bifocals before even addressing my existence.

"Oh, hello there. Are you new here? My name is Gus Santor, been working round' here for seven years now, seven of the best years of my life. How can I help you today, sir?"

My patience was wearing thin. "Like I said before, I just need to see the current residents list, that's all."

"You look like you are in a real hurry mister, don't know why. There is so much here in Boston that..."

I lost my mind. "Listen Gus, I just need you to get me these files. I need to see my family and I can't do that if I'm stuck in a history lesson."

He looked offended, but he finally listened to my request. He waddled over slowly to a large stack of binders and lifted a bulky burgundy colored one from the top of it. Gus then made his way back to the desk and passive aggressively threw it down in front of me.

"Have a wonderful day, sir."

I tore through the pages like it was giftwrapping on a new king-sized mattress. They were listed in alphabetical order by last name, so all I needed to do was make it to "F", and I would have my answer. I arrived in section F in a flash and began to scroll down the relatively short list of fifty names. Felger, Fern, Fester, Filch, Finnigan...Foley. I rubbed my eyes and tried again, thinking that I must have missed something. Felger, Fern, Fester, Filch, Finnigan...Foley. I teared up and tried again. Felger, Fern, Fester, Filch, Finnigan...Foley. I slammed the book's cover and pounded the desk. Gus jumped at the sound and began to shout at me from behind a bookcase. I didn't care in the least, I was furious, and I was broken. My sweet Delilah was not here. My lovely wife was not here. My family was not here.

Epilogue: Tomorrow

Jack kept his poker face, but Ez could tell that he was tearing up. All of that effort, all of those risks, all of those triumphs, all for nothing. Ez felt contrite for Jack. He felt sorrow and pain, he felt his loss and his misery. Ezekiel stood up from his bag and hugged his new friend.

"It's going to be okay Jack, it's going to be just fine."

Jack wiped his eyes in an old handkerchief and recomposed himself. "Thanks, little buddy, you're a life saver."

Ez took pride in those words, finally a compliment worth remembering. During the long pause, Ezekiel noticed the sun was setting. Jack's story had claimed the entire day. The light dimmed behind the many towering landmarks in the colony, and a pinkish color filled the atmosphere. The warehouse had finally grown cooler and less humid, so the two friends could at least sit comfortably in their silence. After a few minutes, Jack finally felt as though it was time to push the stalling conversation onward.

"So, little buddy, that's how I came to be here now. Did you learn anything about the outside world during the story?"

Ez nodded. "Yeah, I think I have learned more than I ever thought I would, just in one day too."

Jack grew a snide grin across his face. "Well I guess this was all worth it then. You have to remember Ez, Boston is a wonderful place and the people here have a lot going for them. Outside these massive iron walls is a land of unforgiving savagery and the constant unknown. If anyone ever even wanted to think about going out there, they would have to show one hell of a lot of grit. Heck, they might even have to be some type of crazy."

"Do you think I will ever be that strong?"

"I'm sure of it, little buddy."

Another long pause followed the compliment. Something was

eating at Ez now that the story was over. It was a small question, only two words, but perhaps it was the most important question that he could have asked all day. He knew Jack probably didn't even have an answer for it, but it had to be mentioned. Ezekiel gathered up the stomach to put his question into light and then pushed the two short words out of the back of his throat with some spit and the force of repressed curiosity.

"What now?"

The words were choppy and sputtered out in a fast, unclear manner, but he was sure Jack heard them. He seemed almost confused, as if the answer were obvious.

"What do you mean?"

"Well, I just wanted to know, well…what comes next? Do you need a place to stay? Because my mother and I live here in a bigger apartment, just the two of us, and I am sure we have room for at least one more person."

"Kid, that is very kind of you, but I'm afraid I have other plans."

"Plans? What does that mean?"

Jack stood up, tore open the bag he was sitting on, and loaded some spare briquettes into the back flap of his pack.

"Well, it means that I haven't given up just yet."

The more Ez thought about it, the more he realized something had not added up about this man. The ministers always had refugees seeking permanent residency stay in an old hotel one mile from the docks until they became full-time citizens. Jack, a refugee, wasn't anywhere near the hotel. And the gun. All people seeking citizenship were forced to relinquish weaponry until they took the proper classes and earned permits. It was all policy, and none of it applied to his new friend. This all could only lead to one conclusion.

"You aren't staying, are you?"

"You got me kid. Someone smart like you was sure to figure it out at some point. I don't think my heart would ever let me stay. You see Ez, I sheltered myself after realizing they weren't here. I went and removed my name from citizen registration immediately after looking at the records. There was nothing for me here after all. I took a day or two to pack up some new gear, and I was ready to head back out entirely by myself. However, one scorching afternoon earlier this week, Mountain found me in the marketplace and dragged me over to a nearby alleyway to talk. He told me he heard rumors. Rumors of another colony a hundred miles away from here, and that was big news. Do you know where that colony is Ez?"

Ezekiel shook his head. He had never heard of another camp anywhere except for Boston.

"Well, that colony is in Dartmouth. Right on the seaboard, five miles from my old front doorstep. If they are going to be anywhere, it will be there. I'm getting another chance to find closure here, Ez."

"Incredible. We had a colony on our doorstep? And I never even heard of it?"

"Apparently not."

"Are you still making the trip by yourself?"

"Not quite. I'm getting a little help from a couple friends."

Their little chat was ended moment later by a voice that rumbled louder than a lingering crack of thunder.

"Hey Beanstalk, stop being a greasy pedophile and get your gear together."

Ez whipped his head around to see the figure in the twilight. It was a massive, stern looking black man with a dusty face who towered well over anybody that Ez had ever seen. His biceps were the size of sandbags, and probably just as heavy too. Jack stood up and greeted his friend with genuine enthusiasm.

"Hey Mountain, come here, I want you to meet a friend of mine. This is my buddy Ez, and Ez, this is Mountain, the big dumb and ugly one from the story."

Mountain clapped his right hand off of the back of Jack's head. The colossus then reached his arm down and shook hands with the boy.

"It's a pleasure to meet you squirt. Has Jack here been telling you any lies about me?"

"No, of course not."

Seeing Ez retreat made Mountain relax himself a bit more. "Good, I don't expect anything less from my good pal, right?"

"Yeah, sure, right...whatever." Jack replied

The two of them shared a quick laugh, and Ez more formally introduced himself. Mountain told Ez a quick story about how Jack tried to carry half his gear after the battle in New York, but dropped it all on his own foot. Soon after, Mountain looked down at his wristwatch.

"Ah shit. We're behind schedule. We should probably get going Beanstalk, the others are waiting for us."

"Others?" Ez seemed surprised.

"Yeah kid, there are a small cluster of other survivors who want to explore the other settlements around here, and they have elected to join us on our adventure."

Jack jumped into the conversation. "That's right. I guess not everybody around here likes this place, so we're bouncing. It's almost like we are conducting a Train of our very own. Sort of, anyway. Just like The Train, we got a schedule to keep. Mountain, why don't you go ahead, while I say my goodbyes."

"Okay, just don't be late. I would hate to leave you here to bother this kid any longer than you already have. Well, it was nice to meet you Ez, but it looks like time for me to roll out. Just get real big, big like me some day, and tackling the wasteland won't be a problem for you." The towering figure turned around and started jogging toward the main gate.

Ez turned to face Jack, who was now hastily stuffing spare equipment and food into the smallest pocket of his backpack. Once he finished with the scraps and old junk, Jack slung it over his back and nodded back at him.

"Well kid, looks like it was just about time that I shoved off too."

Ez picked up the white crate and the bag of medicine. "Alright Jack. You be careful out there. I want you to let me know some day if you find what you're looking for. I don't care if you have to crawl to get back here, I want you to promise me that you will."

There was a hint of doubt in Ezekiel's voice, and Jack picked up on it immediately. "Listen Ez, I know that you might think that at some point in this story I started to exaggerate or overstate a point to make it more dramatic or moving, but I promise everything I said was true. I told it the only way I know how. Simply. The world is crooked and falling apart, and there are difficult and trying times occurring outside that gate, but one thing remains certain. The simple fact is you keep finding something you are willing to push on for, even if you don't want one, and that will make you strong. That, little buddy, is exactly why I won't be coming back to tell you a thing."

The last sentence caught Ezekiel off guard. His face grew red and his fists clenched tightly like a vice.

"What do you mean you won't come back? Don't you think I at least deserve to know what finally happens after all of this?"

Jack kept his cool. "You didn't let me finish. I see something in you, kid. Something I've never seen in anyone else out there. You got spirit, and a lot of it. It is formidable and powerful and sharp and it is yearning to break free of this place. I think you know exactly what I am talking about. You want to climb the highest mountain and place your feet in foreign dirt and conquer new frontier. You got a little adventure somewhere in there Ezekiel, and that's something you have to harness for yourself. That is why I will not come back to you, but you will be the one to come to me. When you are stronger, wiser, and matured, I challenge you Ez. I challenge you to take that big step and come find me. Then you can have the ending to the story that you wanted. Anyways, at the end of the day, what's the point of a story if it doesn't inspire you to do something?"

Without saying another word, Jack spun around and started to stroll down the alleyway. Before he completely disappeared from sight, Ez sprinted after him and grabbed hold of his mud-stained shirt.

"Wait, hold up."

"What is it?"

"Thanks...for everything."

Jack smiled and took a handful of the colorful, brilliant fruit from the child's outstretched hand.

"No need to thank me little buddy, I think I learned as much from you as you learned from me. I'll see you around sometime, or maybe not. Guess that's in your hands now."

Just like that, the traveler left in all his tattered and ragged glory. Awaiting his arrival was a crowd of a dozen or so thin men and women with backpacks and half grins. Just then, Ez realized just how much Jack meant to those people. Believing the story wasn't so hard anymore.

A few of the generic city guardsmen pushed and shoved the enormous gate inches at a time and eventually forced it to close. The brave and adventurous nomads were gone now without a single trace, and Ez thought to himself, *I doubt anybody in the city will even realize they're gone.* On top of the briquette bag where Jack had sat, there was a long, thick box which was coated in dirt and dust. Quietly, Ezekiel crept over to the slanted package and gently lifted its lid up only a few inches. Just enough to look inside. Within the silk wrappings of the case was a sturdy black instrument which had been withered by time, but still kept a certain luxurious glare to them. He lifted the gadget out of its fancy lining and held it up. Its two front lenses shimmered and glistened in the faint light from the stars.

For a moment, Ezekiel believed Jack accidently forgotten them on top of the bag, but after he mulled the situation over for a few moments, Ez realized Jack was far smarter than that. He had abandoned the field glasses so that Ez could keep them, or return them someday. Ez set the exquisite item back into its soft casing and replaced the lid. While he fumbled with the supplies, there was a highly audible, melodic screech above him. Streaks of color, both red and green came streaming down the skyline in thick, single lines. Curfew in Boston was a strict regime, and ignoring the warning is considered a very serious offense. Anyone seen after hours on the streets would be arrested and persecuted by the local guard as any other petty criminal or thief. Ezekiel didn't have time to handle a criminal indictment. He had medicine to deliver.

~ * ~

Under the shadows of the towering skyscrapers, Ez began his stealthy escape from the docks. The streets, which were full of life and activity mere minutes ago, had completely dissipated into a few local beggars and homeless families who hid inside crates and truck-beds to evade capture by the night watchmen. The curious sound of concerned, chattering voices muffled through pane glass windows could be heard coming from the lower floors of housing complexes. Old newspapers and plastic bags rolled down the street in herds. Alley cats digging through mounds of garbage, the sounds of shoe rubber sliding across concrete.

Once he made it away from the frequently-patrolled area near the docks, Ez found time to think and reflect about the day's events. As he mantled over old wire fences and squeezed through barely ajar doorways with his packages, Ez contemplated what he would do now that Jack had galvanized him to leave everything behind. There was a lot to consider before undertaking such a huge and ridiculously dangerous task. Someone does not simply 'leave' Boston. Everybody had a role to play in the city, and blindly vanishing without concern for that role seemed foolish and risky. Ez had a home, and while being strict and mundane, Boston was more than kind and nurturing to those who wanted to survive and exist in peace. But thinking about things like that only begged another important question; is that what he really wanted?

The full moon rose higher into the nighttime sky, illuminating the slumbering city with an intense grey light. Guards patrolled the main roads, carrying their torches and batons. Their black leather uniforms were intimidating, but no matter the case, they never dared enter the alleyways alone. The west side of Boston was the poorest district in the entire colony, and by no small margin. This area usually held new residents and incoming refugees, like the survivors from The Train, scavengers, street salesmen, wall-maintenance workers, prostitutes, and a cavalcade of other commoners. People were so despondent and downcast that residents from other sectors frequently referred to the whole zone as *The Thieves Den*. If any well-endowed northerner or east sector gentry had the misfortune of finding themselves here, it was more than likely that they would be robbed or mugged before they made it to town square.

Luckily for Ez, the folks who lived in the rat-infested hellhole had a great deal of respect for their neighbors. If you came from the west side, you held respect from west-siders. That was how it had been for all of Ezekiel's life. If one member of the community grew too sick to work, or too hungry to stand, all those who could afford gave food or medication to their fallen brothers or sisters. That's how the poor survived. It was a comforting thought. Everyone around this part of town knew of Ez, the boy-wonder who could scavenge the tightest spaces of any building in the city. He was a hero in their eyes. They all knew how hard he worked to take care of his mother, and even the vilest being around would tip their hat and pay their dues. His mother, Jamie as she was affectionately known, had always run a small shop selling the goods that Ez brought home every day, and for a reasonable price too. Between the two jobs that the mother-son family had, they managed to scrape together enough coins for two meals a day. It was a living.

~ * ~

There was an old warehouse that once produced plastic storage containers that stretched for hundreds of yards from end to end. Now it was home to a small gang of homeless men who tended to spend their existences smoking homemade hallucinogens through large wooden pipes. They were friendly, so Ez figured it would work perfectly as a segue from there to the polluted building Ezekiel called home. A set of toppled over wooden pallets sealed the southern entrance, but there was a small opening in the top left corner of the doorway. Gently, Ezekiel lifted himself up onto the decaying square and scooted himself across to the microwave-sized hole. Gently, Ezekiel reached the arm carrying the field glasses through the gap and dropped the box onto the concrete floor. Next, he pushed the container full of strawberries through the slot and let them drop as well. Some spilled out of the white crate and bruised, but they were all salvageable.

As he lifted his slim figure and pushed himself through the tight spot, Ezekiel continued to think to himself. *The stuff Jack described in the story all seemed so dangerous. Existence is a threat out there. Could I even handle all that? I don't want to just throw my life away over this. Between the feral animals, raiders, toxic air, and roamers, I just don't know if it is safe enough to try. Then again, when have I ever cared about safety?* He mulled the question over in his head as he fell face-first into the cold concrete floor. The collision stung for a moment, but relatively soon after, he was up and walking with his packages again. As he passed by the old men who were smoking a foul, rubber smelling substance from a peace pipe, he waved pleasantly to them. In return, the high old men waved back while laughing manically at something completely unidentifiable. Ezekiel figured he must have missed a joke and carried on.

Ezekiel hopped up onto a rusty, stalled conveyer belt and skipped between the cracks. *But still, how much of Jack's story was exaggerated? Maybe the Acolytes weren't all dead. Maybe he left out something that would scare me off. Oh, what am I saying? He wouldn't do something sick like that. Jack seemed to be an honest man, more honest than anyone around here anyway. Maybe he did give me all the details, and I'm just trying to give myself a reason not to go. Maybe I should just stop focusing on the negatives and think about the reasons that I should go instead.*

The northern end of the factory was only blocked by an old door which had fallen to shambles ever since it closed down. Some locals mentioned the door was stuck, so recently, a crew of misfit scrappers came along and completely took the hunk of metal off its hinges. That much iron could have been sold for quite a hefty sum to wall maintenance workers on the north side. Going through the door, Ezekiel found his way back onto the sidewalk adjacent from his housing complex. Ezekiel took cover behind a pile of trash bags and searched for guards. Luckily for the boy, his dark green shirt matched the color of the bags, so he was completely camouflaged from the sight of a nearby watchmen who, by the look of it, was clearly intoxicated beyond his limit.

Ezekiel knew he could sneak past the drunk if he ran fast enough. So as the guard went to take another swig from his whiskey bottle, Ezekiel sprinted across the road toward the front entrance of the twenty-story high-rise. Ezekiel barely made a hint of noise when jolting across the sidewalk. With an incredible burst of speed, the boy-wonder passed through the inlet without a single soul catching sight of him. He let out a sigh of relief once his feet passed through the busted sliding glass doors and his skin was graced by the presence of artificial lobby lighting. The front desk was covered in dust and scratch marks. It was mostly common knife graffiti, but Ezekiel had always been fond of the doodle of the stick man on the moon. The chairs in the lobby had been torn to pieces a great many years ago, but their feathery remains were still strewn about on the cheap, plastic, tile floors. It was an unsanitary, ugly, detestable environment, but Ezekiel didn't mind it as his home in the least bit.

He began the lengthy trek up the one hundred and fifty steps that lead to his flat, and thought about all of the reasons why he wanted to leave the city. The first thing that came to Ezekiel's mind was the detailed descriptions of forests and deserts. Ezekiel had been in the city for his whole life, and even from his youngest childhood memories, he couldn't recollect what a forest looked like. There were a few shrubs and limp, dying trees where the local farmers operated, but they were few and far apart. The grass there was short and brown as well, and expansive patches of ugly weeds consumed anything else in their path. It was blighted and sullied. Ezekiel wanted to see life. Real life.

Another subject that often beckoned to him from outside was his curiosity about other settlements. Ezekiel had gathered a pretty good idea of the ins and outs of life in Boston, but now that he knew that there were more survivor camps around the country, he wanted to learn more about them. *Did they have walls and gates to protect them like he had here? Were there markets and refugees and guards and government?* Maybe if he visited some of them, he could get a better idea of how the world around him actually worked. As he walked up flight after flight, Ezekiel began to notice some of the patrons in the complex sitting about in old lawn chairs, reading magazines published dozens of years ago. They were uninterested in the world around them and held blank, unenergetic stares as they turned the pages of ancient pop culture magazines. An actress. A sex scandal. The usual pulp. This reminded young Ezekiel of the most imperative reason that he wanted to leave this sloppy, parasite of a place behind. It was because he wanted to live life as it was intended to be lived.

Free.

Everyone in Boston was disgustingly content. The thought of complacency made Ez uncomfortable. Fear gripped his friends and family since the day he was born, and to Ez, that was a waste. People sat in their dark, dank abodes and casually forfeited their lives with no hopes of finding a real purpose. Boston was a place of scheduled, boring, mediocre continuations. He reached the thirteenth floor of the building and exited the stairwell. Room numbers lined the hallway to his left and right. Some with their doors entirely removed, while others had been completely bolted shut. Ezekiel found his way to room 1317. Home sweet home.

~ * ~

Connor Harding

Pulling a well-hidden key from underneath a pile of old newspapers, Ezekiel unlocked the door and shoved it open. Its metal hinges shrieked like banshees in the night while the hunk of heavy wood slowly pushed across the shag carpeting. Ezekiel tiptoed his way inside and let the bulky object swing itself closed. He slid into a walk-in closet near the door that served as his room and set the field glasses under a plain white sheet and small throw pillow. Once the box was tucked neatly away under the covers, he strolled out into the common room to see his mother impatiently tapping her foot on the shag carpet.

"You're late Ezekiel. Things get dangerous around here at night you know. You better have a good explanation as to why you were gone all day."

Ezekiel's mother was a stern woman, but she was also well versed. Her complexion was wrinkled and her hair was a wispy silver. She had always loved Ez dearly, but she had a bitter outlook on existence. Ezekiel tensed up. He could tell Jamie had broken into her private stash that night, and that never put her in a good mood. He once tried to explain to Jamie that he wanted to learn about the outside world after she had polished off a bottle of vodka, but it was met with a scolding speech about how foolish it would be to leave Boston for any reason. If he were to tell her about Jack and his story, Ezekiel was sure it would be met with the same frustrated response. So on the spot, he had to try and form a white lie about his whereabouts to throw his mother off of the trail.

"Well, the local courier needed my help this afternoon. He was behind schedule, and if he didn't deliver a package to the far east side of the city to a merchant, he would have been fired. I decided to help him with the job by carrying a big, heavy box to the docks in exchange for a reward." He deceived. She looked down at him with a savvy, contrary glare.

"Why should I believe that? How did the courier reward you for your work? You weren't out running drugs for those damn street urchins, were you?"

Ezekiel, thinking fast, lifted up the quarter-eaten package of strawberries and gave them to Jamie.

"He gave me these."

243

She sat back onto her queen-sized bed and lifted one of the berries up into the lamplight.

"Really? Wow. I guess you weren't joking round then. Hand em' over. Just please, next time you take a day trip to help a stranger, let me know. Alright?"

"Sorry, I guess I just forgot to."

"Well just don't forget. You're a smart kid. Now go get some sleep. You need to be up by six tomorrow if you want to reach the outskirts before the birds get bitchy. Don't want you getting blinded in one eye by a grouchy finch."

Without another word, Ezekiel retreated back to his closet and shut its sliding door behind him. He sat down on the plain white blanket in the corner and dug out the black box from beneath it. He was exhausted, but before he went to rest, he wanted to get one more good look at his newfound treasure. There was a tiny, silver flashlight the size of Ezekiel's ring finger sitting atop a nearby dresser. He promptly picked it up, flipped the on switch, and shined the fluorescent white beam at the ceiling.

Gently sliding the equipment out of its wrappings, Ezekiel lifted the small black instrument into the light and watched the radiance dance along the graveyard of metallic scratches. Ezekiel was fixated by the way it kept its prestige, even though it was coated in the wares of the world. He took a strawberry out of his pocket and quickly popped it into his mouth. The treat was sweet and bitter at the same time, but it still held an earthy texture that Ez rarely got to savor. As he swished the seeds from one side of his mouth to the other and watched the light flicker from the exquisite tool, Ezekiel came to realize something. The feel of the rusty, beaten binoculars in his hands felt almost right. It was almost as if they belonged there, with him. A key to a thousand locks, or a thousand answers. Ez knew that one day, he would become stronger and faster and wiser. He also knew when that day came, he would be ready to fulfill his calling and use those field glasses the way that they were intended to.

To Ezekiel, the world hadn't ended, it was only reborn, and now it was ripe to be explored and conquered a second time. Every animal, every sight, every charming, forgotten noise. The thoughts of those sweet and forbidden lands filled Ezekiel's mind again, and as he swallowed the remaining piece of delicious fruit, he set his mind straight. He would fight the evils of the land, and he would travel the most dangerous of landscapes, and he would rediscover things the world had left long buried. Ez felt the spirit of adventure fill his lungs like a raging flood, just like they always did. One day, he would see it all for himself, no matter what.

About the Author

Connor Harding is a new author on the scene, with *The Train* being his first major published work. He hails from northeast Ohio, where he grew up reading adventure novels and watching Steven Spielberg movies. Nowadays, he attends the Ohio State University as an undergraduate English major and outspoken champion for the Oxford comma. With a love for a good story being his life's creed, Connor undertakes every work with the intent to fully entertain his reading audience and maybe even change the way they think about things.

FOR THE FULL INVENTORY
OF QUALITY BOOKS:
http://www.roguephoenixpress.com

Rogue Phoenix Press
Representing Excellence in Publishing

Quality trade paperbacks and downloads
in multiple formats,
in genres ranging from historical to contemporary romance, mystery
and science fiction.
Visit the website then bookmark it.
We add new titles each month!

www.ingramcontent.com/pod-product-compliance
Lightning Source LLC
Chambersburg PA
CBHW051944220626
47052CB00004B/790